THE ETERNITY WAR: EXODUS

In my real body, I'd been hurt and in pain. My reactions had been dulled by my time in the prison. I knew that I was worn out and tired. But this skin was fresh. The simulant's senses were needle-sharp, and the rush of adrenaline and hormones and combat-drugs that hit my bloodstream was very nearly a religious experience.

I wasn't Keira any more. I wasn't weak.

I was Lieutenant Jenkins. I was strong.

And I was angry.

THE ETERNITY WAR:

EXODUS

Jamie Sawyer

www.orbitbooks.net

ORBIT

First published in Great Britain in 2018 by Orbit

A CIP catalogue record for this book is available from the British Library.

ISBN 978-0-356-51006-4

Typeset in Stempel Garamond by Palimpsest Book Production Limited,
Falkirk, Stirlingshire
Printed and bound in Great Britain by CPI Group (UK) Ltd, Croydon CR0 4YY

Papers used by Orbit are from well-managed forests
and other responsible sources.

To Mum, for always believing in me

PROLOGUE

For a long, hurt moment Clade Cooper – former Alliance Army Ranger, more recently turned head of the Black Spiral terrorist organisation – was back *there*.

No more. Not again.

Cooper spluttered, cried out. Gasped for breath like a drowning man. The burn in his chest felt so real that he put a hand there, and held it. Clutched at his own beating heart.

It's a dream. Just a dream. Nothing more.

Finally, when Cooper knew he could accept it, he sighed to the dark. Let his breathing fall into a rhythm, and was glad when the hot, dry air filled his lungs. That was the good hurt. But the nightmare lingered, a guest outstaying its welcome, and that was the bad hurt. The horror had been warm, and very wet, pervading every element of his body.

"Does that hurt?"

"Of course it hurts. Everything hurts."

One leg out of the bunk. Foot to the cold floor. Pain crept through the limb and it took all of his strength not to scream, but the sensation was passing. Cooper rolled his body

I

around, allowing the bedsheets to grate against his skin – causing another ripple of discomfort through the mass of scar tissue that was his flesh – and sat up.

The room around him was dark, and empty, but that didn't mean that he was alone. The place was filled with ghosts. They gnawed at the edge of Cooper's consciousness. Threatening to drag him down into the Deep.

"We want to do everything we can to make you comfortable."

"I'll never be comfortable again."

There was a communicator beside Cooper's bunk, and it chimed once, an indicator light warning of an incoming communication. Such a simple, innocuous thing – part of everyday life aboard a starship – but it evinced a sudden reaction in Cooper. He snapped his neck around to respond. Desperately trying to stop himself from falling back into the nightmare. Into the wet. Into the shadow . . .

"This isn't going to be easy. No one has ever survived this procedure."

"I don't care. Not any more. Not without them."

A face appeared on the communicator's small screen, throwing a thin light over the chamber. As much as Cooper hated to admit it to himself, he was grateful for the illumination, and glad to see the face there. It was one of his Disciples; a small, greying man, with a middle-aged face.

"Sir?" the Disciple said. "Your cabin activated the medical alert. I thought that I should check on you . . ."

The Disciple's nation and planet of origin were unknown, but he had once been a doctor. That didn't matter any more, because now he had no title. It was the Black Spiral's way: none of the Disciples had any proper rank. It was, Cooper supposed, a consequence of his response – his *rebellion* – against the structures that had once bound him. He had known many doctors, once, but he was no longer that man.

"There are certain technologies that would allow you to retain your identity, but with a new skin . . . You should consider a body-sculpt. A complete physical overhaul."

"I wouldn't be me any more."

Cooper could remember her eyes, most of all. They were almost pleading, because no one could live in that much pain. Not if they wanted to remain human.

"Sir?" the Disciple asked, calling him back to the here, to the now. "Are you experiencing more night terrors?"

"I am fine," Cooper growled.

"Do you need assistance?"

"I was dreaming. It is one of the many consequences of my history."

"Yes, sir. Of course." The Disciple swallowed. He was almost mesmerised by Cooper's face. That was a universal reaction, something that Cooper had grown accustomed to. Finally, the other man bowed his head, clutched the symbol at his neck. "They seem to be getting worse as the fire spreads. Would you like more pain relief?"

"This isn't going to be easy."

"Nothing ever is."

"Yes. Send me more drugs. More oblivion."

"As you wish."

Cooper reached over and activated the pain-relief system set into the bunk control console. The effect was instant: the cool spread of analgesics spreading through his dry, tortured body. He felt as though he was inflating inside his own skin, becoming more alive with each heartbeat. The nightmare's shadow quickly receded, leaving nothing more than a psychic stain. He felt a brief stab of resentment – of displeasure that he had to rely on the machines around him to live, to endure any sort of quality of life – but it was passing. Whenever

Cooper slept, he did so attached to the apparatus. The machinery constantly flushed his blood of the poisons that accrued there, and was a requirement of being outside his armour. The filtering device was a fact of life, nothing more.

"Thank you, Disciple. You are a good man."

"It is all for the glory of the Spiral."

"Have they found the target?"

"Lieutenant Runweizer has reported." Runweizer was one of many agents deployed on Old Earth, within the structure itself. Like many military converts, Runweizer was less willing to give up his title than other Disciples. However, such operatives were a necessary evil. "He has visited the target's last known location," the Disciple said, but left it at that, hesitant to give the full report.

"And?"

The Disciple's voice dropped. "The target was not present."

"That is disappointing, although hardly unexpected. Tell the lieutenant to keep looking."

"Yes, sir. There . . . there is something else."

"Go on."

"As you know, we are desperately in need of more materials . . ."

Pain relief and medical supplies, as well as other essentials for shipboard existence, were growing sparse. Another fact of life aboard the starship, and one that Cooper felt acutely. The Disciple looked on with doleful eyes. Perhaps it was the doctor in him; still seeking to understand what was happening to Cooper. That made a smile jerk at the corner of Cooper's mouth, because he didn't really understand this himself. He doubted that anyone understood what was happening to him.

"Our stock of the retrovirals is almost depleted," the Disciple muttered. He swallowed, staring off-screen, pained to admit it. "I . . . I'm not sure how much longer I will be able to administer treatment to you, sir."

"Understood."

"We should conduct another raid," the Disciple suggested. "And soon." His eyes misted, noticeable even over the comm-link. "While I am still able to help you."

"Very well. I give the order."

"As you wish, sir."

"Alert me when we get to the next Gate."

The Disciple went to open his mouth, to speak some more, but Cooper cut the comm. The after-image of his grey, aged face lingered on in the dark for a second or so, then Cooper was alone again.

"Wouldn't it be easier," said the doctor, "to just . . ."

What had she meant to say? It had been many years since their meeting, and Cooper had often caught himself wondering what she had sought to tell him. Had she wanted him to die? To give up?

Never. While I live, their memory continues. They live.

Cooper's eyes fell to his armoured suit. It sat in the corner of the room, illuminated in its charging cradle. He couldn't remember having activated it, but that wasn't new. Increasingly, he had found the armour switching on without his permission: the wrist-comp flashing as it connected with unseen networks, the weapons systems cycling up of their own accord. It was as though the armour itself was becoming sentient, reaching out to other machines around it.

Cooper stood on pained legs and wandered to the suit. Its black plating was scratched, battered. The manpower-amplifier was an older pattern, the attenuators and strength-augmentation system partially exposed on the arms and legs. Still, every threat-marking and kill-score had been painstakingly restored: the skull-motif glared back at him from the helmet. He reached out, caressed the armour. Felt a prickle of static touch his skin, and more exquisite agony erupt inside of him.

"Who am I?"

"I am the Warlord of the Drift," he answered, "and I will bring it all down."

There was work to do.

The old gods were coming back, and they were hungry.

CHAPTER ONE

BROKEN

Private Chu Feng manned the UAS *Santa Fe*'s navigation console, and read the results from the terminal. His eyes were wide, the words rolling out of his mouth on automatic.

"We're in Asiatic Directorate space," he said. "Riggs has jumped us directly into Directorate space."

Silence stretched across the *Sante Fe*'s bridge, and for a heartbeat no one dared to move or speak. I was frozen in time and space, unable to draw my eyes from the tactical display as it gradually populated with data. Not even Captain Miriam Carmine, the erstwhile and irascible officer in charge of the *Santa Fe*, could bring herself to question the results.

Corporal Daneb Riggs, second in command of Jenkins' Jackals, as well as my sometime lover and confidant, had just betrayed us in the most spectacular way imaginable. He'd flown the *Santa Fe* into one of the most dangerous locations in the known universe.

The dam finally broke.

"We're . . . we're in Directorate space?" Lopez stammered,

dumbly, in utter disbelief. "How can that even be possible? The *Fe*'s equipped with diplomatic protocols, right?"

Lopez was talking about the navigational inhibitors with which all Alliance starships were equipped. In theory, that meant that the *Santa Fe* wouldn't be capable of jumping into a diplomatically sensitive area. Unless . . .

"Riggs overrode them." Feng jabbed keys and cursed in rotation. His face crumpled in an anxious grimace. He looked to me. "This is bad, ma'am. Very bad."

"Explain," I said. I couldn't see how things could get any worse than they already were.

"This isn't Chino territory."

In ordinary circumstances, Private Chu Feng was young, hot-headed and a decent son of a bitch. He had been vat-grown by the Asiatic Directorate, designed to be one of their elite Special Operations troopers, but fate had a different destination for Feng. His liberation from a Directorate training facility had resulted in his induction into the Alliance Army Simulant Operations Programme. Somewhat ironically, Directorate Spec Ops clones made decent simulant operators, and Feng was a good example of this principle. His Asian features were boyish in a way that betrayed the purpose of his muscular body. Right now, his brow was sweaty, short dark hair swept back from his darker eyes. He looked like a frightened kid, which I guess in a way he was. Feng had been born fully grown, and was only a few years out of the vat.

"You just said that we jumped into Directorate space," Lopez said. She sounded angry, and in no mood for discussion on this topic. "Now you're saying we're not in Chino territory? Make up your mind, Feng."

Gabriella Lopez: Proximan and proud, the only daughter of one of the most powerful political figures in the Alliance.

8

Lopez had joined up with Sim Ops to prove a point to her old man. She'd come to me young, beautiful and full of arrogance. Her military career had once been a joke. Now, I hardly recognised the hard-edged, stern features of her face – the way that her jaw bounced as she assessed the tactical display. I liked her a lot more this way. Long dark hair pulled into a ponytail, gene-sculpted face still covered in bruises and lacerations from our last operation, this Lopez meant business. Although, strictly speaking, shipboard regulations prohibited it, Lopez carried her Revtech-911K pistol holstered on her thigh.

"Yeah, well, there's a lot more to the Asiatic Directorate than just Chino territory," Feng said, eyes still to the monitor in front of him. "And we're somewhere so much worse."

"Such as?" Lopez pressed. It spoke more of her sheltered upbringing than anything else that she didn't know that the Directorate was made up of dozens of nation-states.

"We're in Asiatic Directorate space claimed by Unified Korea," Feng answered.

"Uni-Kor?" I said. "Shit. That is worse."

Korean space. Of all the Asiatic Directorate member states, Unified Korea was the most bloodthirsty, the most fervent. The Uni-Kor had never recognised the end of hostilities between the Directorate and the Alliance, and I doubted that they ever would. Their region of space was secluded and well armed; a stronghold against the rest of the universe.

Just then, Private Leon Novak burst onto the bridge. The life-prisoner was still recuperating from multiple injuries – walking with a protracted limp, his face and shoulders covered in abrasions – but none of that seemed to stop him.

Novak shook his head. "Ship says we are in Asiatic space!" His blunt Slavic accent was painfully matter-of-fact, his tattoo-covered features creased in alarm. "We are fucked, yes?"

"Welcome to the shitshow," said Lopez. "You're a little late."

Novak had been recruited from a prison in the Russian Federation, and had joined Sim Ops because every transition – every death – gave him a little more life. His enormous arms were scored with self-harm injuries, each marking a successful transition in a simulant, his muscled body barely fitting inside his shipboard fatigues. I had sent Novak down to the docking bay, to check on what we'd assumed was a faulty door sensor. He'd been too late to stop Riggs from launching the Warhawk, the *Santa Fe*'s only shuttle.

"Are you sure about this, Feng?" Lopez whispered. Strength seeped from her voice as she spoke. "Maybe the navigation console is malfunctioning."

"Of course I'm sure!" Feng shouted back, pounding a fist against the terminal. "Do you think I'd make a mistake about something like this?"

Captain Carmine spoke up. "The boy's got it right," she said. "We're in Uni-Kor space."

The *Santa Fe* was Carmine's command. She sat in her captain's throne, hunched over the console. Also known as "the Carbine", Carmine was an ageing Californian with attitude, and one of the oldest, and best, starship captains that I'd ever had the pleasure of serving with. Strands of silver hair escaped from beneath her service cap, her frame whip-like, left leg replaced by a crude Navy bionic. She clutched a holo-picture of her three daughters in her hand.

"Take it easy, Chu," said Zero. Although I wasn't quite sure of the detail, Zero and Feng had a thing going on: she was the one to calm the savage beast. "You're doing just fine."

Sergeant Zoe Campbell, aka Zero: some kid I'd rescued from an Alliance colony world during the Krell War, who had grown up to become my friend and eventually join Sim Ops. Smaller than the others, with the physique of a pen-pusher rather than a trooper, Zero was our designated intelligence and operations analyst – the back-room ops manager, if you will. She'd wanted to be a simulant operator, aspired to be just like me, but Feng wasn't the only one to whom fate had dealt a surprising hand. Zero was a "negative". Her body had rejected the data-port technology, and as such she couldn't operate a sim. Ginger-haired and freckled, Zero wasn't used to being in the thick of the fighting. Our last mission – into the Maelstrom – had given her a taste of how hot things could get. That was surely a cakewalk in comparison to our current situation . . .

"Where exactly in Korean space are we?" I asked. "We need solutions, not problems. Give me specifics."

Feng worked for a moment, then replied, "Joseon-696."

The tremble in his voice pretty much told me everything I needed to know, but Captain Carmine confirmed the rest.

"We're in orbit around the third world," she said. "It's a prison planet. Goes by the name of Jiog, and if even half of the rumours are true, this place will make Novak's *gulag* look like paradise."

The curve of an angry pink orb appeared on the viewscreen. A sparse band of white cloud claimed the equator, while the surface was sprinkled with vast black conurbations of industry. There was a lot of space traffic out there too, and several orbital facilities. This was not a backwater colony planet, but the heart of a busy, populated system.

"Jiog?" Lopez asked, looking around the bridge for answers.

"It's one of the Alliance's top three locations of interest," Carmine said. "The planet's exact location has been highly classified." She raised her eyebrows. "Until now, that is. Your man Riggs must've known some pretty complex quantum-space equations to jump us here. We get out of this alive, and we'll get a Christo-damned medal."

"Fucking Riggs!" Lopez said. "Fucking bastard! How could he do this to us?" She put her hands to her head in exasperation. "Can this day get any worse?"

Lopez probably meant that rhetorically, but she got her answer anyway.

The *Santa Fe*'s sensor-suite was just about the only thing that still functioned aboard the vessel, and that was currently painting several hostiles advancing on our position. A dozen warships burst through the dark and converged on our location. The lead vessel was an angry black arrow that speared space as it made hard burn.

"Incoming communication," declared Lieutenant Yukio. She was a small Japanese woman, and Carmine's dedicated executive officer. One of only four Navy crew that had survived our last mission into the Maelstrom, and loyal to Carmine until the very last.

"On-screen," Carmine said.

The tactical display filled with an incoming transmission, and the Jackals went quiet. A military officer appeared. Wearing a dark uniform, a tunic buttoned to his neck in the formal Directorate style. The man's face was hard, eyes dark, and his chest bustled with medals. I knew enough about Directorate protocol to say that he wasn't Navy, but his exact branch of military service wasn't clear.

"I am Captain Mariam Carmine, of the UAS *Santa Fe*," Carmine started. "We are currently experiencing technical difficulties, but should—"

"I am Commander Kwan Ryong-ho," said the figure, speaking over Carmine. "Your identity is irrelevant."

I'd heard of the name, and so had the *Santa Fe*'s AI. Intelligence on the subject filled the nearest terminal screen, and with growing unease I scanned it. The guy was a walking war-crime: the last of a long line of Directorate dictators and military despots, a relic of a past age. Exactly the sort of person we could do without right now . . .

Zero began to babble in a low mutter beside me, "That ship is the *Furious Retribution*."

"They sure know how to pick those names," I said.

The *Furious Retribution* was a huge, ugly ship. They didn't make them like that any more. She carried several flight-bays – capable of carrying a whole squadron of fighters – and bristled with weapon points.

Zero kept talking. "She's believed to be the private command post of Commander Kwan Ryong-ho, head of the Directorate's Bureau of Shadow Affairs."

"What's Shadow Affairs?" I whispered back.

Zero's verbal diarrhoea continued unabated. "It's the Directorate's internal security force; their equivalent of Military Intelligence. The Directorate wouldn't even confirm its existence until a few years ago."

"Fucking marvellous," I said. With each word Zero spoke, my heart dropped a little further.

And she wasn't even finished . . . "Remote psych profiling indicates that Commander Kwan is paranoid, confrontational, and prone to acts of sudden aggression. Highly unstable. When the Directorate broke up, the commander seized control of the Joseon system – established his personal domain." She swallowed, voice dipping. "He's also wanted in ten Alliance territories for atrocities against humanity."

"Our presence here is accidental," Carmine attempted again, addressing Kwan. "My ship's navigational computer has suffered a catastrophic malfunction—"

Kwan ignored Carmine. "You are in violation of the Border Treaty, and your presence within this system is impermissible."

"What do they care for treaties?" Feng asked, off-camera.

The Asiatic Directorate had once been the Alliance's great enemy – engaged in a cycle of hot and cold wars that had claimed generations on both sides of the divide. But several years ago, the Directorate's internal power balance had irrevocably shifted: with a number of member states leaving the union. The Directorate lingered, sure, but the beast had been declawed. The result was the Border Treaty.

It had to be said that there was some small irony in Kwan's response. The Koreans had never agreed to any damned treaty, and the break-up of the Directorate had been so thorough that no one had been left to agree to the terms anyway. It had left a ragged line of impoverished and desperate systems between Alliance and Directorate space, which had led to the liberation of several clone-crèches like that Feng had been born into.

"This really isn't necessary," Carmine said. "If we can just—"

"This discussion is over," Kwan declared. "Prepare for boarding operation."

That last comment wasn't directed at us, I realised. The bridge of the *Furious Retribution* was visible behind Kwan, and a dozen military officers, all dressed in black uniform, were busy at tactical stations. Kwan waved a hand at the closest.

"Wait!" I broke in, unable to let this play out. "This isn't deliberate! I'm Lieutenant Jenkins, of the Sim Ops Programme—"

"An officer of the Simulant Operations Programme?" Kwan said. "That is interesting." He paused, then added, "Do not resist the boarding party."

The transmission ended.

I turned to Carmine. "Can you get us out of here? Q-drive, thrusters: anything?"

I knew that the chances were slim. The *Santa Fe*'s quantum-drive had got us this far based on a combination of blind faith and iron determination, and I had no hope that we were going to be able to jump out of the Directorate space anytime soon.

Carmine stared at her console. "All my systems are locked out." She shook her head. "Riggs did a proper job on my ship."

No one on Carmine's crew disagreed. Riggs had programmed the quantum-jump sequence that had taken us out of the Maelstrom, and as such he had been left in control of the *Santa Fe*'s systems for days. I felt a stab of anger and remorse. I'd trusted him, had let him in. This was all my fault.

"I've got multiple hostiles moving on our location," offered Lieutenant Yukio.

"Do we have null-shields? Weapons? Sharp fucking sticks?"

"Nothing," Carmine said. "We're a sitting duck."

"What about the simulators?" Zero suggested. "You could skin up and take on the Directorate."

Just mention of the simulator-tanks sent a thrill through me. I could already imagine stepping into the warm amniotic, making transition into a fresh new body. In the tank, everything was all right . . .

"I don't think that you understand me," Carmine said. "We've lost control of *all* of the ship's systems. Engines, simulators, the whole deal. That our life support is still functioning is a minor miracle."

There were several copies of the Jackals on ice in the *Santa*

Fe's cargo hold; racked and tubed and ready for deployment. But without operational simulator-tanks, they were just useless meat.

An alarm sounded across the bridge.

"We're being targeted," Yukio said. "The *Retribution* is engaging."

"The Directorate are firing missiles on us?" Lopez asked, looking down at the scanner-feed.

"Hell, no," I said. "That's the boarding party."

On the tac-display, smaller signals began to coalesce and take shape. They were being fired from the *Furious Retribution*: crossing the void of space between our ship and theirs in a heartbeat. To the uninitiated – and I had to remind myself that the Jackals hadn't fought the Directorate before – they looked very much like missiles. But I knew otherwise. These were troopers wearing flight-rigs, hard-suits specially adapted to the rigours of a starship boarding action.

"We can't let them onto the ship," said Feng.

"You're Directorate, Feng," Lopez said. "You'll be just fine."

But Feng's face had drained of all colour, and he shrank inside his fatigues. "Do you have any idea what the Directorate does to traitors? Because that's what I am to them: a traitor."

Lopez went quiet. There was no smart quip to that.

I didn't add anything to the discussion, because morale was already at an all-time low, but it wouldn't be much better for Lopez. Once they found out who she was, and her connection to the infamous Senator Lopez . . . She would be as much a prize for the Directorate as Feng.

Carmine took control. "Lieutenant Yukio, prepare to erase the *Fe*'s memory-core. Burn the data-stacks."

"Aye, ma'am," Yukio said. "Burn initiated."

"How long will it take?" I asked.

"T minus ten minutes until complete purge," Yukio said.

"I don't think we have that long," Lopez implored.

"Riggs' shuttle is leaving the system," Zero said, frowning. "See: it's flying away from the fleet."

Riggs had stolen the *Santa Fe*'s only shuttle. That was a Warhawk model, incapable of supporting its occupant for more than a few days. It had just broken away from the *Fe*, and contrary to my expectation was actually taking a course out-system – avoiding the Directorate attack group altogether. What was the bastard doing? Riggs' betrayal was beyond doubt, but to whom he was defecting: that was still open to debate.

"He planned it like this," I said, my eyes flashing between the tactical display and the monitor showing Riggs' progress. "It was a fucking trap."

"What about Pariah?" Zero said. "It's still in Medical."

Pariah was the only talking – and truly *thinking* – Krell that I'd ever encountered, and I knew that its value to the Alliance was immense. It was a unique communication bridge between us and the Krell Collective. But more than that: Pariah had become our ally, and had assisted us several times during our mission into the Gyre. As of now, the alien was still hibernating in the medical bay, recovering from integration into the wider Silver Talon Collective. I had no way of knowing whether the failure of the ship's energy supply had interfered with that, but I knew that Pariah needed to be warned about the Directorate.

Carmine read the expression on my face, and sighed. "You've grown too attached to that fish," she said.

"I didn't hear you arguing when P saved our asses in the Maelstrom, Carmine."

"A fish is a fish," she muttered back at me, but the words didn't have much force, and I knew that she didn't mean it.

"P needs to be warned," I said.

"All right," Carmine replied, unhooking herself from her terminal and staggering to her feet. "Then you need to get down to Medical and see to it yourself."

With that, the spartan bridge crew – four Navy staffers, including Carmine – jumped from their terminals. Carmine unclasped a carbine from under her console; the antique Fabrique Multiworld MN rifle that had become her trademark weapon and earned her the nickname "Carbine". She looked impossibly old, but also impossibly stubborn.

"This is it. This is where it ends." She loaded her rifle, braced it across her chest. "We'll cover you." Carmine fixed me with her gaze. "You get back and I don't, tell my daughters that I love them."

She reached out a hand and opened it. Inside, she held the tri-D picture of her family, crumpled with age. I took it.

"I swear," I said.

"We don't have time for a long goodbye, Jenkins. Go, now!"

"Defend the bridge," I said. "Break out the armoury. Jackals, you're with me. We'll move on Medical."

The Jackals filed through the *Santa Fe*'s corridors, bouncing and twisting as the ship's artificial gravity field failed. The overhead lights had gone the same way: emergency bulbs flashing. The *Fe* was a smaller Alliance-pattern corvette, barely a warship at all, and she surely wasn't made for this sort of frontline activity. But then again, few ships were. This was a mission-fatal incident. The *Fe* wasn't coming back from this, and we all knew it.

We covered the distance to Medical just as the first breachers boarded. There was a muted thump through the

Fe's space frame, and a pressure wave went through the deck, through the whole damned ship.

"They're using demo-charges," I said. "Sounds like it came from the bridge."

"Do you think that Carmine is all right?" Lopez asked.

"I don't know," I said. "Just move."

Controlled atmospheric depressurisation followed. All around us, in the various sub-chambers that branched off the *Fe*'s main corridor, pressure hatches began to close. At least those were still operational; either because they were being driven by some AI sub-routine that Riggs hadn't managed to subvert, or maybe because the Directorate were being careful not to lose atmosphere. If it was the latter, I knew that wasn't out of any sense of humanity; rather, they wanted live captives.

Medical was plastered in red light. The simulator-tanks sat powerless and empty; so much useless metal and plastic in our current situation. Zero's operations console was also dead – the various monitors from which she would ordinarily be able to observe the mission now blank.

"In, in," Novak said, herding Lopez and Feng into the chamber.

"Get that door sealed," I yelled.

The Russian did as ordered, and the blast door slammed shut. The door was six inches of reinforced plasteel but it didn't make me feel any safer.

Pariah's hibernation capsule was still powered, although the device's control panel was filled with error messages and warning codes. No time to examine what any of those meant; instead, I just rapped a knuckle against the armourglass canopy.

"Wake up, P."

Inside the glass tube, the pariah-form had folded in on

itself. Six long limbs, each tipped with claw-like appendages, and a barrel-chested body that was covered in a scaled hide; Pariah gave ugly a whole new meaning. Granted, the xeno was no more and probably no less attractive than the rest of its species, but we had to serve with this particular fish. Its eyes were shut tight, head resting against the inside of the capsule. Awkwardly grafted to the alien's chest was a voice-box, a device that allowed the alien to communicate with us. Pariah was the brainchild of Dr Claus Skinner, also known as the Fleshsmith. The doctor had been killed by the Black Spiral on North Star Station.

"Do you hear me, P?" I asked, angrily now. "Wake up!"

Suddenly, Pariah's eyes snapped open, and it stirred inside the capsule.

"Jenkins-other," it said, through the control console. "We are in hibernation. Our wounds are not yet healed—"

"Yeah, well, healing will have to wait. We're in some pretty bad shit here, P."

The alien paused, then said, "Define 'bad shit'."

"As in 'fucked beyond reason'," Lopez shouted back.

She unholstered her pistol – a weapon given to her by her brother, which had saved us on North Star Station – and braced at the hatch, ready to fire on intruders.

There was another *boom* through the ship's frame, closer now. The air temperature immediately dropped, tasted of burning. My ears prickled with the shift in atmosphere. The ship's failing life-support system was struggling to compensate.

"You felt that, right?" I asked.

P lethargically opened its limbs. "We felt that."

"There's a lot I should've told you," I said. "I – I don't know how much you know about the world outside North Star Station, or what Dr Skinner taught you, but you need to know that this situation is critical. We're being boarded by Directorate forces. They'll want to take us – and *you* – prisoner."

"What is 'Directorate'?"

"There's no time to explain. All you need to know right now is that the Directorate are the bad guys, and they are enemies of the Alliance. They'll want to know what you know. You cannot engage with these people. Understood?"

The alien writhed inside the tank. "Human-other rivalries are not our concern," it said.

"I'm not asking you to take sides," I said, speaking faster now. "I'm telling you that these guys mean business. If you've learnt anything from me, then know this: do as I say, and don't answer their questions."

P considered that for a moment, and I noticed how badly injured it was. Lacerations laced the alien's body; impacts pocking its carapace. Zero was no medic, and although she had tried her best to heal the fish, it needed time. It was in no fit state to fight.

"We understand," it finally responded.

"They're here already!" Feng said.

The side wall of Medical was transparent, allowing a view of the *Fe*'s main corridor, and that was now filled with hulking figures. Troopers in vacuum-rated battle-armour, black and shiny, with full-face helmets and flight-rigs mounted on their backs. They were accompanied by an army of semi-autonomous breaching spiders, each as big as my head. The mechanical swarm spilled across the walls and deck: clutching every surface for purchase.

One breached the hatch to Medical, and detonated. The door instantly gave way. Red-hot debris was thrown across the chamber.

Lopez started firing. It wasn't much by way of resistance,

but the closest Directorate trooper took a hit to the chest. In heavy armour, the trooper shrugged off the impact, flipped a grenade through the hole in the hatch.

"Fire in the hold!"

The stun grenade detonated. Light and white noise filled the room.

I rolled left, hit the deck as fast as I could, but only managed to take the edge off the explosion. Images were plastered across the insides of my eye-lids.

Another spider-bot went off, creating a larger hole.

Medical descended into chaos. The Directorate filled the space with their armoured mass. Armed with heavy shock rifles, these guys weren't here to kill us. No, they had come to capture. They executed their mission with crisp precision; working as one, as though they were a single hive-mind. These, I knew, were Directorate Special Forces. The squad had probably been born together, the product of Chino-Korean advanced genetic engineering. They would not stop, would not pause, until their objective was complete. What chance did we stand?

Lopez was screaming, one of the spider-bots clambering over her, pinning her to the deck. Feng was lashing out with arms and legs, slamming into armoured bodies. Novak slashed with a makeshift knife, the blade useless against the boarders' hard-suits. The Directorate had already taken Zero; a single trooper dragging her unconscious from Medical.

Through a red haze I watched each of them go down.

My squad. My people. Jenkins' Jackals.

Other soldiers had already surrounded P's tank.

"Remember what I said, P!" I shouted.

There was something in the alien's eyes. Some spark of understanding: our minds in synch. Did Pariah represent a cure for the virus currently spreading through the Maelstrom?

If it did, then it couldn't be allowed to fall into Directorate hands. We exchanged that knowing without words.

The nearest hostile waded through bodies, red-eyed goggles glaring down at me. The chest-plate of the trooper's armour was filled with insignia – the Directorate badge, Uni-Kor's flag, and a Taijitu symbol. Words were scrawled across the armour plating in Standard, scruffy like a child's handwriting: SIM-KILLER.

"Fuck you!" I screamed.

I grasped for the lead trooper's helmet, pulled at the sealed face-mask segment. It came free with a hiss of escaping atmosphere. I was stunned to see a face that I recognised starring back at me.

"Feng?"

No, not quite Feng. This version was different. If Feng was Mark I, this bastard was Mark X: older, battle-scarred, world worn. Surely this soldier's selection for this mission couldn't have been deliberate, but the effect on me was immediately disarming.

One side of the soldier's face was covered by an intricate fire tattoo, and it came alive as his lip lifted in a snarl. He slammed the stock of his shock rifle directly into my head. It connected with my temple, and pain exploded in my skull.

Another soldier appeared at his shoulder, face-mask removed as well. A third version of Feng, except this soldier's face was covered with an intricate snowflake tattoo.

Fire and Ice. Twins.

I stumbled backwards. Carmine's photo fell from my hands, and I scrambled for it. Pariah had finally come awake, was violently thrashing its limbs against the inside of the capsule. Too little, too late. Around me, the Jackals were being restrained by the boarding party.

"Targets acquired," Ice said, in American-Standard. His

electronic voice sounded so flat, so empty: at odds with the cold fury behind the face-mask. He nodded. "Objective is secure. We have them."

Meanwhile, Fire just kept hitting me and hitting me. Until, eventually, it all went black.

And just like that, it was over.

CHAPTER TWO

THE BODY REMEMBERS

Six days later

A lamp, fierce as a spotlight, shone down on me. So bright that it was very nearly blinding; rendering everything else in the room in harsh, black outline. There was little option but to look straight at it though, because two metal stanchions on either side of my skull held my head in position.

"Is she awake?" came the curt male voice.

I tried to make out the speaker, but got nothing more than a silhouette.

"Yes," was the response. "Her vital signs have stabilised."

"Good."

"She is fascinating, Honoured Commander. Truly fascinating."

That was shadow number two. Sounded female, breathy. Excited?

I stirred from the table. It was stainless steel, freezing cold against the skin of my back. The clamps had just enough give that if I tilted my head, I could see my own body: the mounds of my breasts, the perfectly immaculate flesh of my limbs. *They won't stay that way for long*, I thought.

More relevant than that, I also caught a glimpse of my surroundings. My eyes adjusted quickly, and I saw that the rest of the room was unkempt, worn out. There was medical equipment stacked in the corners; tiled walls that had collected a lifetime of grime, stained and splotched by viscera, mired by blood and dirt. Generally unsanitary. Not the sort of place you'd want to be naked in, for sure.

A torture chamber. That was what this place was.

The sense of vulnerability was unbearable. I tried to move some more, and found that I was spread-eagled, like a butterfly ready for dissection. I wriggled, really fought against the field holding me in place, but it was pointless. Breathing was hard enough. I was on a gravity-plate; and the field it emitted was strong as any physical bond.

I'm screwed, I concluded. *Totally and utterly screwed.*

While I'd like to think that I wouldn't have ended up in this position except with consent, that wasn't the case. I couldn't muster the energy for a quip on that. There was nothing funny about this, not at all.

"Can she hear me?"

"I think so," the female answered.

"Respond, Prisoner."

"Perhaps she requires some motivation."

The figures moved around the edge of the table, dipping in and out of clarity. One carried a probe of some sort, its tip lighting with a bright spark. That promised pain on a level that I really didn't want to think about.

"I'm awake," I managed. On the G-plate, talking was difficult, but not impossible. "I'm fucking awake, all right."

"Good," the male answered. "That's very good."

Small, short, with Asian features. Unified Korean.

Kwan. His name was Commander Kwan Ryong-ho. I recognised him from the transmission to the *Santa Fe*. Now that my eyes were adjusting to the light, I was beginning to make out the details of my captors. Kwan was past middle age, but with the edges taken off: the effects of a partial rejuvenation-regime showing in the lines around his eyes, in the new hair growth that struggled to take root on his pale pate.

"Welcome to my world," Kwan said. The words were spoken in precise, fluent Standard. Kwan's high cheekbones were etched with blue light; subdermal circuitry that looked almost cosmetic, but allowed him to make head-to-head comms. "You are my prisoner."

He lingered a distance from the arc cast by the lamp, with his hands clasped behind his back. He was always moving, his body always fidgeting, radiating impatience. He wore the black uniform of an Asiatic Directorate officer, with service-regulation trousers topped by a tunic that was buttoned to his neck. A physique that, while not fat, was not that of a soldier either. He was shorter than me, I'd guess, and physically didn't look like much of a threat. But if Zero's assessment of the man was even partly accurate, his physical prowess wasn't the issue . . .

"My colleague is Surgeon-Major Tang Li-na," Kwan said. The second figure, the female, gave a slight bow of her head. "The Surgeon understands your kind, and will be conducting this interrogation."

"It will be my pleasure, Honoured Commander."

Kwan continued, "You will answer my questions, Prisoner. Is that understood?"

I had no choice but to lie there, but that didn't mean I had to like it. "Fuck you," I replied.

"She has spirit, this one," said the Surgeon.

Her face was brilliantly lit as she positioned herself over me, and I could see her more clearly as well. Surgeon-Major Tang wore a surgical mask, tight over a defined chin, and was younger than Kwan, although I couldn't say by how much. She pushed a shock of bright blonde hair – striking against her similarly Asian features – from her forehead, where an ocular medi-viewer was fixed. The multi-lensed apparatus clicked and whirred as she focused it on my body.

"We are of the Asiatic Directorate," Tang said, "and you are in the star system Joseon-696, on the planet Jiog. This is a sovereign colony of Unified Korea." She paused. "Under Council Directive 988, we have permission – indeed, we have a *duty* – to investigate any potential threat to the national security. Be aware, Prisoner, that the Honoured Commander has authority to execute any and all who trespass into Directorate territory."

Although I already knew this, Tang seemed to take great pride in informing me of it. She was a patriot through and through, this one. I knew that I wasn't getting out of this alive, no matter what these people said.

"We will start at the beginning," Tang said. "Why were you sent here?"

"I'm not telling you a Gaia-damned thing," I answered.

"What is your mission?" Kwan said.

Now there was a question. The European Confederation vessel *Hannover* had been our mission objective. We had been sent into the Maelstrom, into the Gyre, to recover the starship, or at least to search for survivors. There had been none, but we'd secured the *Hannover*'s black box. All well and good, except that the box and all of its data had been stolen . . .

Kwan asked, "Were you sent here to kill *me*?"

When I didn't answer, Tang said, "Her silence speaks for itself."

"It is exactly as I thought," Kwan said. He wore distrust like a cloak. "The Alliance would love to finish the Directorate once and for all. I am an easy target."

Tang nodded enthusiastically, very much taken with that idea. "Yes, Honoured Commander. She is an assassin. Her ship was filled with military technology."

"Make no mistake, Prisoner," Kwan said, ignoring Tang. "I will get answers. We have access to your ship's mainframe. It will take time, of course, but eventually we will discover your mission."

Then you don't need me, I thought.

Kwan pre-empted that conclusion and said, "But things will be easier for you, Prisoner, if you talk. Who sent you here? Was it the Senator?"

That could only be Senator Lopez: the father of Private Gabriella Lopez. His political aspirations, to become Secretary General of the Alliance, appeared to be a constant no matter where in the universe we travelled.

"We already know that his daughter was among your squad," Tang added.

I knew that it had been too much to ask for that fact to go unnoticed by the Directorate. Although I tried to hide it, Kwan must've seen the reaction that the surgeon's comment stirred in me.

"We have pored over your ship," Kwan said. "Have no doubt that every scrap of intelligence has been secured, and will be analysed accordingly. Her callsign is 'Senator'. Why is that?"

Lopez was an unexpected prize haul for the Directorate. She would be a bartering chip to be used against the Alliance, against a rising political star. I didn't like Senator Lopez much, that was for sure, but the fact that the Directorate now had his daughter in their custody was a major blow to the Alliance.

I ground my teeth and looked up at the ceiling.

"I suppose that it would be a badge of honour for him to claim the head of Commander Kwan Ryong-ho for the Alliance," Tang suggested. "It would shatter the Directorate for good."

"Which is exactly why you will not be getting free," Kwan said, glancing down at his fingernails. "I take it that she is drugged?"

Tang gave a small shrug. "Yes. It is difficult to be precise, given her condition, but it should be enough to keep her under control."

"You continue to impress, Honoured Surgeon," Kwan muttered.

"I am grateful for your praise."

Tang wore a medical smock that had started as white, but was striped with red and brown stains: worn more proudly than the various Asiatic Directorate emblems of service that adorned her lapel.

"Get a fucking room," I growled.

"So you will speak?" Kwan replied. "Then we will begin," he continued, eager to hurry this along. "Why are you here? If you have not been sent here to assassinate me, then what *is* your mission?"

"My name is Keira Jenkins," I said, by rote. "My rank is lieutenant. I am serving with the Alliance Army Simulant Operations Programme. My serial number is 967253."

"What is your mission?" Kwan repeated. "Why are you in Directorate space?"

In the process of searching for the *Hannover*, we had discovered that the Krell had been infected with a plague. The contagion was spreading through the Maelstrom like wildfire, and many Collectives had already become infected. We had agreed to help the Krell search for a cure, and I had made contact with a navigator-form: a higher-function fish head, capable of speaking for the whole shoal. That ad hoc alliance had been shattered when the Black Spiral attacked the Krell ark-ship. I'd seen the Spiral's leader, codename Warlord, deploy some sort of capsule, and I suspected that the Spiral were responsible for spreading the virus.

"Are you an infiltrator?" Tang asked. "Perhaps sent here to find state secrets? To steal information for your masters back in the Core Systems?"

Commander Kwan tried a different approach. "Your comrades have already spoken," he insisted. "But I want to hear this from you, the mission commander. Think of this as an opportunity. Should you speak, you have my word that things will be easier for your subordinates."

"My name is Keira Jenkins . . ." I replied.

At the edge of my vision, I could just make out two more figures, standing at what I assumed was the hatch to the torture chamber. Both were armed; with AUG-30 PDWs – personal defence weapons – crossed over their enormous chests. These were the twins: Fire and Ice. Their presence was ghostly, slightly otherworldly, and their bug-eyed goggles reflected the light back at me. A battered medical drone also watched on at a safe distance, recording the proceedings for broadcast on the Directorate's only remaining government news channels. Footage like this was pure gold for the propaganda effort.

"My rank is lieutenant. I am serving with the Alliance Army Simulant Operations Programme . . ."

Tang loitered at the head of the table. Her own ocular headset flashed and flickered, recording and analysing everything that I did and said.

"Should I make her speak for you, Honoured Commander?" Tang enquired. Her Standard was stilted, overly formal, but her eyes were dark wells. The aura of excitement that prickled about her was very nearly pheromonal. "I can, through the application of certain drugs, *encourage* compliance . . ."

"Not yet," Kwan said. "She will break. She knows that this is best for her." His authority reasserted, Kwan began again, "I am giving you one more chance. Let us start with your capture. Tell me the story of when you first arrived at my facility. How we found your ship drifting in space."

"Controlled space," Tang added. "*Sovereign* space."

"Directorate space," Kwan concluded, with a nod.

I focused on the light overhead. "My rank is lieutenant."

"There were five simulators on your ship," Kwan said, voice a quiet growl. "And yet we have recovered only four operators. We know your callsigns, your operator's credentials. We know that the fifth tank was used by a soldier called Daneb Riggs."

Kwan's eyes narrowed. He had hit on a nerve, and he knew it. I fought to control the unconscious reaction to the line of interrogation, but it wasn't easy. Tang's medi-viewer ticked and beeped as it registered my shifting bio-rhythms.

"Where is the fifth soldier?" Kwan asked. "Was he killed?"

"Or has he already infiltrated our facility?" Tang suggested.

I had no loyalty to Riggs, not any more. He had betrayed me, betrayed all of us . . . Kwan and Tang stood, waiting for my account.

But of course, I told them nothing. I wouldn't give the Directorate the satisfaction of confirming even a single detail. I retreated to my safe place.

"My name is Keira Jenkins. My rank is lieutenant. I am serving with the Alliance Army Simulant Operations Programme. My serial number is 967253."

Commander Kwan let out a sigh. I got the distinct impression that he was someone who expected to get what he wanted on the first request. In that case, he and I weren't going to become friends anytime soon.

"Please, give up this pathetic charade," Kwan said. He sighed again, showing his exasperation. "As an Alliance Army operative, you are an enemy of the state. An enemy of the Asiatic Directorate."

What Directorate? I wanted to scream back. *You guys are supposed to be gone. The Directorate is finished.*

Tang nodded profusely. "We know who you are. Former member of the Lazarus Legion. You served under the terrorist known as Lieutenant Colonel Conrad Harris."

Now, that got the better of me, and I answered despite myself.

"I'm not that person any more," I said, strength rising in my voice. "I'm not *anyone* any more."

Kwan smiled. It was a cruel, but somehow tired, expression. "You are an asset of the Asiatic Directorate, and as such you will answer my questions. Why was your ship carrying a Krell bio-form?"

Pariah's history was special. The Directorate already had the alien's body. They were probably torturing it just as they were torturing me.

"What do you know about the virus spreading through the Maelstrom?" Kwan followed up. "Tell us why the Krell are evacuating their homeworlds."

This was new information, but I knew that it was all part of their interrogation technique. I was probably being drip-fed the intelligence because I wasn't leaving this room alive. A second passed as Tang and Kwan waited for my response.

And, eventually, I did reply.

"My name is Keira Jenkins. My rank is lieutenant . . ."

Commander Kwan's hackles rose. He seemed to increase

in size, his jaw set. He spoke over me, in his quiet, commanding way.

"They say that simulant operators are selected because of their insensitivity to pain," he muttered. "Is that right?"

"I am serving with the Alliance Army Simulant Operations Programme . . ."

Kwan nodded his head, just once, and Tang turned her back to me. There was a trolley behind her. It held a selection of implements that would make a torturer proud: metallics glinting as they reflected the chamber lights. Tang selected a laser scalpel and activated the blade. The brilliant flash brought with it an involuntary gush of memories; made every muscle in my body seize up. Tang saw my reaction, and her brow creased with interest.

"The body remembers what the mind tries to forget," she remarked. "That is most interesting."

"We have methods of retrieving your memories," Kwan said. "A full neural download, for example, will allow us uninhibited access to the contents of your head. The process is painful."

"*Excruciatingly* painful," Tang echoed.

I knew that choice of words – "*the contents of your head*" – wasn't accidental. The sentence was spoken with real threat. From any other organisation in human space, I would've thought it was just bluster. But the Directorate were – or at least had been – masters of this technology. They'd been stripping prisoners of their memories and their skins for longer than I'd been in the Army, and the stories of what they were capable of made even the most grizzled veteran's blood run cold . . .

"The procedure is universally fatal," Kwan said, reining in Tang's enthusiasm, "but the results are not always reliable. So, it would be better for all concerned if you gave us answers now."

The drone overhead watched and watched. Its red eye glimmered maliciously.

"My name is Keira Jenkins . . ."

"Fine," Kwan said. He didn't even look in my direction as he gave the order. "Take her apart."

"Of course, Honoured Commander."

She flipped the ocular display over her face, protecting her eyes from the scalpel's intense, burning light.

Tang had been wrong. The mind well remembered this pain. I started to scream; the noise echoing around the chamber, echoing around my own head.

Like I said, I was screwed. Totally and utterly screwed.

None of it was real, of course.

I was in a simulant. My real body was in a simulator-tank, held somewhere else in the prison. It hadn't taken our captors long to figure out how to use the technology once they had recovered it from the *Santa Fe*. They had seized the stock of sims in the ship's hold, and now they were putting them to a use for which they had never been intended.

The Surgeon-Major did her thing, and for all its engineered perfection, the simulant didn't last long. The Directorate knew torture, and Tang had honed her technique: knew just the right flesh to peel, muscles to cut, bones to break. In a real skin, you have a pain threshold. Once that's crossed, you go into shock. There's only so much damage a real body can take. But simulants don't have that safety mechanism. Tang just kept going and going on the simulant until there was nothing left of it, and even if I had wanted to speak I doubt that I would've been able.

Eventually I extracted, but it didn't stop there. When Tang had finished with the first body, we went again.

And again.

And again.

I lost track of how many transitions and extractions I made. Still, I didn't talk.

Kwan finally made the call.

"We are finished for today," he said. Pressed down his uniform. Picked a little lint off the chest. "Perhaps some reflection will assist the prisoner in making the right decision."

I knew that it wasn't over, but for today it was done.

In the circumstances, that surely had to be some sort of victory.

CHAPTER THREE

ENGINEERED PERFECTION

Fire and Ice appeared in front of my simulator-tank, and hauled me from inside. The conducting gel necessary to operate the tank had turned a filthy green, filled with floating debris, and it flushed out across the floor, poured over the boots of the waiting troopers.

I wasn't in the torture room any more, but this chamber wasn't any better than the last; like everything else on Jiog, dirty, empty, hopeless. Tang stood a safe distance from my tank, at the edge of the room.

"Hold her there," she said, logging data on a slate. "I need readings."

Fire grabbed one arm, Ice the other.

"Stand," grunted Fire. "Now."

I made a perfunctory attempt to resist them, but I knew that it wasn't worth the calories. Both were fully armoured in black hard-suits, and my fists bounced off their hides. The Directorate clones never seemed to remove their armour, but they were always bareheaded. I suspected that was deliberate – a destabilisation tactic – because they looked so much like Feng. Had they been born from the same cloning crèche? Dark hair shaved close to scarred scalps, faces covered with proto-Taoist tattoos. Fire on the right of his face, Ice on the left. Their faces were otherwise identical: blunt-featured, broad-nosed, slabs of men. They even appeared to have scars in the same place.

Ice shook my shoulder. "Hold still."

They both spoke perfect Standard. Probably part of their birthing download.

"You're bastards," I spat.

"Do we have to go through this again?" Tang asked. "Your comrades are far less obstructive."

She spread her arms. Through aching eyes, I saw the other simulators positioned around the room. The tanks were currently empty, but I could tell that they had recently been used from the pools of conducting fluid on the ground. Every Jackal except Zero was operational. I had no doubt that they had undergone torture and interrogation in their own private hells.

Ice flipped a shock-baton from his belt. The two-foot truncheon crackled with blue light, filled the air with the smell of ozone. The scent was much better than the cloying smell of faeces that lingered in the chamber.

A Directorate medtech checked me over with some sort of handheld device. This body – my real body – was still in one piece, but only just. I was naked, dripping wet with conducting fluid, and covered in bruises, cuts and burns. I glanced down at my limbs and noticed how much weight I'd lost. We'd only been here six days, by my reckoning, but six days was a long time in Directorate custody. Malnutrition had hit me hard. I was losing muscle mass, and fast. The tattoos of my present and former military service had faded, become barely visible against my filthy skin.

The medtech appeared again, a folded prison uniform placed across her open hands. Ice took it, and under duress I dressed. The uniform was coarse-fibred, uncomfortable, and it had no insignia, no identifiers. Shackles at the wrists and ankles completed the ensemble.

Tang started, "I want to see if . . ." but her words trailed off.

Something rumbled all around us, and the walls of the prison shook. Tang's eyes panned the ceiling, expectantly. Fire and Ice froze in position. The vibration came up through the soles of my feet; was strong enough to loosen a layer of dust from the ceiling, fat motes drifting past the bare-bulb lamps.

"What's happening?" I asked.

"Nothing," said Fire. "It'll pass."

"Get her out of here," Tang said, abruptly. "Take her to the hole."

"Yes, Honoured Surgeon."

Before I could ask any more questions – not that I would get answers – I was dragged out of the room.

Jiog prison complex was a sprawling mess of gantries, walkways and chambers. Hundreds of individual cells lined the walls of this cell block: each holding a prisoner behind old-fashioned bars. The main block extended for as far as I could see – reaching into shadow in the distance. There was no telling how many prisoners were being held here, but at a guess it was in the thousands. The sound of so many detainees in one place was overwhelming; the clattering of metal against cell doors, of whoops and yells and screams. Filthy hands reduced to claws by starvation reached from between cell bars as we went. Most of the prisoners here were Alliance servicemen and -women. Some wore military uniforms, others prison outfits, others yet just rags. It made me feel sick.

Hope was as alien to these prisoners as the Krell. Kwan and his men had this place properly sealed up: failsafe upon failsafe. There were armed guards everywhere, both above and below me. Wearing tactical vests and carrying shock-batons, shotguns across chests. Propaganda posters lined the walls, repeating the mantra HONOUR, OBEY, SERVE in Standard. Walking guard stations, called Prowlers, patrolled the edges of the prison complex. The bipedal machines swept every gantry and deck with mobile spotlights, their riders panning heavier automatic weapons across the banks of cells.

Fire and Ice dragged me along the main corridor, and we passed work-gangs in filthy orange survival-suits. I had no idea what the workers actually did on Jiog's surface, but they seemed selected from the larger, healthier prisoners. The workers were manacled together in a ragged column, their chains *clank-clanking* as they marched to another sector of the prison.

"Novak . . .?" I called, as I recognised a familiar face. "Is that you?"

The Directorate had probably realised that Leon Novak had no information to give – that, as a lifer, he wasn't worth interrogating. His enormous muscled frame, face covered in gang-tattoos and nerve-studs in his brow, was unmistakable.

Novak grinned an unhealthy smile, but we were ships passing in the night, nothing more than that. His work-gang was gone before I had a chance to speak with him. *He looks okay*, I thought, reassuring myself. Of all the Jackals, I knew that Novak was the trooper most likely to adjust to life in the prison. Many of his group looked like they carried similar gang markings, familiar script tattooed over faces and scalps. Perhaps Novak even had some friends in here.

"Keep moving," said Ice.

"We're almost home," added Fire.

We reached the junction of a prison block. Korean characters were printed overhead; words that I didn't understand, but I had come to recognise. *Solitary confinement.* The door slipped open.

They pulled me further down the corridor. Through a security gate, and a chamber that scanned me with blue light. More guards armed with pistols worn on the hip . . .

"Don't even think about it," said Fire.

A shock-baton slammed into the back of my legs. I didn't give them the satisfaction of going down; instead, whirled about to face them. Fire and Ice paused, waiting, watching. Challenging. Fire had his baton fully racked. It crackled with energy.

"Just give me any excuse," he said.

I relaxed my posture. "Not today, boys."

They looked almost disappointed. Another guard opened the hatch set into the floor. It settled with a loud *clunk*.

"Inside," said Ice. "Now."

Fire grabbed one arm, Ice the other. They tossed me down the hatch. I hit the floor hard.

"Fuck you both," I yelled to the dark.

The hatch slammed shut above me.

In the distance, I could hear a scream. It sounded a lot like Feng.

Had it really been six days since we'd arrived on Jiog? It was, I realised, impossible to say with any certainty. Without a day–night cycle by which to measure the passing of time, my circadian rhythm was a distant memory. We could've been here for weeks, for all I knew. The disorientation was all part of the scheme; a classic interrogation technique.

The screaming stopped, eventually. I sat on the dank, mouldy floor. The wall at my back was as wet as the ground. I was hungry, cold and angry. Not a good combination.

The stigmata left from the torture session were all over my body. A neat welt across my shoulder. An incision that stretched from gullet to gut. Dissection marks at the limbs, at every major joint. The red, psychosomatic line that marked where Tang had just opened my sternum was particularly bright and painful. None of the injuries was real, but all of them were remembered. I pulled my prison uniform a little tighter at the neck and tried to forget.

The Asiatic Directorate had been a feature in my life since before I could remember. My father had fought them during the Deimos Campaign. He was filled with old war stories of what a treacherous and dangerous opponent they could be, and he was keen to tell anyone who would listen. Still, in those early days – when I'd been a teenager, and we'd been living in San Angeles territory – he showed a certain kind of grudging respect for the Directorate. While he didn't approve of their behaviour, as a military man he could appreciate their training, discipline and determination.

All that changed when my younger brother had been killed in a bomb-blast outside of a shopping mall in Diego District. There was no rhyme or reason for the atrocity – when tensions between the Alliance and the Directorate were at their peak, there rarely was – and that somehow made it worse. His name had been Robin, and he had been thirteen years old. Theodore Jenkins' only son had been swept up in a conflict that had been going on for generations. The Directorate claimed immediate responsibility for the dirty little nuclear device that decimated a good portion of Diego District, and that was it: Robin was gone, and Teddy was left with his disappointment of a daughter for consolation.

After the incident – Mom never called it "murder", and as a family we'd settled on the neutral terminology that seemed to imply there was no real fault on anyone's behalf

– Dad's attitude to the Directorate changed. Hell, his attitude to life changed. He was withdrawn, inward-looking and damned well critical of everything I did.

"Sorry, Dad," I said, just to hear the sound of my own voice. "I let you down again. Let you down real good."

My father had never wanted me to join up with Simulant Operations. He'd wanted Army kids, had wanted us to enlist in a proper military service. I'd tried doing that, just to please him, but when the opportunity to join Simulant Operations had come up, who was I to say no? Sim Ops – riding the galaxy in a body that wasn't really yours – wasn't his thing. He couldn't understand why I had decided to transfer out of regular Army, and enrol in the Programme. Of course, he'd never made a transition; never known the way a true operator feels when they get to inhabit another version of themselves.

But maybe he was right, I thought. *Where has Sim Ops got me? Trapped on a Directorate rock.*

Not that it particularly mattered where I was, but I took in the detail of the cell. It was a few metres cubed, walls covered with dirty ceramic tiles. I'd already tried peeling those away, but after long hours of effort I'd given up. There was a light above me, distant: as though I was at the bottom of a deep well, looking up a shaft.

"It's real cold in here, huh?" came a voice, in the dark beside me. "Not what I'm used to, that's for sure."

I swallowed, sat up.

"Who's there?" I asked.

"Tau Ceti is a long way from Jiog, and Ceti V is warm like you wouldn't believe. Peaceful, too. We never had to worry about the Directorate when I was growing up."

But I recognised the voice. *This isn't possible. You know that it isn't.* A shape disentangled from the dark in one corner

43

of the cell. Face caught by the single shaft of light from above.

"Don't be like that, Jenk," he said. "You and I used to get on just fine."

Daneb Riggs stood over me. He wore his Alliance Army uniform, slightly dishevelled, open at the neck to reveal his muscular torso. His dark hair was tousled just so, broad arms crossed over his chest. He looked as young as I remembered him: a perfect replica of the man who had betrayed us – had betrayed *me* – during our flight from the Maelstrom.

"You've lost weight," he said, rolling his head disapprovingly. "You should watch that. Your strength will suffer."

A tide of hate and anger and disgust crashed over me. It was only quelled by the fact that I knew Riggs wasn't really here: that he was a figment of my imagination. Too little sleep, too little food, and too much torture can do strange things to a girl's mind.

"They've done a job on you," he said, shaking his head again. "The Directorate sure are bastards."

"You can hardly talk. You're worse than them."

Riggs' face creased as though he was disappointed at my reaction. "I was a member of your squad, once. I was your second in command. I was your golden boy. I was a *Jackal*."

"And now you're a traitor."

Riggs gave a half-hearted smile, his broad features open and honest and completely devoid of malice. "Come on. Don't be like that. I did what I had to do."

"Fuck you."

"Watch your language."

"Why'd you do it, Riggs?"

He sighed wistfully. "It wasn't an easy call, Jenk. Believe me when I say that."

"I don't believe anything you say."

Not least because you aren't really here . . .

"It's complicated," Riggs said. But as he drew nearer to me, I saw that he had something in his hand. He was holding a crudely machined infinity spiral, on a chain, looped between his fingers. The Black Spiral's icon.

"You're one of them?" I said. "You're working for the Black Spiral?"

Riggs smiled. "You don't *work* for the Spiral. See, that shows how wrong you've got the whole system. It's why you people can't stop Warlord. You don't work for him; you become *part* of the Spiral."

"And now you've got the *Hannover*'s black box . . ."

"Not personally," said Riggs. "Not any more, anyway. But yeah; the Spiral has the box now."

"You used me!" I said, my voice a muted hiss.

Riggs crouched. He wore heavy, Army-issue boots: the soles crunching debris as he moved.

"You let me do it, Jenk. You've got to take some responsibility for what happened."

"I don't have to do a damned thing, except die in this hellhole."

"That's true, I guess. Die again, and again, and again . . ." Riggs whispered. "You ever stop to think there has to be an end to all this?"

"I'll end you, for what you did."

"Calm down. I get that you're angry, and I'm fine with it. That's not what I meant."

"You don't mean anything," I snarled. "Not to me. Not any more."

"*I* might not," Riggs said, pressing one of his big hands to his chest. "But you want to ask yourself a question: how many times can you do this? How many times can you die before it begins to *matter*?"

45

"Fuck you."

"You've said that already," he said. Grinned some more. "And we already have, as well. Lots of times, as I remember. You seemed to like it."

"You're not real, Riggs. You're not here, and I'm not wasting my energy talking to you."

"It was so damned easy to get under your skin. You were a soft target. Older woman, younger man. Disaffected with her job." He shrugged. "After what happened with your last big outfit, the Lazarus Legion, you were just so desperate to be loved . . ." Riggs pulled a face now, an exaggerated look of disapproval. "It was pretty gross, to be honest. You reeked of desperation."

I snarled. Lunged across the cell, my fingers turned to claws. Riggs pulled back, into shadow.

"You'll have to be faster, next time," Riggs whispered. "But chin up, Keira. You'll get through it one way or another."

"I'm going to find you, Riggs. Find you, and kill you."

Riggs' outline was gone now; completely melded with the shadow. But I could see the slits of his eyes, reflecting the low light, and I heard his last words clear enough.

"You don't know what's coming, Jenkins. None of you do . . ."

His voice trailed off, just as another vibration hit the walls of the cell. Was it more violent than the last episode? It felt like it was. I reached out with a hand and steadied myself against the wall until the noise and motion had passed.

"You in there?" came another voice.

I expected at first to see Riggs again, but it wasn't him.

"Ma'am? You there?" it repeated.

"Novak?" I said, on my hands and knees now, searching the mouldy cell wall. That was where the voice seemed to

46

be coming from. "Where are you? How – how are you?"

"How am I talking?" he asked. "Cracked pipe, in wall. Am in next cell."

"How's that possible?"

Novak chuckled. "This is prison. I am lifer, yes? I know prisons, ma'am. I know places like this."

"Thank Christo."

"Keep voice down," Novak said. "There are guards up there."

"Please tell me that I'm not imagining you too . . ."

My chest suddenly felt tight with emotion. This was the first time I'd spoken to a member of the Jackals since our capture, and I hadn't expected the stir that it caused in me.

"If you were imagining a member of the Jackals, wouldn't you be imagining one of the others?" Novak asked, his tone amused.

"Fair point."

"Are you hurt?"

"Not badly," I said. "I can walk. I can fight."

"Good."

"I saw you today. I saw you in the prison—"

"Yes, yes. I work. I am in gang."

"That was fast," I muttered. "We've been here, what, six days?"

I heard Novak inhale sharply. "We have been here long time. Weeks, ma'am."

Although I'd expected as much, Novak's words still shocked me. I was losing control in here, and things were only going to get worse.

"Have you seen the others?" I asked. "Have you seen Zero? Did Carmine make it out?"

Zero and Carmine: they couldn't make transition. They didn't use the simulants like the rest of us. Were the

47

Directorate torturing their real bodies somewhere in the prison?

"They are alive," Novak said.

"Are you sure? How do you know?"

"Like I say, I know prison. World is different: system is the same."

"We have to get out of here, Novak."

"I know," he said. "We will. Be careful what you say. They are listening."

The ever-present threat of surveillance wasn't just paranoia. A spy-eye – a black half-globe, shiny and new, very out of place with the surrounding features of the cell – was attached to the ceiling. It winked the occasional light down at me, reminding me that I was being watched, being listened to. Everything and everywhere in the prison was bugged.

The cold ceramic tiling of the wall suddenly began to vibrate, and I jumped back. Another shockwave, or whatever it was, thundered through the cell. Followed by a distant roll of thunder, that dissolved into something like boots drumming on the deck.

"Do you know what's making that noise, Novak?"

"It's happening," Novak said. "They're coming."

"Who's coming?"

"Soon," Novak whispered. "It'll happen soon."

"What will happen? Tell me!"

"The voice knows."

"What voices?"

"Not *voices*," Novak replied. "*Voice*. The Voice. In my head."

"Okay," I said. My heart sank with disappointment. "Okay."

"It tells me things, and it will tell you, too."

"What things?"

Novak paused, then answered, "Sleep, now."

I collapsed back against the wall. So that was it; Novak had finally gone mad. Deep down, I wasn't surprised. He hadn't exactly been sane before our capture, and Jiog had tipped him over the edge. My hope that he had an actual plan to get us off this rock was fleeting, and I felt it drain from me as I lay in the dark.

There was another noise overhead; the clatter of a baton against the security hatch. A figure up there, glancing through the observation window. I recognised Fire's broad face, the tattoo on his cheek just visible, watching me down in the dark. But he just moved off, disappeared.

When he was gone, I whispered, "Novak?" I searched the wall for a crack, a seam, some shred of evidence that Novak was on the other side. "Novak! Are you there?"

But there was no answer.

I sat alone in the whispering dark, and pondered his words. *Soon. It'll happen soon.*

CHAPTER FOUR

REDACTION

The observation hatch cracked open; bright light pouring down the shaft. A face appeared at the lip of the portal.

"Get up."

I didn't sleep in the hole, not really. The space was too wet, dark and unpleasant for any downtime to count as actual rest. But I had been dozing, and now I stirred.

"Hands open," barked Fire. "Away from the ladder."

I did as ordered, and an extendable metal ladder slipped down the shaft, clanking noisily as its feet hit the floor. Ice and another anonymous masked trooper began the descent into my cell; Fire covering them with his AUG-30.

"I'm not trying anything," I said. *Not yet, anyway.*

Ice gave that same disappointed look as he reached the base of the ladder. He folded my arms behind my back and slapped a pair of magnetic manacles around my wrists. Pushed me forward, into the stress position. This was uncomfortable, painful even, but nothing new, and nothing like what these bastards were capable of.

"Up," Ice said.

"You really should ask a girl if she's busy before you take her on a date," I said.

"You're not funny," Ice replied.

"I'm not trying to be."

Up the ladder. Through the main prison chamber, and towards the medical wing, escorted by Fire and Ice. Tang and a gaggle of medtechs were waiting there, but something else caught my attention.

"Jackals!" I called. "Report!"

Feng and Lopez, manacled, eyes forward, were flanked by guards. At the sound of my voice, the troopers turned. They were both badly dishevelled, beaten, malnourished. It hurt to see them this way. Feng in particular had a face full of bruises, and angry red welts lined his neck: injuries that had probably been caused by an active shock-baton. But despite his condition, Feng's face split in a smile when he saw me. I noticed a missing tooth when he did so, and that his left eye socket had ballooned.

"Ma'am!" he said. "You're alive!"

"I knew that you would be," Lopez said.

Lopez was barely recognisable. Dark hair hanging in lank strands, her face streaked with dirt. She swayed as she spoke, and a trooper propped her up.

"Guards," Tang said, "ensure that the prisoners remain pacified at all times. If any of them misbehave, you have my permission to use force. Non-lethal, in the first instance."

A dozen soldiers, each with the physique of Fire and Ice, milled around the medical chamber. All wearing kevlar vests and head gear, decked out with personal defence weapons and shock-batons. The bay should've been crowded with so many personnel, but I realised that something was different.

The simulators were gone. I loathed the reaction, but my data-ports – where I made connection with the simulator, which would allow me to make the neural-link to my waiting sim – had started to buzz with anticipation. That sensation evaporated, to be replaced by rising anxiety.

"What are you doing, Tang?" I asked. "What've you done with the simulators?"

"Not your concern, Prisoner," Tang replied. "Prepare them."

We were stripped naked, manacles removed.

"They're ready," said Ice.

"Do it," Tang ordered.

An army of medics, carrying hypodermics, descended on us.

"Where's Zero?" Feng shouted. His voice was achingly hoarse, as though he had been screaming or shouting for a long, long time. "Have you seen her, ma'am?"

Zero wasn't here. Neither she, Novak nor Pariah were present. Novak was probably still on work duty, and I doubted that the Directorate would risk putting Pariah on release, but where was Zero? Panic gripped me.

"Where's my officer, Tang? What have you done with her?"

"If you've hurt her—" Feng started, but his words were lost as a guard slammed an activated baton into his chest.

There was no time for further argument.

I felt the spike of a needle in my arm, and the world immediately started to lose clarity.

"Commence procedure," said Tang.

Immediately, this was different, and immediately this was much, much worse than what had come before.

I woke, but I was in my real body this time. Standing up, more or less; restrained, pinned to another gravity-plate. I had never been inside one of the torture chambers in my real skin before today, and I didn't like it much. Feng and Lopez were here too; arranged in a triangular formation, a distance between each of us. Restrained in the same way: facing forward. Feng's body flexed and bucked with un-bridled fury. Now that he was naked, I could see just how badly he had been beaten. Not simulated injuries; these were for real.

"Zero?" Feng said.

Zero. Sergeant Zoe Campbell. She knelt on the floor. Head lowered, but when she heard Feng's voice she looked up with red-rimmed eyes.

"It's okay," she said, so quietly that I could barely hear her. "I'm okay."

She so obviously wasn't. The room closed in around me, and the Jackals dissolved into shouted protestations, insults, threats. But it was useless, and we knew it. The restraint equipment was simulant-proofed. What chance of escape did we have in our real skins?

"*You motherfuckers!*" Feng shouted. "You touch her, and I'll rip you apart with my bare hands! I swear it!"

And not just Zero.

"Carmine . . ." I said.

She wore the remains of her Navy uniform, and had seen almost as much attention as Feng. The old captain's face and shoulders were a seething mass of colourful bruises; a mouth-watering range of blues, greens, browns. She looked up at me and nodded. Yeah, that was Carmine. Too strong to give the Directorate the satisfaction of breaking her. She'd hold out until the very end, and then some.

"Don't worry," Carmine said. "I'm fine too. It'd take more than these ten-credit operators to finish me, that I can tell you."

She still had spirit, but she looked so frail, so old. At her age, she was taking this worst of all of us. Her bionic leg was positioned awkwardly, the trouser hem of her uniform torn. Dried blood caked a wound on her cheek.

"Silence."

Commander Kwan and Surgeon-Major Tang stalked the perimeter of the chamber, a safe distance from each of the gravity-plates. Fire and Ice were present too, both fully armoured. A flock of drones hovered overhead.

Lopez and I fell quiet, but Feng didn't have that sort of control. He was rabid as an infected Krell; his eyes bulging, teeth snapping, foaming at the mouth. Kwan observed him with a contemptuous stare.

"How the mighty have fallen," he said. "A proper Directorate trooper values loyalty. It is truly incredible that this one was birthed of the same crèche as my personal cadre."

Tang nodded in agreement. "I was the progenitor of the cloning programme," she said, looking in Feng's direction. "Does that surprise you, Prisoner?"

"The surgeon is known as the 'Mother of Clones' in some circles," Kwan muttered. "She was even on Delta Crema, although before your birthing."

Delta Crema was the place of Feng's inception. The Alliance had liberated him from a crèche there, and it had once been a major cloning facility under Directorate control.

"I can do incredible things with the flesh," Tang muttered. "It is a gift, and one that I proudly dedicate to the good of the Asiatic Directorate." She smiled; a chilling, horrible expression. "The loyalty of my troopers is, ordinarily, unsurpassed." She paused in front of Feng's gravity-plate and evaluated him with her oculus. "But my work is not as flawless as I would have hoped. To a proper clone, loyalty is as vital as food and air." She sighed. "Without it, most wilt. They simply cannot live."

Feng growled at Tang, and she shrank back.

"That is no way to speak to your mother," she said. "Of course, when an errant child does not appreciate the reasons for its existence, like any good mother I have methods to bring it back into the fold . . ."

"Damn you all," Feng roared.

Kwan had grown bored of this discussion. "Shut the traitor up," he said.

Fire stepped forward, and snapped his shock-baton across Feng's stomach. The noise the impact produced was sickening. Feng was strong, and he kept ranting for a while, but after another few blows he got the message. The scent of burnt flesh, caused by the shock discharge, was thick in the air. I could feel the pain radiating off the young trooper, and it was almost too much to bear. Feng finally gave up: his snarls reduced to ragged gasps for breath.

"Good," Kwan said. "The dogs learn."

"We're Jackals," I spat. "Not dogs."

"You will all learn," Kwan said. "Sooner or later."

Zero turned away. Eyes fixed on the floor, she didn't want to see the beating. She looked so much smaller than the rest of the squad. Her prison overalls swamping her thin body, she appeared painfully resigned.

"If you've hurt her," I said, with as much poison as Feng, "I'll kill every last bastard on this planet!"

"You'll do no such thing, Prisoner X-563," said Tang.

She was already fussing over her tools. She selected a small electric saw and activated it. The saw's razor-blade wheel buzzed to life. Tang waved it menacingly over my naked stomach. I had a sudden, retch-inducing memory of every other death I'd suffered on this planet.

"Please – don't," Zero said, haltingly. "I'm okay, Jenkins. Th-they haven't hurt me.

None of this is real."

"Shut up, Prisoner X-233, also known as Zero," Kwan said. Then, back to Tang, "Restrain yourself, Surgeon-Major. You will have your chance."

"As you wish, Honoured Commander."

Kwan paced into the middle of the room, circling Zero and Carmine. The commander was dressed in an exo-suit – like the rest of his commandos, ready for deployment at a moment's notice – and the armour hummed quietly as he moved. He even had a slim-line thruster-pack on his back; a mobility unit that would allow him to jump and fly short distances. The chest-plate of his suit was covered in various medals and badges, the product of a lifetime's service in the Asiatic Directorate, and a heavy sidearm that looked more ceremonial than functional hung at one hip, a sword with a mono-blade at the other. His air of intimidation was magnified tenfold, which I guessed was exactly what he had intended.

"Today someone will break," Kwan declared. "Today, someone will tell me exactly what I want to hear. Activate the display."

Although it had that same torture-chic decor as the last, the chamber we were in today was different. One wall was filled with downloaded schematics, with tri-D plans and tactical reports. Mostly in Korean and Chino, but also Standard. This was everything that the Directorate had obtained from the *Santa Fe*'s data-stacks and mainframe; our entire surviving intelligence package. That was it then: Yukio had failed. Her attempt to burn the *Santa Fe*'s stacks had been unsuccessful. It wasn't surprising, but it was still disappointing.

"The Greater Asiatic Directorate does not have a Simulant Operations Programme," Kwan said. "The technology was withheld from us, by your Command. By your masters."

"You stole enough of it," I muttered. I glared at Kwan, and he continued pacing.

"The Alliance," he said, rolling the word around his mouth with obvious distaste, "is so eager to think of the Directorate as broken. As a spent force. There you are, with your superior technology and your Core Worlds, and your Shard Gates. And here we are, with our decimated prison worlds, our rag-tag fleet of starships, our shattered military.

"But we are not the spent force that your government would have you believe. We are simply biding our time. And your arrival here, in my system, makes me think that this time is *now*. I am the man to make it happen."

I sniggered. "You're nothing, and no one!"

Kwan exhaled slowly. He radiated danger. "I have power," he said. He spread his hands in a gesture that encompassed the world beyond the chamber. "*This* is real power."

"This is a shithole of a prison, Kwan."

He gave a world-weary grimace. "On the surface it might look like that. But I can assure you that the reality is very different. Having something that others want: *that's* power. Having the ability to change the universe, to influence galactic destiny: *that's* power.

"The Bureau of Shadow Affairs was once the premier intelligence agency in the Directorate. I could reel off the names of the many Alliance personnel we are responsible for assassinating. We were the Director-General's right hand; the agency that he turned to when all others failed."

Kwan looked to Fire and Ice, and they shone with pride at the commander's words. He clasped each by the shoulder.

"But all of that changed when the Directorate collapsed. Now we are an organisation without purpose. A body without a head."

Tang's eyes flared at that expression. Kwan was giving her ideas.

"I can change that, though. The other candidates for the Directorate's leadership are nothing more than pretenders, charlatans. *I* am different. I can see the long game, and I can reforge the Asiatic Directorate into something great. Into something better than it once was."

"And how are you going to do that?" I asked.

"We know that something is happening to the Krell. We know that something is happening in the Maelstrom. And now, thanks to our interrogation of your starship's data-stacks, we know that you have recently been into Krell territory. We know that there is a war going on. Reports had already started to reach us, but your intelligence confirms it.

"Where there is war, there is opportunity. I believe that your ship was sent into the Maelstrom to investigate a weapon. A weapon that your Alliance intends to use against the Directorate. I want you to tell me what you were searching for in the Maelstrom, and I want you to tell me right now."

Carmine laughed. It was a wet, bedraggled sound, but it was a laugh nonetheless.

"Same old Directorate," she managed. "You haven't changed at all. You won't get a damned thing from this old girl, that's for sure."

Kwan nodded, as though he had expected that reaction.

"This one – Prisoner X-567 – speaks often," Tang said. She stood behind Carmine. "Too much, in fact. It is a shame that none of what she says is important."

"They call me Carmine the Carbine," she answered. "And that's for two reasons. One is that I talk a lot. I ever get a chance to break out of these bonds, lady, I'll show you the other."

"Quiet, Carmine," I ordered.

"I'm Navy," she said, looking up at me. "You can't give me orders, Jenkins. When you've served for as long as I have, you get to understand people like this."

"Quiet!" Kwan roared.

"I've seen enough of them. Small men, with big ideas—"

"I said, shut up!"

But instead of focusing his wrath on Carmine, Kwan stopped behind Zero. He looked down at her with such malice that Carmine actually stopped talking. An even colder sensation settled deep in the pit of my stomach.

"I am told that what makes a true operator of simulants is the capacity to take suffering," he said. "That is what differentiates you from the average Army trooper. You have a much higher pain threshold."

Tang nodded. "Your flesh-puppets – your simulants – have an admirable capacity to take injury, to absorb damage. It is quite something."

"But these two are different," Kwan said, indicating Zero and Carmine. "Neither prisoner carries the data-ports."

Feng gave a sharp intake of breath. His jaw worked angrily, but the words wouldn't come. Not this time.

Tang moved forward, on cue, and tugged at Zero's overalls. Revealed her forearms, the back of her neck, where the data-ports necessary to interface with the simulant technology had once been. There were scars there, tiny reminders of Zero's abortive field career.

"Don't touch her," Carmine said. "I'm old. I can take it. Kill me instead."

But the Shadow agents were focusing their attentions on Zero.

"She is your intelligence officer," Tang said. "Yes?"

I watched Zero for a moment. I couldn't bring myself to reply.

"Answer the Honoured Surgeon," Kwan said.

With grim reluctance, I nodded. "Yes. She is."

"See how easy that was?" Kwan remarked. "Hands behind your head, Prisoner X-233."

"I said, stop this!" Carmine complained. "I'm growing fed up of this prison. It's cold, and my knees ache. Well, my real knee, anyway."

"Carmine, whatever you're trying to do, please be quiet!" I said.

The old captain nodded at me. Went to wink. "I know exactly what I'm doing," she said. "Tough as old boots, me. We'll have quite the story when we—"

Carmine's head exploded.

I couldn't compute what had just happened. Fire stirred behind Carmine's body, his gun at his hip. The old captain's corpse collapsed forward.

Oh shit. Carmine was dead. Actually fucking dead. Rage and horror and pure, unadulterated hate flooded my system.

Lopez immediately burst into scream. *"No! No! No!"*

"You bastards!" I shouted.

"Hands behind your head, Prisoner X-233!" Kwan repeated.

Carmine's execution had the desired effect, and Zero complied immediately. Despite her obvious efforts to hide it, she was shaking. Zero's head was blood-spattered. Not just any blood: Carmine's blood. It matted her hair, flecked the side of her face.

"Prisoner X-233 is what you call a 'negative', as I understand it," Kwan said, carrying on as if nothing had happened.

"She's a Jackal," Feng shouted. "Just like the rest of us!"

"For all her faults," Kwan said, "she is quite brave, this one. You can all hide inside your flesh-puppets, but she has no such armour."

"Don't touch her," Feng said. His voice dropped, cracked with emotion. "Don't even think about it."

Kwan ignored him though, and fixed his eyes on mine. "What is happening in the Maelstrom?"

When I didn't immediately answer, he flipped the catch on his pistol holster. Drew his weapon in the same fluid motion. He raised it, showed it to the chamber. The sidearm was bulky and multi-chambered, of a type I didn't recognise. That alone set off warning bells. There were very few weapons in current use that I didn't know . . .

Kwan aimed the pistol at the back of Zero's head. Jammed the muzzle against her skull, through the tangle of auburn hair. Zero froze, eyes wide, still staring on the patch of floor in front of her.

"Do you know what this is, Prisoner X-233?"

"N-no," Zero stammered.

"Address the commander with his proper title!" Tang said.

"No, Honoured Commander," Zero said.

"This," Kwan said, indicating the weapon, "is a redactor."

The muzzle of Kwan's pistol transformed, peeled open like a metal flower: became a dozen thin probes. Each was tipped with a needle.

"I warned you that it would come to this," Kwan explained, "and now you leave me no choice. The redactor will extract the prisoner's memories. Each probe," and the silver-tipped implements that made up the gun's muzzle quivered at that, as though they had a life of their own, "burrows deep into the subject's brain. The process is extremely painful, and extremely dangerous." Kwan shrugged. "There will not be much left of her when the procedure is complete."

"Nothing, really," Tang added. "Less than nothing. Less than Zero."

Kwan said, "We've tried this on meat puppets but it does not have the desired effect. The redactor only functions on original test subjects."

"Don't do this!" I said. "It doesn't have to happen!"

"No!" Feng shouted.

"Shut him up for good," Kwan ordered.

Fire and Ice descended on Feng, their shock-batons at full charge. The assault was short-lived but brutally effective. Blood spattered the floor and the table on which Feng was restrained. He hung there, barely conscious.

"I will ask again," Kwan said. "What is happening in the Maelstrom?"

"We don't know anything!" Lopez wailed.

"You actually expect me to believe that?" Kwan said. "You were sent out there to find a weapon. I want to know what happened in Krell space. I want to know why you were carrying a Krell bio-form – a *talking* Krell bio-form – on your starship!"

Kwan's arm was rigid, the pistol held firm. The arming stud on the side of the redactor flickered, taunting me. *What choice do we have?* I asked myself. I couldn't let this happen. Couldn't let Zero die like this.

"We . . . we were on a mission," I started. It was hard to find the words, to explain myself. I fought my natural instinct to remain silent in the face of interrogation. "A mission to find a missing starship. Please; the rest of my squad knows nothing. I'm their commanding officer. I'm responsible."

A glare around the room told the others not to dissent from that. Lopez remained frozen in place. Feng just lay against the medical table, his body plastered with fresh blood. His brow was so damned swollen that he was struggling to see out of his eyes.

"Go on," Kwan said, weapon arm unfaltering. The redactor's probes shivered in a horribly organic way.

"We were searching for the Euro-Confed starship *Hannover*. It went missing inside the Maelstrom, in the Gyre."

"While searching for a weapon?" Tang pressed.

I went to shake my head, but found that I couldn't do it under the field created by the gravity-plate. "No. It . . . It was on an exploratory mission," I managed. "But we never found the ship."

"You expect me to believe that?" Kwan said.

"It's the truth," Lopez chimed in.

"Leave this to me, Lopez," I ordered. "We didn't find the *Hannover*, but we discovered her black box, her flight data."

"Where is this flight data?" Kwan barked. "Tell me everything."

"It's gone."

"Lies!" Tang exclaimed. "Tell the Honoured Commander the truth!"

"There was a traitor onboard the *Santa Fe*," I said. "The fifth member of my squad. You saw his simulator. He Q-jumped us here, and then escaped with the data."

Kwan slammed the body of his pistol into the side of Zero's head with shocking abruptness. The noise was startlingly loud in the closed space; gut-churningly so. Zero folded without a sound, kept her hands on her head.

"This is your final chance," Kwan said. "Tell me everything, Lieutenant Keira Jenkins, of the Jackals, formerly of the Lazarus Legion, sworn enemy of the Asiatic Directorate."

"The traitor's name was Corporal Daneb Riggs!" I implored. "His callsign was Jockey, and he was a Marine aviator before he joined Sim Ops. He left the ship in a

Warhawk shuttle! He must've had accomplices nearby, maybe in your organisation!"

Kwan smiled grimly. "Now you accuse my men of disloyalty?"

"Check the *Santa Fe*'s log!" Lopez said. "You'll see that the shuttle left the *Santa Fe* after we jumped here. He could've been working for someone else – maybe the Black Spiral!"

"Lies! Lies! Lies!" Kwan snarled.

The pistol went to Zero's head again. She closed her eyes: tight, so tight.

It's okay, honey. You're going to be okay. Be brave for me.

"Kwan! No! Don't do this!"

"Her blood will be on your hands—"

A deafening boom spread throughout the facility. The quake drummed right through me, made the entire room shake. Tang's torture implements rattled on their tray. It was like the last time I'd heard the noise, but much, much louder. Closer, I decided.

The Directorate paused. Kwan's eyes became unfocused, lights twinkling beneath the skin of his cheek. That was the result of in-head comms: someone was communicating with him from outside of the room. He nodded, back becoming ramrod straight. At the same time, Tang began to wring her hands uncomfortably: her attention decisively diverted from the room.

The quake wasn't the only disruption. There were other noises, coming from all around us. Voices; yelled shouts from somewhere outside of the room.

"What's happening?" Lopez asked. "What's making the sound?"

"Be quiet," Kwan said.

The expression on his face told me enough. I was more chilled by that than anything I'd seen or heard so far. *He's scared*, I realised. Kwan and Tang were frightened by whatever had caused the noise . . .

Kwan shifted his attention back to Zero, still kneeling on the floor in front of him.

"Let her go, Kwan," I said. "We've told you everything. Killing her won't achieve a damned thing!"

"I don't believe you," Kwan said, through gritted teeth. "What is the Aeon? Where can we find it?"

"*Aeon?* I have no idea."

"They know more," Tang said. "They *must* know more!"

Lopez intervened, "We don't! You have to believe us!"

Fire and Ice were shouting something in Korean, speaking fast. Kwan's face was alight with activity. He was close enough that I could see much of the in-face circuitry was damaged. He looked like a particularly bad alcoholic, with a network of burst capillaries beneath the skin. But whatever he was being told did nothing to change his mind, and the redactor remained aimed at Zero's head.

We made eye contact, Zero and I. Her lips were pursed. She looked so tired.

"You're going to be fine," I mouthed, slowly. "I'll get us out of this."

Zero tried to smile but she was a smart girl. She knew my words were empty, and that made it hurt all the more.

Back to Kwan, I screamed, "Don't do this!"

Another quake hit the chamber. The glow-globes in the ceiling winked, throwing the room into dark, then light.

"Go from here," Tang ordered Fire and Ice. They reluctantly did so they were told, retreating out of the chamber through a side door.

"As commander-in-chief of the Bureau of Shadow

Affairs," Kwan began, "and by the authority vested in me by the Greater Asiatic Directorate, I hereby declare you all enemies of the state."

"Let her go!" Lopez shouted.

Feng was yelling too, but he wasn't making much sense.

"We need to go, Honoured Commander," Tang said, drawing back towards the door of the chamber. "Now."

Kwan stared up at me.

"I hereby authorise use of the redactor mind-probe. Commencing procedure."

CHAPTER FIVE

DISGUSTING PRISONERS

The lights went out again, and this time the blackout lasted longer. Several seconds passed.

When the lights came back, Zero, Carmine's body, the Directorate and the drones were gone. All gone. The space where Zero had been kneeling, where Kwan had held the redactor against her head, was empty.

"Zero?" Feng managed. His speech was slurred, so unclear that I could barely understand him. I guessed he'd bitten his tongue during the beating. "Where . . . is she?"

There was a grinding noise, the sound of a mechanism being forced. Some shouting in a language I didn't understand. Then part of the wall came away, revealing a secret door out of the room.

"You're fucking kidding me . . ." Lopez said.

"Why would I be kidding?" came a Russian accent. "Is not funny at all."

Novak stood there, framed by light from the chamber beyond. Dressed in a grubby worker-gang uniform, he carried a powered cutting tool in both hands. A dozen prisoners were lined up behind him, all wearing the same overalls, peering back with tattoo-covered faces.

"We are disgusting prisoners," Novak explained.

"You mean this is a prison revolt?" I asked.

"Exactly. Just like I said. Hurry; is not much time."

With a blunt exchange in what I took to be Russian, the other prisoners moved on Novak's word.

"What's happened to . . . to Zero . . .?" Feng said.

Novak nodded. "Was hologram. Hard light. Very realistic."

"*Very* realistic," Lopez agreed. "Then where is she?"

"Not here," Novak said. "We go now, find her."

"The thing with the redactor wasn't real then?"

"Probably was real, but not happening here."

"Does that mean Carmine is okay too?" I asked. There was hope here; fleeting, but possible. We could rescue both Zero and Carmine . . .

But Novak put paid to that idea. "I doubt it. They execute her for real. She was no use to them. We must go; must find Vali."

"Vali? Who's Vali?" Lopez asked.

Novak flinched at mention of the name, but recovered fast. He set his jaw. "I said Zero. Must act now, yes?"

Fire and Ice had been for real. Feng's injuries were testament to that. Kwan and Tang had kept themselves safe, while risking their subordinates.

"Need to . . . get her out . . ." Feng tried to say.

"Yes, yes. You first."

"How do you know any of this, Novak?" I said. Although I was grateful for the rescue, I was still unconvinced as to the source of Novak's intelligence.

"No time now. We talk later. Zero; she is in real danger."

"Let's just get out of here and worry about the rest when we can," Lopez said.

Novak and his compatriots were already inspecting the grav-plates, testing whether they could be broken with the equipment they had with them.

"These guys friends of yours?" I asked.

Novak shrugged. "Like I say; prison is prison. I am prisoner for life, yes? We know each other, from *gulag*." Novak tapped a finger to one of the markings on his forehead. "Sons of Balash. Is gang."

"Is *bratva*," agreed another prisoner. "Balash *Bratva*."

"Friends turn up in the craziest of places, I guess," I muttered.

Every one of the prison-workers had the same Cyrillic script on their faces, their gang tapestries very similar to Novak's. The winged icon above each eye obviously denoted membership of a gang or crew. How they had ended up here wasn't exactly clear: one paused to leer over me as I stood naked on the bench. The black-toothed grin suggested that on the outside, in any other circumstance, he and I would most certainly not be allies.

"Get us out of here, Novak," I said, staring back at the prisoner.

Another quake hit the chamber. The place shook violently, the prisoners stumbling to keep their footing. One waved at Novak, speaking in Russian. Novak nodded in grim agreement.

"Hold still," Novak said.

He had a massive pair of powered cutters; a heavy, oversized tool, now made lethal. Blue energy danced around the device's tip. The blades looked capable of cutting through a starship's hull, let alone the gravity-plate.

"Just do it," I said. "And make it fast."

"Always," he grinned back.

"On my mark . . . Go."

I closed my eyes, fully prepared for Novak to snip off a

hand or foot, even if only accidentally. Thankfully, that didn't happen. Novak sliced into the table's concealed generator, and it stopped working. I slid off the bench.

"Easy," Novak said.

The other prisoners did the same for Feng and Lopez, and both Jackals were soon free. Lopez had to help Feng get to his feet, and I tried not to notice the bright red stain that he made as he slid free of the plate.

"I'm . . . okay," he muttered, fighting off Lopez's assistance.

"No, you're not," she said.

"I can . . . walk."

"Get dressed," Novak suggested. "Here."

He produced three orange worker overalls, and three pairs of sturdy work boots. We dressed quickly: I was glad to have some clothing between my naked body and the prisoners' eyes.

To Novak, I said, "Tactical report, trooper. Do you know Zero's location?"

"She is through there."

"Then let's go," Feng said.

"Hold on," I argued. "We need to save Zero, but how is this possible, Novak? Did you plan all of this by yourself?"

I didn't want to insult Novak, especially after he and his friends had just saved our asses, but there was no way that Novak had executed this alone. He and the other prisoners were gang heavies; not strategic masterminds.

Unsurprisingly, Novak shook his head. "No. Had help. Followed voice. In head, in ear."

"Again with the voice, huh?" I said.

Lopez shared my incredulity, and rolled her eyes in disbelief. "Right, right . . . So you followed a voice in your head, and it led you here?"

"Voice is real," Novak said, defensively. "It say to give this to you, ma'am, when time was right. Guess that is now."

He held out a dirty hand, and I realised what he was trying to say. There was an earbead in his palm. It winked a red eye at me: indicating that it was active, receiving a communication from somewhere. I frowned and took it from Novak.

"Where'd you get this?"

"From prison," Novak said. "Another man, he give to me. Tell me that I should listen to voice, yes?"

The comms-bead flashed again, and Novak nodded his head encouragingly. It felt like the bead was beckoning me, inviting me down the rabbit hole. Hands shaking, I raised it to my ear. A voice at the other end instantly became distinct.

"It's about time," it said.

The words were spoken in Standard, but the audio was filtered, making the vocals distort into an electronic warble. Must've been using some sort of scrambling technology, maybe a locational displacement package as well. That would account for the distortion. The technology would make it both very difficult to identify the speaker, and to trace the location of the transmission.

"This . . . this can't be happening," I said. "Identify yourself, speaker. Are you real?"

"I'm real, all right, but that can wait," the voice answered. "You don't have long. You need to do exactly what I tell you."

"Why?"

"Because I want to get you and your squad out of this alive," the Voice said. "And because this has taken a lot of planning."

Novak spurred me on. "Voice tells truth. Has not let us down yet."

The prisoners nodded and murmured in agreement.

"This is happening across the prison," the Voice continued.

"The place is in revolt. It was the best cover we could get, in the timescale available."

"What do you mean?" I probed.

The Voice sighed impatiently. "We're trying to get you off-planet, using the prison revolt as a distraction. It will hopefully divert Directorate resources to elsewhere on the planet."

"That's all very convenient," I argued. "Who are you?"

"Later. We can talk later."

"I'm not risking my people on the say-so of some mystery—"

"I'm getting you of out there," the Voice insisted. "Okay? That's all you need to know right now. We have audio, we have visual, and your sergeant is in danger."

Feng and Lopez both looked at me expectantly.

"I'll need answers," I said, "but I suppose they can wait."

"Good," said the Voice. "Your officer isn't far from here. You need to get out of that room. Use the main door. It's unlocked. Be quick or be dead."

"Copy that."

Cautiously, we entered the next chamber. It was a long, rectangular room. No Directorate at all, lit only by the glow of various monitors and terminals: holo-screens displaying colourful graphics, equipment that was decidedly more high-tech than anything I'd seen on Jiog so far. We crossed the threshold into the new room, and the hatch hummed shut behind us, making me jump with surprise.

"Through the room," the Voice directed.

As we passed them, the monitor screens lining the edge of the chamber flickered, overhead glow-globes flashing erratically. The interruption was brief; gone before I'd properly considered it.

"Are you causing this?" I asked, nodding at the screens. Could whoever this was actually see that gesture?

He – I had the feeling, although I couldn't say why, that I was talking to a guy – answered anyway, "No. Not intentionally, anyway. Move on."

I checked the exits. Two options: one at the end of the chamber, and another on the right.

"Which hatch do we take?" I asked.

"Right flank," the Voice replied.

"I don't have a weapon. Will I need one?"

"The prisoners have tools. They can use those if you meet resistance."

The hatch was big, blast-shielded. Covered with warning symbols and Korean text.

Lopez, one arm still wrapped around Feng's shoulder, inspected the control console. "I think that it's unlocked," she said, with surprise.

"It is," Feng nodded. "I can read the text."

Novak raised an eyebrow. "Chino can read Korean, yes?"

"I was bred for joint operations," Feng said, with a brittle grin. "Of course I can read Korean."

"Open the hatch," said the Voice.

"Do it, Novak."

Novak activated the door. The panels slid open—

And a wall of wind hit me so hard that I was almost floored. The Jackals stumbled backwards.

What the fuck?

Hand protecting my face, I braced in the doorway.

Saw where we actually were.

A train.

We were on a moving train.

"I should probably have warned you about that," the Voice offered.

"Yes," I said. "I think that you should."

73

"Better late than never. You're on a train, travelling cross-country."

"And that seemed like something you didn't need to mention *why*, exactly?" I asked. I turned to Novak. "Did you know about this?"

Novak frowned, and his reaction struck me as genuine. "No! Directorate put us in box, move to work place. We work, go back to prison."

The train, I guessed, was an advanced magnetic-levitation job. It was almost silent, except for the low electric hum of the engine; and that was easily dismissed as the running noise of the prison. The other effects of the train's operation were probably being contained by an inertial dampener field, much like those used by starships. That would explain why we hadn't been able to feel the effects of the intense speed at which the train was travelling.

"Have . . . have we been on a train all along?" I asked.

"No," the Voice said, with a little irritation. "You were in Jiog's primary prison complex, which is several klicks south of your current location. Kwan had you loaded onto the train for interrogation. He was planning to take you off-world."

Everything outside was moving, and moving fast. An industrial wasteland spread out in every direction for as far as I could see. An angry, ugly landscape lit by a pale star that barely managed to make its light felt. Black spires lurked in the distance – were fixed points of reference – but the sectors surrounding the track were nothing more than blurs of colour, rendered smears by the speed at which the train travelled. In the extreme distance, way, way behind us, was a collection of stout black structures, surrounded by a fortified grey wall. That, I guessed, was the prison; where we had been held for the past few days.

74

"Do you expect us to go out there, ma'am?" Lopez asked, shouting to make herself heard above the roar of the wind.

I swallowed. "It looks that way."

"Feng's in bad shape," Lopez said.

"I'll make it," Feng said. "Stop making excuses for yourself."

One of Novak's crew shouted, indicating to the door behind us. Pounding came from the other side. Had to be Directorate troops, coming to investigate.

I turned to my squad. "Come on."

"I – I can't," Lopez started, showing the true reason for her objection. "I'm sorry, but I just can't do this—"

"No such word," I said. "Novak, help Lopez with Feng."

"Go now," the Voice insisted. "Out, and along the side of the train."

I peeked my head outside. Already I could feel the foul, acidy taste of the polluted air at the back of my throat, filling my mouth. I'd need a respirator, an oxy-tank, to breathe for anything more than a few minutes out there . . . The wind stung my bare face, but I braved it. *If I can do this,* we *can do this*, I told myself.

Slowly, cautiously, I put an arm outside. The train was armoured, its skin plated like the hull of a starship: grey, battered, mostly featureless. I gripped a panel, fingers finding the gap between two plates. It was a handhold, although not much of one.

The pounding on the door behind us increased in volume.

"Jackals, follow me," I barked.

Both hands gripping the outer skin of the train now. My boots found a lip just below the hatch panelling. It was far from easy: my muscles ached with the tension of holding on to the moving train, wind rushing past, my ears, face, neck stinging with the cold.

"This is fucking insane," Lopez said.

But she too came out of the train, copying me. Then Feng, Novak following him. Novak's prison buddies at the tail end. As soon as we were all outside the train, the blast door slid shut behind us.

"Was that you?" I asked the Voice.

"Of course. It's another obstacle between you and them."

I got my first glimpse of the true scale of our transport. The train was a long, sterile snake of a thing, stretching out in both directions. Each train cabin was twenty or so metres in length, and several metres wide; big enough to accommodate internal chambers. It was quite frankly enormous. Titanic in length, like nothing I'd ever seen before.

"Keep your eyes forward," the Voice threatened. "Keep moving. You need to get to the next carriage. Don't look outside."

"I'm trying not to," I said.

"Try harder."

What was out there that I shouldn't be seeing? Shapes sailed past. Towers, the shells of blackened buildings. Something like an oil derrick appeared out of nowhere – suddenly *there*, right beside me. The train was moving so damned fast that I didn't notice it until it was already hurtling by: so close to the train's flank that it almost brushed my ass. There were dozens of skeletal structures all around the train tracks, some half-toppled into the sand-banks, others drooping overhead as though they had once had some function connected to the railway—

A brilliant, bright light filled the sky.

I froze for a moment. We all did; eyes to the falling star . . .

The noise. The same sound that I'd heard in the prison, then again in the interrogation room.

I instantly identified what it was.

A starship engine. Something landing in the desert.

"Holy mother of fuck," Novak said.

A ship came down in the wastes. Streaking fire, it hit the ground hard. Its engines roared, made the air vibrate, the train shake.

And not just any ship.

"That was a Krell ship," I shouted, to the others. "A bio-ship!"

"I told you not to look," the Voice said.

Distracted, my fingers slid against the train's hull. I slipped.

"*Shit!*"

Before I knew it, I was losing purchase.

The train took a bend. Tilted at just the right moment. My weight shifted, body suddenly against the train's hull again. My fingertips braced the shallow details of the armour plating. A surge of adrenaline threatened to engulf me, my heart thundering in my chest: my whole frame humming with the vibration of the train.

"Move," the Voice insisted. "You need to get to the ladder between the next two cabins."

"There are more of them coming down!" Lopez said.

The sky was filled with falling stars, with Krell starships. They were moving too fast for me to get much of a look, but I could see enough. This wasn't a chance encounter. It was an invasion. The Krell had come to Jiog.

"This is what Kwan was frightened of, isn't it?" I asked the Voice.

"We can discuss this later. That sector is about to become hot. Just keep moving."

I did as ordered. There was no thought here: no rational chain of action. One foot after the other, then one hand after the other. I filtered out everything else.

"I'm here," I said. "I'm on the ladder."

"Go up."

I nodded at my team. "Lopez, you and Feng go first."

"Copy that."

Lopez and Feng painstakingly climbed the ladder.

"Novak, you next."

He yelled orders to his fellow prisoners, and they exchanged words in Russian.

"My people will follow after you," he told me.

"Whatever. Just get up there."

Novak hauled himself up, and I started the climb after him. I thrust out a hand, snagged a rung. It was slick, the metal so cold that it bit into the flesh of my palm. Once I was halfway up, Novak extended a hand and I grasped it. He dragged me onto the train roof, waving to the rest of his gang that they should follow.

The wind whipped around me as I reached the roof of the cabin. Hair flying about my face, slapping against my neck. On both feet, I kept low to reduce air resistance. The drag was intense.

"Holy shit, this is bad," Lopez said. "This is bad. This is really bad . . ."

"Stay with it, Lopez!" I ordered.

But try to reassure Lopez as I might, I shared the sentiment. Dozens of Krell ships were on the horizon – their bloated, shelled construction impossible to mistake – and bio-pods rained across the desert. Each impact produced a deafening thunderclap, threw up a column of dirt and smoke that stained the skyline. At this distance, I couldn't identify what Collective the invaders came from – or, more pressingly, whether they were infected or otherwise. It didn't much matter, I decided. They would probably kill us either way . . .

78

Meanwhile, the train powered onwards through the wastes like a—

Bullet.

"Down!" Novak yelled.

The crack of a kinetic pistol. A round sailed past me.

Directorate troops spilled from a service hatch in the roof, further down the train. I counted three of them, and the first was already up and out of the cabin.

"Keep going," the Voice ordered.

More rounds spanked the train's roof. Sparked off the armour plating. Bright detonations in the dark: tracers and explosive-tipped rounds. Only the best for the Directorate's Bureau of Shadow Affairs.

The train tilted left on its mag-lev rail, shifting to one side. I reacted instantly and went low. The balance of my body followed the motion of the train. The Jackals copied and managed to hold on.

Not everyone was so lucky. Only a couple of Novak's crew had succeeded in getting onto the roof, and the others were still hugging the train's flank. Several lost their footing. They tumbled off the train.

The closest Directorate commando – the asshole who had been firing on me – reacted a second late as well. The commando's bulk slid sideways. Clutching at the roof, he went the same way as the prisoners: over the edge.

In the blink of an eye the commando and the prisoners were gone. Our team's number had been slashed. Novak just hunched there, his expression unreadable.

"They knew risks," he said, without explaining himself. "Get up here, rest of you."

The other prisoners hauled ass. In an effort to move faster, most of them had abandoned their weapons.

"Proceed ahead," said the Voice. "Objective is next carriage."

"Easier said than done," I replied. Speaking was tough; every time I opened my mouth the freezing wind seemed to fill my lungs. "Jackals, move up."

We skulked low.

Behind us, both surviving commandos were fully deployed from the hatch. They crouch-crawled along the roof and were gaining on us, fast. Not for them the blistering cold wind – their suits were fully sealed, impervious to such weather conditions.

"Watch your left flank," the Voice said.

"Left!" I yelled to the others, aware that they had no communicators.

There was a flicker of light out of the corner of my eye. *Something* was racing alongside us: beside the train tracks, keeping pace.

"Is that you?" I asked, hopefully.

"No," the Voice said. "It's not."

A combat buggy coalesced out of the dust. Wireframe military model, with six big wheels and an open crew cabin. Xenon headlamps piercing the gloom.

"Oh shit, oh shit, oh shit . . ." Feng said under his breath.

The buggy's engine roared as it was pushed into overdrive, the small vehicle swinging left and right to avoid debris beside the track. For one heart-stopping moment it lurched close enough to the train's flank that I managed to make out the passengers. Six figures in full hard-suits, faces concealed behind masks, goggles pulled over their eyes. The buggy's back was hunched with some kind of pintle-mounted heavy automatic gun, and as the vehicle pulled alongside the train, the weapon shifted on its mount to track us.

"They aren't going to use that on us, surely?" Lopez asked. "I mean, we're just escaped prisoners, right?"

I glanced back down the train. There were dozens of shapes

on the roof now, all heading in our direction. I picked out the familiar orange of prison gang-workers – probably escapees like Novak's crew – but also other, more agile shapes . . .

The train was infested with—

"*Krell!*" someone shouted.

The Krell crept onto the train roof. Its long, sinewy limbs allowed it to move with relative ease, and it advanced on the two remaining commandos. The closest was focused entirely on us, lining up a burst from his PDW.

I almost felt sorry for the fucker. The Krell primary-form lurched upwards, claws outstretched, and reduced the commando to nothing but a red mist: body torn from the mag-locks, sailing free from the moving train.

The second commando hunkered down, and started to fire at the Krell. The xeno went down in a splatter of ichor.

But where there's one . . .

Dozens of alien bio-forms clambered up the train's roof.

And Lopez got her answer. The buggy's cannon opened fire on the Krell.

"Fish heads are infected," Novak said, pointing at the closest alien.

The Krell were grotesque bastards, and ordinarily I'd struggle to tell one Collective from another, but this alien was different. In the briefest of snapshots, I saw the xeno's pallid, diseased skin. Its bio-suit was tattered, hanging from its skeletal frame like strips of meat, and its carapace was burst in numerous places. Worst yet was the thing's expression. Vacant, uncaring eyes: silver orbs that reflected back the carnage around it. Webbed hands extended, using its upper limbs to stabilise itself, the alien crawled onto the roof. It moved with all the grace of animated roadkill.

"Not like Pariah at all . . ." I whispered to myself.

The Directorate commando put a round in the monster's head, but that wasn't going to stop the Krell. There weren't enough rounds in that pistol to put down the swarm of aliens converging on the roof.

"We've got to get out of here," said Feng. "This place is turning into a warzone."

"Agreed," I said. "Move."

We fell back into formation, and I got a glimpse of the length of the train ahead. Dozens of identical carriages, and through the fog and pollution-banks, I couldn't even see the train's driver cabin. The idea of walking all of those carriages made my spirits plummet.

"Please tell me that we don't have to get across all of those," I said.

The Voice answered by implication: "Just the next carriage. Door seal X-23."

But my attention was elsewhere. A Directorate commando with an RPG – a rocket-propelled grenade launcher – had taken to the buggy's flatbed, and was aiming at the train. There was no way that the RPG was going to be capable of derailing the transport – it was simply too huge – but it would surely be capable of throwing us off the roof.

"*Brace!*"

The rocket hissed as it discharged from the launcher, the buggy backing off slightly as it launched.

The rocket wasn't aimed at us, and I didn't see where it hit, but that didn't really matter. We were caught in the blast zone as the warhead detonated. The backwash hit me like a fist; intense and sudden, hot enough to singe my hair. Something extremely sharp hit me in the right arm.

The train abruptly shifted course again, and suddenly I was falling, falling, falling.

CHAPTER SIX

ZERO PROSPECTS

I slid over the edge.

The pain in my right bicep was excruciating, threatening to overcome me. I tried to fight it, and reached out for anything that I could get my hands on.

It was useless. The armour plating gave no purchase . . .

. . . but the ladder fixed to the side of the train did.

Hold on. Hold on!

The fingers of my right hand – my injured arm – grazed a rung—

And snagged it.

I slammed into the train. Something crunched as I made impact. Probably broken ribs: shards of pain erupted in my chest.

Stay with it! Stay with it!

I just about managed to remain conscious. Wrapped another hand around the ladder. Holy Gaia, it hurt like nothing I'd ever experienced before.

"Are you still alive?"

The Voice was tinny and distant, and I realised that the

comms-bead had almost come free from my ear. I plugged it back in.

"Only just!" I gasped, struggling to speak. "I'm bleeding."

A piece of shrapnel had hit my right bicep. Penetrated all the way through flesh, likely muscle too. But it wasn't just the open wound. My whole arm was in torment.

"I think . . . . I think I've broken something in my arm."

"We'll worry about that later."

"I'm not sure that there's going to be a later."

"Not with that attitude, there won't."

"My . . . my squad," I said.

What had happened to the rest of the Jackals? Had they also fallen from the train, or were they still on the roof? I couldn't tell from my position, but didn't relish the idea of dragging my sorry ass back up there . . .

"They're fine."

"You can tell that?"

"Hmmm. Sure. I can tell."

There was no time to test the Voice's rather unconvincing response. "Then tell me what to do, hotshot."

"You need to go back into the train." The designation X-23 was printed on the side of the carriage in big, bold lettering, just beside me. "Use that hatch between the carriages."

I lurched along the ladder, this time into the tight gap between X-23 and the next carriage. The windshear decreased just a little. There was an armoured door into carriage X-23, but the control console glowed with green icons. It was unlocked.

"Get inside, then left flank."

"Why?"

"You'll know once you're in."

The hatch peeled open, and I collapsed into the new cabin.

There was an instant shift in temperature and atmosphere. It took a second or so for my tired eyes to adjust to the low light.

Zero!

The scene we'd witnessed in the interrogation chamber played out at the back of the carriage: Zero kneeling on the floor, Commander Kwan towering over her in his exo-suit, flanked by Fire and Ice. Carmine's almost headless body remained in position in front of them, blood pooling around the corpse. But something had changed here. Although Kwan still had the redactor aimed at Zero's head – the probes tunnelling into her hair – his expression was neither victorious nor composed. Surgeon-Major Tang was at his side, waving her arms in exasperation. There was shouting, much shouting.

The hatch hummed shut behind me, and such was the chaos that no one noticed my arrival. Not immediately, anyway. That gave me a precious moment to think about how best to solve this problem, about how I could get to Zero. She was at the other end of the chamber. The module was double-length and rectangular, crammed with more scientific equipment. Medics and technicians manned the machines.

Left flank, I remembered. That had been the Voice's command.

And suddenly I understood why.

One of the *Santa Fe*'s battered simulator-tanks sat beside me. Canopy up, control panel lit, ready to mount. The word CALIFORNIA – my callsign – was stencilled there. This wasn't just any tank. It was *my* tank.

Of course, a simulator without sims would be useless. Which made the Directorate's decision to store the simulator and my skins in the same location incredibly foolish.

The room contained my simulant stash. Every body, I guessed, that remained from the *Santa Fe*'s salvaged supply. A half-dozen cryogenic capsules lined the walls: emitting a soft blue glow, each containing a pristine, fresh-as-the-day-they-were-farmed copy of me, in fetching deep blue neoprene undersuits. Although frost crept across the outer casing of the capsules – the skins were supposed to be kept on ice until they were needed – it was already cracked, thawing. The sims were not in deep-freeze. They were ready for deployment.

Oh hell, yeah.

The scent of the place reached the back of my throat, invaded my body. An almost sexual desire stirred in my bones.

Finally, someone noticed my arrival.

A Directorate medtech shouted in Korean, reeling away from me.

Surgeon Tang's head snapped in my direction. Her eyes widened in shock, in horror.

Zero, the redactor still attached to the back of her head like some bizarre metal crab, swayed as though she were in a trance. But she managed to pull herself out of it for just a second, and saw me. *I'm here for you, Zero.* I prayed that I wasn't too late, that Zero could still be saved.

"No!" Tang screamed. "Do not let her get into that tank!"

A guard powered across the room, sidearm drawn. The pistol fired—

I was in the tank. The round bounced off the canopy, which was already slipping shut.

NOT READY, flashed the tank's interior control panel. AMNIOTIC CYCLE NECESSARY. INITIATE REBOOT.

I was hurt, and bleeding, but I could work one of these machines in my sleep. The tank was as good as an extension of my own body. I slammed the CYCLE AMNIOTIC command on the control panel. The technology was largely automated; made for operation by meatheads like me.

Fluid began to fill the tank. I grasped the data-cables, methodically slipping each into my waiting ports. The prison overall came open easily, and each new connection caused an eruption of ecstasy inside me. A respirator hung inside the tank. Again, that was sloppy. I plugged it over my face. The tank was almost filled with amniotic now.

NOT READY, complained the tank. INITIATE REBOOT—

OVERRIDE. EMERGENCY TRANSITION.

Rounds impacted the tank's canopy. Spiderweb fractures appeared across the armourglass.

Hold. Hold. Hold!

The simulator-tanks weren't frontline equipment, but they were made to withstand small-arms fire. I'd seen the combat specifications, and read the technical manual a dozen times. Although I knew that it wouldn't hold out forever, the canopy would take a decent amount of punishment. The hood would be able to take a blast from a PDW.

At least, I hoped so.

COMMENCING TRANSITION . . . PLEASE WAIT . . . COMMENCING TRANSITION . . .

"I want every commando on this train in this room!" Kwan shouted, his eyes bulging from his head, the internal circuitry in his face glowing, such was his anger.

The Voice was probably speaking to me, but I tuned it out. Couldn't hear anything above the rush of blood in my ears, the hammering of my own heart. Everything else was falling away.

SELECT TARGET FOR TRANSITION, suggested the tank. Now that I was hooked up, one with the machine, we were communicating over the neural-link: the tank just another voice in my head. POSSIBLE TARGETS IDENTIFIED . . .

"She cannot be allowed to operate that tank!" Tang yelled.

Too late, Tang.

ACTIVATED, the simulator said.

The world around me disappeared.

My perspective shifted. I wasn't in the simulator any more. Instead, I was inside one of the cryogenic capsules.

Transition confirmed.

I looked back at the simulator. Christo, the body inside looked alien to me, and I couldn't actually believe it was mine. Floating almost peacefully: eyes open but unseeing. Blood trailing from the open wound in my arm, curdling with the blue gel inside the tank.

That skin wasn't mine, I decided. Not any more.

In my real body, I'd been hurt and in pain. My reactions had been dulled by my time in the prison. I knew that I was worn out and tired. But this skin was fresh. The simulant's senses were needle-sharp, and the rush of adrenaline and hormones and combat-drugs that hit my bloodstream was very nearly a religious experience.

I wasn't Keira any more. I wasn't weak.

I was Lieutenant Jenkins. I was strong.

And I was fucking angry.

Tactical assessment: three commandos. Tang. Kwan. Fire and Ice.

The nearest commando continued firing on the simulator-tank.

I could imagine his confusion – could almost read it, coming off him in noxious waves – as he saw that there were *two* bio-signs on his HUD . . .

Tang realised what was happening. She yelled a warning. *"Aim at the simulants!"*

Did the commando see me before I struck?

I hoped so.

The capsule's control panel flickered with activation lights. The content – the simulant – was now live.

I slammed a hand through the plasglass of the capsule's canopy. The cryogen pods weren't combat-rated, and they were made to be disposable, more or less. The glass was toughened, but not like my simulator. It broke in jagged shards, and cryogenic fluid poured out. I'd almost forgotten how strong a simulant body actually was.

The commando turned. Gun up.

I lurched out of the capsule. Both hands to the target's neck.

His pistol fired. Once, twice.

I lifted the commando with every ounce of strength that my simulant could muster. Slammed the body against the row of capsules behind him. Hard, harder. More canopies shattered. Something broke inside the commando's armoured suit, and the body went limp.

"The power!" screamed Tang. "Cut the power!"

Gun.

It fell to the floor, out of the soldier's lifeless hands. I crouch-rolled forward, through more broken glass, grabbing for the weapon. Touched the cold metal stock—

Another commando behind the first.

He raked the floor with gunfire from a compact defence weapon.

I was wearing a neoprene undersuit. It offered no protection, and the salvo scythed right through it. Detonations of pain exploded across my body.

Not even a simulant could survive that.

But no matter: there were plenty more where that came from.

Neural-link severed, I snapped back to the simulator-tank. Into my own skin.

EXTRACTION CONFIRMED, the tank told me.

I saw the commando stooping over the dead simulant, popping rounds into the spent body just to be sure.

Smart.

He turned to look at me now. Gun raised, the red lenses of his goggles flickering.

But not smart enough.

COMMENCE TRANSITION, I ordered.

TRANSITION CONFIRMED.

The remaining cryogenic capsules were now mostly ruptured, and I became one of the simulants opposite the body I'd just occupied.

Lightning-fast, I was on the next commando. Before he had even had a chance to register what was happening – his own weapon still trained on the simulator, on the ruins of my real body – I reached for the sidearm holstered at his thigh. As I pulled it free, he twisted to face me.

I flipped the pistol's activator stud.

Fired.

The commando spattered across the chamber. Dead.

"Stop her!" shouted Kwan.

Tang made for a terminal across the room – perhaps the power control; that would shut down the simulator tech. The various techs were all making for cover, too panicked to follow orders.

"I'll do it, Honoured—" Tang blurted.

Despite her lofty rank, the Surgeon-Major wasn't a

soldier. She slipped on a pool of cryogen, babbling to herself.

I made a split-second decision. As much as I wanted to kill the Surgeon, she would have to wait. Fire and Ice were closing on her, and firing on me too.

Threat evaluation: that was what this called for. More troopers were at the hatch now, entering the cabin. Three more advanced on the room with PDWs drawn. They took in the decimated chamber, and although I couldn't see much of their faces beyond the goggles and breather masks, I could sense their surprise.

Too slow.

I fired the pistol at the lead trooper. He stumbled forward with puncture wounds across his chest. But the second and third commandos crouched low and made it into the room—

Another spray of PDW fire, and the second simulant was history.

I jumped back into my real body – felt the sting of gunfire across my chest—

—not my chest: just a simulation—

A commando loosed a volley at my dead skin—

—not dead: really me—

I roared in defiance as rounds bounced off the simulator-tank's canopy.

Kwan grabbed Zero, pulled her to her feet.

COMMENCE TRANSITION.

Another simulant, out of the capsule.

I'd never made transition so many times in such a short period. The pattern of being born, dying, reborn – it had a kind of rhythm to it. A perverse calm settled over me; my senses so hyper-alert that I wasn't scared of dying any more.

Another commando advanced on the terminal Tang had been trying to reach: what I took to house the controls to the power supply. That was lucky, I suppose. Because this technology wasn't native to the Directorate, they had not managed to fully integrate it into their systems – which meant someone had to manually flip the switch in order to shut it down, rather than do it wirelessly.

Well, we can't have that, I thought.

I body-slammed the commando. His fire went wide, PDW spraying the ceiling as he collapsed under my weight.

Words came to me through gritted teeth, and I spoke as I worked.

"My name . . ."

The third commando was on me.

". . . is Keira Jenkins . . ."

I twisted. Fast and lithe: making the most of my unarmoured state.

Gunfire sliced the air—

—bounced off the simulator-tank—

I closed a hand round the muzzle of the lead trooper's weapon. We wrestled momentarily, but there was no contest.

I was a sim. He wasn't.

I forced the weapon low and thrust a fist into the trooper's face with lethal force.

"My rank is lieutenant . . ."

I grabbed the PDW as the man went down. It was small and delicate in my oversized hands. The closest commando became my next target. I fired a volley from the PDW. The trooper crumpled as gunfire hit him full-on in the chest.

Act. React. Act. React.

One hand to the body on the floor. Without even thinking, I unclasped a grenade from the commando's body-harness. The cylinder had a red tip. If the markings on the Directorate's equipment were anything like those on standard Alliance munitions, that meant that the grenade was a standard fragmentation type. In a closed environ like this, a frag grenade would work wonders.

I sprayed the open hatch with weapon fire, using the compact machine gun one-handed, absorbing the recoil through my right hand. With my left, I activated the grenade. Tossed it through the hatch. The commandos shouted warnings to one another, and scrambled away from the grenade. That gave me a second's grace.

"Danger close, Zero!" I yelled. I was so wrapped up in the carnage that the warning was nearly an afterthought.

I vaulted to the hatch. Slammed a hand to the door control. It slipped shut.

The grenade went off. The detonation made the deck rumble, but the hatch took the force of the explosion and held firm. In that contained space, I knew that there would be no survivors.

"I am serving with the Alliance Army Simulant Operations Programme . . ."

How many of them were there? Not enough. I wasn't done yet. The kill-frenzy had me now. I was riding the wave of simulant euphoria so high that I barely noticed how many Directorate there were lined up behind the first attacker.

They had to die. They *all* had to die. I took out everyone I could: techs, commandos, every target.

"No, no, no!" I heard Tang repeating.

The Surgeon-Major was at my feet, desperately scrambling away. Fire and Ice fired pot-shots at me, obviously trying to close on Tang, but they knew that anything more intense might endanger the officer. I made the most of that, and dodged their gunfire.

"Please, no!" Tang screamed.

She threw her hands over her face, smock spattered with the blood of her own soldiers. I grabbed her by the shoulders and put my weapon to her temple.

"*Cease!*"

Kwan stood mere metres from me, at the end of the cabin. He held Zero across his chest, an arm locked around her neck. His own pistol was rammed against her head; not the redactor, but something more instantly lethal.

"Stop this," Kwan said. "Immediately."

I fought the rage. Controlled it. I'd destroyed the medical chamber. Bodies, armoured and unarmoured, were strewn over smoking consoles, over the remains of the Directorate's burgeoning Simulant Operations Programme. I didn't even remember killing some of them. Only Tang, Kwan and the twins were left. We had ourselves a standoff . . .

"I will terminate her," Kwan said. "Understand?"

Zero wriggled against the strength of Kwan's exo-assisted arm. He restrained her effortlessly, and ignored her protest.

I answered by twisting my gun a little harder into Tang's head. "You harm her, and the Surgeon gets the same."

"I know what she knows," Kwan said. "I have her intelligence. I have *the* intelligence." He didn't explain what that meant, but said, "Let the Surgeon-Major go." He tossed his head. "Comply. Now."

"Why would I do that?" I asked. "I'm disposable."

"You might be," Kwan said, "but you value your squad, and you value the sergeant's life." His eyes flickered over my shoulder, to the simulator-tank. To my real body. "Your real skin has almost expired. You know this. Surrender now, Prisoner."

Tang was limp in my simulated hands; her sense of self-preservation almost too much for me to stomach. Both Fire and Ice covered her, training their AUG-30s on me.

"Kill them both!" Zero said, her voice rising in pitch. "Just do it, Jenk!"

It was nice to know that Zero's mind wasn't any more scrambled than usual, but I wasn't about to risk my friend's life. Zero was a Jackal. My anger was blunted, cooled, when I noticed Carmine's body out of the corner of my eye. Kwan wasn't blustering. He really would kill Zero. My squad: Kwan knew that was my weakness.

I lowered my weapon. Released Tang.

"You comply," breathed Tang, her relief palpable. "How very wise."

"Now let her go, Kwan," I said.

"This is for the best," Kwan said. "The Directorate will achieve greatness again. The Aeon will be ours."

"Quit this Aeon shit," I ordered. It didn't mean a damned thing to me. "Let Zero go."

The subcutaneous circuitry under Kwan's face flared with activity. He took a step backwards, still holding Zero. Towards the door at the back of the chamber, which would take him further up the train. Fire, Ice and Tang followed him, Tang making sure to place herself behind the big commandos.

"We've got all we need from this one," Kwan said. "The redactor was not allowed to run its full course, but we have enough." He locked his arm a little tighter round Zero's neck, and she struggled some more, face turning red. "Make peace with your maker, Sergeant."

The train rocked with new vigour.

"What—?" started Tang. She was almost thrown off her feet again.

As tactical situations went, this was off the scale. The list of potential threats that could end us on this train was too long for me to properly assess.

"Zero!" I yelled. "On me!"

Kwan's grip on her momentarily relaxed, and Zero saw her chance. The commander stumbled backwards.

The sound of tearing metal filled the air, and the cabin roof peeled back. The rent sucked out the module's processed atmosphere, instantly filling the chamber with Joseon-696's sickly pale light.

Zero was in my shadow now. Not safe, but safer.

"Stay down," I ordered.

"S-solid copy," she stammered.

Something enormous swooped from the hole in the roof.

Kwan, Fire and Ice opened fire on the shape that came through. Rounds bounced off a carapace shell.

He might be insane, but Kwan knew when the game was up. His eyes flashed to the tear in the metal deckhead, and he saw his opportunity for escape. He yelled something in Korean – an order – and the joints of his exo-suit popped and whined as he activated the thruster-pack on his back.

Fire and Ice obeyed Kwan's command. One grabbed for Tang, the other glaring back in my direction.

"This isn't over," Fire said.

"I think that it is," I shouted back, raising my PDW.

With that, Fire activated the mobility pack on his hard suit, the thrusters glowing white hot, sending out a ripple of heat in the closed space. Zero put a hand to her face, but I weathered the blast as the Directorate bastards left the train.

The enormous creature that had just landed, literally, in the middle of the carriage turned to face Zero and me. Zero gave a sharp intake of breath. Recoiled closer to me.

It was Krell, that was for sure.

Words escaped my lips. "Well I'll be damned . . ."

CHAPTER SEVEN

REUNITED

This wasn't just any Krell, and it was immediately obvious that this fish was different to the others on the train. It wasn't infected, for a start: that much was clear from the pallor of the alien's skin, and the way that it moved. But more than that; this was *our* Krell.

"We are here," said an electronic voice.

"Pariah!"

Although I recognised the alien's carapace patterning, the sweep of its crested head, its shape had changed. Newer, fresher, *angrier* injuries covered the alien's torso and head, and the xeno had gained muscle mass, become much bigger than when I had last seen it aboard the *Santa Fe*. The alien stomped its feet impatiently, and shook its body like a wet dog just out of a river. Ice crystals covered its carapace, cryogen dripping from its six limbs.

"We are here," it repeated. "We have sustained injury."

"Right, right," I said. Nodded.

"The not-Alliance requested information," Pariah replied, as though that were some sort of explanation.

"It's okay, P," I said. "I can see that you're angry."

"We followed your directive, Jenkins-other. The not-Alliance are enemies of the Kindred. We wish to get . . ." the alien said, pausing to cock its head. "*Even.*"

"I hear that," I said. "You'll get your chance, P."

"Hold your fire," came another voice. "We're coming in."

It was Lopez. She, Feng and Novak – his gang reduced to only a handful of prisoners now – lingered at the lip of the hole in the roof. They rapidly clambered down into the cabin, with Novak going first and pulling the others through.

"Whoever the fuck is helping us just freed Pariah," Lopez said, expressing unlikely support for the alien. She brushed hair out of her face, and tried to compose herself. "It was being held in the last cabin."

"We are grateful," it said, in an electronic monotone that almost reminded me of the Voice.

Pariah's speaker box – the apparatus that allowed it to communicate with us – was still fused to its chest, but the flesh around the device was puckered and swollen, as though someone had tried to prise it free.

Feng was the last through the hole, and Lopez helped him down. Zero's face illuminated at the sight of him.

"Chu!" she said, throwing her arms around him, despite – or maybe because of – our situation. "Are you hurt? What did they do to you?"

"I'm fine," Feng said. "I'm good, honest."

"You don't look it."

"What about you?"

Zero gave a weak grin. "My head hurts like you wouldn't believe."

Feng's hand went to Zero's head, gently pulling hair away from an ugly series of burn marks that covered her scalp. It looked as though the redactor's probes had been responsible for those injuries, and the smell of burning hair lingered in the air.

Zero shrugged off her condition though. "I . . . I don't think that Kwan finished the process," she said.

"That's good."

"You've lost a tooth," Zero said, more concerned about Feng than herself. "Let me see—"

Lopez rolled her eyes. "This isn't the time or the place. Feng'll live, Zero, and that's all you need to know right now."

She had a good point. Another, more violent impact rocked the train, and the pair parted, all business now.

Novak stepped up. "Fish," he said. He put an enormous hand on the xeno's shoulder, or at least where a shoulder joint might've been beneath the rows of shell-like carapace plating. "Glad to have you back."

Novak's gang didn't look so impressed with the alien's arrival, and they kept a safe distance. I guess they'd never seen a talking fish before.

"We are glad to be back," the alien said. "The not-Alliance threatened termination. The experience was . . . unpleasant."

"Is Kwan dead?" I asked, speculatively. Hopefully.

Feng shook his head. "No. We couldn't go after them. They used flight-rigs, took off further down the train."

"Let the train take care of them," suggested one of the convicts. "They will not get far."

"We're on a train?" Zero asked, staring up at the hole in the roof in disbelief.

"Yeah, we're on a train," I explained. There was little time to bring her up to speed, so I gave her the abbreviated version. "The Directorate were taking us cross-country, although I don't know to where, exactly. The prisoners are in revolt, and we've been in touch with an interested party via a mystery communicator."

"Okay . . ." Zero said. Of course, she was struggling to take all of this in. I couldn't blame her for that. "And you haven't suffered any recent head injuries . . .?"

"This is for real, Zero. I'm not imagining this shit. The others will vouch for me."

"The lieutenant is telling the truth," Feng affirmed. "I know it's a lot to deal with, but we can explain properly when we have time."

"*If* we have time," Lopez added.

"Ever the optimist, huh?"

"I'm just saying, is all," she muttered back.

"Who are these guys?" Zero asked, indicating the prisoners. She obviously had the same impression of them as I did.

"They are okay," Novak said. "Are with me. I swear for them."

How that was supposed to provide reassurance, I wasn't quite sure, but Zero left it at that and didn't ask any more questions.

"This bucket is full of Shadow commandos," I said. "We've killed some, but it feels like the whole Bureau is stationed here."

"Must be one big train," Zero suggested. She still didn't sound very convinced.

"You can see for yourself, soon enough."

"Is not all good news," Novak grunted. "You forgot to tell best part. Infected fishes are everywhere."

All remaining colour drained from Zero's face. She looked a paler shade of white. What with malnutrition and the incident with the redactor, there hadn't been much there anyway.

"We should get out of here," Feng said. He stood a little taller, throwing off some of his injuries, or at least burying them. Either as a result of Zero's discovery, or perhaps because of his enhanced clone physiology, he already looked as though he was recovering from the punishment beating. It was impressive.

"Affirmative, trooper," I said.

"Ah, ma'am," said Lopez. "Can you walk in your own skin?"

I sighed and looked down at my simulated body. I knew that I was going to have to lose this skin. My real body had started to reflexively curl up inside the simulator. The golfball-sized wound in my bicep was still bleeding, but inside the simulant, I was impervious to the pain.

"That your tank's canopy held out during that was quite something," Feng suggested, inspecting the mass of cracks across the armourglass.

Lopez tapped the casing experimentally. "You're going to need something for that gun wound," she said.

"And you're all going to need weapons if we're going to get off this planet in one piece," I said.

I palmed one of the Directorate personal defence weapons, passed it to Lopez. She took it and inspected it.

"Works just like any other gun," I said. The AUG-30 was a Chino mass-manufactured submachine gun, made for close in-fighting and personal defence. "Point and fire."

"Got it. Nothing for Novak?"

"Do not need a gun," Novak said, grinning. Although I hadn't even seen him do it, Novak had broken off a piece of plastic from something inside the carriage, and was now testing the makeshift weapon in his bare hands.

"Guess that you can make a shiv out of anything, hey Novak?" I said.

Novak nodded. "Is true."

As the Jackals stripped the Directorate commandos of anything useful, I paused in front of Carmine's body. She was face-up, staring at the deckhead. Head blown apart. Her uniform was bloodstained, dishevelled in a way that – in life – she would never have allowed.

"I'm sorry, Miriam," I whispered. "But I'll make them pay."

Zero stood at my shoulder, trying her best not to look at Carmine. It could so easily have been her.

"What's our next move?" she asked me.

In my real ear sat the communicator-bead, our only channel to the Voice. I needed that for our next instruction. For all I knew, it had been trying to contact me throughout the assault, but in the simulant, I couldn't hear it.

"Looks like we're about to find out."

I extracted back to my real body.

Lopez taped a medi-pack over the wound on my bicep, which dealt with the blood loss. The pain in my forearm was pretty wild, but I could still use the limb, so maybe it wasn't broken after all. I knew I had at least one busted rib though, because I could only take short, painful breaths. But a hypodermic that Feng assured me was filled with pain-reliever – only he could read the instruction text – and a handful of uppers saw off any immediate risk of giving in to my injuries, and we got on with what mattered.

I left the carriage in the same way as I'd got in; wedging myself between two cabins.

"You there, Voice?"

"I copy."

"We've cleared the modules, and I have my officer."

"Good. Follow the carriages towards the driver cabin. You can take the roof again."

In convoy, the Jackals, Pariah and the prisoners scrambled up the side of the train.

"Always with the fucking roof," I said, shaking my head.

"Quit griping. I got your fish out."

How did the Voice know about Pariah? P was a black op, and very few personnel in Science Division and Military Intelligence were aware of its creation. As soon as we got to a place, a time, when I wasn't being shot at, stabbed or threatened with mortal injury, I had some serious questions for the Voice. As it was, everything had to wait. Being given instruction was far easier than having to sort this mess out for myself.

"You looked like you were enjoying that back in the lab," the Voice said.

"Is that an accusation?"

"Not at all. It's just nice to see you enjoying your work."

"You can see us then?"

"Sometimes."

"You want to explain that to me?"

"We have limited control of the train's security cameras," the Voice said, sounding a little irascible. "Enough to tell you there's a shitload of Directorate commandos on that transport, and that you really should just get on with this instead of asking so many questions."

"We're ready for them."

"They aren't the enemy. Not any more."

I laughed, and realised that it had been a long time since I'd heard myself do that. "From where I'm standing, the Directorate are very much the enemy."

"Yeah, well, things have changed."

"How do you know all of this?"

"We were able to override the security protocols from orbit."

That wasn't quite what I meant, but the answer revealed enough. "Marvellous."

"Things might be bad down there now, but they're going to get much worse."

The train was subject to regular and repeated explosions, although the conflict seemed focused on the rear carriages. The Directorate were having a hard time suppressing the prison revolt – there must've been hundreds of prisoners being transported via the train network – and a whole fleet of ramshackle civilian vehicles was racing alongside the tracks. A dozen or so buggies and trucks, I guessed, moving at maximum speed to keep pace.

"What are they doing?"

"Those prisoners want off-world, just like you," the Voice answered. "That train is the only option."

"They're pretty desperate," I said.

As the buggies drew parallel with the train, bodies leapt from open crew cabins and clutched for the flank. Several failed to make it, and were either smashed against the hull, or crushed under the wheels of their own vehicles. Of the handful that did – miraculously – manage to board the train, most were cut down by Directorate gunfire. There were now dozens of Directorate commandos on the train's hull, just visible through the dust, focusing their attentions on the incoming threat. Tracers illuminated the area surrounding the train tracks as the Directorate and the prisoners exchanged fire.

"No sign of Kwan," Feng yelled at me, above the noise, looking back down the train.

"Maybe the Krell got him," Lopez said.

"We can only hope," Feng added. He sounded surprisingly bitter. It was unusual for him.

"Heads down!" the Voice ordered.

I reacted fast, and went prone. The others copied.

An engine roar filled the air, loud enough that it made my teeth rattle, the bones of my jaw vibrate. A dark shape descended from the clouds and fell in alongside the train.

"What the hell . . .?" Lopez asked, her voice trailing off.

It was a Raven-class gunship, instantly recognisable from the profile.

"Please tell me that's for us," I said to the Voice.

"You wish. No, that's Directorate heavy support."

The gunship carried four gun-pods on its belly. Each appeared to have a life of its own, twitching as they independently tracked ground targets. The gunship weaved left, right. It was so close that I could even see the crew inside the battle-scarred cockpit, the Korean unit badges on the nose.

I braced. Expecting to be blown off the roof by those gun-pods at any moment . . .

But the flyer dipped low, almost recklessly so, and fell back. I allowed myself the luxury of breathing and felt a spike of relief run through me.

"That was close," Lopez said.

I watched as the multiple guns on the ship's belly sprayed the prisoner convoy with gunfire. There were explosions, the snarl of engines as vehicles took evasive action. Meanwhile, the Raven dodged a volley of RPGs and small-arms fire. The prisoners must've plundered an armoury . . .

"You need to get inside the train again," the Voice remarked. "You've reached your destination, and it isn't safe out there any more."

I relayed that to my team. "Move up, people. We're going back inside."

"Got it," Novak said. "Next carriage. Hatch is in roof."

We'd reached the very nose of the train. This was it. I crawled alongside Novak. The Jackals readied a collection of makeshift and stolen weapons, pistols and PDWs taken from the Directorate casualties back in the lab carriage. I checked the ammo load on the PDW I'd slung over my back. The read-outs on the weapon were all green.

I nodded at Feng. "Keep Zero behind you and make sure she's safe. The rest of you, kill anything that looks Directorate."

"Go! Go! Go!"

I popped the hatch and was first in, stolen weapon panning the cabin's interior.

There were crew in here, a dozen or so personnel poised over command consoles resembling those of a starship bridge. While they wore Directorate colours and carried weapons, they obviously weren't military, and we caught them by surprise. Perhaps they hadn't expected the fight to reach them quite so quickly, or maybe the Voice had somehow interfered with their access to the security feeds. I wasn't going to question good fortune.

"Stand down!" I shouted. "Everyone be cool—"

They didn't listen. The nearest – a man with a young face and a shaven scalp – grappled with a pistol at his belt and stood from his console. He barked orders at the others.

Pariah vaulted over the console before I had a chance to react.

It speared the crewman with a claw, right through the chest. He wore no armour, and the new, improved Pariah had no difficulty in lifting the body. The man yelped. His pistol fell from dead hands.

Another crewman took a pot-shot at Pariah. The slug bounced off the alien's head, and it whirled around to face the new threat.

That was all the encouragement the Jackals needed. We let loose.

Feng capped who I took to be the driver before he'd even left his chair. Novak took another man who looked to be running for the security shutdown – a sealed red button on the wall. He used his shiv to stab the crewman, grunting and swearing in Russian as he repeated the action again and again. The rest of the crew were mopped up with gunfire, and the cabin was suddenly empty and quiet. No casualties, no injuries. Not Alliance, at least. Nice and neat.

"We're clear," I said. "Does everyone feel better now?"

Pariah turned to me sharply, and I was struck again by how big it had become. The creature barely fitted inside the cabin. Not just bigger, but more aggressive, more dangerous. This wasn't the same alien we had known. The grafted bio-armour that most Krell wore had become thicker, reinforced, and the xeno's musculature strained beneath it.

"That was satisfying." It bristled. "We remember what the not-Alliance did to us."

Exactly what *had* the Directorate done? I'd heard that some Krell Collectives exhibited a sort of stress-reaction, being capable of rapidly evolving certain warrior castes when necessary. I'd never heard of an individual bio-form undergoing a spontaneous change, but maybe that was what had happened here. It would certainly explain the rapid shift in the xeno's biology.

"The Directorate will pay for everything," I promised.

"Just do not go mistaking Feng for one of them . . ." Novak said, wiping his shiv against the edge of the nearest console.

Lopez aimed her pistol at the bloodied corpse at Novak's feet.

"You sure that one's dead?" she asked.

Then, before the Russian could answer, she fired at the body. Stared down at it, lip curled in a twisted grimace.

"Well, I am now," Novak muttered.

Lopez nodded. "Let's not take chances." She looked up at Pariah. "The fish isn't the only one who wants blood for what happened in the prison."

The Voice coughed at the other end of the connection. As a result of the vocal distortion, the noise came out like an electronic warble.

"You do know that you're on the clock here, right?"

"Of course," I said. "Close the hatch, Lopez. Seal us in."

"Copy that," she said.

"Get to work," the Voice commanded. "You need control of the train."

I dragged the corpse from the driver's console. The body was still hooked to the terminal, the Directorate equivalent of data-ports running into the man's neck, with jacks tethering him to the station. I unplugged those and made space at the console. The desk was lit with red warning icons.

"Zero, come look at this," I said.

Zero cracked her knuckles and took up the station.

"Might as well make myself useful," she said. "Let's see what we can see . . ."

Novak glanced at the controls. "Is not Standard," he grunted. "You speak Chino?"

"I don't," said Zero, typing some commands on the main keyboard. "But some of the commands are a typical arrangement."

"Feng, get over here," I said. "Translate this shit."

He settled into the seat beside Zero. "Actually, Novak, most of this is in Uni-Kor, not Chino."

Novak sucked his teeth. "So?"

Zero and Feng got to it. They worked fast, and a surveillance feed from the outside of the train appeared on the main console. Buggies loaded with prisoners were on both sides of the tracks now, and like enormous black birds, two Raven gunships dipped in and out of the confusion: spraying the attackers with gunfire.

The terrain was shifting too. The skeletal structures out in the desert were closer to the tracks on each side. We were in a more built-up area. Archaic-looking chimney stacks rose out of the industrial wastes, belching thick black smoke clouds across the horizon. As the train plummeted onwards through the poisoned landscape, we entered a fog-bank that was so dense it temporarily blinded the sensors. A heartbeat later, and we were back out.

A Krell bio-ship sailed into view.

One of the Directorate Ravens banked sharply – too sharply – to avoid plasma fire from the Krell ship.

I felt a prickle over my skin, aware of what was coming next.

At high speed, the Raven slammed into one of the derricks beside the tracks. It exploded, and spectacularly, showering the Krell, the Directorate, the prisoners and the train with burning debris. It was several carriages back, but enough of the bird hit us to cause a violent shiver down the train. The Jackals collectively flinched, me included.

"The Kindred are succeeding," Pariah said. "An ark-ship of the Long Tooth waits in orbit. This is only the start."

Long Tooth: one of several Krell Collectives. Science Division had given the various shoals names, and they hadn't been very imaginative about it. Long Tooth was not a Collective I knew much about, but I guess I knew enough: the Collective was now infected with the plague that was twisting the Krell into something else . . .

"Get us control of the train," I ordered Feng, with fresh determination.

"Can you do that?" Zero asked Feng.

"I . . . I think so," he said. He didn't sound very sure, but we didn't have much of a choice.

We hit another smog-bank. This one was so thick that the Directorate and Krell forces were only visible by tracer- and laser-fire; flashes of light on the camera-feeds.

A face appeared on the main terminal.

Kwan.

"There are fugitives on this train," he said. The address appeared to be train-wide, not directed just to the driver cabin. "They will be found. All prisoners will be recaptured. Those who resist will be terminated. Security forces are inbound, and moving up this train. Make no mistake—"

"Cancel that feed," I said. "It's not doing us any good."

"Affirmative," said Zero.

"What can he do?" Novak asked. "His men have other things to worry about."

It sure looked like the Directorate were being overpowered. The Krell were making the most of the destruction of the Raven, flooding the train.

"But it proves that he's still alive," I said, morosely.

"Which is the worst news I've heard all day," Lopez added.

". . . and we're done," Feng declared. Green symbols danced across the control board.

"What next, Voice?"

"Activate the route planner. And work faster: there are multiple hostiles closing on your location."

"Call up the route planner," I said to Feng. "Now."

"Copy that."

A schematic appeared on the terminal screen. Like the branches of a tree, train tracks spread across the wastes, offering dozens of different routes.

"Select Route Sixteen."

I relayed the order. Feng did as requested.

Another smog-bank. The train shook again, very hard now. Pariah began that weird alien clicking at the back of its throat; a noise that I took to be disapproval.

"We've got new course directions," Feng said.

"Where's it taking us?" asked Lopez.

"Does it matter?" Novak grumbled. "Must be better than here."

"I'd like to know where I'm going to die," Lopez said.

A laugh rumbled up from Novak's stomach. He sat awkwardly at one of the crew stations, his bulk so big that it barely fitted at the terminal.

"Is because you are Senator, yes? Because you like to be in control."

Lopez frowned. "It's not that at all, Novak, and I can't believe that you're still going with the senator thing after all this time."

"Maybe we should change name to 'shooter', yes?" Novak suggested.

"Not funny," Lopez said, cradling the pistol in her hands.

"Tell her no one is going to die," the Voice remarked.

"Then where *are* we going?" I said, sympathising with Lopez's comment.

"Jiog Port," said the Voice. "You're only a few klicks out."

"What about the Krell and the Directorate on the train?"

"You're going to leave them behind. Disconnect the carriages."

"You want us to do what?" I asked in disbelief, a finger to my ear, holding the bead in place. I thought that I'd misheard the order. "Feng is doing what he can, but—"

"You have no time left. The Krell are everywhere. Disengage the rear carriages."

I swallowed, nodded. "Feng; Voice wants you to disengage the rear carriages."

We emerged from the smog-bank, suddenly back in a region of light. Ahead, rising through the smoke and fog was a tower-like structure: black, ill-maintained, crumbling into the desert. Its outline was blurred by the poisoned atmosphere. This must be Jiog Port. Anti-air batteries chattered away at the sky around the base of the structure. Was this the last bastion for Directorate – and human – forces on the planet?

"You need to time this just right," said the Voice.

Feng was poised over the controls, Zero at his side. I could sense their anxiety: the stress showing on both their faces. Feng licked his lips, a fine mist of sweat forming on his forehead.

"Next bank," the Voice said.

The Jackals were silent. Still.

This cloud was particularly thick with particulate from whatever pollution plagued the surface of Jiog.

"Go," the Voice ordered.

Feng worked fast. Fingers jabbing at the console.

An alarm sounded.

"What was that?" Lopez enquired. "Did it work?"

"I – I don't know," Feng said, still trying.

"You're doing good, Chu," Zero said. "You're doing good."

The train roared through the smog but there was a sudden flash of illumination behind us. So bright that it lit the particulate in the air, caused the entire scene outside to become a milky blur.

"Directorate gunship," the Voice said. "Another one just went down."

Feng nodded, worked wordlessly. More sweat on his brow. A schematic of the train appeared on his monitor: crawling with dozens of warning markers. He checked off each carriage in turn, overrode alert boxes that popped up on the holo-screen.

One of those carriages contained what was left of my sims. I seriously baulked at that, because I couldn't remember the last time I'd been without a stock of simulant bodies. Even when I'd been in the prison complex, the sims had been there. They had been my armour, my protection, despite Kwan using them against me.

The train was still inside the smog-bank . . .

"Hurry," I said.

"I'm trying!" Feng objected.

"I mean it."

The smog began to thin.

"Now," the Voice yelled. "Now!"

The deck vibrated. Something *clunked* behind us.

Feng sighed. "It's done."

The train suddenly gained speed. The cabin shuddered. Readings on the control panel showed that we were being pushed into the red.

The smog-bank abruptly cleared, and the train's sensors came back online.

Yes.

The other train carriages had disengaged, were rapidly losing speed. Meanwhile, the control cabin had shifted to another track. The Voice's plan became obvious to me. Inside the sensor-blind of the smog-bank, we were hidden: had effectively managed to change course without being seen by the Directorate or the Krell. The rest of the train trailed behind, still in the dense smog.

"Shit," Lopez sighed, shaking her head. "Have we actually lost them?"

"I think so," I said. "I hope so."

Novak nudged Feng in the shoulder. "You are okay, for Directorate, yes?"

Feng managed a weak grin. "Thanks, big guy."

"So now all we have to do is get off this rock," Lopez said.

Pariah shifted. It had been quiet throughout the process. Now, it hooked a claw towards the view-port. At Jiog Port.

"The infected are still coming," it said. "There is not much time."

"How exactly are we going to get the fish in there?" Lopez said. "No offence, Pariah, but that's a Directorate facility. They'll shoot you on sight."

Pariah flexed its limbs. A pair of barb-guns popped out with a wet *shucking* sound, making Lopez jump. The weapons looked like pistols, but were made from gristle, bone and shell. Although this was the alien's primary armament, and I'd seen the xeno do this trick many times before, I'd assumed that the Directorate had somehow removed Pariah's weapons.

"You could've just used those earlier, you know," Lopez suggested.

"Unnecessary," countered Pariah. "Physical force was sufficient to neutralise the not-Alliance."

"They're called the Directorate," Zero offered. "And Lopez has a point. How are *any* of us going to get through security?"

"We have an idea," said the Voice, "although I don't think that you're going to like it."

CHAPTER EIGHT

TOO CLOSE TO THE SUN

"This is the best that you could come up with?"

"In the circumstances, yes, this is the best we could come up with," said the Voice. "It's better than getting wasted, isn't it?"

"Maybe."

But only just, I thought.

The Jackals had stripped the train crew's uniforms, and then put them on. Simple as that: we were now dressed in full Directorate attire. As plans went, this wasn't exactly a strategy.

"These guys sure like black," Zero said, pressing down her suit. Every feature of the uniform was consistently black; rubberised, capable of covering almost every inch of the wearer's body.

"It's a lifestyle choice," I muttered. "Just make sure that you keep the hoods up, people."

The uniforms were equipped with built-in respirators and atmosphere-hoods covered with a transparent face-plate; semi-mirrored, obviously a safety precaution for use on the surface. A long, trunk-like breathing tube reached from the respirator to the control unit on the chest.

"We look ridiculous," Novak said.

"*You* sure do," Feng chided.

Of all the Jackals, Novak looked the most out of place. The Directorate uniform clearly wasn't made with the physique of a Russian convict in mind . . . Novak's gang didn't look much better than him.

"Try to hunch or something," I said to Novak. "Make yourself look smaller."

He grunted, and slumped forward. The suit was strained over his massive shoulders, at least a couple of sizes too small for him. Even his head looked crammed in behind the face-plate of his hood.

"At least you got the suit without bloodstains on it," Lopez complained. Although we'd chosen the least damaged uniforms, many were holed by gunfire or torn by Novak's frenzied assault.

"And you're ready, too, P?" I asked.

Pariah twitched aggressively. "We are aware of the plan."

"Even if you don't like it, huh?" Lopez said.

Pariah lifted its thin lip in a thoroughly, and uncomfortably, human gesture of disdain. Its whisker-like barbels bristled.

"We do not," it said. "But we understand the need."

We'd found some restraints in one of the security lockers, and Pariah's front limbs and legs were shackled. The manacles were strong and heavy. Lopez had activated the mag-locks in an attempt to make Pariah's custody look convincing, but they still looked woefully inadequate given the alien's size.

"How do we know that the Directorate won't shoot Pariah on sight?" Zero asked.

"We don't," I said. "It's a tactical gamble."

Feng glared out of the train's windscreen. "Automated docking is commencing. We need to move."

The train had begun to slow. We passed under the shadow of Jiog Port; its outline cast a silhouette by the setting sun. A docking station was visible at the base of the structure, a black tunnel waiting to accept the train.

"Do you have transport arranged, once we get in there?" I asked the Voice.

"It's been taken care of."

"I hope it's a nice, fast ship."

The Voice chuckled. "I never said anything about a ship. Off-world transports are restricted."

"So there's no ship?"

Everyone paused, listening in to one side of my conversation with the Voice.

"Of course there's no ship. This is a prison planet, in case you hadn't noticed."

"So why are you sending us to the spaceport? It's going to be crawling with Directorate forces!"

"Calm down. Like I said, it's been taken care of. You're travelling freight class."

Closer still to Jiog Port, I made out several thick black lines – heavy cables – that connected the port to the sky above. Each disappeared into the ugly clouds.

Space elevators.

"Head towards the cargo sector," the Voice said, "and keep your heads down. You're taking the lift."

We emerged into Jiog Port, the Jackals surrounding Pariah as though transporting a prisoner of war. The alien plodded along in time with our march.

"Are you sure about this?" Lopez asked me. She was having a sudden, and very understandable, crisis of confidence. "I mean, we're dressed as train crew. Why are train crew transporting a Krell prisoner?"

"Of course I'm not sure," I said. "But it's not like we have much of a choice. Now just try to look like Directorate."

Feng jabbed Lopez in the shoulder with his weapon. "It's because the planet is under an evacuation order," Feng suggested, "and Pariah is a priority prisoner."

"That sounds marvellous," I replied. "We get stopped, that's exactly what you should tell the Directorate."

This was crunch time, and it was hard not to feel anxious. If we were discovered, we could expect a slow and painful death.

"Keep your visors polarised, hoods up," I ordered, "and your communicators tuned to this channel, at all times."

The uniforms carried a short-range suit-to-suit comms system.

"We're doing just the same as everyone else," Feng muttered, by way of encouragement. "No different to thousands of other worker-proles."

And Feng was right about that. The station teemed with black-suited civilian workers, completely anonymous, totally faceless. All wearing the same gear, more or less, as the Jackals. They gave us a wider berth because of P – not even the Directorate wanted to stand within scent distance of a fish head – but the alien was otherwise attracting surprisingly little attention. Pariah wasn't the only Krell in captivity down here. Other specimens were being moved as well; either herded by military escorts, or sealed in cryogenic capsules. They didn't look infected, but from nerve-plugs to flesh-grafts each and every one showed signs of Directorate experimentation.

"Chu, do you know which way we're going?" Zero asked.

Feng nodded, indicated ahead. There was Korean text

printed on the wall. "Cargo terminal is through that sector."

"You should be able to see the elevator when you reach the checkpoint," the Voice said, over the joint comms. Feng had also aligned the suit-to-suit communicator to the same channel as the Voice was using, and now everyone was treated to the Voice's pearls of wisdom . . .

"Right, right," Lopez said. "But I'm still struggling to understand why you couldn't arrange a shuttle."

"Struggle away," said the Voice. "It couldn't be organised, okay?"

"But if this doesn't work, we're basically trapped down here. A ship would be so much easier."

"PMA," the Voice replied. "'Positive mental attitude'. Look it up sometime."

"If I get the chance, I might just do that," Lopez said.

Zero prickled. "Company incoming, people."

Squads of troops marched past, boarding tracked armoured personnel carriers, mounting dropships that sat on landing spars above us. The soldiers moved in tight drill formation, with a precision that I doubted any Alliance Army unit had ever achieved. Hundreds of personnel, from several military branches.

"The infected have breached the cordon around this facility," Pariah declared. The alien's vocals were being piped directly into our comms system as well. "They will be here soon. They will terminate the not-Alliance."

Pariah watched the movements of the other xenos with what I took to be curiosity.

"Can you feel anything from those Krell?" I asked. "What do the Directorate want with them?"

"Cannot sense others," P said. "Not of Collective."

"The Directorate should have quarantine protocols in place," Zero suggested. "I mean, we know that Pariah can't be infected, but what about those other specimens?"

We really didn't know that as a fact at all. Exactly how vulnerable or otherwise P was to the plague was one of many unknowns that surrounded the bio-form. Still, P didn't correct Zero, which perhaps told its own story.

Lopez squirmed beside me. "Can . . . can *we* be infected?"

"You're not a fish, Lopez," Feng rebuked. "You keep asking this question."

"We've all seen the mess that the virus makes of the Krell," Lopez said, churlishly. "Pardon me if I'd rather not end up like that."

"So far as we know, it's species specific," I said. Again, I really didn't know that as a fact. "No need to worry about it, Lopez."

Lopez muttered back, "That's not very reassuring, ma'am. Those infected fishes still give me nightmares."

"Is like dead, yes?" Novak said, struggling to express himself. "We have word for this, back in Norilsk. Is *strigoi*."

"They were more like a Christo-damned zomb—" Lopez started.

"Don't," I said. "Just don't say it."

Because saying it makes it real, right?

"But what about the other Krell in this port?" Zero said. "That's my point. It's something the Directorate should be thinking about. The infection could be airborne, for all we know. There's a real safety risk here—"

Zero's words were cut off as a flight of security drones scattered overhead, and the Jackals unconsciously paused beside a metal arch. The drones disappeared back the way that we had come, towards the train station.

"We need to go through here," Feng said.

The flow of personnel was interrupted by a security gate. Directorate soldiers in light armour were checking civilians as they approached. They wore helmet-mounted scanning apparatus. Like docile animals, the civilians paused to be examined, face-plates becoming transparent as they were inspected by the security detail.

"Ah, fuck it," Lopez said. "So close!"

"You got any ideas, Voice?" I asked.

The Voice paused. "No. You're going to have to get through this on your own."

We were beginning to hold up the tide of civilians, and one of the guards was eyeing us from his post. Granted, that could've just been my imagination – paranoia is a powerful master – but we couldn't stand around here for long without drawing attention.

The guard suddenly barked something and waved towards us.

"What did he say, Feng?" Novak asked.

"He wants credentials," said Feng.

Lopez's hand went to the holstered pistol at her belt. "Shit. Our cover's blown."

"Wait," I hissed, pushing Lopez's hand away. "Not until I give the order."

There was motion to my left.

At first, I thought that something had landed in the crowd; had fallen from overhead. There were gantries and walkways up there, interlacing the open hallways. But quickly I realised that was not the case. The crowd was moving, forming a circle around something on the concourse . . .

A worker detail had been transporting a Krell, lining up with the other evacuees. This particular specimen was a slimy-wet primary-form, much smaller than Pariah, with nerve-staples pocking its torso and head. It didn't look well, but then they never do, and it was impossible to tell whether the alien had started out this way or its condition was a more recent development. Its hide was speckled and blotched red – maybe of the Red Fin shoal, although I was no expert in Krell identification. Like P, the xeno was chained at the limbs, but also had a shock collar clamped around its neck.

The alien sort of stumbled, falling into its handlers. One carried a shock-baton, and slammed it into the xeno's leg. The alien pitched forward some more . . .

And vomited a torrent of blood and mucous.

What happened next was almost mesmerising. The alien spasmed, pulling at the bonds holding its wrists. Black splashes were visible across its hide. Those shifted. Even as I watched, they grew.

I guess that Zero had her answer.

The handler hit the alien with his baton again. Bright blue light crackled across the fish's carapace, and it almost went down.

But not quite. A limb broke free from the bonds. The xeno grabbed for the handler, and threw him into the air. He came down among the civilians, with a sickening crack.

The Krell had now completely broken free, and its body was more black than green. Silver filigree spread across its head, and its eyes had turned completely dead.

Pariah had enough tactical acumen to restrain itself from acting, although I could sense that was no easy decision for the fish.

"It's happening," I said. "The virus is spreading."

Even the smaller Krell bio-forms were much taller than the humans that made up the crowd, and they were visible as islands in the sea of workers. Other Krell were also turning now. Several were rebelling against the Directorate. Had the virus become airborne, or was this the result of something the Directorate had done? For all I knew, these specimens could've been infected before their capture.

A ripple of panic spread through the crowd, workers jostling us. Novak pushed some aside. A tannoy began to drone on in the background, the words lost to me, but the intent clear. The place was being evacuated.

The guard's attention was elsewhere. The tide of workers and soldiers swelled. A gun went off behind us. There was shouting, then the scream of dying Krell. An explosion.

"They're here," the Voice said. "You've got to get out of there."

Then the crush started.

A handful of civilians breached the security checkpoint, and the guards didn't even try to stop them. It wasn't that they had lost discipline, but rather that there were bigger – *much* bigger – things to worry about.

That was all the distraction we needed.

"Stay together!" I hollered. I struggled to compete with the noise and chaos spreading through the hall.

Novak yelled the same order at his convict crew, but their numbers had already thinned. Several disappeared beneath the crowd.

"P, do your thing!"

Pariah flexed its limbs and the manacles holding them snapped apart. The xeno took up battle-stance, both barb-guns extended, its upper raptorial limbs deployed like those of a massive praying mantis.

The effect was immediate. The crowd parted around us.

"Take Cargo Rail Three," the Voice said.

"This way!" Feng called.

As one, we vaulted over the checkpoint. A stampede of civilians followed us.

The next terminal was filled with metal crates and de-activated robotic loaders. Against the far wall, twenty or so metres away from our position, were four cargo rails: vertical tracks, each loaded with a heavy industrial lift. Three of them were ready for launch, with pods the size of large elevator carts docked at the base of the rail.

Zero waved. "There! Those cargo pods will go up the track, and into space."

"Sounds great," Lopez said. "Let's move."

Everyone seemed to have the same idea. Lopez fired a volley of warning shots into the air, clearing the way to the nearest rail. The crowd surged around us. Several civvies scattered into the forest of cargo crates, using them as cover.

"Those pods aren't for human use," Feng said, nodding at the closest signage.

"Then it's lucky that we're Jackals," I said. "So this is your flight plan, Voice?"

"It's the safest way off-world," the Voice said. "Don't worry; the pods are pressurised."

"Really?" I asked.

The Voice paused before answering. "Yeah, sure. Probably."

We found Cargo Rail Three. Feng activated the pod controls, and the iris-style metal door slid open. Inside, the pod was a metal box a few metres across, empty save for a cargo crate in one corner. It had a small scratched and battered window, and a rudimentary control panel by the door.

We were finally in, although the door sat open behind us.

"We ready?" Feng asked.

I nodded. "Do it."

Some controls inside the door flickered green. I hoped that was atmospheric control, but who knew? There was no time to check.

"They come," said Pariah.

"You need to get that door shut, Feng!" Lopez exclaimed.

Whatever Collective these Krell had originally come from,

they now shared the kinship of infection. As one, they made their own push for the gate. Could infected Krell communicate with each other? That seemed likely; simultaneously, across the concourse, several broke through a hole in a wall. They began to butcher the closest targets – throwing aside eviscerated bodies. Directorate soldiers opened fire on them, and met immediate resistance from bio-weapons.

The remaining civilians began to run for the pods. A soldier with a rifle yelled a warning, firing a volley into another group of evacuees.

"Launch the fucking pod!" Lopez shouted, more insistent now. "Do it!"

Some of the Krell broke the line. Crushing anything underneath them, the xenos used all six limbs to close the distance to the cargo rails. There were suddenly so many of them.

Red lights filled the console. Feng was jabbing at the controls, cursing to himself.

"What's the hold-up?" I asked.

Lopez started shooting, the harsh report of each shot bouncing off the closed walls.

"Just go!" she shouted.

"Saying it won't make it happen!" Feng said. "We're locked out of the controls—"

Pariah opened up with both barb-guns.

I went prone. "At least get the hatch shut, Feng!"

"I'm trying! I'm trying!"

We weren't equipped for this. PDWs and pistols were for personal defence, not protracted combat ops. Instead of armour piercers and uranium tips, we were packing frangibles and small-calibre rounds. The Krell were armoured, and their morale was unshakeable. Boomer-fire – hot as plasma – strafed the pod's entrance, and stray bone-rounds pinged off Pariah's carapace.

The pod door began to hum shut . . .

. . . but the Krell kept coming. Metres from the hatch now.

"*Mudak!*" Novak yelled.

One of his crew – the only one left, I suddenly realised – had taken a hit to the chest. The big man dragged his comrade further into the pod.

"I'm in!" said Feng. "I have control!"

Then the hatch shut.

"Nice work," the Voice muttered. "Very nice work indeed, Jenkins."

"Just launch us, Feng," I said.

"Affirmative."

The pod accelerated upwards, on nothing more than an energised rail that led into space. It was a cargo lift to the stars.

The craft was made for getting materiel off-world to waiting freighters, but it turned out that the promise of a pressurised interior was true enough. I discarded my head-gear. Although the pod's cold atmosphere made my skin prickle, we were all happy to get out of the survival-suits and throw off our Directorate disguises. I sat quietly, appreciating the throb of blood through my veins.

We're alive. We're almost off Jiog.

It was the *almost* that troubled me. The immediate thrill of surviving – of escaping the surface of Jiog in one piece – was beginning to wear off, to be replaced by abject exhaustion. My body was bruised, battered, aching. I'd forgotten about my arm and ribs during the escape, but now the pain had come back. I wanted to sleep so badly, and hunger gnawed at my stomach, reminding me that I hadn't eaten properly in what seemed like an age.

Novak sat with the only member of his work crew that had made it off the surface. The man was sprawled on the deck, a nasty breach in the crew-suit showing where the ganger had been hit: a ragged hole that had probably punctured a lung, if not worse. I didn't want to remember how badly that sort of injury hurt. A blackened spine – a Krell barb-round – poked from the ganger's open wound. Those were particularly painful. The bone splintered inside the body, poison-tipped fragments worming their way to vital organs. The prisoner had been making a wet hacking sound for the last few minutes, and everyone except for Novak tried not to notice. I'd searched for medical supplies – for something that could ease his passing, because I was quite sure that he was going to die – but the pod didn't carry that sort of equipment.

The man clutched Novak's hand, and spoke gently in Russian. Novak talked back in the same language, pausing every few minutes so that his comrade could catch his breath.

"Life is pain, my friend," Novak muttered, breaking into Standard.

The dying ganger grinned some more. He had blood on his teeth. "For some."

Back to Russian. I pretended not to listen, not to hear, but I picked out some words. The ganger gave a name: Mish Vasnev. Then a rank: major. That didn't mean much to me, but it had a surprising impact on Novak.

He gripped the ganger's hand a little tighter. I could see tension on his face. "Major Mish Vasnev?"

"*Da . . .*"

"Where is Mish Vasnev?"

Who is Mish Vasnev? I asked myself. Novak had never mentioned him or her; not to me.

"She lives . . ." said the ganger, but his voice trailed off.

Then, with one final, eruptive gag, he went still. His glassy eyes looked up into space. Novak watched for a moment.

"He is dead," he finally said. His disappointment was obvious.

"Shit. I'm sorry, Novak."

"Do not be," Novak said, still holding the man's hand. "He will not be missed."

"What was his name?"

"Was called Alexei." Novak crumpled beside the body, fingers locked over his knees. "He was an asshole."

"He helped us."

Novak nodded, distantly. "We were brothers. Both Sons of Balash."

Alexei's dead eyes just stared on.

"He . . . he was Sim Ops too," Novak said. "Another lifer. Like me."

I sighed. "You'll get your credit for every transition you did in that hellhole," I said. "I'll make sure of it."

That was the deal: every time Novak died, a little was knocked off his sentence. Given enough transitions, he would be a free man. Novak's eyes flared at mention of his credit.

"Good," Novak said. "Is good."

Novak wasn't usually this talkative. He and I had once been taken prisoner aboard a Krell ark-ship. Sure that he would die in the fish prison, Novak had entered a sort of trance. I learnt how he had tried to leave the *bratva* – more specifically, the organisation that I now knew to be the Sons of Balash – and his wife and child had been murdered. He had subsequently been blamed, and that had resulted in his life sentence. The setting might be different, but I got just the same vibe from Novak as I did during that conversation. I almost asked him who Vali was. That was the name he had mentioned back on the train, when he had first rescued us from the interrogation chamber. His reaction on being pulled up on it by Lopez had been telling. But as I watched on, saw how shattered he was, I thought better of raising it now. It was another on a very long list of questions that I needed to ask if we ever got out of this alive . . .

"Take a look out here," Zero said. She was crouched at the view-port.

"Not more shit, I hope," Lopez said. She sat in another corner of the pod.

"Depends on your definition of shit," Zero replied, with a tired smile on her face. "But you should take a look, Jenk."

I dragged myself off the deck – despite the resistance that every muscle and bone in my body seemed to scream – to take a look through the view-port. We were almost up the rail now, reaching the mesosphere, and our position gave a bird's-eye view of the planet below.

Jiog's surface was claimed by a dozen black eyes – burning pits of destruction – that stared up into space. Nukes, plasma warheads or some more exotic weapon; whatever had caused the devastation, the effect was the same. Jiog was being razed to the ground.

"Lovely," I said, sarcastically. "I'll be glad to see the back of it."

"You haven't seen it all yet. Check that out."

She pointed out the sky above us, where the clouds gradually thinned.

There were Krell warships anchored in orbit above the planet. As P had told us, one of those was an ark-ship: bloated and lethal, swarming with smaller Krell bio-ships—

An explosion in low orbit was so bright that I had to shield my eyes.

"That could've been an energy core going off," Feng said.

"Going to be raining metal on the surface for a while,"

Lopez suggested. "Your buddies are doing a good job on the Directorate, Pariah."

The alien had been so quiet since our launch that I had almost forgotten about it.

"Others are not 'buddies'," it replied. "Others are infected."

"Whatever," Lopez said. "The Directorate and the infected are welcome to each other."

Kwan's mobile command station, the *Furious Retribution*, was up there somewhere, but I was quite sure that she was big enough and ugly enough to live through this battle. Kwan had survived the attack on the train. I had no doubt that he had a contingency plan in place, to ensure his safety if the planet fell.

Lopez crossed her arms over her chest, shivering. "How long till we reach our destination, Feng?"

Aided by Zero's technical knowledge, Feng now had access to all of the pod's systems via the control panel. I had the feeling that this operation was stretching his understanding of Korean to the limits, and despite his clone-class stamina, the kid looked completely exhausted. Everyone had their breaking point, and I could tell that Feng was approaching his.

"We're headed to a cargo platform in low orbit," he answered. He anxiously wetted his lips. "We'll dock in five minutes, maybe."

I looked down at the communicator-bead in my hand. I couldn't even remember having taken it out of my ear, and now I saw that it had started blinking with an incoming signal. I settled it into my ear again, ready to listen to another round of the Voice's instructions.

"Do you copy?" the Voice asked.

"That's an affirmative," I answered. "We're heading up the rail."

"We see you."

"And?" I pressed. I detected a hint of reticence in the Voice's mechanical tone, and I didn't like it.

"We have a starship in low orbit. Once the pod docks, stay put. We'll move into synchronous orbit, dock with the platform and take you aboard. But it's going to take some time for us to reach you."

"What's your ETA?"

"Ten minutes, minimum."

"Ten minutes? That's too long."

"It's the best we can do."

Bing!

An alert chime sounded over the pod's comms system. As one, the Jackals scanned the sky and the land outside, searching for an explanation.

"Sitrep, Feng. What's happening? I can't see anything out here."

Feng answered, "There's another pod, coming up behind us."

The control console began emitting the pitched beeping of a radar system. A graphic illustrated that the second pod was chasing us, adopting the same approach velocity, on Cargo Rail Two.

Lopez's shoulders slumped. "Well that is just typical . . ."

The Voice broke in on the comms again. "We're detecting another pod heading in your direction."

"You're a little late with that intel," I said. "Can you reschedule the exfiltration?"

"No can do. Do you have spacesuits?"

I stared down at the stolen crew-suit. It wasn't rated for use in hard vacuum. "No, we don't."

"The other pod's accelerating," Zero said, her knuckles turning white as she grasped the edge of the console. The read-out on the screen flickered, mocking us, counting down faster and faster. "Less than eight minutes until interception."

"It's Kwan and Tang," Feng said. "It has to be."

"Mummy wants her baby back . . ." Novak muttered.

We were escaping Jiog's upper atmosphere now. More explosions, source unknown, rippled across the horizon. I could make out the cargo platform above us, running lights flashing against the void. The facility looked so damned close.

"Is there anything you can use in your pod?" the Voice asked.

I turned to the Jackals. "Search this place. Fast!"

The squad immediately did as ordered. There were lockers around the perimeter of the capsule, but they contained only emergency respirators and a box of space flares. No good. Lopez tackled a metal crate that was locked to the deck, and which looked more promising.

"Novak," she said, "help me with this."

With a snort, Novak levered the lid of the metal crate with one of his many shivs. It cracked open.

"Jackpot, yes?" the Russian said.

There were a half-dozen glossy black suits stockpiled inside. Lopez pulled one of them out. The tech was undoubtedly military-grade – much bigger and more heavily armoured than the crew-suits, endorsed with the Directorate Navy seal. The armour had grapnel launchers on each arm, and was equipped with a full helmet for use in vacuum. Lopez prodded the oversized thruster rig attached to the back of the unit.

"Is this a flight-pack?" she asked.

"Fucking A it is," Feng muttered. "They must've been loading them onto one of those warships."

"Whatever," I said. "Don't question good luck."

IK-5 "Ikarus" suits. I recognised the armour, and repressed the memory of our last few minutes aboard the *Santa Fe.* The Directorate Navy had been using this armour. It was pressurised, heavy-duty tech: would withstand the rigours of vac-exposure, of a prolonged EVA. In short, it was exactly what we were looking for.

I wasted no time. "Feng, do you know how to use these suits?"

Lopez tossed one of the suits to Feng.

He nodded at me. "I know how to use them."

"You're going to show the rest of us. Are they powered?"

"Fully charged and ready for use," Feng said.

"Then get dressed, people." To the Voice, I said, "We've found some Ikarus flight-suits."

"Very convenient," the Voice said. "Use them. Stay in contact."

"Affirmative. Team, saddle up. We're going EVA."

"I've never used an Ikarus suit," Zero suddenly broke in, as we all began to climb into the armour.

"That's kind of stating the obvious," Lopez said. "None of us has. It's Directorate-issue; Feng will know what to do."

"But I . . . I've never used a spacesuit at all," Zero said. "Like, never even spacewalked."

"Not even in Basic training?" Lopez ventured.

"Not even," Zero confirmed. "The techs found out that I was a negative before I got that far through Basic, and, well, there didn't seem much point in going through with the Vacuum Operations training if I wasn't going to be able to use a sim . . ."

"Shit," Lopez said. "Is this going to be a problem?"

"I'm not saying I won't do it, but I'm not sure that I *can.*"

"First time for everything," Novak offered. "Feng can carry you, yes?"

Feng nodded. "I'll take care of you, Zero."

Zero grimaced. "I guess so."

"What about fish?" Novak said. "Has no suit."

"We could adapt an oxygen bottle, maybe fit a mask," Zero suggested.

"Didn't know that you cared," Lopez said, as she finished fitting her own suit.

Pariah's bio-suit and respirator were gone, and plainly none of the human-grade equipment would fit.

"Unnecessary," Pariah declared. "We do not require protection."

There was not time to argue with P about that. I'd already clambered into the lower half of my new suit, and started zipping up the inner body-lining.

The chiming from the console had now increased in pitch, becoming more insistent.

"You're making a habit of wearing Directorate uniforms," the Voice said over the comms. "Try not to get too comfortable in them."

"I'll try."

CHAPTER NINE

SUITED AND REBOOTED

The cargo pod slid into the docking terminal. There was a gentle clunk through the hull, a rumble through the structure around us, and we were finally still.

"Comms?"

"Check."

"Suits sealed?"

"Check."

"Internal oxygen supply?"

"Check."

"Ready?"

I stared back at my squad, now all suited and booted and ready to roll. Helmets locked in place, fully vacuum-sealed. Nods all round.

"Then open the hatch."

There was no airlock on the capsule. No going back once the pod was breached. We'd have to live with it, or die with it, as the case may be.

"Breaching," Feng said, holding up a gloved hand.

The pod door cracked open. There was an immediate rush

of venting atmosphere, and we braced to avoid being sucked out into space. The hurricane was intense but brief.

Then the silence.

"Keep your comms and beacons on at all times," I ordered. The suits were networked, to allow the wearers to operate as a flight wing.

"The Ikarus is closer to a one-man space craft than an armoured suit," Feng explained. "It's got everything that a trooper needs for a deep-space operation. Life support, cooling system, grav-stabilisers and a flight-rig."

We slowly crept out of the pod, onto the cargo platform. Magnetic-locks in the soles of each boot automatically activated. I grappled with the exposed steelwork of the terminal to steady myself.

"What about a heat shield for re-entry?" Lopez asked, speculatively.

I felt the touch of vertigo as I looked over the edge of the platform. The vista outside had been replaced with an ugly layer of cloud below us, and space above. I swallowed. It was a very long way down to the surface of Jiog, but if we happened to break orbit, that would be the least of our concerns.

"There's no heat shield," Feng said. "But don't worry about that. You get pulled into the atmosphere, the drag will kill you."

"You'll burn up," I confirmed. "Simple as that."

Lopez nodded. "Right. I'll try to avoid doing that then."

"Would help if knew what controls mean," Novak said. He was struggling, breathing hard over the communicator. Novak never did like zero-G, and this op was no different.

"The flight control systems are in the gloves," Feng hurriedly said. He spoke automatically, the words spilling out of him: more deep-knowledge. "Flex your right palm to activate thrust. Left to use grav-assist."

"Well, that was the quickest flight lesson in history," Lopez said, bobbing free of the platform. "But these controls look a lot more complex than that . . ."

The helmet HUD was painted with unidentifiable symbols and text, glowing neon graphics that meant nothing to me. Meanwhile, there was a computer built into the suit's left arm, and that was also flashing with a series of images. The Ikarus suit clearly wasn't made for Alliance soldiers.

"A trooper could get hurt using hostile tech in these conditions," I decided.

Zero was probably in the worst condition of all. Sure, she was fit and healthy, if you discounted the fact that she had just been almost redacted, but she was strictly rear echelon. Operations officers didn't go into the field – or at least they weren't supposed to. Zero's breathing, verging on hysterical, was even more pronounced than Novak's.

"You okay, Zero?" I asked her.

"All good," she said. She made deliberate eye contact with me, and repeated: "All good."

"Breathe in," Feng said, quietly over the comm. "Breathe out. Keep the rhythm nice and slow."

"Jesus, Feng," Lopez retorted. "Give it a rest. You're freaking me out."

"He's only trying to help," argued Zero.

Feng took Zero's arm, and added, "Stay with me, and you'll be fine."

The cargo terminal was an empty platform, a tangle of steel girders and docking berths. Fully open to vacuum, it was manned by a dozen robot dockers. Those currently sat inert, locked to the deck by mags. The platform was big enough to hold several pods and freighters at the same time. Starlight was visible through the open space between gantries, but the structure didn't look like it had suffered damage.

"We've got company," Lopez said, indicating Cargo Rail Two.

The second cargo pod was behind us, closing fast on our position. A red warning light flashed on its roof as it accelerated up the track.

"On me," I said. I moved further along the structure. "Make safe distance from the pod's dock."

I plodded across the platform. The Jackals followed, with Pariah scuttling alongside, using all six limbs. It was as adept at moving in zero-G as in any other environ, but already the effects of vacuum were taking their toll. Ice crystals were forming on the alien's carapace.

"P, how long can you survive out here?"

"Long enough," it said, without looking at me. The xeno's gills and mouth were clamped tight shut.

"That's not very encouraging."

"It is the truth."

"You never mentioned that you could survive in vacuum before. I seem to remember you wearing a bio-suit last time we went EVA."

"Things change."

"I guess they do." I toggled the Ikarus suit's comms channel. "Voice, do you copy? We're on the cargo platform."

"We're still several minutes out," the Voice said.

"Fuck it. The Directorate are coming up the rail."

"Do you have weapons?"

I laughed. "Very funny."

We still had the salvaged PDWs and pistols. None of them was rated for space combat, and the recoil off a semi-auto in zero-G? Yeah, I had every right to laugh. If it came to a firefight in space, the Jackals were as good as cooked.

"You need to hold your position," the Voice insisted.

"What's the terrain like on that platform? Can you deploy into cover?"

"It's bare metal!" I retorted. "There's nothing up here."

"What about an evacuation-pod, or a lifeboat?"

"It's big. We don't have time to search it."

"Any sort of manoeuvrable craft?"

"I don't know!" I said in exasperation.

"Hold on. We'll be with you soon."

Lopez waved towards the pod dock. "They're almost here! What do we do, ma'am? Where's our evac?"

"Good question, Lopez."

Space around us was busy. There were hundreds of ships out there, their running lights and chemical thrusters visible against the black of space. But without proper equipment, it would be impossible to identify a specific vessel. That and, looking out across the prospect of space, everything seemed so impossibly *distant*.

"We will assist."

I turned to Pariah. The exposed antennae on its back wriggled in agitation.

"We can read communication-waves," it said, bluntly. "We can hear it; read the craft that sails stars."

Novak nodded enthusiastically. "Is fish skill, yes? Can follow Voice's communication!"

The idea seemed obvious in hindsight.

"Sixty seconds until the bogey reaches dock," Feng declared.

"Are you sure about that?" Lopez said to P. "How can you tell which ship we're looking for?"

Pariah seemed unconcerned. "We can read waves."

"This is crazy," Zero said, shaking her head. "I . . . I think that we should wait. Help's on the way and—"

"There's no time," I said. I was already imagining the pod docking, Directorate assholes spilling out and taking us back down to Jiog. "P, can you guide us to the ship if we use these suits?"

"We can."

"For sure?"

"We can," the alien repeated.

"Because if you aren't sure," I continued, "we're finished. There are a lot of ships out there. We get the wrong one, we're going to end up plastered across the hull at best, captured by the Directorate again at worst."

Pariah wasn't cowed. "We have no wish to self-terminate, either."

That was good enough for me. "Voice, we're coming to you."

"That's not a good idea," the Voice argued. "The variables are—"

"Fuck the variables. This is my squad, and I'm making the call. We can't stay here."

"Twenty seconds to pod dock," Feng said. "If we're doing this, we have to do it now."

"Then let's go. Pariah, hold on to my back," I ordered.

Pariah grabbed my flight-pack. It would've been funny if not for the imminent risk of death by vacuum: P was twice my size, and in anything other than zero-G would be an unmanageable weight. Not so long ago, being this close to a Krell would've repulsed me to the point of nausea. *Christo, things* have *changed*, I thought.

"Disengage your mags!"

In an instant, I was free of the platform. As one, the Jackals disengaged too.

"Activate flight-packs!"

The Ikarus' thrusters ignited, and acceleration kicked in. The suit's flight-pack hurled me onwards; moving faster and faster, at a breakneck speed.

I was no stranger to planetary drops, and I'd done my fair share of deep-space operations. But this? It was something else, on a different scale. This was proper, seat-of-your-pants, shit-yourself-scary. I was doing this for real. Not simulated. No safety net: one foot wrong and I was wasted.

Lights spun past me at an alarming rate. Explosions, debris, wreckage. Rather than being distant, everything suddenly felt far too close. Orbital facilities were either taking fire, or self-terminating. Coordinates tracked over my HUD, symbols flashing across the black of space.

Pariah tugged at my right shoulder. Pain speared my arm. I swallowed it back.

"There," it said.

The alien was giving me directions, but they were so vague as to be next to useless. I couldn't differentiate the many lights that were scattered across the vista, and I really had no idea where I was being directed. But I did my best, and veered in that course. The sharp turn made my gorge rise. Was I actually going to be sick inside the suit? *First time for everything*, I thought.

"Stay in formation," I ordered the Jackals.

The squad changed course. It was a messy manoeuvre, but it was good enough. I tracked them visually on my HUD; tiny glowing graphics projected onto the interior of my face-plate. It was impossible to know how close we were to the target, how much longer we had to do this for.

"Maintain thrust."

We followed the curve of Jiog's atmosphere and kept pace. If we slowed, we'd be pulled down into the planet's mesosphere: would eventually burn up on re-entry. That thought alone kept me moving at full tilt. Technically, we were in orbit around Jiog. Sure, it was an assisted orbit thanks to the Ikarus tech, but we followed the same principles of physics as any other orbiting body.

"Ah, what does this flashing red icon mean?"

That was Lopez. Her voice trembled, a by-product of the tremendous velocity at which we were moving.

"Which icon?" Feng asked.

"The flashing red one. Like I just said."

Lopez was at the rear, trailing back a little.

"Ignore it," Novak said. "Maybe will just go away, yes?"

"It's not going away," said Lopez. She sounded remarkably calm, given the circumstances. "It . . . it could be a motion tracker."

I turned my head, just slightly: took in the others, moving in a jagged arrow-shape behind me. What with Pariah still on my back, it wasn't easy to see what was happening.

"Is just debris," Novak said. "Probably floating junk . . ."

"It's not debris," Lopez countered. "It looks like it's moving – coming up behind us . . ."

I saw it too now.

A cluster of blips appeared on my scanner. Glowing red stars: too fast to be debris, adopting too tight a trajectory to be random.

"We're being followed," I said. "Hostiles incoming!"

But even as I spoke, Feng flipped out of formation.

He and Zero hurtled off-course. A beam of hard light sliced the sky, barely missing the pair as they tumbled back towards Jiog.

The Directorate were giving chase.

My mind was a jumble of half-remembered Army physics lessons and space operations training courses.

Zero screamed. It was a gut-wrenching sound, made all the more painful by the fact that there was nothing at all I could do to help. If she was hit, if her suit was breached, then there was no force in the universe that could save her.

There were a half-dozen hostiles in pursuit. They were currently a good distance behind us, but closing the gap fast. They moved with perfect precision; firing the thrusters of their flight-packs, accelerating harder and faster than us. The Jackals were rank amateurs in comparison.

"We're taking fire!" Lopez shouted.

Lasers stitched the area. It wasn't easy to shoot and fly at the same time, but the Directorate Shadows managed it well enough. Their accuracy would only get better as they got nearer . . .

"Hold your altitude," I ordered. "I'm coming back—"

"Stay in formation!" Feng barked. "I've got this!"

He fired his thrusters, just managing to correct his approach. Zero clutched his side, making him a larger target, and more ungainly too. They trailed behind, dodging more fire from the Directorate. Feng's flight path dipped.

"Am coming, Feng," Novak rumbled.

"I'll do it," I said, powerless to stop the Russian.

Novak ignored me. He altered his course, following Feng. He was a speeding bullet: a blue smear against space. I saw his hand reaching out to Feng, saw him grasping for Feng's flight-pack . . .

And then he had him.

Feng, Novak and Zero accelerated to catch up.

"Signal is close," P intoned. "Remain on course."

The alien's carapace and skin was frosted with a sheet of ice, body shivering violently. Whatever P said, I knew that it didn't have much longer out here in the cold of space.

My head was spinning, my heart thundering. I dodged a piece of debris as it span past, then more laser-fire—

"I . . . I see it," I said, through gritted teeth. "Voice? Do you read me?"

Gradually, as we got nearer, a starship began to take shape.

She was a transport vessel; grey and austere and not very memorable at all. With nacelle-mounted thrusters and a segmented hull, the starship was a battered old warhorse of a thing. Her running lights were flashing cyclically; beacons against the black of space.

I'd never seen anything so beautiful in all my life.

"We're going to make it," I said. Started repeating the words over and over. I wanted them to be true. "We're going to make it. We're going to make it."

But the Directorate closed on us: were almost among the Jackals now.

Without explanation, Pariah let go with one claw.

"What are you doing?" I yelled.

"Saving my Kin," Pariah said back at me.

Pariah held on with two claws, but released both of its upper limbs. Barb-guns popped free from the xeno's fore-arms. P opened fire with them, peppering our retreat with living ammunition.

At this distance, I saw a glimpse of the trooper's face: saw that it was Ice. The clone's features creased in surprise – a reaction I hadn't yet seen from the Directorate thugs – and he brought up his rifle to take a shot at Pariah.

P responded.

Ice took a volley of barbs to his face-plate. The commando's suit popped, decompressed, and the corpse folded. Immediately began to drop towards Jiog. Burnt bright as it hit the upper atmosphere.

Pariah wasted no time. It re-adjusted its position on my back, and opened fire on the next target.

It was Fire. This one didn't go down so easy.

"P!"

"We are undamaged."

The Ikarus suit's face-plate was fogged with condensation

from my breath. I probably should've been panicking, but there really wasn't time. Everything was happening so fast.

Fire altered his course. It briefly looked like he was going to evade Pariah, but the xeno kept shooting.

An alarm sounded in my ear. Not from the ear-piece, but from the Ikarus suit itself. Red text flashed on the HUD. I didn't need to understand Korean to know what it meant. *Impact warning.*

"Coming up on destination!" Lopez said. "Target ahead!"

The starship's thrusters were muted, and she waited there in space ready to receive us. As we closed, I saw that hope had a name. PALADIN ROUGE was stencilled on her hull in bright white letters. The plating was stamped with the French and Alliance flags.

"Voice! Require assistance! Directorate on our six!"

Weapons pods on the *Paladin*'s spine swivelled in our direction, tracking targets.

"Danger close," came the mechanical reply. "Danger close."

The flak cannons opened fire.

A Directorate signal disappeared from my scanner. Then another. P kept shooting too, my body quivering with each discharge.

The *Paladin* had a rear cargo hold typical of a smaller freighter, and that hung open: a target to aim for, an entrance to the ship. But at this distance, moving this fast, it seemed an impossibly small mark to hit . . .

With another thrust of his boosters, Fire came up almost alongside me, shooting his laser rifle at Pariah. I jinked, or did my best impression of jinking, while trying to retain speed.

Beep-beep-beep!

"We can do it!"

145

Feng, Zero and Novak tumbled below me. Only one chance at this.

BEEP-BEEP-BEEP!

Novak's flight-pack flared. He was losing pace, spinning. Fire saw an easier target, and veered in Novak's direction.

"Correct that path, trooper!" I screamed. "Stay with me! Do it for your daughter!"

Novak roared.

Then Pariah had Fire in its sights. Twin barb-guns firing, the alien peppered the commando's body with living ammunition. P kept shooting as the body spun away, as it fell towards Jiog. I should've felt some vindication, some sense of relief. Fire and Ice were bastards. They deserved everything they got. But I could only *wish* that I felt something as I saw the last of the twins . . .

BEEP-BEEP-BEEP!!!!

I had tunnel vision. Eyes only for the target of the freighter's open hold. I was suddenly close enough that I could make out every detail of the cargo bay's interior. It was a large, empty chamber: probably big enough to hold a couple of shuttles. Well lit; as though inviting us in.

"Brake! Brake! All brake!"

The suit's HUD was filled with warnings.

The rear of the cargo bay came up to meet me – *all of us* – with such speed that there was no way I was going to stop in time.

Then I was in the ship.

Actually *inside* the ship.

I felt the tug of artificial gravity, my suit's stabilisers kicking in.

I'm wasted. There's no way that I am going to slow down fast enough . . .

But . . . but . . .

Every organ in my body was squeezed, squashed, compressed. Gravity and velocity and momentum and whatever else took their toll. I tumbled across the starship's metal deck. Pariah was loose, bouncing free. Came to a stop further along the deck.

The Jackals did the same. Feng, Novak and Zero rolled in a ball of arms and legs and bodies that almost certainly spelled broken bones. Lopez skidded on her chest, arms outstretched, making a better landing than the rest.

I'm alive. I'm alive. I'm alive.

"Everyone with me?" I finally asked.

I could hear breathing, so that was good.

"Not dead," Zero said.

"Only just," Feng added. "Thanks for the save, big guy."

"Is not problem," replied Novak.

Lopez swallowed, gasped. "That . . . that was hardcore."

Pariah gave no verbal response, but was moving. Wisps of smoke rose from its body.

"Seal the deck. Get this place pressurised."

A half-dozen figures watched us from the other end of the hold. They were armed with pistols, wearing re-patched survival-suits with respirators and hoods pulled up over their faces. Not Directorate, but they weren't wearing any Alliance military uniform I recognised either.

I rolled onto my hands and knees. I was so damned tired of this shit, and my arm not only hurt like all hell, but was wet with blood inside my suit. I grappled with the PDW holstered at my belt. My hands shook. But after what we had just been through, what was one more fight?

A member of the group came forward, the others parting to accommodate him.

"Welcome to the *Paladin Rouge*."

It was the Voice.

I recognised a voice-disruptor at the figure's neck; a transmission scrambler that probably accounted for the weird vocals. The figure disconnected the apparatus and tossed it to another of the group.

"I swear to Jesus, Gaia, and whoever else is listening," I said, getting to my feet now, "if you don't tell me who you are in precisely three seconds, I will shoot."

The Jackals closed ranks around me, readying for whatever came next.

I held the gun rigid – aimed very directly at the hooded figure – but whoever this wise guy was, he didn't flinch. The idea of a full clip from a machine pistol didn't seem to give him much concern.

"I am not fucking with you! Identify, or I will shoot!"

"Lower the gun, Jenkins," came the growl of a response.

Oh Christo. I recognised that voice.

"You already know who I am."

The hood fell with a single motion.

"I'm Lazarus."

CHAPTER TEN

RESURRECTION

Lieutenant Colonel Conrad Harris stood in front of me.

The man also known – *better* known – as Lazarus. At the peak of the Krell War, Harris had been commanding officer of the Lazarus Legion – once regarded as the finest fighting formation in the Alliance Army.

I hadn't seen Harris in many years. He was tall, broad shoulders filling the survival suit, with dark hair clipped short, but still slightly unkempt. Rough-shaven; a sprinkle of whiskers over his chin. His face was stitched with pockmarks and scars, each recalling a battle in which we had fought together. *Now there's a face that tells a story*, I thought. Harris was middle-aged in a non-specific way that some men are; and save for the addition of some creases to his face, another layer of cragginess to his brow, he was more or less how I remembered him. He stood there, watching me intently with his brown eyes.

Is this actually happening? I asked myself. It was so unreal, so far-fetched, that it simply couldn't be true. Was I lying in a Directorate interrogation tank, subject to a bizarre and convoluted simulation somehow designed to secure intelligence? But in the end, it wasn't Harris that convinced me that this was real. My emotional reaction to seeing him was like a gut-punch: the result of so many memories fighting for release. We'd served together in the Simulant Operations Programme for years, and we had been through the worst that the Krell had to offer. No one but the real Lazarus could have that effect on me.

I lowered the gun and ran to him.

"Long time no see, Jenkins," he said.

Harris accepted the hug awkwardly. That was as much of a greeting as I was going to get from Lazarus. Hell, the man never was very good with personal affection, and the intervening years hadn't changed that.

"He's . . . you're alive?" Zero murmured, getting to her feet. Despite her condition, and what we had just been through, she brimmed with excitement like a small child.

Harris' face remained impassive, but I detected the slightest hint of amusement around his eyes; the twitch of his lips.

"He never really died," I said.

The Jackals were in a state of abject amazement. Lopez sighed in astonishment, and even Novak was quietly impressed. To be rescued from Jiog was one thing. To be rescued by *Lazarus* – hero of the Alliance, and a man whom everyone thought was dead – was another altogether . . . Everyone in Sim Ops knew Harris; his myth had become as much a part of the Programme as the tanks and sims themselves.

"We used to call you the Red Demon," Feng said. He'd pulled off his helmet now, and his hair and face were bathed in sweat. "You were the man who could not be killed."

Now Harris did smile. It was a half-hearted expression;

the smile of a man who rarely used it, or perhaps rarely had the opportunity.

"Tell that to the medics," he said, his voice the crunch of wet gravel. I hadn't heard a Detroit accent like his in a long time. "They say that I had the opposite problem."

"He died too many times," came another voice.

One of Harris' entourage had removed their headgear too.

"Dr Marceau . . .?" Zero said. "How can this . . .? What are you both doing here?"

Dr Elena Marceau: another Sim Ops legend. She'd been one of the doctors at the heart of the Simulant Operations Programme, as I understood it, and also Harris' lover. Along with Harris, she had gone into hiding at the end of the Krell War, when High Command had declared Harris dead.

Dr Marceau shook her hair free from her suit, and gave a curt nod in my direction. She was slender and pretty; big dark eyes, and long brunette hair tied back in a plait. But I knew not to be fooled by her looks – although Dr Marceau wasn't military, she was a damned tough cookie. It'd been a long time since I'd last seen her too. Her sharp features carried the years well, and she still had a cold and precise beauty.

"It is good to see you, Lieutenant Jenkins," she said.

"And you, Dr Marceau."

"Please, call me Elena. We've been through this before."

Elena spoke with a French accent, thicker than when I had last seen her. That figured: she had gone into hiding in Normandy, Old Earth, on a farm somewhere so I'd been told. It made sense that the *Paladin Rouge* was a French ship, or at least Euro-Confed registered.

"Aren't you supposed to be retired?" Zero asked, of Elena. "I mean, I'm not trying to sound disrespectful, but . . ." She shook her head. "I'm just struggling with this."

Dr Marceau wasn't one for smiling either – she and Harris were kindred spirits – but now she too looked amused.

"We were hiding from the Directorate," she said. "But when the regime collapsed, there didn't seem much point any more."

"You just can't keep a good woman down," Harris muttered. "I don't like the word 'hiding', though. We were just under the radar for a while, is all."

"Then what changed?" Zero said.

"We figured we could be a lot more useful out here on the front than back on Old Earth."

Elena glared sidelong at Harris. "*You* thought that we would, Conrad. Let's not forget that it wasn't my idea to come out here, *mon amour.*"

Harris shrugged. "The details don't matter. It looks like we turned up just in time."

Pariah rose to full height beside me, with both of its barb-guns deployed. This situation no doubt made less sense to the alien than it did to me, which was saying something.

"Does other require termination?" it asked me.

Elena stepped forward. Now it was her turn to look amazed. Fascination played across her eyes, her scientific mind already questioning the Pariah's existence.

"So this is the pariah-form about which we have heard so much?" she muttered, nodding her head.

"That is our designation," said Pariah.

"Most impressive."

The rest of the *Paladin* team eyed the alien cautiously. I could understand their reaction, but they seemed to be taking this a lot better than I would've expected. Elena and Harris clearly knew more about the Project Pariah than they should have, given the operation's classified status.

"It's the first fish head that we've ever had on the ship,"

Harris said. He sniffed the air. "The first uninfected one, anyway."

Pariah stared at Harris. The xeno was in a bad condition, steam rising from open wounds across its body. That it was alive at all was astounding.

"I killed thousands of your kind," Harris said, "back when it was allowed. Back when the Alliance needed me."

"We are Pariah," P said, flatly. "We are Kindred."

I held out a hand. "Listen, Harris. The fish is with me. It comes to no harm."

"Wouldn't dream of it," Harris replied. He evaluated the rest of my squad. "So these are Jenkins' Jackals, huh?"

I expected something like disdain from him: the Jackals were no Lazarus Legion, and they were in a strung-out state.

"That's right."

Harris grunted a laugh. "Then welcome to our ship, Jackals. Make yourselves at home."

Elena stepped forward. "There will be time for proper introductions later. But right now: we need to get to the Q-jump point, and out of this star system."

At her say, the crew scrambled. I was reminded that Dr Marceau – Elena – was as much a leader as Harris ever was. She'd seen things, been places, that very few humans could ever hope to . . .

"Gustav will make sure that you receive medical attention," she said.

"I can wait," I replied, shaking my head. "See to my squad first."

Elena pulled a tight grimace. "She's ever your protégé, Conrad. As you wish, Lieutenant."

"I'm glad you made it out of there, Jenkins," Harris said to me, as the Jackals followed Elena out of the cargo bay.

"Thanks for coming back for us."

"Leave no man, or woman, behind," he said. "That's the rule. And I could hardly let you die down there."

It might've been my imagination, but his eyes looked as though they had slightly wet on saying those words: echoes of a memory long forgotten.

"Still, I owe you one," I said. "You didn't need to do that."

Harris looked at me in a very particular way. "I never said that the rescue wasn't without a price."

"What do you mean?"

But Harris had already turned away from me. "We'll talk later," he said. "Take it to the bridge, Jenkins. We're not out of trouble yet."

"Covering fire on portside," yelled a crewman. "I want those missiles gone from my scanner."

"*Oui, chef,*" replied another. "Firing solutions locked."

The *Paladin*'s crew occupied all stations on the bridge, hooked to weapons terminals. According to the tri-D command display, space around Jiog was currently thick with hostile targets.

A Krell ark-ship sat in low orbit. Her vast hull was criss-crossed with impacts and unhealed injuries, like the face of a meteor-rained moon. The ark trailed tendrils of living matter behind its bulk, swarming with infected bio-fighters and other space-borne assets. *Flashes of polluted seas. Sacred coral desecrated. Breeding chambers, flooded with corrupted bio-matter. And the navigator-forms: their distended bodies riddled with the virus . . .* I blinked away the visions, fought against the strength of feeling.

"We wish to fight infection," Pariah intoned.

The comms-antennae on Pariah's back bristled softly, as though reading transmissions.

"Another day, fish," Harris said. "Another day."

The Krell were not the only threat out here. A harried and ever-dwindling Directorate fleet, consisting of a handful of battlecruisers and heavy assault transports, was positioned in orbit around Jiog.

"Will the Directorate follow us?" Zero asked.

"They won't," Harris said. "Captain Lestrade will see to that."

"I am taking care of the Krell," replied the man at the command terminal, who I took to be Lestrade. "The girl is seeing to the Directorate."

Novak nodded at Lestrade. "He is big one, yes?"

Lestrade was taller than even Novak, but exceptionally thin with it. His skin was drawn tight over his bald head; not as old as Carmine, but well past his prime. Still, he and the others were doing a good job of keeping us out of enemy fire lanes.

"Is a piece of cakewalk," answered a girl's voice from a booth in the corner of the room.

Zero took an immediate interest. "Is that an interface booth?"

"You got it," said the occupant. She poked her head out of the booth for a moment; looked over at the Jackals.

"The fish is with us," I said, throwing a thumb at Pariah.

The girl just shrugged, unimpressed. In her teens, she was waif-like in appearance, skin a dark oak. A mane of electronic cables wired to her scalp mingled with her dreadlocked hair, and a mass of fibres sprouted from the data-ports on her forearms.

"The kid's called Nadi," Harris declared. "She's the best damned hacker this side of the Asiatic Rim. A recent recruit."

"That was how you manipulated the Directorate's data-network, I take it?" Zero asked.

"Yeah," Harris said. "We couldn't have done it without her. She's a pain in the ass, but she's good."

"I *can* hear you, old man," Nadi answered.

"Sorry, Nadi," Elena said. "You know that he doesn't mean it."

"It's okay. I liked the part about the 'best hacker this side of the Asiatic Rim'. But I'm not a kid. I'm fifteen standard!"

"Which makes you a kid," Harris said. "Less of the old man, and the saying is 'piece of cake', by the way."

"Whatever . . ." Nadi said.

"She's currently so far in the Directorate's systems that they don't know what's real and what isn't," Elena explained. "She was instrumental in your recovery from the surface."

"What tech are you running there?" Zero asked, leaning into the booth. The girl hacker was surrounded by jury-rigged keyboards and several beaten-up computer terminals.

Nadi smiled and laughed. "I'm running a modified second-generation intercessor script," she said. "Illegal, mostly. It'd get me ten in the slammer in most Alliance territories, but I'm using a closed system, see? All of my tech is homemade."

"You and me need to talk, Nadi," Zero said, impressed.

"Anytime."

The conversation was interrupted by another crew station chiming an alarm.

"What've we got, Gustav?" Harris said.

"There she goes," Gustav said. He was a younger man with blond hair and rugged good looks. "Big enough that you can see it on the view-port."

The blasted face of Jiog confronted us: a muddy mixture of pinks and blues and greys. The curve of the planet escaped above and below the view-port, and all around us there were explosions. Some of Harris' crew gasped in surprise as the face of the world burnt.

"The infected will not be stopped," Pariah said.

"Fish talks truth," Novak added. "Will there be any Directorate left?"

"There will always be Directorate . . ." Elena answered, with more than a hint of bitterness in her voice. She had taken up one of the crew posts near the captain's terminal, looking as natural as could be at the station.

Harris nodded. "But not on Jiog. Looks like they're pulling out and burning their own facilities."

"The Shadow Bureau will evacuate everything of tactical importance, and abandon the rest," Feng said. There was certain knowledge in his eyes; a strategic assessment grounded in his genetic heritage. "It's a standard Directorate tactical response. By the books."

"Jesus Christo," Lopez said. "There are still prisoners down there. Can't we help them?"

"There's nothing we can do to stop this," Harris said. "This is one battle that we can't win."

Ships screamed across the void. Transports and freighters pulled away from orbital platforms. Some larger battleships held their own against the tide of Krell invaders, but just as many were already wasted hulks, drifting in the dark, or rippling with sub-detonations that could only be components cooking off.

"Why aren't we being hit?" Lopez asked.

"The Directorate don't even know that we're here," Nadi muttered, somewhat proudly. "I've swapped ship IDs a dozen times already. We're a Directorate ship one moment, then a neutral cargo freighter the next."

"And, unless we get out of here soon," Lestrade said, "a piece of space junk the following."

"Is that . . .?" Feng started, pointing at the tac-display. He swallowed, before continuing, "Is that the *Furious Retribution*?"

The *Furious Retribution* sat at high anchor. Running hot, she was throwing wave on wave of firepower at the Krell, popping targets in every direction. Missiles launched from her flanks, the railguns on her spine chattering.

"Get us out of here," Harris said. "We've seen enough."

"Ready when you are, Captain Lestrade," Elena said with a nod.

The captain pulled a face that suggested he would rather not have been here in the first place, and started chanting back coordinates, manipulating the data-feed in front of him. The *Paladin* initiated thrust. More explosions peppered the horizon outside, although the *Furious Retribution* sat stalwart on the edge of the display.

I sighed. Was it really over?

Harris unbuckled himself from his seat. "We'll be safe soon. At ease, trooper."

That was good enough for me.

There was something satisfying about handing over the reins, about giving up responsibility, to Harris and the crew of the *Paladin Rouge*. Of course, the ship stayed on high alert – Harris' team manning the sensor systems and weapon-pods – but it was all taken care of. There was no station for me or the Jackals, and with an insistence nothing short of an order Harris directed that we rest.

"Good," Novak said, rolling his head on his enormous shoulders. "I earn break, yes?"

"I think we all have," agreed Lopez.

The rest of the squad were just as grateful. We got medical attention from the *Paladin*'s surprisingly well-equipped sick bay. The standing ship's physician was a squat and dour woman called Maberry. She didn't tell us anything about her reasons for being on the *Paladin*, or her background, but from the way she dealt with the Jackals I got the feeling she had a military history, maybe a former combat-medic. She certainly knew her way around a battlefield injury.

"Can you believe it?" Zero asked, still incredulous. Her eyes were ruddy, hair unwashed. She looked a lot like the bedraggled orphan I'd pulled from the remains of Mau Tanis Colony, all those years ago. "I mean, Lazarus, right? And Dr Marceau? Not only are they alive, but we actually get to meet them both . . ."

"Simmer down, Zero," I suggested. "We get the picture."

"You are big fan, yes?" Novak asked.

"Of course," Zero said, her face illuminated. "Who isn't?"

Novak shrugged. "Am not bothered."

"Yeah, right," Lopez said. "We all saw your face in the cargo bay, when we first boarded the ship. You were as surprised as the rest of us."

Novak just grunted.

"Hold still," Maberry said. "This will hurt if you don't."

Maberry sealed the wound on my arm with some staples. The auto-doctor did the rest; knitting back together the injured tissue.

"The arm isn't actually broken," Maberry confirmed. "But it was a nasty impact. Same goes for that injury to your bicep; it clipped muscle, but it could've been much worse. You got lucky. The ribs, on the other hand . . . Try to avoid physical exertion for the next couple of weeks."

"I'll try."

Yeah, I'd suffered two fractured ribs. Hardly surprising. Another round in the auto-doc and a medi-pack saw to them, and I pledged to avoid laughing, coughing or doing anything else too hard until Maberry gave me the all-clear.

Gustav – the young crewman from the bridge – showed us to a shared barracks. Though cramped, it was idyllic compared to the conditions on Jiog. Lopez, Novak, Zero and Feng all crashed the moment my eyes were off them, exhaustion finally claiming its due. Elena saw to Pariah, providing the alien with somewhere quiet and dark in which it could temporarily nest. She seemed intrigued by the alien, which I could entirely understand.

As for me, I stripped out of the Ikarus flight-suit and took a long, hot shower.

Everything feels better after a decent shower, and I needed some thinking space. Was it strange that I wanted to be alone after so many days of confinement on Jiog? Probably, but this was different. As I stood under the shower head, let the water rush over me, I was alone by choice.

A shower on a starship – a hot water and soap shower, instead of a sonic cubicle job – is a luxury. So I made the most of it, and no one stopped me as the minutes rolled by. I watched the grime of our time on Jiog disappear down the drain.

But I couldn't rest. We were still in Directorate space. The territory was dangerous enough, only made more treacherous by the unexplained arrival of the infected Krell fleet. There were still so many elements in play here, so many variables. So many unknowns.

I started as the ship's PA system chimed, and a French-accented voice said, "Jump point reached. Commencing Q-jump in T minus ten seconds . . ."

I braced a hand against the cubicle wall. Felt the throb of the Q-drive as it activated, and we shifted into quantum space.

I should've felt something like relief. That would've been natural; the proper reaction to our flight from Directorate space. And yet I couldn't allow myself that. Instead, I felt something darker. Getting away from Jiog was a good thing, but guilt still gnawed at me. *This was probably the same Q-jump point Riggs used to escape*, I thought. I hadn't recognised him for what he was, and I had let him in.

"Q-jump successful," the ship's AI added a moment or so later. "We have successfully left the Joseon-696 system."

CHAPTER ELEVEN

BACK IN THE GAME

A little later, I went looking for Harris, eager to secure some answers from him. The *Paladin Rouge* wasn't a big ship by any stretch, and it had limited crew quarters. When I couldn't find Harris there, I went to the bridge, and asked Gustav.

"Ah," said the young crewman. "Lazarus will be in his war room." He shook his head with a knowing smile. "You ever need the old man, that's where he'll be."

"He spends more time down there, on his planning, than he does with his own wife," Nadi called out from her booth.

"Lower deck, module C-3," said Captain Lestrade.

I followed Captain Lestrade's directions, and found that Gustav's description – of a war room – was very appropriate.

The chamber was one of the larger aboard the *Paladin*, and had been decked out with a highly advanced tri-D tactical display unit in the centre, and monitors fixed to every wall. It had the feel of an animal's lair, with Harris the alpha male of the absent pack; mostly in darkness, illuminated only by the glow of the various holographic projections. Harris was poised over the main display, eyes narrowed as he studied the flow of data. He barely looked up as I entered.

"You're awake."

"Seems that way."

"I hope you got that arm seen to."

"I did. Your medic, Maberry, says that the arm's fine. Or going to be, at least."

"How about your squad? Are they okay?"

"The Jackals are resting. I'm letting them off the leash for a while."

A tumbler of something amber and likely alcoholic sat on the display beside Harris, the scent filling the chamber. He scooped up the glass and took a sip.

"I see that you didn't get around to replacing the hand," I said.

Harris' left hand was a bad-quality bionic. He inspected it, holding up his glass.

"It's a badge of office," Harris said. "I've grown attached to it."

"Are you trying to be funny? They can give you a proper graft now, you know. Science Division has been doing them for a while."

"Yeah, well, I kind of like this one."

He cycled the fingers of his hand. The whole thing was completely mechanical; an Army job with exposed ligatures and metal components that terminated at the wrist. He'd lost the original during one of the Lazarus Legion's most famous missions. A Directorate agent – another Alliance turncoat, as it happened – had been responsible for causing the injury. The Army had repaid Harris with a replacement bionic the likes of which would give children nightmares.

The metal fingers clink-clinked against the glass as he manipulated them with expert precision.

"You want some?" he asked me, referring to the drink. "You know how I feel about drinking alone."

"You made a sport out of it, back in the day."

"It's good bourbon." I wasn't surprised when Harris slid a small silver flask from his pocket, and produced another glass from nowhere. He raised an eyebrow in my direction. "Proximan-brewed, just like that girl on your squad."

"I'm not a bourbon kind of girl," I said, "but today, I'll make an exception."

Seeing Harris' hand reminded me of Carmine and her replacement leg. That had been of the same manufacture.

"They killed Carmine," I said. "The Directorate killed Carmine on Jiog."

"Captain Carmine? The Carbine?" Harris said. He'd known her too; had served with her during the New Ohio operation. He let out a sigh, shook his head in disappointment. "Shit. I'm sorry to hear that."

"Not as sorry as her daughters will be."

"You and her were tight."

"We were, but I hadn't seen her in years."

"Family's important, right? We were like family, once, but you never did come visit me in Normandy."

Without even a thought, I answered, "It was too painful. After what happened, I mean."

"Kaminski?"

Jesus, hearing his name hurt more than I wanted to accept. I hadn't thought of Vincent Kaminski in a very long time. He had been my sometime lover when we served on the Lazarus Legion.

Harris nodded. "Now, *he* came to visit. 'Ski was that kind of guy. Stayed a whole week."

"I'm sure he did."

"Hated every minute of it, too. 'Ski wasn't an outdoors type. But he visited, at least."

We sat for a moment, in companionable silence, both drinking. The bourbon was strong, swilling around my mouth, burning my gullet on the way down. It felt reassuringly warming as it hit the empty pit of my stomach. But I knew that it would never fill the void that had been left behind.

"Sometimes people die, Jenkins. Sometimes the universe is just unfair like that, and that's okay. It's just the way things are."

"Not 'Ski," I said. "Not my 'Ski."

The Lazarus Legion had each gone their separate ways after the Krell War. Harris, into hiding with Elena. Me, back into the military: trying to fight my way out of Harris' shadow, but failing at every turn. I'd heard that Dejah Mason, the youngest member of the squad, had gone into politics on her return to Mars. She was tough, smart and more than capable – she would do well for herself. Elliott Martinez had taken up with gunrunners, and there were reports that he had been fighting alongside rebels for Venusian independence. Like that was ever going to happen. Like Mason, Martinez was another political animal, although of a different sort. That left Vincent Kaminski.

"Funny, isn't it," I observed, even though I didn't think that it was funny at all. "How we survived so much shit as the Lazarus Legion, but six months back in New York, and death finds Kaminski."

There was a dam inside of me, and sitting here like this – with one of my oldest friends, the man who had once been my senior officer . . . I was worried that if I let it open, it wouldn't stop. The tears welled in my eyes.

"You okay?"

"I will be. It . . . It's been an emotional few days."

I shuddered. Rubbed my arms across my body, snagging the black data-ports on my forearms.

"Let's cut through the shit," I said. "What are you doing here, Harris?"

Harris smacked his lips as though the answer to that question required some serious thought. "The place in Normandy didn't quite work out. It was Elena's dream, not mine."

"That's not what I mean. What are you doing *here*: in Directorate space, with a new crew? You're supposed to be a dead man."

"Being dead didn't suit me."

"That's no kind of answer."

"Then let's just say that I came out of retirement. I've been working under the radar with the intelligence services for a while now."

"With Military Intelligence?"

"Yeah, among others. It turns out that there are plenty of government agencies who find being dead useful."

"I'll bet."

"We're currently working with the Watch."

I'd never heard of that organisation, but then deep intel wasn't my line of work.

"You always needed to be the hero," I said.

"That's not true at all," Harris said. "Not now, anyway."

Harris wasn't even an operator any more. The sleeves of his crew-suit were rolled up, revealing blank spaces – and well-healed scar tissue – on his forearms, where his data-ports had once been. On the back of his right hand, the numerals 239 were tattooed. That was the man's final score; his total number of transitions. When the Krell War had ended, and Harris and Elena had gone into hiding, Harris had been made non-operational – his data-ports removed. There was some irony in the fact that the man who had once been the figurehead for the Sim Ops Programme could no longer operate a simulant . . .

Harris continued, "But when I see a wrong, it's hard not to want to right it."

I laughed, although the sound came out sour and humourless. I was very much aware of Harris' eyes boring into me, watching me. I fought the feeling that he was just another man evaluating me, testing me. Just like Riggs, just like Sergkov, even Pariah.

"The universe is falling apart again," Harris said, "and I can't sit by and let it happen. You can't save them all, Jenkins, but you can try to save some."

"We tried," I said, "when we were Legion."

"I recognise the girl, Zero. She's grown up."

"It's been a while since we rescued her from Mau Tanis," I explained. "She's suffering from hero worship syndrome as far as you're concerned. Try not to disappoint her."

"Kid's got smarts then, huh?" Harris said, with a wry expression on his face.

I stared down at the tactical display. "I see that you've been keeping yourself busy."

The tri-D display showed a particularly complex map of space, sliced with numerous battle lines. There was the Maelstrom, every Shard Gate across the region mapped and plotted, then the Former Quarantine Zone, currently clogged with Krell migrant fleets. Every graphic had been painstakingly labelled and catalogued, with the names of various Krell Collectives – Silver Talon, Blue Claw, Red Shell – floating beside each pawn on the chessboard.

"Dozens of Collectives have already been infected with

the virus," Harris said, sighing. "Many Krell star systems have fallen. Every time one goes down, it triggers a migration event. An exodus."

A frightening number of systems glowed red. Where a system or planet fell, the Krell population migrated outwards: like an organic flood, inevitably smashing against the Former Quarantine Zone and threatening to spill into Alliance space.

"Can't we communicate with the Krell?" I suggested. "We have the frequency-beacon."

The frequency-beacon was one of Science Division's breakthroughs at the end of the Krell War; technology that was supposed to allow us to make contact with the Collective's higher intelligence network.

"The freq-beacon?" Harris repeated. "It doesn't work on the infected Krell, and the uninfected Collectives don't seem to want to listen any more. All lines of communication between us and the fishes are gone. We're on the verge of something terrible. This war will be like nothing we've ever fought before. Sometimes the uninfected Collectives trigger conflict as they flee the virus, but just as often the infected reach out and strike against human worlds." He raised an eyebrow. "Which sometimes has its benefits."

"What do you mean?"

"We used the Krell invasion of Joseon-696 as cover. Military Intelligence had been cultivating a prisoner revolt there for months; managed to smuggle in some communicators. The work-gangs aren't as closely monitored as the rest of the prisoners. Your man Novak didn't even know who he was working with. According to Carmine, Command hadn't even known the prison's location. Harris's intel must've been deep."

"That was quite the plan," I said. "But we got lucky. Things could've worked out very differently."

Harris didn't take the bait, but said, "Novak was an enforcer with the Sons of Balash, you know. There were lots of former gang members down there, and several from the Sons."

"I know about all this, Harris. But the Sons of Balash; that's not him any more."

"Maybe, but loyalty like that never really leaves a man."

"They killed his wife and child," I explained. Sudden recall of that disclosure – hanging upside down in the Krell holding facility on one of their ark-ships, somewhere in the Gyre – made me feel sick . . . I drank down the rest of my bourbon, and Harris immediately poured me another glass. "Novak might have his reasons for working with the Sons," I said, "but he's a Jackal now, through and through."

"If you say so."

"How did you know that we were on Jiog?"

"I keep my ear to the ground. When the intelligence came through that you'd been captured . . ." Harris pulled a face. "I couldn't let it go."

"Why did the Krell choose Joseon-696 – Jiog – as their target?"

"It was random, more or less. The infected Collectives don't appear to have any specific objective. They just wander, mindless, into occupied space."

"That figures," I said. I'd seen the infected fishes up close, and I could easily accept that there was no reasoning behind those dead eyes.

"I wish that the Krell virus was our only problem. The Black Spiral are also running rampant: conducting raids on Alliance holdings all along the Former Quarantine Zone, and throughout the Drift."

The map lit with dozens of glowing attack locations, and I saw how busy the Spiral had been in the last few months.

Harris had methodically categorised their various activities, as though he was trying to predict their next target.

"What's the Spiral's objective?"

"As you can see, the Gates have attracted particular interest. For what reason? I don't know. Not yet, anyway."

It was obvious from his tone that this was a problem to which he had dedicated considerable thought. As a military tactician, to understand the enemy meant that it could be predicted, could be measured and estimated. An enemy that could not be understood was a very dangerous one indeed. That the Spiral were focusing their attention on the Shard Gates wasn't new information, but it was still worrying. The Gates were literal wormholes in time-space, and allowed for instant travel between the Maelstrom and sometimes vulnerable locations in Alliance space. No one had thought to shore up the defences of those star systems, because – until recently – the Krell had been on our side. The Shard were the only other confirmed xeno threat, and no one had heard from the machines in a very long time.

Harris continued, "The Spiral are also stealing equipment and supplies. They've attacked outposts across the Former Quarantine Zone. Some military targets, others civilian. Sometimes, the Spiral's purpose seems to be to destabilise defensive lines." He pointed to a location. "Here, they found an experimental research station. Stole stealth missiles, proper cutting-edge technology."

"Stealth missiles?" I asked. I hadn't even heard of such a thing.

"They shoot you with one, you won't see it coming until it's too late," Harris muttered. "Whenever Alliance forces come up against the Spiral, they never know what they're going into." Harris thoughtfully sipped at his bourbon. "So those are the highlights," he concluded. "The universe has gone to shit."

"We were working with Mili-Intel too," I said. "An officer called Major Vadim Sergkov."

"I know about your mission," Harris replied, "and I knew Major Sergkov. He was okay, for Mili-Intel. We already know that the *Santa Fe* was tasked with tracking the ECS *Hannover*."

"You *have* been busy," I whispered. That was supposed to be protected information. "We found the *Hannover*." I shuddered, recalling what we had discovered in the Maelstrom, and the subsequent loss of that intel. "Or what was left of it. But one of my squad – Corporal Riggs – was a traitor. The bastard manipulated me."

Just speaking Riggs' name brought with it a deluge of anger, regret, disgust. I had let Riggs in: let my guard down. Where had that got me? I shivered with rage.

Harris wasn't one for reassurance, but he did offer, "Hold it in, Jenkins. You'll get your chance to get even."

"Is that a promise?"

"As good as. Riggs was a Black Spiral convert. Someone persuaded him join their cause as a result of his background. We know that he was responsible for your capture by Directorate forces. That was a deliberate act, to take you out of the game."

Harris set down his empty glass, and uncapped the flask of bourbon. Swigged from it directly, and passed it to me. I took it.

"Why did he take the trouble to fly us into Asiatic Directorate territory?" I asked.

"Riggs was a cornered animal," Harris explained. "He had no choice but to bail out when he did. Had the *Santa Fe* jumped to Alliance territory, there was every prospect that he would be discovered. We believe that Riggs rendezvoused with a Black Spiral fleet somewhere outside of Jiog's space."

"So Riggs – the Spiral – now has the *Hannover*'s black box," I said, summarising what we knew. "My mission was a failure. In that case, I need to get back to Alliance space, to Unity Base. I need to make a report to Command. Captain Heinrich and General Draven need to know what we found. I made contact with a Krell navigator-form, of the Silver Talon Collective. It showed me where the virus started. If we can trace the contagion back to source, perhaps we can stop it."

Harris looked at me with an unusual expression on his features. "It's not that simple, Jenkins."

"Of course it is! I have intelligence for Alliance Command, and I need to make a report—"

"Command is compromised. The whole structure is riddled with the Spiral."

"The Spiral's a damned terrorist network," I said, feeling the anger rise in me. "The Alliance has been here before, and we'll be here again."

"Command is compromised," Harris repeated, enunciating the words very precisely.

"Don't patronise me."

"I'm not, but you need to know what's happening out here."

"Then what are you suggesting?"

"You need to start working outside the normal channels," he said. "Outside of these structures."

"You sound almost as bad as Warlord . . ."

"Now there's a name we need to talk about," Harris suggested. "But for now, take it from me: if we're going to stop this war, then running back to Command isn't going to help. Your rescue isn't the end: it's the beginning."

This wasn't over. Not yet, and not by a long way. Our recovery from Jiog was one small battle in a long war.

"I have a responsibility to my squad," I said. Christo, I

sounded pathetic, and I knew it. "They're green, Harris. I can't promise that they'll want this any more than I do."

"You're not giving them enough credit. They're a good squad, a solid team."

I never thought that I'd hear Harris describe an ex-Directorate clone soldier, or a lifer, as "solid", but there you go. Jiog had pretty much been the ultimate test of loyalty, and the Jackals had passed.

"Even the fish head," Harris muttered. "Much as I don't like having it on my ship . . ."

"She shouldn't be drinking."

Elena stood at the hatch, looking imperious dressed in a dark blue crew-suit, her long hair immaculately plaited over her shoulder. She always appeared so serious, and now she scowled especially gravely.

"Doctor's orders," she added.

"A little bourbon never hurt anyone," Harris replied.

Elena pulled an unimpressed grimace. "Tell that to your liver, *mon amour*. She should be resting."

"Maybe she's rested enough."

"I *am* here, you know," I intervened.

Elena took a position around the tac-display, and tapped a cigarette from a packet, lit it without offering me one. Like Harris', Elena's forearms were marked with scar tissue: her data-ports had also been removed, and like him she was unable to operate a simulant.

She glanced at me coolly. "Your squad is in pretty good shape, all things considered. Better than they have any right, or expectation, to be." She dragged long on the cigarette. Her fingertips were stained yellow by nicotine. "Sergeant Campbell – Zero – was fortunate to escape redaction with such limited memory loss, and the pariah-form is in especially good condition. The fruits of Project Pariah are promising."

"How do you know about the pariah-forms?" I asked. "I thought that intelligence was locked down tight."

"The Watch is aware of several off-book black operations," Elena explained. "Although we thought that the Project had been burnt. Certain special operations were aborted, and their data lost, as a result of the infiltration of Military Intelligence by the Black Spiral. The service is rife with double agents."

Harris nodded in agreement. "The Black Spiral has people looking for us. They've even sent agents to our place in Normandy."

"More intelligence from this mysterious Watch, I take it?"

Elena gave me a knowing smile, "You are sceptical, *ma chère*?"

"I have every right to be, Doctor."

"Have you shown her the footage?" Elena asked, turning to Harris.

He shook his head. "It's not for the faint of heart. I wasn't sure whether she was ready."

"What footage? I'm ready. Show me everything."

Harris still seemed reluctant, but Elena encouraged him. "Go on," she said.

"If you say so . . ." Harris muttered.

The tactical display filled with a tri-D image: a surveillance feed. A single Krell was curled at the back of a prison cell. A light came on in the chamber, and the Krell's reaction was instant. The bio-form was up, hurling itself against the cell's transparent walls.

"This is recorded footage," Elena said. "It would be far too dangerous to keep an infected specimen aboard the *Paladin*."

The alien slid down the inside of the glass wall, leaving a smear of ichor and slime where it had made contact. But the reprieve didn't last long. Again and again, the alien slammed its body against the inside of the tank.

"What designation is it?" I asked, unable to pull my eyes from the harrowing spectacle.

"It started as a primary-form," Elena said. "But what it is now . . ." She shrugged. "We've taken to calling them thralls. They are nothing more than slaves to the virus."

The Krell's body frame was much larger, bulkier than a typical primary-form. Its carapace was warped, spiked and spined all over, but otherwise free of any markings: as though it had shed its allegiance to its birth Collective. Instead, the monster's hide was stained black, and every piece of exposed flesh was stitched with new capillaries and throbbing veins. The xeno's eyes were silver orbs, completely alien even to the Krell.

"It's infected with the Harbinger virus," Harris said. "That's what Science Division is calling it."

Giving the virus a name should've made it less frightening. It was, after all, the first step in understanding it. Instead, it somehow personified my fear. I wanted to look away as the creature slammed its body against the observation window, but I somehow couldn't. I wanted to see some element of rationality in those dead eyes, in that decayed and wilted face.

Nothing. That was what I saw. A complete absence.

I'd seen the effect of the virus. Seen what it could do, to the Silver Talon ark-ship. That had taken just one man – Warlord, Clade Cooper – to infect an entire living vessel . . .

Elena opened another file on the display. The image that appeared reminded me a lot of Harris' battlefield maps. But whereas those showed the war in macro, this was the conflict in micro. I wasn't sure which was more worrying.

"This footage is the invasion of a Krell primary-form's higher functions," Elena said, staring at the rippling silver forms that corrupted and twisted the Krell's cellular structure. It was almost hypnotising. Cells were unbound and ruptured, neural pathways rewritten. "As you can see, once Harbinger gains a foothold, it moves rapidly, and it is almost universally effective."

The virus usurped the host cells, took over the body. Here was something more organised than even the Krell. It was the perfect hive organism. There seemed some malignant design behind this virus, behind this contagion. It was so singularly effective that I couldn't accept that it was random . . .

"When Harbinger gains a foothold in the host specimen, it quickly supplants higher brain functions. The virus then enters a communicable phase, usually within hours of infection. Once enough primary-forms become infected, the Collective reaches a sort of critical mass. The infected are desperate to spread the virus. Civil war erupts, although there can only be one winner in the conflict that ensues."

"Harbinger's adaptable, capable of infecting all Krell bio-forms," Harris said. "Their ships, structures, bio-technology."

The tri-D projection shifted again, now showing images from long-distance scopes. *Things* advanced through the void of space. Shambling, rotten corpses of starships, hulls universally ruptured, trailing intestine-like innards as their plasma engines burnt. Every biological component had been corrupted, had turned.

"Imagine what this shit can do to a Krell world," Harris said. "It trickles from the warrior forms, to the leaders, to the navigators. Then the bio-ships and arks. Changing them, twisting them."

Elena continued: "The Krell have no natural immunity to Harbinger. Once they overcome a particular strain, it adapts, mutates, and just starts again. Every laboratory in the Alliance is working on a cure for the virus, but every time we find an answer, it just mutates into a new strain."

"The Black Spiral is spreading this shit," I whispered. "We were on an ark-ship, in the Gyre. We encountered Warlord. Maybe Riggs set that up, too. Warlord deployed something – a vial, a canister – to infect a Krell ship."

Neither Elena nor Harris appeared surprised by that information.

"We suspected as much," Harris said. "Where he's getting the virus from; that's the real question."

"So what's your plan then, Harris?" I asked. I knew that he was building up to this – that his explanation had all been part of the sell. "How exactly are you going to stop all of this?"

"We're searching for a counter for this virus," he said. Now there was an interesting choice of words. Not cure, not remedy: *counter*. "That's our priority. That's what we do first. The Black Spiral, the Directorate, those things can wait. The virus is the biggest threat right now, and we have a lead on some intelligence in the Mu-98 system, so that's where we're going."

"And where do the Jackals fit into this plan of yours?"

I knew, then, that Harris hadn't rescued me from Jiog without a reason. He had been planning something. The rescue mission was a demonstration of what Harris' forces were capable of . . . He met my gaze levelly, his rugged features hard as stone.

"We need a simulant team," he said. "For what will follow. Mu-98 is Russian space. It has a Shard Gate. The area may be hot with fighting. Our objective will be Kronstadt."

"What's there?"

"Not what, but who," Elena said.

"There's a Watch contact on Kronstadt," Harris explained.

"A xeno-archaeologist; goes by the name of Dr Olivia Locke. She was once chief science officer examining the Shard ruins on Tysis World. There was a dig there; the remains of a large Shard facility."

"It was one of the first Shard sites to be verified," Elena said. "I . . . I don't know it."

"No reason why you should," Harris replied.

"Let me guess: more dark ops?"

"Something like that. But if Dr Locke has information that might assist in the war effort, we can't let this go. She was senior, very senior, in Sci-Div before she went off-grid."

"So you've met her?"

"A few times," Harris said.

"Why did she turn?"

"She had a difference of opinion with Command. But we can talk more about that later. Right now, I need an answer from you. Are you with us? Of course, if we meet the Black Spiral along the way," he said, with a shrug, "well, that'll be your chance to get even with them."

And there we have it, ladies and gentlemen: the sweetener. The kicker, the dangling carrot.

"In case you haven't noticed, we're a Simulant Operations team with no sims," I said.

"That condition might not be as permanent as it sounds," Harris suggested. "We've identified a Science Division facility, a farm, that we intend to raid. It's in the Thane system; an outpost called Darkwater Farm."

"But if we do this," Elena said, "there can be no contact with Command."

"The mission will be strictly *sub rosa*," Harris added.

"What are you suggesting?" I asked. I wanted to flush Harris out, to make him say the words, but I couldn't help myself. "That we go AWOL?"

Going AWOL – absent without leave – was pretty high in the lexicon of service misconduct. By rote, the relevant military code came to me: *Article 87 – missing deployment, failure to attend at an appointed time. Maximum punishment: life imprisonment.* I remembered more of the Combined Military Code. *Article 85 – desertion. Maximum punishment in times of war: death.* And looking down at Harris' map, I couldn't think of a more apt term to describe the mass of troop movements than "war".

Harris didn't seem to notice my hesitation. "That's right," he said.

Can I do this? I asked myself. Although they were light-years away from me, all I could think about was what my folks back on Old Earth would make of this. That frightened me more than the ranked Krell war-fleets. I could almost imagine the look on my father's face. Ol' Teddy Jenkins, darling of the Alliance Army: reputation dashed because his daughter went AWOL . . .

"I'm not doing anything without the Jackals," I decided. "They're my team, and my people."

"Fine," Elena said. "Speak with them."

"Just remember this," Harris added. "Whatever they say about Lazarus, the only thing special about me was that I kept on going, no matter how much it hurt. No matter what."

CHAPTER TWELVE

BURY THE DEAD

Conrad Harris had never been a by-the-books kind of officer. To him, discipline was a byword for bureaucracy. He hadn't ever let that get in the way of an objective, and because he got results, High Command had rarely interfered with the way that he operated. But the suggestion that we shouldn't report in . . . Well, that was something I hadn't expected. It was something else entirely.

Call it what it is, Jenkins, my conscience said to me. *Lazarus wants you to go rogue.*

I went down to the *Paladin*'s recreation room. The Jackals had claimed it as home, and they sat together in one corner of the chamber. The team was focused on a tri-D viewer set into the wall, but jumped to attention as I entered.

"At ease," I said. I dialled up a cup of hot coffee from the dispenser, and settled down in an uncomfortable chair. "Where's Pariah?"

"Fish is in Engineering," Novak answered. "Has nest now."

Lopez gave a noncommittal nod. "I'm not sure what's

worse: that the fish is building a nest, or that I don't notice its smell any more."

Zero gave a tight grimace, suggesting that even if she was getting used to Pariah, she wasn't quite comfortable with the Krell.

"Y'all keeping up with current affairs, huh?"

The hall's viewer was a window into the outside world, into the universe beyond the *Paladin*'s hull. The Jackals had been watching a news-cast.

"Yes, ma'am," Feng said.

"Then what's the latest?"

Lopez rolled her eyes. "Same old, same old. The Directorate Executive has issued a press release assuring all territories that rumours of a Krell invasion are just Alliance propaganda."

"Tell that to Jiog," Novak said.

"So Harris can get Directorate news channels on the tri-D?" I asked, a little impressed.

"Sure," said Zero. "The ship has a decent receiver."

"Did we make the cut?"

I dreaded seeing images of our capture on the state-sponsored news-feed. There had been drones present throughout our incarceration. When I'd been younger, and the Alliance and Directorate had been at war, such broadcasts had been regular and graphic: constant reminders of the divide between the two camps.

But Zero shook her head. "No, ma'am. Nothing."

I breathed out a sigh of relief. "That's surprising, if nothing else."

"We were probably Commander Kwan and Major Tang's secret project," Feng said. He stared at the screen, but I could sense the anger in his voice. Maberry had fixed his broken tooth with a ceramic implant, and Feng's injuries weren't as serious as they could've been, but that was hardly the point. It's often said that family feuds are the worst, and this was the closest Feng was going to get to a falling out with Ma and Pa.

"What else is happening?" I asked.

The tri-D scrolled with imagery of Krell war-fleets. Some looked infected, others not so much, but I doubted that the average Alliance citizen could tell the difference. The news was careful to refer to the bio-fleets as "limited exploratory forces", as though that would somehow allay panic. Then the cast shifted to a piece on recent terrorist activity in the border colonies – seizures of supplies, personnel, ships.

Lopez continued with the update: "Black Spiral raids are increasing in frequency. Most shipping lanes to the Core are now classified as no-go zones. Pirates, religious freaks, the whole deal. This Warlord bastard; he's sweeping up anyone with an axe to grind against the Alliance. Criminal gangs, fanatics, the disaffected."

"But worse yet," Novak said, portentously, "Senator Lopez has been appointed Secretary of Defence to whole Alliance!"

His raucous and deep laughter filled the room. No one else joined him.

"Maybe this war, or whatever it is," Feng said, easing back in a chair, "will mean that the Senator's plans to cut Sim Ops have to be abandoned . . ."

Lopez sighed. "You guys don't know Daddy like I do. Even if the Krell made it to the Core, I'm not sure it would change his mind. People are – or at least *were* – behind him in cutting the budget."

I drank my coffee and thought about that. Just a short while ago, the very idea of the Krell – infected or otherwise – making it to the Core Systems would've been unthinkable.

Now it was a painful and very foreseeable reality. Senator Rodrigo Lopez was the one man who could change all of that.

"I've seen enough," I decided.

Zero snapped the viewer off, and I was grateful for it.

"So, what's next, ma'am?" she asked me.

"I finish this coffee."

"You know what I mean."

"I don't know what comes next, Zero," I said.

"We're ready."

I laughed at that. "Ready for what?"

"For whatever we're asked to do," Feng said. There was a cool determination to his voice, and the same in his expression. "For whatever's necessary."

The Jackals were still young, and had bounced back faster than I could've hoped. The squad were dressed in shipboard fatigues, not a proper uniform among them. *Does that matter?* I asked myself. They were still soldiers. The uniform, the badge, the guns . . . That wasn't what made a survivor. And that was what we were now: survivors.

"Harris wants our help," I said. "He's working with an intelligence agency, something that calls itself the Watch. They're searching for an answer to this virus."

There was no response to that. Whatever the Watch was, not even Zero had heard of it. That told its own story. Zero was usually prepped up on these things, which meant that the Watch must've been a very deep intelligence agency.

"What does he want us to do?" Feng asked.

"He needs a simulant squad," I said. "And I guess we're it."

"But we don't have any sims," Lopez said.

I noticed that Lopez was fingering the data-ports on her

forearms, unconsciously rubbing the metal plugs. I knew exactly how she felt. My own data-ports had started to throb again, desperate to be connected to a simulant.

"That might change," I offered. "But he insists that we don't report in. We're not going back to Unity Base."

"Then where are we going?" Novak asked.

"We're going rogue," I finally said. "Or at least, that's what he's asking us to do."

To my surprise, the Jackals didn't instantly baulk at that, not even Zero. Was it because they were blinded by the Lazarus legend? Quite possibly. I continued.

"We're heading for a Science Division facility – a farm – for restock. Our eventual objective will be Mu-98, located in Russian Federal space."

Novak nodded, satisfied with that. "Mu-98 is good."

Did I feel good about bringing the Jackals in on this? No, I didn't. They weren't responsible for my decisions, but they would be affected by them.

"You don't have to do this," I explained, "not if you don't want to. After the Gyre, after Jiog: I understand if any one of you wants out. If we're operating outside of our orders, you have every right to—"

It was Lopez who spoke up first. She locked eyes with me.

"Apologies, ma'am, but are you fucking kidding me?" she said. "This is Colonel Conrad Harris asking for our help. This is fucking *Lazarus*."

Zero nodded. "How could we say no?"

Lopez added, "Colonel Harris saved us, ma'am."

"He's just a man like any other," I said, trying to rein the team back in. I wanted them to make an informed decision: to be lead by the head, not the heart. "There's risk here. Serious risk. If Alliance forces come after us . . ."

Lopez didn't back down. "We're all in this, and in deep. We survived Jiog. We made it off a Directorate prison planet. We're sticking with this, seeing it through."

The response stirred pride in me. I'd assumed that Lopez, more than anyone, would want to jump the next ship Coreside, after everything that had happened.

Novak gave a smile of darkened, pointed teeth. "We are all Jackals."

"Where one goes," Feng said, "we all go."

My squad looked hungry for action. Even Zero, to whom until recently field ops would've been anathema.

"Hey, some of us don't have a home to go to any more anyway," she said, with a shrug of her shoulders. "I'm in."

"Just because your planet was blown up doesn't make you special," Lopez said. She threw a light punch into Zero's arm, and Zero yelped in mock pain.

"I need payback," Feng said, solemnly. "And right now, whether that's against the Directorate or the Spiral doesn't much matter to me."

Feng was already psyched up. He balled and unballed his fists, then made an effort not to do it when he saw that I was looking. His anger was the brightest, the hottest.

"So what are we doing in Mu-98?" Lopez asked.

"Harris has a mission," I said, "although he hasn't given me all the details yet. We're going to steal some sims, then make contact with an asset – a former science officer – on Kronstadt, in the Mu-98 system. Other than that, I don't know what we're signing up to. We're going to have to trust Harris."

"He's Lazarus," Zero said, repeating Lopez's words. She seemed reinvigorated. "Does he remember me?"

"Sure, Zero. He remembers you just fine."

I knew that she would follow him into the fire, no matter

what. That kind of zeal worried me almost as much as Feng's need for revenge.

"We'll help in whatever way we can," Zero said. "I've already started tinkering with some of Nadi's tech. She has a good thing going on the bridge, but I'm sure that I can upgrade some of her systems . . ."

"When do we get a briefing?" Lopez asked, all business now.

The squad bristled with energy. They were ready for it.

"Soon," I said. "But there's something we have to do first."

"What?" she asked.

"Let's remember that not everyone made it off Jiog."

Captain Miriam Carmine, my old friend, had been executed.

Hey, Mom, I thought. *I'm going to use the word, whether you like it or not.*

Carmine had been *murdered*.

It was some small blessing that the Shadow Bureau had not broadcast the footage of Carmine's execution. Her daughters deserved better than to learn of her death in that way.

We had to do something to mark her passing. To call the assembly that we held in the cargo bay a "ceremony" would be a vast overstatement. It wasn't a funeral, because we had no body, and there was nothing remotely religious about it. But it was all we could do to remember her, and it would have to be enough.

"Where was she from?" Feng asked.

"Old Earth. She was Californian, like me."

Feng nodded in agreement. "I thought so. Same disposition."

"So I'm a grumpy old bitch, then?"

186

"Sometimes," Feng replied.

"Did Captain Carmine have any particular beliefs?" Zero asked.

"She believed in lots of things. Swearing and tea, for starters."

Zero gave a sad smile. "That's not what I meant."

"I know," I said. "I'm fooling with you. Carmine never talked about anything except for her daughters. They were what kept her going."

Novak nodded in agreement at that. "Is important. I bet she make good mother, yes?"

"She was mother to anyone who came under her radar," I said. "I think that she regretted how rarely she saw her own children."

I didn't even know their names, I realised. Carmine had spoken of them often, during our deployments together. Always favourably, always proudly. I suspected that she had hated herself, just a little, for not going back to Old Earth, for not settling down in her old age. In spirit, she was a little like Harris. She couldn't help but get involved, right up until the end.

Feng, Novak, Lopez and I held our peace in the cargo bay. Harris, Elena and Nadi attended too, although as far as I knew, neither of the latter had ever met Carmine. She would probably have been pleased with the turnout, nonetheless.

Captain Lestrade did his part too, calling "All hands bury the dead" over the ship's PA, and an all-stop to the ship's thrusters. Then, solemnly, he fired the flak cannons three times in quick succession. That was a nice touch. I appreciated it.

I thought of the promise that I had made to Carmine, aboard the *Santa Fe*. I'd sworn that I would tell her daughters that their mother loved them. Whatever happened out here, I would make sure that I honoured that promise. Carmine deserved that. But as I stood there in the cargo bay – without so much as a body to bury at sea – I made another promise, and this one was to myself.

Kwan might've pulled the trigger – fired the bullet – that killed Carmine, but the blood was on Riggs' hands. Her murder: that was on him. Riggs had killed her.

My data-ports throbbed with new vitality. I needed sims, and I needed guns. I was going to make sure that I had both.

I swear that I'm going to find you, Riggs. I'm going to find you, and I'm going to kill you.

The ceremony finished, and the Jackals and crew dispersed.

One more member of the squad to visit before everything was in place.

"You in here?" I asked the dark.

At first, there was no answer. Only the gentle creak and groan of the Engineering deck, the hum of the *Paladin*'s energy core. If there had been any lights in the chamber in the first place, they had now been deactivated, swathing the chamber in shadow. It was hot, humid and more than a little creepy. It also stank to high heaven, the smell so intense that it was eye-watering.

"We are present," came the electronic response.

I felt the xeno's presence before it replied. The alien brushed the edge of my mind.

Pariah had folded itself between some pipework, and there was a clank as it withdrew, its clawed feet hitting the deck. It unfurled its massive body, filling the chamber with its six muscled limbs, and loomed over me, eyes glittering in the darkness.

"Hey, P," I said, trying to sound more jovial than I actually felt. I hadn't appreciated just how much the alien had grown while we were on Jiog. "Are you still hurting? Dr Marceau says that you're in good shape."

"We are no longer injured," it said. Pariah glanced at its own semi-wet body. "We are changing."

And again, I felt that sensation in my head: knew the answer to my question before I'd actually heard it.

"You setting up a lair down here or something?" I asked, taking a step into the chamber. "It looks real homely, although I'm not sure Captain Lestrade will appreciate it."

A sheen of resin had formed on the bulkheads. Mucous dripped from the exposed pipework.

"Others' opinion does not matter."

"What is this stuff?"

"We are acquiring materiel for manufacture," the alien said. "We require a bio-suit and weaponry." It paused, then went on: "The Kindred of Silver Talon are rotten. We must be ready."

"They were your tribe, P," I said. "Are they all gone?"

"The Silver Talon has fallen, but we are Pariah. We will always be Pariah. Silver Talon were of us . . ."

"Listen, there's still a lot I need to explain to you. Riggs was a traitor. He sold us out, to the Directorate."

"We know of this."

"How come?"

Pariah observed me for a second, and I felt the feelers in my head again.

"When Jenkins-other made contact with the Silver Talon's navigator-form," the xeno said, "a connection was formed."

"I remember."

"Jenkins-other touched the Deep."

I still hadn't really got to the bottom of what the Deep was. I only knew that Clade Cooper, also known as Warlord, had once been immersed in it, and that the experience had irrevocably scarred him. Major Sergkov had likened the Deep to interrogation, but it was also so much more than that. It was being one with the Krell mind, being part of the ebb and flow of information . . .

"Are you part of the Deep, P?"

"We are of the Deep, but we are not part of it," Pariah said. "To become part of it is to become Collective. We are Pariah."

"You have to understand that, if the time comes, Riggs is no longer an ally."

"We know this, because you know this," Pariah said.

"He is an enemy. He jumped us into Directorate space."

The alien showed a complete lack of surprise. "Affirmative. When we convene in the same location as Riggs-other, we will express our state of mind."

"We have a new mission," I said, trying to think how best to explain this. "We're going to a new star system."

"We know this also," Pariah said. "The craft that sails stars is moving at full thrust. We will soon sail the quantum tides again. The Gates call to us."

"I wanted to ask if you would come with us. You're a Jackal now. We . . . we're your Collective. Your Kindred."

Many would probably argue that Pariah should have little say in where and when it went, given that it was technically Alliance property. But I thought that P was more than that. It wasn't just a bio-form any more. P was as much a Jackal as the rest of us.

Pariah cocked its head. "We will go with Jenkins-other."

"Appreciate it, P."

The XT abruptly grappled with an overhead pipe, and with a monkey-like motion hauled itself into the mass of conduits in the deckhead. The structures creaked precariously as they took the alien's increased mass.

"We are changing, Jenkins-other," Pariah said. "Something is . . . *happening* to us."

"Maybe you're growing," I suggested. I was well out of my depth here, and drowning fast.

"It is not that. The not-Alliance activated something inside of us."

I felt a stab of emotion, of raw, unfettered anger, and for a moment it was almost enough to floor me. It was a lot like when I thought of Riggs.

"You mean the Directorate? What exactly did they do to you?"

The alien peered at me from above. Its shelled body had contorted, somehow managed to squeeze into another tight space. How the alien could adapt its size according to requirement reminded me of a squid.

"The Directorate-others woke us up," the alien said.

And we have not yet finished . . . echoed in my mind.

"You're still on our side, I hope."

"Yes," Pariah confirmed. "We will inform Jenkins-other when the situation changes."

"That's reassuring, P. Real reassuring."

"Do not be afraid," Pariah said. "We require contact with two organic designations. The Directorate-others, and the Riggs-other."

I laughed. "You and me both, P. You and me both."

P tilted its head again, fixing me with those alien eyes. "Provided Jenkins-other gives us access to those objectives, then we are in alignment."

"We're in alignment, all right," I said.

I retreated through the hatch, and left the alien to its work.

Harris and Elena were waiting for me outside.

"You see," Harris said, nodding into the room. "What

did I tell you? I knew that they would be willing to help."

"You were listening in?" I said, annoyed. "They're my team, Harris. You had no right to do that."

"The fish is building weapons and armour in there. Why wouldn't I keep eyes on it?"

Elena said, "The organism is extraordinary. It's exhibiting a highly advanced rate of personal evolution. I . . . I'm not sure what it's becoming."

"It's a Jackal."

"It's a lot more than that," Elena said. "I've been running some tests on the Pariah's blood samples. You should see the results."

"I thought you said that I should be resting . . ."

"Resting can wait. This is too important."

"So what's our next move?"

"We move on Darkwater Farm," Harris replied. "A planet called Thane."

Farm: slang for the science stations that bred clones for the Simulant Operations Programme. Sims were farmed in industrial-sized depots. These were automated Science Division facilities, ordinarily well guarded and in highly classified locations. By design, most such outposts were far from Shard Gates – the idea being that, in the event of a hostile takeover event, at least the sims would be safe.

"Does Darkwater carry copies of the Jackals?" I asked. "Sim Ops is still a big programme."

Even if Harris and the Watch did know of the location of a farm – which, on the face of it, I was still struggling to accept, given how secret these facilities usually were – that was only half the problem. We could only use simulants derived from our own genetic material; we needed simulants based on the individual genotypes of each Jackal.

"You were out of Unity Base," Harris said. "Trust me:

192

you'll find simulants you can use there. The outpost contains blueprints for every operator in the Eastern Sector. So, what do you say? Are you in, or are you out?"

"We're in," I answered. "But I'm fed up with being kept in the dark. You want my help, then I want to go into this with eyes open."

"Fine," Harris said. "That can be arranged later—"

I shook my head. "No. In your war room, you spoke about Daneb Riggs."

"That's right. He was a person of interest, on the Watch list."

"Then tell me about him. I want to know who Riggs really is."

CHAPTER THIRTEEN

THE HARBINGER

We met in the war room again.

"You sure that you want to do this?" Harris asked me. "You've been through a lot today."

"If I'm ready to help you, and the Watch, raid a Christo-damned farm," I replied, "then I'm ready for this. I want to know."

It went further than that. I didn't just want to know; I *needed* to know. My Jackals watched on silently. I'd summoned them, because they deserved the truth as well. If it came to it, we needed all the intel we could muster. Elena had joined us too.

"Riggs betrayed the Alliance," Harris said. "It was nothing personal. Keep telling yourself that, or it'll eat you up inside. Don't let him do that to you."

"He only did it because I let him," I said, forcefully. "*I* let him get close. *I* gave him the opportunity."

Harris sighed. "All right. Your call."

He tapped some commands into the holo-table, and the display shifted. I did my best to hold back the surge of rage that I felt inside me as Riggs' image appeared there. My fingernails bit into the palms of my hands as they formed into fists. Had I ever hated someone as much as Riggs? Hard to say. I'd once found that face handsome. The small, almost coy, smile. The way the edges of his eyes crinkled when he laughed. Had any of what we had shared together actually been real? Again, hard to say.

"As you know, this is Corporal Daneb Riggs," Harris declared, "former Off-World Marine aviator. Latterly enrolled with the Alliance Army. Elected service with the Simulant Operations Programme."

It'd been his choice, I mulled. *When had the Black Spiral turned him?*

Harris answered my unvoiced question. "We believe that he was recruited by the Black Spiral as a result of his faith. He was a third-generation Gaia Cultist, and some of his more distant relatives are known to have hard-line beliefs. They were responsible for some minor insurgent activity on Tau Ceti. Most of those records have since been expunged – it's unclear by whom – but you can probably draw your own conclusions."

Novak grunted and stood a fraction closer to me. "I never liked him. Too cocky. Is asshole."

Lopez raised her eyebrows. "He's an asshole and a cock?"

"Yes," Novak said. "Is asshole and cock."

The Jackals' brevity did nothing to lighten my mood. I couldn't take my eyes from the holographic of Riggs. The image had been taken from his service record, and Riggs looked the perfect soldier, standing to attention, Army uniform resplendent. Eyes sparkling with promise.

Harris continued, "He did Boot Camp on Tau Ceti V, same world he was born on. Started attending off-base religious ceremonies during Basic training." Harris shrugged.

"He had full American citizenship. No one asked questions. Turned out those ceremonies weren't Gaia Cult meetings after all. Probably Black Spiral. Military Intelligence discovered the cell last year, not long after you went into the Maelstrom."

I swallowed back my anger. "I want to know what made him turn."

What made him do this to me, I almost added. But I didn't go that far, because the Jackals were here. My relationship with Riggs had been secret, and I was only going to reveal it to them if absolutely necessary.

Harris called up another file. Another familiar face appeared there.

"You are aware of the operative known as Warlord," he said, matter-of-factly. "Also known as Clade Cooper. Former Alliance Army Ranger."

Clade Cooper's service file scrolled across the display now. An image of Warlord as he had once been: older, but otherwise much like Riggs. Also dressed in his full service uniform, on a broad chest proudly wearing every medal he'd earned during the years of his service. He too looked handsome in a rugged sort of way; a reflection of Harris, although his was a face without the worry lines and the influence of a lifetime drink problem.

"This was Cooper prior to his last deployment," Harris said. "Military Intelligence sent him to Barain-V. As you may know, that didn't work out so well."

"He was captured by the Krell," Elena filled in. "Spent two years in captivity."

"During which time his family were killed," Harris said. "It was the Red Fin Collective. Shortly thereafter, Cooper was rescued from Barain. He's the only trooper known to have survived full immersion in the Deep."

The Jackals listened on. They had heard some of this from me, after the briefing from our former commanding officer, Major Sergkov. Hearing it again, though, was no less disturbing.

"On his return to Alliance space," Harris explained, "Cooper was destroyed – both mentally, and physically. The prospects of his recertification for service in the Alliance armed forces, certainly as an Army Ranger, were remote."

The holo cycled through a collection of surveillance feeds, showing Cooper's debilitated state. Lopez gasped, put a hand to her mouth, as the last picture sprang to life. Head and upper body, naked, lying on what might as well have been a mortuary slab.

"That should come with a safety warning," Feng said. He plainly wasn't joking.

The man in the image looked nothing like Clade Cooper. I doubted I would have recognised him. Now, his skin was scarred all over; torso a mass of keloid tissue. Limbs and muscles wasted, atrophied. His upper body was pocked by dozens of medical ports, into which tubes ran, shunting compounds to and from his dying body. His head was shaven tight.

Only his eyes showed any real life. In those, I could see hate. Could see horror. Through some twist of fate, his upper face looked largely injured. I had seen that face for myself, seen Cooper wearing a respirator that had concealed the worst of the scarring.

"This was taken during Cooper's medical treatment on Fortuna," Harris said.

Fortuna was the location of preference for veterans about to be drummed out of active service; a paradise-world where troopers were often sent for R&R before they received discharge papers. It had the best tech that an injured serviceman could ask for, but in the face of injuries such as Clade's? It felt like even Fortuna wouldn't be enough to help him.

"This is Cooper six months later," Harris said, switching the feed again.

Lopez braced for more horror, but there was none. The image instead showed something all-too-familiar: a grainy surveillance feed, likely taken during a military operation. Cooper was now dressed in his trademark exo-suit, no helmet, face concealed behind a respirator. His gear was emblazoned with the ubiquitous Black Spiral badge, and he was running and firing towards the location of the camera. The image abruptly terminated in static.

"He made a damned good recovery," Zero said. "Too good, in fact."

"They said that he would never walk again," Elena echoed. "Which is surprising. It was only months after his discharge that he came to the notice of Military Intelligence as a significant figure in the Black Spiral movement."

"How did they fix him?" Lopez asked.

"Unknown," said Harris. "But whatever it was, it gave him the means to execute a very significant grudge that he has against the Alliance."

"That's great," I said, "but where does Riggs fit into this? Why is Riggs working with Cooper?"

"I'm getting to that," Harris said. "One last image."

The display shifted to show the disposition of Army Ranger forces, and then focused specifically on a unit called the "Iron Knights". Squad leader: Sergeant Clade Cooper. I remembered the designation; Major Sergkov had told me that the Iron Knights were Cooper's team. Other names scrolled down the display . . .

"Corporal Marbec Riggs," I whispered. More information

spilled from my mouth, for some reason better spoken aloud than read to myself. "KIA on Barain-V."

"Riggs' father," Zero said, looking from me to Harris, then back again. "Marbec Riggs was Daneb's father, wasn't he?"

Harris nodded solemnly. "That's right. He died fighting the Krell, under Clade Cooper's command."

And suddenly everything snapped into place. It all made horrifying, precise sense.

"Riggs always did hate the fishes," Lopez said. She shook her head, as though trying to dispel the idea but finding that she couldn't. "He hated them because of what had happened to his father."

"Fucking traitor," Novak said. "Is no excuse."

"The Black Spiral was the perfect outlet for Riggs to vent his anger," Harris concluded.

"Why didn't anyone make the connection?" I asked. I was almost yelling now, but I didn't care. "Why didn't Military Intelligence realise that there was a damned mole in Sim Ops!"

"Why would they?" Harris said. "Riggs was a promising Sim Ops recruit. Good military family." He nodded at the image of Riggs again. "Nice hair. Good kid."

If you couldn't see who he really was, then how could they? my inner voice critiqued. I put a hand to my face. Pinched the bridge of my nose and stood there for a long time.

"Are you all right?" Zero asked.

I hardly noticed when she put her hand around my shoulder: a gesture that was wasted, but appreciated. There wasn't much that was going to make me feel better about this.

Nothing but killing Riggs.

"It's just a lot to take in, is all," I said. The words sounded distant and wrong; someone else's excuse.

"This is what we're up against," Elena said. "This is the new war, Jenkins. Now, are you going to help us fight it?"

In the corner of the room, beyond Elena's shoulder, I saw a flicker of movement in the shadow. The not-Riggs that had been taunting me in the Directorate prison. He was smiling – the same smile as on his service record – but the expression had somehow turned malicious, somehow turned dark.

"You're going to have to catch me first, Jenk."

"With pleasure," I said.

The ship's medic, Maberry, was waiting for me in the corridor outside the war room.

"Do you have a moment?" she asked. "Preferably alone. There's something that I need to talk to you about."

What Harris had just told me was still ringing in my ears, and I needed time to think about what Riggs had done – why Riggs had done it – but Maberry's demeanour made it clear that she *really* needed to talk to me. She peered into Harris' war room, in a way that suggested she wanted this to remain between us.

"Sure," I said. "Fine. I'll come now."

"That's probably best."

"Is it about Zero?"

Maberry chewed her lip. "Who?"

"My sergeant," I said. "Zoe Campbell. She was almost redacted by the Directorate."

Maberry shook her head. "Sorry, I'm struggling with the names of the new arrivals. The sergeant was lucky. Miraculously so. Had the redaction process been allowed to run for a few minutes longer . . ." She let that hang, allowing me to draw my own conclusions. "But she'll be okay. Physically, she's tired, but that's not news. The burns to her scalp will heal."

"Then what's this all about?"

"I'll show you."

She led me into the sick bay, and closed the hatch behind us before hurriedly calling up some files on the tri-D display. They looked like medical scans; low-resolution images produced from the shipboard auto-doc. Internal body maps, that sort of thing. They only caught my interest when I saw who the images were of.

PATIENT: FENG, CHU.

"This is your man Feng," Maberry said, pointing out the glowing scan data. "He's a Directorate clone trooper."

"I know that. He has the serial codes to prove it."

"I've seen them. He was liberated from a birthing crèche on Delta Crema station. It's tattooed on his ass, in case you wanted to know."

I lifted an eyebrow. "Can't say I've seen that, but I was aware of the fact. He's a damned good soldier. He's proved his worth ten times over."

Maberry nodded professionally. "I'm sure that he has," she went on, "but you should know about his background."

"He's been fully de-doctrinated," I explained. "I've seen the documentation. His conditioning was broken."

As Kwan had stated, all Directorate clone troops were born indoctrinated. Pre-programmed to the great cause, ready to take to the field with the minimum of training, brought up in military crèches. When the Asiatic Directorate had officially collapsed, many R&D facilities were seized by the Alliance. Some had yielded useful candidates for the Sim Ops Programme. The improved clone physiology was a stable platform for the operation of a simulant. Of course, liberated clones were subject to extensive psychological testing, their Directorate loyalty protocols broken, before they could be declared safe for deployment as Alliance troops.

"I don't doubt that's what you were told."

I didn't like Maberry's tone. "We don't know each other very well, Maberry, for you to be casting aspersions on my squad."

Maberry didn't answer me directly, but instead said, "This scan is from the auto-doc, taken when you first came aboard the *Paladin*."

The image was of the inside of Feng's skull. It looked unexceptional. He had all the usual stuff: a brain, some skull, maybe a little too much space in there, but nothing particularly unusual. But as Maberry manipulated the image, I saw that wasn't quite true. There was a sliver of metal deep in Feng's head. It was printed with a serial code and Chino characters, visible only under extreme magnification.

Maberry crossed her arms over her chest. "As his commanding officer, you should be aware that Private Feng still has something in his head."

"How the hell did that get there?"

"It's been there since his inception, I'd wager."

"What is it?"

"A neural-implant."

"What does it do?"

"Impossible to say without thorough analysis," Maberry answered, unwilling to commit herself. "But if I had to guess, I'd say that it's some sort of bio-module. A neurotransmitter or receiver, maybe? That'd make sense."

"It needs to come out," I decided. "Feng can't walk around on an Alliance starship carrying Directorate technology."

"The boy *is* Directorate technology," Maberry said. "They

made him, and whatever we do to him, he'll always be their product. Can you see how the neural-plant is anchored to the cerebellum by these strands?" I nodded, although I couldn't really see that level of detail from the scan. "It's wired to his brain so deep that it'd be impossible to remove without killing him. At least, with the tech we have on this ship. Maybe a hospital ship, or a Sci-Div facility could help, but . . ."

"What about smart-drugs? Try a course of medication, flush it out."

Maberry shook her head. "Nothing I'm familiar with would be capable of that sort of precision, I'm afraid."

"Then ask Nadi to help. Perhaps she could hack the module, run a bypass."

"This is beyond her," Maberry said. "And I thought it best to speak with you first, before I discussed it with Nadi. She's young; she talks a lot. Once she knows, the rest of the ship will follow shortly after."

"Shit."

"It might be benign."

I gave Maberry an unconvinced look. "Really? The Directorate put something in a clone trooper's head, and it might be benign?"

"Well, whatever it is, Commander Kwan didn't activate it when he had Private Feng in his custody on Jiog."

Surgeon-Major Tang had made Feng. She had been project director, had been responsible for his creation. The Mother of Clones, Kwan had called her. It was beyond question that Kwan and Tang had known about the neural-plant. So why hadn't they played that card, when we had been on Jiog? Although I desperately wanted to believe that the neural-plant was benign, I just couldn't accept it. I knew the Directorate too well for that.

"Does Feng know that it's in there?"

"I don't think so. He was quite proud to tell me that he had been retrained, that his conditioning had been broken."

Feng wasn't a machine, although the way we were talking about him made him sound an awful lot like one. The idea of concealing this information from Feng made me feel instantly guilty. He deserved to know what was going on in his own head, even if he couldn't change it. *I* would certainly want to know. But what was the alternative? Feng had struggled with enough self-doubt to last a lifetime. He was one of my Jackals, and if he was a problem, I was going to have to deal with him myself.

"Feng's a good kid," I said. "Thanks for the intel, but keep this to yourself, please."

"Of course," Maberry said. "If there was any immediate danger, I think we would already know about it."

"That's encouraging," I said, although I didn't feel that way at all.

"You might be on your own out there, soon. I just thought that I should let you know."

We took the Shard Gate in the Canopus system.

It was defended by a heavily armed contingent of Alliance Navy, but Nadi did her thing, fooling Space Control into believing that we had the relevant authorisation codes. We slipped through the military cordon easily enough. They were on patrol for infected Krell forces, and obvious Black Spiral sympathisers: a single French-registered freighter, claiming to be transporting relief supplies to the Outer Colonies, was easily dismissed. Nadi did a good job faking our credentials – she was a real asset to a covert operation, and to the Watch.

After that, we Q-jumped to Polaris. Another Shard Gate

waited there, and we went through the same procedure. No hassle, no problem. It was almost too easy.

I sat up in the rec room, waiting, drinking coffee. Watching the ever-more-depressing news-casts as we sailed on through the void. *Famine on Epsilon Eridani. Jakarta Prime calling for independence. Senator Lopez petitioning the Alliance Assembly for withdrawal of military support for the Outer Colonies . . .*

"What's the Senator's problem?"

I jumped awake. Body rigid, I went into battle-mode immediately.

"Sorry, Jenk," said Zero. "Didn't mean to startle you there."

Zero, looking about as tired as I felt, drifted into the rec room.

"I'm not startled," I said.

She pulled a tight smile, fixed herself a coffee. "Tell that to your face."

"Sarcasm doesn't suit you, Zero."

She sat beside me at the table, repressed a quick shiver as she looked up at the news segment on the viewer – *Krell fleet arrives at Joseon-696: Directorate forces claim decisive victory* – and then blew on her coffee.

"Incredible, isn't it? Meeting Lazarus and Elena, and this ship . . . Just to think that only a few days ago, subjective, we were there, on Jiog . . ."

Just to think that Jiog probably doesn't exist any more.

"Harris doesn't have the effect on me that he does on everybody else," I said. "We served together for a long time. I don't see him in the same way."

Zero grinned from ear to ear. "I'm glad I don't think like that."

"What do you mean?"

"All this; it still excites me. I'd hate to lose that."

"You almost did," I said. "If Kwan had finished using the redactor on you . . ."

Zero sipped at her coffee. "Yeah, but he didn't. And I'm all good."

Was that really true? Zero's ginger hair was pulled back from her head in a tight ponytail, and I could see the flash-burns where the redactor's probes had made contact: where they had literally sought to suck knowledge out of her head. In normal circumstances, an event like that would warrant a full medical assessment, if not leave on one of Fortuna's veteran retreats . . .

Zero was quiet for a moment, and then a little longer.

"Is something up, Zero?" I asked her. "I'm sensing that you're here for a reason."

"No," she said. "I'm not."

"I think you are. C'mon, spit it out."

"Really, it . . . it's not serious," she said, at the same time rubbing the probe-burns on her temple.

I'd known Zero long enough that I could tell something was up. She wanted to talk about something.

"Go on," I said. "I'm listening."

"Well, it's just that—" she started.

Harris appeared at the rec room hatch, filling the chamber with his presence.

"You people should be resting," he interrupted. "Our ETA at Thane is only eight hours."

Zero immediately clammed up, drank down the remains of her coffee. "Yes, sir. I – I was just working on a new programme with Nadi."

"Well get rested. I'll need you frosty tomorrow."

"Got it," Zero said, bobbing her head. "Yes, sir."

"And less of the 'sir'. I'm not military any more."

Zero blushed. "Understood."

She went to back out of the room.

"You want to talk, Sergeant," I said, as she went "then you know where I am."

"Solid copy," she said.

Harris watched her go. "She's turned out well enough."

"She's a good officer," I said. "She wanted to be a simulant operator, you know, after we saved her from Mau Tanis. Do you remember that mission?"

"Of course."

"Liar," I said. "Mau Tanis was just another military operation for you. I doubt you can even remember who was on the Lazarus Legion back in those days."

"I can recollect, well enough."

"Way I remember things, you didn't even want me to go back into the colony and pick that girl up."

"I was concerned for your safety. The whole damned colony had just suffered a Krell bio-bombardment."

"Yeah, that's true. Still, Zero's only here because I found her."

"Things were different then. Easier."

"There was no glory on Mau Tanis, Harris."

Harris' eyes misted, just a little. Recalling a memory nearly two decades old; when the Lazarus Legion had been deployed on Mau Tanis, and Zoe Campbell – Zero – had been the sole survivor of the operation. Harris produced his ever-present silver flask and poured something that smelled alcoholic into his coffee. He did the same for me, without asking whether I wanted any.

"What happened to my apparent and very pressing need for sleep?" I asked.

"You can have one drink with an old man, surely," Harris said. He nodded his head reflectively. "Things were damned good back then. When we were Legion."

"Times change. But they can be good again."

"You have the Jackals," Harris muttered. "And you've got a good outfit there."

"Your team aren't so shabby either," I replied.

"They're okay," Harris said, with typical understatement. "How'd you muster them?"

Harris gave a sort of shrug. "I found them here and there. When you've been in the military for as long as I have, you make connections. Maberry was a Navy Corpsman; did two tours in the Van Diem Straits. She's a real Devil Doc, that one."

"She has a certain manner about her," I said.

There was an opportunity, here, to tell Harris about Feng. I couldn't explain it to myself, but I didn't take it. I let the moment pass. Maberry clearly hadn't told Harris about Feng, either. She knew that he was my problem.

"Don't let that fool you," Harris continued. "Things get hot, Maberry's calm under pressure. Captain Tomas Lestrade was a combat pilot, retired out of Navy service. I found him working for the Euro-Confed merchant navy. The life didn't suit him. Whatever he tells you, he'd rather be running combat ops than living the quiet life."

"And Nadi? What's her story?"

"She's a war-orphan. Same as Zero. Except, instead of the Krell, it was the Spiral who killed her family. She was jumping ships out of the Arcturus Loop, offering her services as a code-hacker. Doesn't have any family left; if we hadn't stepped in when we did, I think she would've ended up in the cubes."

"Unless we stop this war," I said, growing maudlin for a moment, "I guess that there will be a lot more like her and Zero."

"We can change that," Harris promised. "But I've been meaning to ask you: do I still have the record?"

"The record" had been Harris' for a long time. He'd held the top spot in Simulant Operations – been the operator with most transitions to his name – for years after he'd left the Programme, after he'd been declared dead.

"Sorry, Harris," I said. "Captain Ving, out of Unity Base, has the title now. He's a proper, bona fide, grade-A asshole."

Harris ignored my assessment of Ving's character, and focused on what he actually cared about. "How many?"

Given the Watch's apparently infinite resources, I suspected that Harris already knew this information. It was more than public knowledge: Ving was the face of Sim Ops, a rising star in the Programme.

But I answered anyway. "Nearly three hundred," I said, "although not all of those were in hot zones."

That seemed to warm Harris' heart. "Then they don't count. Everyone knows that."

"Sure," I said. "Everyone knows that." I finished my drink. "And talking of hot zones, when am I going to get a briefing on the next operation? My Jackals are hungry to get moving on this."

Harris smirked. "They want new skins, right? I remember that feeling."

A hand dropped to one of my data-ports, and I felt that caustic tang at the back of my throat. Yeah, I was feeling the withdrawal. I needed a new body as much as any of my squad.

Harris slid a data-slate across the table. "Here's everything that you need to know. Consider this to be your briefing." He activated the slate, which threw up a clean-lined tri-D schematic of a space station. He'd already flagged key locations – the Command Suite, Simulant Storage Depot, Birthing Chambers . . . "So far as we're aware, these records are up-to-date and reliable."

"We're expecting resistance, I take it?"

"Of course," said Harris. "It's a simulant farm: we can expect simulants. *Lots* of simulants."

"Then what's our current equipment stockpile?"

"Limited," Harris admitted. "What you brought aboard, plus some sidearms. Nadi and Feng have reprogrammed the Ikarus suits. We've got munitions, so the PDWs and pistols you brought aboard can be repurposed."

"So we're going aboard an Alliance farm dressed as Directorate?"

"Basically."

"This doesn't sound like much of a plan, Harris. There are only half a dozen combat-capable personnel on this ship: the Jackals, Pariah." I paused. "You. How the fuck are we going to take on a single squad of sims, let alone lots of them?"

The words sounded all kinds of wrong in my head, and even worse spoken out loud. *I* was Alliance. *I* was Sim Ops.

"We can do this. Your fish will be instrumental."

"Of course," I said. "P is a Jackal."

"'P'?" Harris asked. "You even have a nickname for it now?"

"All right then, *Pariah* will help. It has a vested interest in settling this war. But I need details, Harris. How are we even going to get aboard the outpost?"

He smiled. "All taken care of, Jenkins, but our approach method is going to be somewhat novel . . ."

CHAPTER FOURTEEN

ASSAULT ON DARKWATER

Thane's star system was officially known as TX-1267, but it wasn't publicly recognised as having been explored. TX-1267 was a pale main sequence star, supporting seven lifeless worlds. None of the planets were capable of settlement without some serious investment, and the system's remote location meant than neither the Alliance, the Directorate nor any other space-capable human faction had therefore paid it much attention.

Thane itself was a gas giant that put out an unhealthy amount of background radiation, with an orbiting ring of asteroidal debris. The planet's atmosphere was mainly composed of hydrogen, helium and methane, and to the naked eye it was an ochre smudge that made me feel vaguely nauseous. Thane wasn't anyone's idea of home, that was for sure, but those same features made it the perfect location for a covert science facility. Within the planet's ring, hidden from view unless you knew exactly where to look for it, was Darkwater Farm.

Becoming increasingly drunk, the previous night I had

studied everything there was to know about Darkwater and Thane. Harris' briefing had been very specific, and he had meticulously planned the assault. In turn, I'd briefed the Jackals, and as a result everyone knew their role in this operation.

"You're right about one thing," I muttered, into the communicator: "this certainly is a novel deployment method."

I was currently clinging to the side of a small asteroid, a lump of rock that wasn't much bigger than me. I used the hand-grips of the Ikarus suit to steady myself, and held on for dear life, poised ready for the next manoeuvre.

"I do not like this very much . . ." rumbled Novak.

"Getting a little queasy, hey, Big Man?" Lopez asked.

"More than little," Novak answered.

Doing this in our own skin? It turned out that it wasn't much fun.

"That planet," said Novak, referring to Thane, "reminds me of home. Air is same colour." His words were peppered with gasps and wet swallowing sounds, as though he was trying to stop himself from vomiting. "Same as Norilsk."

"Your home has yellow air?" Lopez asked.

"On good day, yes. Is like bad place."

"Is definitely like bad place," Feng laughed. "Remind me never to visit you, Novak."

"I never offered," Novak replied.

The HUD on my Ikarus suit was alight with motion, as I tracked asteroids in the debris field. Usually, those asteroids would be barely visible against the silky dark of outer space, but the HUD gave me an augmented-reality view. The Jackals, along with Harris, were using the asteroids as launch-points to approach the objective. Except for Pariah, we were all using commandeered Ikarus flight-suits, Harris wearing the armour that Zero had used to escape Jiog.

"We approach," Pariah intoned.

P was now wearing its self-made bio-suit, and it was the only member of the team that I couldn't visually track. That was all part of the plan. In full fish armour, P would be almost invisible to the farm's scopes and scanners. A single life-sign could easily be missed.

"I have visual on the target," Zero said over the comms-network. "Flagging on your HUD."

Zero, Nadi and Elena were on the *Paladin*, watching the mission unfold through the squad's vid-feeds, at a safe distance.

"Solid copy," I said.

The objective was a much larger asteroid, located deeper in the band of rocks. There, the debris was more closely packed.

I see you . . .

Darkwater Farm clung to the underside of that rock. It was an ugly black hulk of a thing: a space station composed of a dozen or so modules, arranged in a cross-shape, cruci-fix-like. Each of the station's four arms was tipped with a docking bay, labelled Alpha, Beta, Gamma and Delta. A jagged range of sensor masters, radar dishes and weapons placements were scattered across its armoured hull, with the latter tracking targets through the debris field. The whole station was tethered to the asteroid by a series of cables that – on closer inspection – were thicker than my waist.

"The cables and gravity-drive keep the facility in a stable orbit," Harris had explained.

Beneath me, Thane's surface roiled and boiled. Various coloured bands polluted the otherwise mustard surface. I could almost feel the atmo attacking the outer coating of my Ikarus suit, although I knew that was pure paranoia. We'd have to be in a whole world of shit – quite literally – to feel that. The station would have to be knocked out of its orbit, for a start.

"Why bother with the tethers?" Lopez asked the squad at large.

"Plausible deniability," Harris muttered. "If this place goes tits up, Sci-Div can blow them remotely. Darkwater would fall into Thane's atmosphere within minutes. There wouldn't be anything left for the enemy, whoever that might be, to salvage."

"How are those new control systems working out for y'all?" Nadi asked, her voice cheery-bright, without any edge of military discipline at all.

"Great," I replied. "I can actually read controls that are in Standard."

"Now," Lopez said, her voice popping with static, "if I could just get the heating controls to work properly . . ."

Nadi laughed. "You Proximans all same! Want it hot and comfy . . ."

"Easy for you to say," Feng muttered. "You're the one on the nice warm starship."

The *Paladin Rouge* currently sat beyond the range of Darkwater's scanners. We'd been deep-inserted into the theatre; Harris and Nadi had assured us that a half-dozen small targets, approaching through the asteroid field, would be capable of evading the base's point defence systems. So far, that theory had proved to be true.

"Cut the chatter," Harris said. "Are we ready to—"

"Hold!" Zero interrupted. "Check Beta Dock."

The station turned gently in front of me. The farm was used to accepting traffic, and each of its four docks could hold a dozen starships. Most of them were empty, which was what we had expected. One, however, was not.

"Shit," Lopez said, "there's a ship docked down there."

"Scanning now," I said, focusing my suit's scopes on the vessel.

"It's an Alliance ship," Feng said, doing the same. "A Simulant Operations ship, Intruder-class."

Long, sleek, with a pointed prow that spoke of violence, the Intruder was a far cry from the *Paladin*'s squat outline. Weapons pods studded her outer aspect, nestled beneath the sleek nacelles, but the ship wasn't really made for direct combat. The Intruder-class was a proper Sim Ops ship; made for penetrating enemy lines and dropping sims directly into the fray, rather than slugging it out with her own armaments. A ripple of nostalgia crept through me as I panned my scanner back and forth across the ship. Her hull plating was crisp, almost new, and although her null-shield emitters were deactivated, the ship sat in a docking claw ready to launch.

"Strike deployment configuration," I whispered to myself.

"She's a very nice ship," I heard Captain Lestrade saying, on the *Paladin*'s bridge. "That's a drop-deployment bay in her belly."

Instead of a dedicated missile bay, Intruders carried drop-deployment tubes. Those were part of her mission role, and meant that armoured simulants could be fired directly from the ship into combat.

"Can you get any identification off the hull?" Zero asked me, obviously frustrated that she wasn't out here with the rest of us.

"Affirmative," I said. My enthusiasm was tapering off. "I have a name and serial code."

"And?" Lopez asked. She couldn't get a clear view of the ship, not from her location in the asteroid field.

"It's someone we know," I said. "UAS *Firebird*. Transmitting identifiers to you now, Zero."

Zero reacted immediately. What with her near-photographic memory, I knew that she would recognise the name.

"What are Phoenix Squad doing out here?" she exclaimed.

"Phoenix Squad?" Harris asked. "Who the damn are they?"

"That's Captain Ving's squad," I said. "I told you about him, last night. He has the current Sim Ops record."

Ving was a bully and a bastard. I didn't like him, and I liked it even less that he would show up out here. It didn't feel right at all.

"The Jackals and Phoenix Squad have a bit of history together," Lopez added. "And with Captain Ving in particular."

"He seemed to have a problem with me," Feng said, apologetically. "Being ex-Directorate and all."

"Then today will be a chance to settle the tab," Harris replied. "Their presence doesn't change anything. We still have a job to do. Mission is a go. Follow approach path to objective."

I swallowed. Licked my lips. The Ikarus suit's mobility options came online: the thruster-pack attached to my back, currently at full charge, and the grapnel system built into the forearms of the suit. While it wasn't a patch on a proper sim-class combat-suit, I'd grown to quite like the Ikarus. It carried some impressive kit and was well suited to a mission like this.

"Jackals deploy," I said. "On me. Keep thruster activity to a minimum. Full stealth."

"Copy that," Feng replied.

Brief flashes of blue light marked the Jackals' mobilisation. I fired my grapnel. The specially adapted harpoon gripped another rock, a couple of hundred metres to my left flank. The pulley mechanism whined softly as I was dragged across space, into the cover of the next piece of debris.

The farm's null-shield flickered ahead.

"On Proxima," Lopez said, her voice strained, "we have energy fields just like these on our hab-modules."

"So?" Novak asked, grunting with exertion.

"The electric field activates, and attracts insects and other bugs," Lopez said.

"And what happens?"

"It burns the bugs alive."

"Oh," said Novak.

I clutched for another rock, rode it. I was that bug, passing through the anti-insect field. The sensation was far from pleasant, but it was brief, and it wasn't dangerous. Although warnings flooded my HUD, they were gone before the energy field did any lasting damage to me or my suit. The null-shield was an anti-ballistic protective measure, mainly used to disperse laser and plasma fire. It didn't deal well with small targets, and that included the smaller pieces of debris found all over Thane's asteroid belt.

I fired my thruster. Grabbed for yet another rock.

My heart beat sporadically, and I couldn't help but check that the farm's defensive systems had not activated. Incredibly, although they twitched and tracked the asteroids, the defence network didn't fire. Our plan – or more accurately *Harris'* plan – was simple. Ride a rock through the station's null-shield. Get aboard, disable defences. Then dock the *Paladin*, and fill up on sims and tanks and whatever other equipment we could plunder . . .

In truth, Darkwater's greatest defence wasn't its weapons grid, but its hidden location. Out here, in unexplored space, unless you knew where to look for it, the prospects of finding the base were virtually non-existent. That Harris had been privy to that sort of intel put him in a different category to most enemies of the Alliance.

"I'm in position!" Feng shouted. His outline was beneath me, somehow, and I saw that he was crouched on Darkwater's hull.

I tumble-jumped towards him. With an outstretched arm, I snagged the hull, and the magnetic strips in the palm of my glove activated: held me there. I used the mag-locks in my boots too, then managed to stand up. The shift in perspective was almost overwhelming, in my own body, and I fought to keep last night's liquor in my stomach.

Lopez and Novak called in. They were scattered across the hull, but all in one piece.

"Everyone's down," I said. "Jackals are on the deck."

"I'm down too," Harris said. He sounded irritated.

I saw him on my left flank, plodding along the hull to reach me.

"You going to be able to catch up with us, Lazarus?" I asked.

He huffed over the comms. "Of course I can."

"Take care out there, Conrad," Elena suddenly said.

"I'm fine," Harris retorted. "What's our closest entry point?"

"I'm sending you the location of the nearest airlock," Nadi said. "It's fifty metres out; see?"

". . . *withdraw immediately. This is an automated announcement. You are entering restricted aerospace, and your presence is in violation of Military Code 23-98. On threat of lethal force, you are hereby directed to withdraw immediately . . .*"

I winced as the emergency broadcast intruded onto the comm-net. It was loud and insistent, and the machine-emulated voice actually sounded panicked, if that were possible.

"Cover's blown," Zero said. "The station's defences are waking up."

Sure enough, the various weapon systems on the farm's hull came online.

"Doesn't matter," Harris said. "They won't fire now. We're within the friendly fire parameters."

Whoever was on the farm now knew that we were here, but there wasn't a damned thing that they could do about it. I could only imagine Science Division's desperation, as they picked us up on bio-scanners and whatever other sensory tech the station had: knowing that we were coming, that we were now inside their safe perimeter.

"Can someone shut off that announcement?" Harris said. "All that lethal force shit is pissing me off."

"On it," Nadi said.

"And you're sure that the staff won't be able to purge the farm?"

"Sure enough," said Nadi.

This operation was pushing Nadi to the limits of her abilities. While we conducted the boots-on-the-ground assault, Nadi and Zero were attacking the station's soft security systems.

"Pariah, are you in position?" I asked. "What's your status?"

There was a slight pause before the xeno's reply – just enough for me to suspect that P might've been wasted somewhere out there in the asteroid belt – but eventually I got my answer.

"We are ready," it said.

The alien was further down the farm's hull, too far out for me to see where it had landed.

"You remember what you're supposed to do?"

"We remember."

"Then radio silence from here. Good luck. Jenkins out."

The comm-line fuzzed with static, and I could only hope

and pray to Gaia and anything else that would listen that the fish would actually do what it was supposed to . . .

Lopez was positioned over a service hatch in the hull.

"I have our entry point," she said, although she didn't sound impressed. She pulled a face behind her visor. "It's a waste-disposal tube."

I sighed. "Only you could be bothered by that in a situation like this, Lopez."

"Just get the hatch open," Harris ordered.

"Do not fire until we have no other choice," I said. "And that includes you, Novak. The personnel in there are Alliance citizens. Our war isn't with them."

The Russian grunted over the comms. "Affirmative."

The Jackals and Harris assembled around the hatch, and Lopez fixed a low-yield demolition-charge to the outer lock.

"Do you remember the last time that we assaulted a space station?" Feng asked.

"It was Daktar Outpost," Lopez said.

"Feels like long time ago," Novak added.

I grimaced. I knew that Feng didn't mean anything by it, but Daktar Outpost had been an outright disaster.

"This is going to be different," I countered. "Safe positions, people."

"Setting charge." Lopez bounced a clear distance. "All clear."

The demo-charge activator winked at me, then there was a rumble through the farm's hull as the charge detonated. The hatch blew outwards. There was a brief rush of escaping atmosphere, and then we were in.

Up the trash chute, and into the station.

"Keep that hatch sealed until we've secured the theatre," I ordered, as we clambered out of the chute and into a corridor. "We've got gravity, and we've got atmo. Let's try to keep it that way."

Novak knelt over the hatch, spraying it with sealant. The foam hardened immediately. The read-out on my HUD indicated that any lost atmosphere was being replenished by the farm's life-support systems.

"Hatch sealed," he declared.

"Corridor is secure," Feng said.

"That was easier than I thought it was going to be," said Lopez.

"Don't speak too soon," I replied.

The corridor was industrial and bathed in an amber glow from the emergency lamps in the ceiling. A siren wailed in the distance.

"Move on the Command Suite," Harris said.

A map of the facility appeared on my HUD. So far, Harris' clandestine intelligence looked pretty damned accurate. Signage on the station's walls pointed out COMMAND SUITE, SIMULANT DEVELOPMENT, STORAGE BAY, DOCKING BAYS ALPHA – BETA . . .

"Take down the security eyes as we move," Harris ordered.

"On it," Lopez answered.

She popped pistol-fire into the security cameras studding the deckhead of the next junction, sending out a rain of sparks—

"Stop right there, you Directorate bastards!"

The amplified voice cut right through me. The owner sounded very, very angry. That, I decided, was only going to get worse.

Harris used the corner of the corridor as cover. Fired off a warning volley.

"I said not to shoot until necessary!" I yelled.

"It's necessary, okay?" answered Harris. "Plus, I'm guessing that the security team is going to be simulants! Grenade out!"

Harris primed a grenade, bounced it down the corridor.

"Incoming!" shouted another trooper.

"Christo damn it!" I exclaimed. "This is an Alliance facility, Harris."

It was a stun grenade, and it detonated a second later. The security team reacted as one, their armoured suits clattering as they took up a defensive position.

"We've got multiple signals converging on our location," Feng said, his face grim behind his visor. "Looks like a full squad."

Phoenix Squad. Had to be that they were on-station, and acting as security. Had Captain Ving been demoted? That would've been a sweet explanation, but I somehow doubted it. More likely, he was just here through coincidence. If the Spiral had been taking out space stations and closing down access to Shard Gates, then it was entirely possible that Darkwater represented a significant Alliance asset, maybe requiring additional security.

"We'll take another route," I declared. "On me. Watch those corners!"

"Weapons-free, people," said Harris, despite my objections.

He laid down more gunfire with a Directorate carbine, and retreated back up the corridor. Bulkhead hatches were whining shut around us, systems already in turmoil. Another security team were converging on the next junction, planting portable energy shields in the corridor's deck to establish a cordon.

"All hostiles cease activity!" roared the station's AI. "You are contained within this level."

"Push on through!" I yelled. "Keep going!"

My nerves jangled. Another grenade went off behind us, Novak weathering a storm of frag. Feng tossed a smoke grenade, creating portable cover.

There was motion above me. I panned left, my suit identifying a possible target—

A sentry-gun dropped out of the ceiling. Twin-linked kinetic cannons swivelled in their mount, targeting lenses focused on me, painting me with their infrared optics. I brought my gun up to respond, yelled a warning that we should all *get the fuck down*—

The sentry-gun fired.

The deck vibrated as it absorbed the impact of armour-piercing rounds.

I bolted around the next junction, through a bank of smoke. I could make out the words COMMAND SUITE in glowing text ahead of me, as well as STATION IN LOCKDOWN: REPORT TO SAFE LOCATION.

"Surrender your weapons!" yelled a figure beneath that sign.

Bio-signals closed on our position, from every direction. Ten figures in total, advancing on us. A double-strength Sim Ops Army squad. Just to reinforce the point, another sentry-gun activated in the ceiling, mechanism whining softly as though to warn us that it could fire at any time.

"We're trapped," Lopez said.

Novak stroked one of his blades, taped across his chest. "Could always go down fighting, yes?"

Harris grunted in disapproval, his PDW aimed down at the floor. "Wait."

"Stand down!" came that angry voice again.

"Maybe this wasn't such a good idea after all . . ." Lopez muttered.

The security teams advanced behind glowing energy shields that were almost as tall as me, in a nice slow march. Shields clattered as they locked to the deck. Heavy shotguns were aimed through the gaps between the shields.

"This is an Alliance Simulant Operations facility, and you are trespassers. Drop your weapons."

I recognised that voice, and just hearing it made me angry.

"They're simulants, yes?" Novak grunted. "Like Lazarus says."

"Maybe we should ask," Lopez said. "I volunteer you, Novak."

The security detail closed tighter. They wore full combat-suits, emblazoned with Simulant Operations badges. The lead officer deactivated his shield, and it instantly disappeared. Only his head poked from the collar-ring of his suit, but he was most definitely a simulant.

"Mark 15 combat sim," I said, over the external speaker of my Ikarus suit. "Am I right? And you're Captain Ving."

He was close enough that I could see the picts stencilled on his armour; his callsign PHOENIXIAN proudly displayed across his chest, fire birds dancing up the outer sleeves of his arms. *How long does it take these guys to mark up their damned armour?* I wondered.

Now it was Ving's turn to freeze. He frowned at me. His head was shaven, face broad and pristine, suggesting that this sim was freshly hatched. Notwithstanding that, he looked like a veteran of the Programme; the way he carried himself, and the practised ease with which he'd herded the intruders – *us* – into a trap.

"What did you say?" he asked.

"I asked if those are Mark 15 combat sims. Your skins, I mean. And if you're Captain Ving, of Phoenix Squad."

"Who wants to know?" he said, squinting at me.

"I guess that I'm an easy face to forget," I said. "In Directorate battle-armour, at least."

"Jenkins?" he said, still paralysed by disbelief. "Keira fucking Jenkins, of the Jackals?"

"That'd be right. Although Keira Jenkins works just fine."

Someone else on Phoenix Squad chortled, but Ving shot him a look that silenced the noise.

"You've been gone a long time," Ving said.

"You don't seem pleased to see me."

"Why the fuck should I be pleased to see *you*?" he asked. "You were a damned mess when you were Captain Heinrich's platoon. We all thought you'd got yourself wasted in the Maelstrom. Bought the farm during the exodus, or something."

That provoked more laughter from Phoenix Squad, and Ving didn't bother to stop it this time. His words provoked quite the opposite reaction from the Jackals, who visibly tensed. Out of the corner of my eye, I saw Novak's hands on his knives. I prayed that he wasn't going to do anything stupid; that he was just going to let me handle this . . .

"I see you've got your Directorate friend with you, too," Ving said. He looked at Feng. "And now it all makes sense. You're fucking traitors, right? All of you."

"It's not what it looks like," I said.

"What did you do to get security detail, Ving?" Feng argued. "You must've pissed off the brass mighty to get a shit job like this. The real war is about ten light-years that way." Feng indicated with a thumb behind him.

Now Lopez laughed.

That seemed to offend Ving's suffocating sense of bravado. "I'll ask the questions here. As of now, you are prisoners of the Alliance."

"Sure," I said. My throat was dry, the grip on my AUG-30 tight.

"Drop your guns."

"That wasn't much of a question, Ving," I said.

I wasn't dropping my gun for anyone, but there were only five of us. If it came to it, this would only end one way.

"Where's the damned fish?" Lopez muttered, suit-to-suit.

"Do we rush them?" Feng offered.

"Just stay calm. No one do anything until I say."

Ving unholstered a pistol from his belt. Took a step forward.

"This corridor is sealed. The room behind you is in lock-down. The sentry-gun overhead is armed. What are you doing here?"

"Ah, it's kind of complicated," I said.

"Leave this to me," Harris insisted.

"Stay where you are!" Ving ordered again.

"It's okay," Harris said. He reached up, popped his helmet. "I think you'll know me."

With that, Harris revealed his face.

Ving might be an asshole, but he knew his Sim Ops stuff. He was old enough to recognise Harris. To recognise *Lazarus*.

"He's supposed to be dead . . ." muttered one of Ving's troopers.

"Lazarus is gone . . ." said another

"It's . . . this is a damned trick," Ving said. I wondered if that sounded as dumb in Ving's head as it did spoken aloud. "A Directorate trick!"

I felt a jolt of something run through me. A psychic shockwave, if you will. A communication unfolded in my head.

We are here.

"It's in position," I said.

"Shut up!" Ving shouted at me, looking suddenly very confused. I guessed that his tiny brain couldn't process all of this at once. It was a lot to take in for a shaved ape like Ving. "You're dead. You're all dead!"

"No," said Harris. His hands were up now, palms open. That struck me as a ridiculously brave – or foolish – thing to do. Every shotgun in the corridor was trained on him. "It's you who's dead, my friend."

One of the troopers collapsed. The body crumpled, combat-suit losing rigidity like a puppet with its strings cut. The trooper's armour noisily clattered to the deck, shield failing with a fizzle.

"Hold position!" Ving yelled, over the wail of the security siren.

In turn, each of the simulants collapsed to the floor. Harris just stood there.

"This is a trick!" Ving shouted, his pistol up. "This is a damned—"

He fell before he had a chance to finish the sentence. The pistol dropped from his hands, gloved fingers immobile.

The corridor was suddenly quiet, still.

Two minutes earlier.

Darkwater Farm had kilometres of service tunnels. They were tight, dark, dank. Just how the fishes like it.

Must be a holiday for you, P, right?

Pariah had got onto the station easily enough – unlike Lopez, it had no fear of using waste hatches, and it welcomed the closed spaces. Once inside the facility, it used its heightened spatial abilities to navigate the insides of the station. The creature needed no maps or schematics to find its way to its target. Fish senses were keener than that.

P paused in one shaft. Smelled the air. There was a

wrongness aboard the station, and if P could feel it, then I could too. There was something beyond the walls, flowing through the air-currents . . . but despite its sharpened awareness, Pariah couldn't identify the wrongness, and so moved on. The objective was not far.

A chamber filled with humming machinery, with devices that sang with data and transmitted perpetually. The others had a name for this place. It was a *Simulant Operations Centre*, containing ten simulator-tanks – glowing bright blue, an operator lying in each. The tanks, the equipment used to operate the sims, was all technology of the other; not something which Pariah knew how to operate. But Pariah understood how to follow the data-waves and the info-streams, no matter what the language. That was Kindred knowing, and was intuition on a genetic level.

I saw this in my mind's eye. Felt it all through a compressed data-burst, as though I was experiencing it first-hand. As though I saw things through the alien's eyes.

How is this happening?

We are here, P said.

Pariah paused over a certain tank. The words printed there meant nothing to the alien, but I knew them. VING.

"*It's in position*," I said.

We act, Pariah told me.

P activated both bio-guns, and they folded out of the xeno's limbs. It fired into the nearest terminal, and one by one the simulator-tanks went dead. That was the noisiest machine – the device sending the most data. The neural-link to each sim was severed.

The SOC's emergency protocols kicked in, and the mainframe failure triggered an emergency extraction. Ving and Phoenix Squad's tanks soon began to purge, the operators emerging from their cocoons still wet with amniotic, shivering and shaking.

P stood there, both barb-guns trained on the room, covering ten operators at once.

"Others should not move," P said, "if others wish to continue existing."

On newborn legs, quaking with extraction-shakes, the operators looked on in stunned amazement. Phoenix Squad might be stupid, but they weren't suicidal. Not in their own skins, anyway.

Ving immediately surrendered, and the rest of Phoenix Squad followed suit.

The connection – or whatever I had just experienced – between P and me broke.

I stumbled, unsteady on my feet. My legs had turned to rubber and I felt as though *I* was one of those damned operators, and *my* neural-link to a sim had been cut . . .

"You okay, ma'am?" Feng said.

I shook my head. "I'm fine. Dazed, is all. Pariah has the operators down on C-deck."

Harris nodded. "You need to have a word with that fish. It cut that way, way too close."

"Sure," I said. "It . . . it got delayed."

Lopez raised an eyebrow at me, as though to ask *You know this how?* but said nothing.

"Those operators won't stay in one place for long," Harris said. "They need to be secured."

"P has them covered," I said. "For now, at least."

Nadi broke in on the comms. "You need to get into the Command Suite. I'm reading a breach in my firewall."

Harris was already on the door. "Can you remotely open the hatch?"

"Let's see what I can do," Nadi said.

"They're sending a communication off-base," Zero explained.

"That's all we need . . ." said Lopez.

"On me," Harris ordered.

CHAPTER FIFTEEN

A NEW SKIN

"... repeat, they are on-station! We have multiple hostiles inside the facility!"

With weapons up, the Jackals deployed into the Command Suite. This was Darkwater's operations centre, with several consoles, monitors and staff stations. A view-port set in the far bulkhead gave a sweeping view of the asteroid field.

"Stand down!" I shouted, as we stormed the room.

There were a dozen or so technicians manning the suite. Dressed in white overalls and Sci-Div smocks, the geeks mostly surrendered immediately – with hands up, wide-eyed expressions of fear on their faces. One made a bolt for the door, and Novak caught him with an open palm to the chest, the impact almost flooring him. The tech quickly submitted, and went to his knees with the rest.

But not everyone was so eager to give it up. One tech was bent over the comms console, talking as she operated the relay. The woman saw us, knew that we meant business, but kept going anyway. She repeated the same request, or some variation on it, as the other techs surrendered.

"We need immediate assistance!" she said. "They are on-station! Immediate assistance requested from all available assets—"

Feng trained his pistol on the woman.

"Away from the console, ma'am," he said. "We're in control of the farm now."

Lopez pushed the woman aside, but with admirable tenacity she scrambled back to the machine.

"Immediate!" the woman continued, yelling into the communicator. "I said *immediate*!"

The tech was young, her skin bronzed, and with long dark hair. She was fairly nondescript; certainly no hero type. But as Lopez dragged her away from the console, she saw Harris, and something snapped behind her eyes.

"She's armed!" I yelled, my AUG-30 panning up.

The tech was whip-quick. Pistol out. Firing.

A single shot. Aimed at Harris.

He grunted, flinched, as the round hit his shoulder.

The tech snarled, went to fire again—

But never got the chance. Feng put her down with a sharp bark from his own weapon. The woman collapsed over the terminal, torso pouring blood.

There was a half-second of indecision from the Jackals.

"Harris!" I shouted. "Are you okay?"

"Jesus," said Harris, morosely, "that's going to sting."

He was still standing, and cycled his shoulder, groaning. The shot hadn't breached the Ikarus suit, but had dented the left shoulder guard pretty badly.

"Saved by Directorate armour," said Harris. "I'll never live it down."

Lopez swallowed, looking at the dead technician. "You killed her, Feng."

"I – I didn't have a choice," Feng said.

"Is okay," Novak muttered. "Killing Alliance is what he was made for."

"She shot Lazarus!" Feng insisted.

"Keep these people covered," I said, nodding at the other techs. They looked terrified by what had just happened. "That was . . . unfortunate, Feng."

"I didn't have a choice," Feng said again.

"I know. But like I said: these are Alliance citizens."

"Thanks for the save, kid. You did good," Harris said, but kept rubbing his shoulder. "This damned armour doesn't have a medi-suite. I'm going to find some analgesics, but I'll live."

Lopez nodded at the dead woman. "She didn't like you much, sir. Did you know her?"

"Don't recognise her," Harris said.

The other technicians remained frozen, although someone whimpered.

"No more heroes," I said, to the room in general, "and no one else will get hurt. Do we understand each other?"

"Y-yes," stammered an older man who looked like he might've pissed himself.

"She was new," said another woman, whose hands were locked behind her head. "Mori, I mean."

"That didn't need to happen," I said. "And if you all do as we tell you, it won't happen again."

Novak prowled the edge of the group, leering behind his open visor. I couldn't tell whether he was doing it deliberately or not, but his aura of intimidation was stirring the group into a frightened compliance. The Russian stroked one of his sheathed knives, taped horizontally across his chest, and the man who looked like he had pissed himself did actually piss himself.

"How many of you are there on Darkwater Farm?" I queried.

"Thirty-two science-grade technicians," answered Piss-man. "We're . . . we're a skeleton crew. Most of the facility is automated."

"See, just like I said," Harris muttered.

Harris had predicted that the station would have a small standing staff. The farms were largely unmanned, monitored by an AI. It didn't take much to oversee simulant production. Mostly the simulants were grown in tubes, and after that it was only a matter of keeping them on ice before they were shipped out for distribution.

"How many simulant operators?" asked Novak. That was the real resistance.

The man swallowed, quivering hard. "Just Phoenix Squad. Ten troopers."

"Then we have them all in lockdown," Harris said. "I don't think that the other techs will put up much resistance."

Piss-man shook his head. "No. They won't. I'm station supervisor. My name is Dr Vernon. You can tell them I give permission to surrender."

"That's very helpful, Dr Vernon," I said.

"What's happening here?" asked the other female tech. "I mean, who are you people? You're wearing Directorate armour. But . . ." she looked at Harris, then over at Lopez, who had removed her helmet now, dark hair spilling from the collar of her suit. "He looks like Lazarus, and she . . . she looks like Gabriella Lopez."

"Looks like you've got a fan club, Lopez," Feng said, shaking his head in disapproval.

Lopez's eyes burnt, angry that she had been recognised. I guess, in her own way – being an heir to the Lopez throne – she was even more recognisable than Harris. He had faded into legend, into myth; become part of Alliance history. Senator Lopez's story was still current.

"Forget that you ever saw her," I said to the woman. "It doesn't matter who we are. You behave yourselves, you'll get out of this alive."

"S-sure," she said.

"Herd these people up, Lopez," I said. To Harris: "Did your admirer manage to get a signal off-station?"

Harris prodded the dead woman aside, and she slumped to the floor. The console was streaked with blood, monitor spattered with claret. Harris wiped it so that he could read the info-stream.

"Not sure," he said, frowning. "But standard operating procedure in case of a station takeover would be to send out a mayday."

"Help him, Feng."

Feng did as ordered, accessing the terminal. "She wasn't sending a mayday, ma'am."

"Then what was she sending?" Harris asked.

"I'm not sure. The stream is encrypted." Feng shrugged. "Maybe she panicked."

"It's not a very good distress signal if no one can unencrypt it," I said.

The dead woman, MORI printed on her lapel ID, lay still on the floor. Regret rippled through me. No doubt about it; we had properly crossed the line now. I shunted the emotion to one side. I couldn't think about this now.

Harris rubbed his chin thoughtfully, then spoke into his communicator. "Nadi, Zero: I want you to run a decryption package on that signal. I want to know its intended destination as soon as you can get it."

"Sure thing, boss," said Nadi, chirpy as ever. "But it might take a while."

"The nearest Alliance outpost is light-years out," Zero explained, speaking over the comms. "The farm has a tachyon-relay, but even allowing for faster-than-light communications, any response is likely to take days to reach the nearest Alliance outpost. If you factor in time-dilation, and then consider that Alliance space forces are badly stretched, I'd say we're looking at a much longer—"

"Okay, we hear you, Zero," I said, speaking over her. "You're saying that it's not an immediate threat, right?"

"Exactly," Zero agreed.

That took the heat off a little, and it was good enough for Harris. He gave the all-clear for the *Paladin* to dock with Darkwater, and began to rattle off orders to his team over the comms net.

"Lestrade, get down to the *Firebird*. Maybe we can cannibalise some of those parts, or commandeer the ship."

"Yes, sir," Captain Lestrade said.

"It's a combat ship. Should be right up your space lane."

Lestrade chuckled; the first time I had heard him laugh. "I see her. She is a lovely ship."

"Gustav, secure Docking Bay Alpha. Nadi, keep the station's AI in check . . ."

He continued to issue commands to the crew, ever the leader. They each responded crisply over the comms.

"Hey, ma'am," Feng said. "I've found something."

The Jackals assembled around Feng's terminal. He'd accessed a data-feed.

"What's it supposed to be?" Lopez asked.

"It's a security warning," I said. "From Rimward Traffic Control."

Feng nodded. "Exactly."

"So?" Lopez said.

Feng shook his head, dismayed that Lopez couldn't see the importance of the intel. I guess that she still had a lot to learn, no matter what we'd been through together.

"Rimward Traffic Control is responsible for policing the former border with the Asiatic Directorate," I said. "They're reporting a potential incursion into Alliance space."

"More specifically, it's from the Joseon-696 system," Feng completed. His face had taken on an ashen appearance, and I knew that it wasn't just as a result of what had happened in the control room. He looked sideways at me, pursing his lips. "The Directorate could be searching for us," he said.

"How many ships?"

"Report says a single quantum trail, so probably just one," Feng read. "But that's all Kwan needs."

"Can you identify the vessel?" I muttered.

"I can't," Feng replied.

"Is big galaxy," Novak said. "Could been anyone, yes?"

"Forward that intel to Zero," I said to Feng, a hand to his shoulder. "I want her to analyse possible flight and jump patterns. Anything we can use to outrun them."

"Solid copy," Feng said, still staring at the terminal screen. "You ever think there'll be a time when the Directorate are out of our lives?"

I gave a short laugh, and wished that I could give him some reassurance, but all I could think about was the metal in Feng's head.

After the Command Suite, the invasion was bloodless and over in all of ten minutes. Dr Vernon made an address over the station's PA system, and the remaining scientific staff surrendered soon thereafter. Most had gone into hiding. None had thought to arm themselves, and there were no further acts of resistance. Whoever Mori was, she was obviously made of sterner stuff than the rest of the crew. I almost felt sorry for her.

Hands locked behind heads, fastened with cable-ties from

the general supply, the sci-techs were a quivering, terrified bunch. Many still wore bio-hazard suits from working in the cloning vats. I prowled the ranked bodies, my weapon on hip, trying to look more in control of this than I felt.

"*Paladin* docking in five minutes," Harris said, over the station's PA.

"Have you swept the decks for any remaining crew?" I asked Feng.

He nodded. "Yes, ma'am. Everyone's accounted for."

"What are we going to do with them?" Lopez asked.

"We could kill them," Novak said. "We should probably kill them."

I scowled at Novak. "We're not doing that. None of them is to be hurt, understood? What happened in the Command Suite was a necessity. That girl was fighting back."

"Ving is hole in ass," Novak said, unapologetic. "Could do just him, yes?"

"Not even Ving," I said. "Whoever they are, Phoenix Squad are still Alliance personnel." Going AWOL was one thing; killing Alliance citizens – and in particular Sim Ops – was entirely something else. We weren't going down that path. "Round them up, get them into the evacuation-pods," I ordered.

Lopez paused, looked a lot like she might baulk at that, but then set to it. I could understand her reaction. Now that we were actually here, aboard Darkwater, I was beginning to feel the enormity of it all. Did I feel bad about loading the farm's crew into evac-pods? Yes, I did. I felt damned well terrible. But if we left the crew on-station, they could either follow us, or arrange for the dispatch of a response team. The girl who had activated the distress signal was proof of that. The station had to be neutralised, definitively, with as little loss of life as possible.

Darkwater's evacuation bay was a long corridor with a series of circular openings on each bulkhead that connected to its two dozen pods. The hatches were open and waiting for occupants.

Like prisoners of war, the techs were marched into the pods. Darkwater Farm had enough craft to evacuate everyone, although it would be cramped and far from comfortable. The pods were quickly filled up, but the prisoners didn't give us any trouble.

The atmosphere changed as Ving and Phoenix Squad appeared at the end of the corridor. They were all dressed in station-side fatigues now, but still wet from the tanks. Although Novak and Pariah kept them covered with their weapons, I could detect their animosity. I didn't blame them for that – had I been in their situation, I was sure I would've felt a good deal worse. But if there was a flashpoint, where this would turn nasty, it was now. These were hardened operators, not desk jockeys. Pariah's enormous shadow, both guns deployed, seemed to provide sufficient encouragement – or threat – to keep them in line for the time being, but I wanted this part of the operation done, and fast.

I took in Phoenix Squad; a team that had been Captain Heinrich's darlings. Even out of his sim and combat-suit, Ving was an imposing figure, competing with Novak in height. However, Ving and his squad were all too well muscled, primped and preened, to be mistaken for frontline troopers. Everything about him and his people was too perfect, too manufactured. Indeed, I'd heard rumours that Ving had even had muscle tissue sculpted and implanted, so that he was closer in appearance to his simulant. Which was, in itself, pretty weird, as it was based on a copy of him . . . Ving's hair was cut very short, with markings shaved into his scalp, and his brow was permanently lowered in a simian scowl. Now, he just looked plain confused, in complete shock as to what had happened.

"What *are* you?" Ving said, pausing to inspect Pariah.

"We are Pariah," the xeno said. "Move. We have orders not to terminate others. But that could change."

"This has to be some kind of trick," Ving said. He shook his head in dismay.

"You keep saying that," Feng said, "but it doesn't make it any truer."

"So the Directorate are working with the Christo-damned fishes now?" Ving suggested.

"It's more complicated than that," I said.

"I'm all ears, Jenkins."

"You wouldn't understand," I muttered back.

P prodded the line of operators with its bio-guns.

"What the fuck is that fish?" Ving questioned again. "Is it some kind of Directorate project? Because I've never heard of anything like it, and Phoenix Squad has been places."

Ving's squad murmured agreement.

"So Lazarus – Colonel Harris – is a turncoat as well, now?" someone yelled. I detected a hint of disappointment in that question. Harris had fought the Directorate, had been there during some of the key events that precipitated the Great Enemy's downfall. To think that he might be working with them was almost too much for these operators to bear . . .

Phoenix Squad might well be asses, but I was very nearly drawn into a discussion with them. I felt driven to explain myself, to tell these bastards exactly what we were doing out here. Yet I knew that to do that, I would be risking the whole operation.

"Like I said, it's complicated," I answered. That would have to be enough.

Ving shook angrily, his jaw dancing.

"This conversation is over," I said. "Do it, P."

"Into the craft that sails stars," Pariah ordered. The troopers shuffled aside to avoid being touched by the wet muzzles of the xeno's weapons.

"They're not used to a talking fish," Lopez muttered.

"A while ago, neither were we. Get them into the pods."

Ving turned to me. "You could just send us out on our ship, you know? The *Firebird* is still docked."

"I'm not stupid, Ving. I send you off on a ship, you'll be right back in our faces before we know it. The evac-pod is the best that I can offer." To Feng, I said: "Have you deactivated the transmitters?"

"It's done," he said. "The evac-pods have short-range emergency beacons, but I've removed the comms modules. They'll broadcast standard pick-up codes, but they won't be able to send any directed transmissions."

Ving just shook his head. "I always knew that you were a bitch, Jenkins. I never liked you."

"Feeling's mutual."

"Neither did Captain Heinrich."

"So he's still around, huh?"

"Of course he is. And General Draven, too. They'll come after you," Ving said, lowering his head as he clambered into the pod. "No one has ever hit a farm before. General Draven and Captain Heinrich won't leave this."

Heinrich and Draven: my two immediate superiors. Draven had, in the mists of time, served with my father when he was an active Army officer. Despite myself, I felt a pang of contrition deep inside. The emotion resonated through me. What would my folks think of me now, hijacking an Alliance station, going so far outside my orders that I was almost as bad as Riggs?

Stay focused, Jenk. This is the only way.

"You just sit tight and enjoy the flight," Lopez suggested, with a patronising grin. Trying to sound more confident than I knew she really felt.

"And we know who you are," Ving said, pausing at the hatch of the evac-pod, nodding at Lopez. "Your father, the Senator, is a great man. What in Gaia's name are you doing out here helping these people? He'd be disappointed in you, and he'll send people as well."

That hit a nerve with Lopez, too. She kept her weapon trained on the squad leader, but exchanged an uncomfortable glance with me. What Ving lacked in intelligence, he certainly made up for with unpleasantness.

"Just get in the pod, Ving. You'll be picked up in a few days, if you're lucky."

"Keep telling yourself that," Ving said, "and maybe you'll even believe it. This far from the Core, from occupied territory, we could be drifting for years."

"Then you better make those ration-packs last," Feng recommended. To me, he added, "That's the last of them. All crew and operators are loaded."

I nodded. "Seal them in."

"Solid copy."

On my command, the hatches to every pod simultaneously hummed shut. Green lights showed above each craft's hatch. Ready to go.

"Fire the pods."

"Affirmative," said Feng.

There was a series of thumps through the station's deck as the pods launched, and it was done.

"Visual confirmation of successful launch," Lopez said, glancing at the view-ports set into the corridor wall.

The pods initiated hard-thrust away from Darkwater, arcing out towards deep-space, where they would then begin to transmit emergency beacons in an attempt to attract passing ships. At least, that was the theory. They had food, water and heat in those things, but Ving was right. There was no telling how long it would be before they were rescued. Meanwhile, the baleful eye of Thane glared up at me, its sickly yellow surface crawling with storm-clouds.

There was another brief rumble through the deck.

"*Paladin Rouge* has successfully docked," came Harris' voice over the comms. "We're tracking those evac-pods. They've broken Thane's orbit."

"Affirmative," I muttered. "And yet I still don't feel any better about myself, Harris."

"I find that alcohol helps."

"I mean it. This . . . this is some heavy shit."

"*Necessary* shit."

I couldn't help shivering a little. "Stop trying to be glib. We've never done anything like this before."

"No regrets, Jenkins. We're doing what needs to be done. The *Paladin*'s crew is coming aboard, but I don't want to stay on-station any longer than we need to. Double-time it, trooper, and get that place searched." Harris was back to issuing orders like I was still under his command. "The *Paladin* is ready to receive when you are. Elena and I will secure simulator-tanks. Gustav will be ready for immediate dust-off, as soon as Captain Lestrade has checked out the *Firebird*."

That was everyone accounted for. Now that we had control of the farm, and all hostiles were taken care of, the *Paladin*'s personnel could move about as they wished. I suspected that, in truth, some of the crew wanted to stretch legs, to get a couple of hours off the ship.

"Understood. Jenkins out." I switched comms bands, to the Jackals-only squad channel. "Zero, do you copy?"

"I'm here," she answered.

"Have you managed to crack the message decryption package yet?"

Zero sighed, and I could tell that she was frustrated. "No, ma'am. It's not Alliance-standard."

"All right. Keep trying."

"It might help if I come aboard as well," Zero said. "I'd like to check out their comms array, see if I can lift anything directly from the mainframe."

"You do that."

"We've found something else."

"Go on."

"The farm has a dark sector. Nadi can't access part of the mainframe. One of the farm's central modules is completely sealed off."

"Do we need to explore it?"

I could hear Zero's shrug. "I'd like to, if I can."

"All right. Work on the mainframe access first, then you can think about cracking the dark sector. It's not a priority."

"Roger that. Nadi's staying on the *Paladin*. I'll upload whatever I find."

"We'll run a sweep on the base, and get loading. Jenkins out." I turned to the Jackals, now assembled in the empty corridor. "Lopez, run an inventory on the Supply Deck. Feng, you take the armoury. I want armour, weapons, grenades. Whatever we can get."

Feng grinned. "That, I can do."

"And me?" Novak asked. "You want I should search this 'dark place' Zero is talking about?"

"No," I said. It wasn't that I didn't trust Novak in an unexplored area of the base, but rather that I'd feel better knowing where he was. "Check out Simulant Processing. Secure anything useful down there."

244

The Russian grunted in approval.

Pariah chittered softly next to me. "We will go back to the craft that sails stars," the xeno said.

"Sure," I said. "Stay on the comms, people."

"Where will you be?" Feng asked.

I smiled. "I've got a personal appointment."

I descended the station's levels in the elevator, and the temperature dropped as I went. I tried, and failed, to control the throb of my pulse. The adrenaline of the firefight was wearing off, but it wasn't just that. My data-ports were positively on fire with expectation. It was excitement, pure and simple.

SIMULANT STORAGE BAY A appeared on the elevator control panel, and the doors hummed open. Although this was ordinarily a highly restricted area, Nadi had already broken all of the security protocols. I unbuttoned my helmet, clipped it to my belt. I wanted to experience this first-hand, with every one of my senses. The waft of fresh cryogen hit me full-on and I got the strongest headrush in the universe. No matter what their line of service, no matter where they came from, this place was Mecca to any sim operator.

Glow-globes illuminated in response to my presence as I entered the chamber, but it was so big that the perimeter was still shrouded in shadow. It was a warehouse of flesh: bank upon bank of cryogenic storage capsules, piled so high that they reached the ceiling. The capsules were glass-fronted so that the bodies could be seen inside, with electronic read-outs indicating user names.

This is what we came here for, and this makes it all good.

And it was true. Whatever we had done to the crew, being in here it all felt justified. It felt *right*. I needed to be reunited with my sims, as though their genetic code called out to me across space. Machine-valves and life-support modules hummed and wheezed around me, maintaining the skins in a state of readiness. Nothing down here gave off a bio-sign, because every body was kept in a specialised state of cryogenic suspension: the sims were not independently alive, after all.

I passed through the vault with near-reverence. Very few simulant operators, rogue or otherwise, got to see an operational farm, and I'd never seen so many skins in one place. The simulants were grown in gestation-tanks, to specification on Science Division's instructions. Every operator in the Sim Ops Programme was catalogued in the mainframe, and the farms then produced sims based on each operator's genetic code. Harris had explained to me that Darkwater was the main production facility for the entire Eastern Sector, which meant that it housed simulants for military teams working out of Unity Base.

Although the whole facility was kept on ice, the cold meant nothing to me. I made my way to the centre of the cathedral-like space – more lights flickering on as the station tracked my progress – and with shaking hands I activated one of the enormous robotic loaders. The words SQUAD DESIGNATION? appeared in glowing text on the viewscreen.

JENKINS' JACKALS, I typed.

ORDER CONFIRMED. SECURITY OVERRIDE ACTIVE.

With a whine of hydraulics, the service bot rearranged the cryogenic capsules. Each capsule contained an inert simulant, dressed identically in deep blue neoprene undersuits, stamped with the badge of the Sim Ops Programme.

Faces and bodies passed in front of me as the capsules cycled, as the machine searched for the Jackals' sims. The facility stored thousands of bodies, could be used to grow millions. I recognised some of those faces, knew of them from my assignment to Unity Base.

The machine finally stopped cycling. Hydraulics purred as a series of capsules settled in a row. Copies of the Jackals stared back.

I swallowed, shouldered my PDW. For some reason, I was suddenly very much aware that I was wearing Directorate armour. It felt wrong – disrespectful even – to be standing here, in the uniform of our enemy . . .

My hand rested on the outer casing of one of my sims. The body inside was unblemished. Then Lopez, much the same. Feng: this body without the brutal injuries caused by our incarceration on Jiog. Then Novak. No gang-tattoos, no prison markings. No nerve-studs in his forehead.

I paused at the last tank.

RIGGS, DANEB.

The traitor. The body inside looked completely at peace. Eyes shut. His muscular torso was relaxed. I'd laid my head there. I'd seen sweat gathering on his pecs after we'd done our thing. His hair was short, dancing softly to the current of the cryogenic fluid inside the capsule.

My communicator chimed, interrupting this private moment.

"Ma'am, you copy?" asked Novak.

"I'm here," I said. I almost felt annoyed with him for the intrusion, but there was a hint of urgency to his voice that wasn't normal. "What's your situation?"

Novak sucked his teeth. "Have found something. Is very—"

The signal suddenly swarmed with static, and I winced at the noise. I retuned the communicator band, searching for a stable frequency.

"Novak, do you copy?"

No answer. I tried for another connection.

"Zero, you read me?"

"I read," Zero said. She too sounded panicked. Of itself, that might not be unusual. But together with Novak's reaction, I was starting to become concerned. "Where are you?"

"I'm in Simulant Storage. I have the sims, and I'm using the robot loader to send them to the docking bay."

"Copy that. I've been trying to comm you, ma'am."

"My suit didn't register any incoming message," I said. "Maybe Nadi isn't as good as she thinks she is . . ."

Zero kept talking. "You need to get out of there. Now."

"All right, calm down. I'm almost done."

"*Now!*" Zero said. "Everyone needs to get off the farm. The message: it was—"

The comm-line went dead, and I thought about Zero's words. She had sounded pretty insistent. Instead of trying to reach her again, I decided to activate the robot loader for the simulants.

DOCKING BAY ALPHA, I selected on the terminal.

ALL SUBJECTS?

LOAD SELECTION: JENKINS, NOVAK, LOPEZ, FENG.

INITIATE.

The machine hummed as it shuttled capsules into the loader. They would be swiftly dispatched to the docking bay, where the *Paladin* waited. Our simulants loaded rapidly, green lights flashing as the bodies were launched through the network of tubes that connected storage to the docks.

I paused in front of Riggs' bodies.

"Fuck you, Riggs," I said. I opened the terminal's main menu.

INITIATE PURGE COMMAND.

His bodies would be gone for good. Deleted. Sure, he could grow some more, but that was hardly the point. This was as close to satisfaction, to revenge, as I was probably ever going to get.

"*Sayonara*, Riggs," I said, staring at the simulant in the tank. "I'd say that it was nice knowing you, but that would be a lie."

Riggs' eyes sprang open.

CHAPTER SIXTEEN

DANGER TIME

You know that feeling just before the shit hits the fan? When you know that something bad – *incredibly* bad – is going to happen, but you just can't accept it? I was there, in that place, suffering from a sudden and debilitating disconnect between brain and body. Because it was so improbable, one element couldn't process and act on what the other element was experiencing. Hell, more than that: what I was experiencing was fundamentally *impossible*. Various possibilities raced through my mind.

It's a reaction to the purge command.

I've accidentally activated something.

I'm imagining it, and the whole damned thing is in my head.

That last one seemed the most likely, because I had been hallucinating Riggs. I'd seen him on Jiog, even spoken to him.

Yes. That has to be it.

But Riggs – or his simulant, at least – yanked at the respirator plugging his lower face, and shivered off droplets of cryogen.

PURGE COMMAND CANCELLED, the read-out on the tank flashed.

The capsule lid engaged. The body inside stumbled out; all shiny and new. Light wisps of steam rose from the neoprene undersuit, in reaction to the change in temperature. The undersuit clung to Riggs' body, perfectly illustrating his simulated, sculpted physique.

Adonis-like.

Hair just right. Messy, but not really untidy.

His skin a perfect tan, an advert for descendants of Tau Ceti V.

His eyes. Deep, inviting, a little bit naive.

Incredible that I could still think that, after all he had put us through. He looked, for all intents, more like a kid playing soldier than a proper operator. Maybe that had been part of his appeal, I reasoned, or maybe it was just a practised front. It had certainly got me to trust him.

A single bio-sign flickered into existence on my HUD. Riggs was very much alive.

Finally, my body starting working. I fell back, reaching for my PDW. It didn't do me much good though; my legs collapsed beneath me, and I landed on my ass.

Riggs pulled at the cables connecting him to the capsule, and they came loose easily. He stared down at me, and his expression was surprised. I suspected that my face told just the same story.

But then he smiled. It was a perfect simulant grin, every tooth in his mouth a bright white. He held out a hand.

"What the hell are you doing here, Jenk?"

I shook my head. That would make it okay. That would make this all go away.

"You're not real," I said. "You're not fucking real!"

"I can see why you'd say that," Riggs muttered, "but I am real. I'm here."

And then realisation hit me. The pieces snapped into place. Riggs was using a simulant-tank to link to this new skin. A simulator wasn't easy technology to come by, but the Spiral had been raiding stations up and down the Drift. Given the sort of noise that Thane's star was throwing out, the real Riggs had to be somewhere nearby. The neural-link would degrade, would become useless, at anything other than close range. That meant Riggs – the Black Spiral – had a ship, and must be close. They had probably been using the asteroid field as cover; the *Paladin* wouldn't see them coming until it was too late. Zero's warning, Novak's last transmission: everything made sense. The Black Spiral had come to Darkwater.

I backed away from Riggs. My fingers found the bead in my ear, fumbled with the communicator. I had to warn the others.

"Zero!" I screamed. "The Spiral are here! Riggs is in Simulant Storage!"

Riggs watched with a look of near-amusement. "No, no," he said. "Don't do that."

Then he sprang at me.

I rolled left. The bead whined in my ear – *no comms!* – and I grappled with the Directorate PDW. I felt like I'd lost control of my own body.

Riggs slammed a foot down on the gun. Its plastic casing cracked, split. The weapon was useless. I hadn't even managed to get off a shot.

"Zero! Novak!" I screamed. My voice echoed through the empty storage depot, lost to the metal walls and hissing machinery.

"Just stop this," said Riggs. "Things don't have to be difficult."

He stood over me, face awkwardly neutral, his boyish features failing to portray any remorse, any guilt. *Maybe he's sorry*, a soft voice whispered in my ear. That was the weak me, the me who had listened to his carefully spun bullshit for the entire length of our deployment together. *Maybe he wants to come back into the fold . . .*

But *that* me didn't answer. Armoured Jenkins took care of it.

"You're a fucking asshole, Riggs," I spat, snarling. I spun back, a cornered cat. "And I'm going to kill you."

Riggs shook his head, smiling. Did he really think that I was that harmless?

"Don't be silly, Jenk. You're not going to do anything like that. I'm in a simulant, and you're not. Might is right."

I scrambled left, boots kicking at the floor as I tried to stand. The immediate flood of anger and hate threatened to overwhelm me, and I fought to keep it in check.

"Fuck you, Riggs."

Riggs pounded after me. Grabbed my leg, yanked hard.

I slammed an armoured boot into his shin. He barely noticed.

"Warlord once tried to turn you," he said. "Do you remember when he spoke to you on North Star Station, when we first picked up that stinking fish? I was disappointed when that didn't work."

I kicked out again. With both hands now, Riggs pulled me back.

"Get off me!" I screamed, struggling to get loose of his grip.

Riggs was stronger than me, by quite some margin.

"I thought that the Directorate would've finished you off on Jiog," he said, as he worked. "You're Lazarus Legion. You were on their most-wanted list. I thought that it would've been a nice, clean execution." He paused. "It's a shame."

"You sold me out. You sold *us* out!"

"The Jackals?" he asked, as he dragged me to my feet. He pulled me so close that our faces almost touched. "They're nothing, Jenk. A bunch of useless no-hopers, the worst of the worst. You know that, right?"

I thrashed my legs, pumping them hard, but Riggs got me airborne. Swung me across the aisle. I hit a bank of cryogenic capsules so hard that my teeth chattered, and I tasted blood at the back of my throat.

The capsule behind me broke, and something gaseous started venting from inside. Amber warning lamps flicker-flashed overhead, throwing Riggs into lighting from some bad horror-movie. An alarm began to sound in the distance, bouncing around the chamber.

All of that detail came to me in snippets, because the pain was all-consuming. I'd hit my back, and it felt an awful lot like something had broken in my ribcage. Could've been a new injury, could've been something not yet healed from Jiog: it didn't much matter. The Ikarus suit wasn't equipped with a medi-suite; but I rode it out, unwilling to give Riggs the satisfaction of seeing me hurt, and sprang back to my feet.

Riggs followed up with an overarm blow with his right fist.

At the last possible moment, I slipped free. Slid right. He hit the canopy of another capsule. From the yowl of pain he made as he connected, it sounded as though it was hard enough to hurt. More cryogen vented across the module, and glass fragments crunched noisily beneath my feet.

Revenge could wait, I decided. I had to get out of here.

I broke away from Riggs. He was bigger than me – faster in a sim – but size was my advantage.

"I'm supporting He Who Cares," Riggs yelled. "I'm trying to help us all."

I dodged another swipe, made off through the row of capsules. But I hadn't managed more than a half-dozen paces before my right leg gave out. The Ikarus suit's power attenuators – the hydraulic cabling in the leg that amplified speed, force – squealed in denial, and I barrelled left. Riggs bore down on me again.

"You're a maniac, Riggs."

"I hoped that you'd see this differently. Warlord said that you would."

"Warlord is even worse than you!" I shouted. Could someone hear me, trapped in here? Where were the rest of my squad? Into the communicator again: "Zero! Nadi!"

"Things are over between us," Riggs suddenly said. He dragged me upright. I continued flailing, balling fists and landing blows all across his chest and shoulders. He winced with each, but it was pointless. "I mean it. After everything that the Krell have done to us – to me, to you, to humanity – we're selling out to the damned fish heads! Why can't you see this?"

"I know about your father," I said. "I know why you turned."

"And you think, somehow, that gives you power over me? That's a low blow, Jenk."

"I never said that it gave me power. But I know how your mind works, and I know weakness when I see it."

"There is no weakness in the Black Spiral. There will only be a pure, dark dawn."

"So you gave in," I said, buying time. "You gave in to whatever lies Warlord and the Spiral are spinning. I know about Tau Ceti, about your family—"

"It wasn't like that!" Riggs implored. His words were at odds with his actions, as he dragged me in front of the next bank of sims. "Warlord knows what's best for all of us! He was once like you, like me. He's seen the One Truth!"

"He's been into the Deep, Riggs. That's all this is: the Krell's intelligence pool—"

"He's seen the other side!"

"You're spreading the virus," I said, because to keep talking gave me something to grasp: something to which I could anchor this nightmare. "The Black Spiral is starting a war between the Alliance and the Krell!"

Around me, copies of simulants stared back. So much power here, so much force, and yet I could use none of it. I kicked out, hit Riggs in the leg somewhere. He scowled this time. Lifted me off the floor again. Hands locked around my neck.

"It's not that simple," Riggs said. "We're finishing the Krell. They'll be gone: the Maelstrom will be empty. You really have no idea. It'll be so fucking glorious!"

A light ignited behind Riggs' simulated eyes. I'd seen that sort of expression – beatific, dogmatic, fanatical – on the faces of street-preachers and religios. This version of Riggs was so far from the one I'd known that I barely even recognised him. He had become radicalised, so indoctrinated that nothing I said could've changed his mind.

"He Who Cares is all that matters," Riggs shouted. "The Dominion will be born again!"

"This is madness!" I screamed. "You're insane!"

"I'm finishing this now. I'm tying loose ends. I should've never left you on Jiog, Jenk. I was weak. I'm going to make up for my mistake."

"Zero!" I yelled again.

My communicator dangled loose from my neck. With sim-fast reactions, Riggs grabbed the comm and tore it from my head. Tossed it away, put both hands back to my neck.

I gasped. Choked. Hands grappling at Riggs' shoulders;

gloved fingers digging into his neoprene suit. Feet off the floor now.

"I really did care for you," he said. "I want you to know that. What happened between us wasn't right. It didn't go down how I wanted it to, and I'm sorry."

I heaved. Choked some more. Felt my kicks connect with Riggs' body somewhere. Slammed a foot into his groin: watched the pleasing look that spread across his features. He relaxed his grip just fractionally – enough for me to take a gasp of cold, cryogen-laced air, but not enough to get free—

"Shhhh," Riggs said, his voice just a whisper, carrying the intimacy of lovers. "Shhhh. Quiet now. Quiet."

Riggs slammed my head into the canopy again and again and again. The malice on his features was so alien that he almost looked demonic, possessed. He was murdering me; and quite successfully at that.

"It's okay," he said. Some reassurance, huh? "It's going to be okay. You always did have a death wish, Jenk. This is fine. It's what you always wanted. This is a good day to die. Once you're gone, there'll be nothing left to stop us."

I lashed out senselessly, without purpose. This was survival, pure and simple.

"Fu – ck," I managed, "yo – u—"

"You've said that already," Riggs said. "You could've joined us. It didn't have to be like this."

"Tr – ai – tor," I said, my larynx collapsing.

Everything started to feel numb. Not like cold numb, but dissociated numb. There was pain, but it was distant. As though this wasn't really happening to me. My heart rumbled, throbbed. My data-ports cried out for the simulants around me; each inert and useless and beyond the reach of my dying fingers.

Riggs looked back at me with those naive (filled with secrets: dark secrets) *eyes. His body glistening with sweat* (cryogen) *from another session in bed.*

"*You're beautiful,*" he said. "*You do know that, right?*"

"*You know that was the last time,*" I said, firmly.

"*You said that last time . . .*"

"*Well this time I mean it, kemo sabe.*"

Riggs nodded, but that idiot grin (filled with malice) *remained plastered across his* (twisted) *face.* "*See you down there, Jenkins,*" *he said.*

I was fading, fading, fading . . .

I stood on the very brink of an abyss.

My Jackals were with me, but not just them. General Draven, Captain Heinrich, the crew of the *Paladin*. My mom and dad: disapproving faces glaring back at me from the edge of the crowd. Would they ever actually forgive me for joining the Simulant Operations Programme? Probably not. But what I'd done on Darkwater overshadowed that decision by a long way. There were others there too. Captain Carmine – dear old Carmine, now dead, her remains consigned to Jiog, lost to Directorate space. Even Senator Lopez, dressed in a dark jacket and slacks that screamed that he was a serious politician, but he could still be trusted.

"Fuck," I said. "So this is how it ends, huh?"

"Maybe," said another voice. Not just one, I realised, but all of those gathered.

"I always thought that it would be less colourful."

The abyss was filled with light. Swirling, incandescent streamers, like distant star-nebulae but moving. It was kind of beautiful, and the glow filled me.

"This is the Maelstrom," said the voices.

I was looking into Krell space, and it was looking back at me.

"It's changing, right?" I asked, frowning. Which was quite difficult, as I realised that I had no actual body. I was just a thought, a reflection. "What's happening?"

"Exodus," said the voices. "We are leaving."

The lights were disappearing. Only blackness remained. A great, gnawing darkness appeared beneath me.

"There will be nothing," answered the collective chorus. Many voices at once, but no longer speaking in unity. Instead, they formed a discordant chorus that hurt to listen to. "There will be nothing to stop them."

"To stop whom?" I cried out.

"Don't let this happen," said the voices, now crumbling, speaking out of rhythm. "Stop the Great Dark. Stop the Dominion."

And then I was teetering on the edge of it. The Great Dark: the abyss itself.

There was nothing left any more.

For an eternity, I wasn't sure whether I'd fallen into the abyss, or simply become it.

Fade, fade, fading . . .

. . . back, back, back!

"Get back!"

The voice scythed through the mists of my failing consciousness and pulled me back from the edge. Things went from dark, to monochrome, to something approaching colour. The experience was far from nice, and far from exhilarating, but I realised something. I was alive. And sometimes, just being alive is good enough. This was one of those times.

Riggs glared sideways, something attracting his attention. "Wh — what?" he stammered.

His eyes widened in what I took to be disbelief, and his face dropped. I couldn't make out what he'd seen – who he'd spoken to – but whether I lived or died, it was a reaction I was glad to see on the bastard's face.

"I said, get back!" the voice yelled again.

Riggs' grip on my neck loosened further. Not by much, but enough so that I managed to gulp down some air. There was a sudden rush of oxygen into my lungs, and that was enough to kick-start my body. I reacted instantly. I flexed, wriggled free. Slipped through Riggs' hands.

"You're not supposed to be here," Riggs opined. His voice had taken on an unpleasant whining tone; a child whose Alliance Day party had been spoiled. "You're *dead*!"

Cryogen filled the aisle, creating a bank of white mist, and Harris emerged from the gas. Wearing his Ikarus suit, his AUG-30 PDW trained on Riggs.

"You'd be surprised how often I hear that," Harris snarled. "But I'm Lazarus."

Riggs stepped back. The floor was now covered in wet fluid, a chemical mixture caused by the capsules that had been damaged during the fight. The sprinkler system had initiated overhead, showering the damaged aisle with water.

"That's—" Riggs said, his body tensing, regaining just a modicum of his threat-aura.

"Enough talk," Harris replied.

He sprayed Riggs' body with a volley from the AUG-30. The weapon's report was loud and brash in the closed environ, and at this range it was as deadly as it sounded. Riggs had no room to evade, and took the storm of gunfire full-on. He crumpled beside me, eyes empty. Extracted.

Harris evaluated the simulant coolly, then reached out an open hand in my direction. He helped me up.

"Are you okay?" he asked.

"I'm fine," I said.

"You're lying, but we'll worry about that later. Can you walk?"

I nodded. I put a hand to the collar of my suit. The armour section was badly deformed by Riggs' attack, but my neck was in an even worse condition. Just swallowing was agony. I felt as though I'd been run over by a juggernaut.

I wasn't going to let Harris see that, though. "I can walk," I confirmed. "How did you find me?"

"Sprinkler system," Harris said, water running down his face already. "When it was set off, I heard the alert."

"What the hell's happening?"

"I don't know," said Harris, shaking his head. "No comms. Did you shuttle the sims to Alpha Dock?"

"I – I think so," I said. The robotic loader mechanism was still now, most of the Jackals' simulants having been transported from storage through to – I hoped – the docking bay, where the *Paladin* waited. "Zero was trying to contact me, when—"

The capsule loader began to operate. Above the din of the emergency siren, new simulants were being prepped for use. And not just any simulants.

Riggs' simulants.

Riggs had just extracted, and was remotely initiating transition. Starting this whole process again. A new version of Riggs loaded from above, right in front of the one Harris had just killed.

TRANSITION INITIATED, the capsule read-out said.

There were ten – twenty, a hundred – copies of the asshole above this one, each racked and ready for deployment.

ARMOUR AND WEAPON ORDER CONFIRMED, the same panel flashed. STAND BY FOR DELIVERY.

Riggs' eyes opened inside the capsule. He was already

tearing the respirator from his face, the canopy rising with the hiss of escaping atmosphere—

"Come," Harris commanded. "We're leaving."

He dragged me along the aisle. At first my legs refused to work, partly because the Ikarus suit had taken damage during the attack. The Directorate obviously didn't make suits as durable as the Alliance's combat-armour. We fell into a loping rhythm through gas-banks and puddles of smoking chemical fluid, the arch of the exit flickering with amber security lamps.

Riggs' capsule opened. He slid out, not even bothering to disconnect himself from the life-support cables. Immediately, he began to give chase. Legs pumping, feet splashing through the pools of fluid as he picked up speed.

"Keep moving," said Harris. He half turned back the way we'd come, and sprayed the aisle with carbine-fire.

Riggs ducked. Sim-senses and all that. His jaw was set, grim determination painted across those boyish features.

I slammed a hand onto the exit hatch control panel. The hatch started to peel open, so fucking slowly.

Riggs saw what was happening, and he didn't like it one bit. He picked up pace. Arms cycling as he broke into a proper run.

Harris paused, fired another volley. A round clipped Riggs' shoulder, probably bit bone, but he barely flinched. He was a goddamned monster.

Meanwhile more machinery had activated. Another robotic loader slid by overhead, revealing itself in the rafters of the warehouse. A giant metal claw delivered a cargo container to the corner of the room. *Armour and weaponry.* Riggs was going to suit up, equip himself for war. He'd have access to plasma, explosives, whatever else Darkwater Farm had in its armoury stockpile. As the place was in the business of war, it would have a proper arsenal.

The hatch ground open just enough that we could get beneath it.

"Get through!" I shouted to Harris.

We ducked under the plate in unison. Riggs' footfalls seemed to make the deck quake as he moved – faster and faster and faster.

"Shut the hatch," Harris said. "Now."

As soon as I was through, I moved on the control panel on the other side. I had to get the hatch sealed.

"It's already too late!" Riggs roared. "We're all part of Warlord's plan!"

The hatch reversed, began to close. Riggs was a second too slow, even in a sim, but I wasn't taking any chances. I ripped a red-tipped grenade from my suit harness, thumbed the activator. Flung it under the hatch, just as it slid shut. Although my view of him was restricted by the closing door, I saw that Riggs paused, retreating from the grenade.

"*Sayonara, kemo sabe,*" I said, with a wave of my gloved hand.

The hatch rumbled shut, and the grenade detonated. The blast door vibrated, but held firm.

"That should slow him down," I said, shaking my head. There was still too much noise in my ears, as though someone had turned up the volume produced by the beating of my heart, the pumping of my blood.

Harris nodded in approval. "We need to get back to the *Paladin*."

"Agreed."

"This way."

A mechanical shudder hit the station, reverberating through the corridor. We paused for a moment, steadying ourselves against the wall.

"That was a ship docking," I said. "They're boarding the farm."

The station's AI reported a second later, confirming my suspicion: "Station breach. Station breach. Unauthorised vessel in Docking Bay Theta."

"That's the other end of the station to the *Paladin*'s location," Harris said, getting his bearings from the flashing direction signs on the corridor wall. "We have some time before they reach us."

Unconsciously, I put a hand to my neck. It hurt like holy hell. "I need a gun. Riggs will be on our tail."

And he'll have weapons and armour this time.

Without pause, Harris pulled a heavy pistol from a thigh holster, and tossed it to me. I racked the pistol's slide, checked the load out.

"Armour-piercing rounds," said Harris. "Be careful how you pick your targets. I don't have any more ammo."

"Solid copy."

Harris' craggy face settled into a grin. "Just like old times, huh?"

I smiled back. "Just like old times."

The Ikarus suit's map facility, loaded with Darkwater's schematics, indicated various routes through the station. I squinted at the holo, plotted our path to the *Paladin*'s dock.

"We'll go through Simulant Processing," I said. "Novak is there. We could do with another pair of hands."

Harris flexed his mechanical fist. "Not funny," he said.

"It wasn't supposed to be a joke. Feng was in the armoury, Lopez in Supply."

Both were close to Alpha Dock; there was a reasonable chance that they'd made it out. Simulant Processing, on the other hand, had access corridors that led to Storage.

"Captain Lestrade was on the *Firebird*," Harris said.

"That's Docking Bay Beta." He shook his head. Beta was at the other end of the station; Lestrade would be on his own aboard the *Firebird*. "We'll have to worry about him when the time comes," Harris decided.

"Then we better get moving."

CHAPTER SEVENTEEN

DESPERATE MEASURES

A whole sixty seconds later, running as though the devil himself were behind us, we breached Simulant Processing.

If Storage was heaven, then Processing was a lot like hell. Hot as the Proxima Colony, and humid to boot, it was lit only by the occasional hiss and sputter of working machinery. There were plenty of possible hiding spaces in here, and as soon as we entered, our pace slowed to a near crawl; covering each other as we advanced an aisle at a time, corner by corner.

"This place isn't suitable for human occupation," Harris muttered, under his breath, as we moved. "It's supposed to be fully automated."

"Figures," I said.

Simulant Processing was a flesh factory. As vast as Storage, but filled with production lines, manufacturing runs, hydraulic presses, robotic manipulators. There was a lot of activity down here, a lot of motion that acted as a distraction. All of that played havoc with my bio-scanner, although in truth, very little of what was around us was actually *alive*. Aisles were lined with cloning vats, where the simulants were birthed; filled with chemical soups, hormonal concoctions that drove the specimen down a particular developmental path. Bodies in various states of growth glared back at me. A spinal column here, grafted with bionic implants. A skull with simulated eyes there. Then a row of corpse-things with exposed muscle fibres.

As Harris said, everything here was automated, and the machines continued to operate regardless of the developing crisis. A conveyor belt still churned out gleaming metal implants – purpose unknown. Elsewhere, a robotic welding arm fizzed and sparked, attaching components to armoured suits. Technology and biology were unified here; the sims and equipment were supposed to be used together.

"Where's the lifer?" Harris said in a loud whisper, so as to make himself heard over the throb of the surrounding machinery.

"I . . . I don't know," I said. "He called in before Riggs attacked. He should be here." I'd ordered Novak to search Simulant Processing. This was where he was meant to be. Even so, I wasn't surprised not to find him here. "It isn't the first time that he's gone missing during an operation," I muttered.

Harris shrugged. "We don't have time to look for him. Riggs won't be far behind us."

We prowled on to the next junction. The chamber's chemical stink sank to the back of my throat and sat there.

"Novak?" I called. "Novak!"

A shape moved at the end of a row of machines. A bio-sign appeared on my scanner, reflecting the movement. I detected other sporadic signals in the vicinity.

"Incoming," Harris said. "Get lively!"

I ducked a volley of gunfire. The shooter accompanied the attack with a battle-cry: "Purge the fishes! No peace!"

I caught a glimpse of the tango as he moved between pillars further down the aisle. The man wore a black survival suit, taped and holed in equal measure, with a white spiral printed on the chest-plate, Cult of the Singularity iconography plastered over the sleeves and leg-modules. Backlit from behind by a fizzing robot welder, the man was a ragged and fanatical figure. His assault rifle – even in trained hands, a spray-and-pray weapon – blazed inexpertly, sending rounds across the factory floor.

Harris fired back, using a piece of industrial machinery as cover.

"Head through the vat section," I said, slapping Harris on the shoulder. How far behind us was Riggs? How long until he got here? The noise would surely attract his attention. "We can't afford to get bogged down in here."

Harris nodded. We went flush to the wall, moving as fast as possible.

Sprang! A kinetic hit the deck, too close to my left boot for comfort.

"Shooter," Harris said. "Twelve o'clock. Gantry."

He returned fire into the metal catwalks that criss-crossed the area. More gunfire chased us into the shadow of a cloning tank.

"Dead end," declared Harris.

The factory floor was a maze of machinery, and we had been backed into a blind alley. On one flank, machinery processed the torso units of combat-suits with enormous pressing pads. On the other, cloning vats churned and glowed.

"They're over here!" yelled the fanatic.

"Comms are still down," Harris said, bracing against a pillar and drawing a bead on the only direction in which the hostiles could come at us. "We're in this alone."

"As ever," I said.

"Take out as many as you can," Harris suggested.

"If it comes to it," I said, more battle-cries sounding across the factory, more fanatics drawn to our presence, "I've got a grenade." I patted a hand against the tactical webbing, where my last frag grenade was holstered.

The shooter on the catwalk fired again, landing a shot even closer this time. I guessed that he was armed with a sniper rifle. Range and visibility conditions weren't ideal for sniper-fire, but trapped as we were, it was only a matter of time before we got swarmed. All the sniper had to do was pin us down.

Another shape rounded the corner, waving a knife in the air, wide eyes suggesting that he was stimmed to the gills. I popped his head, and backed up alongside Harris. Bodies were starting to pile up, but still more figures were clambering over the hydraulic machinery beside us. Small-arms fire pattered off the deck.

"Less than half a clip left," Harris said, matter-of-factly.

The sniper rained another shot down from on high. The round went wide, hit a nearby console.

"I'm out," I said, tossing my pistol away. It would do me no good empty.

"Stay behind me," Harris ordered.

The Spiral closed on us. They knew that we were almost out of ammunition, could sense the kill was near. These were not professional soldiers, but they were professional maniacs. The first guy we'd encountered down here was at the head of the group, his rifle lowered, his dirty ginger beard parting to reveal a smile.

"We have them, Disciple Riggs," he said, into a communicator at his neck. Even zealots had comms, it seemed. "Simulant Processing. Come now."

The sniper rifle sounded again.

Then a yell from on high.

A body fell from above, directly onto the lid of a cloning vat. The sniper's shout was abruptly cut off by a wet crunch. The distance between the roof of the vat and the gantry was reasonable; clearly enough to kill or seriously injure the attacker.

"Malvern?" shouted the lead fanatic.

The group's resolution wavered, then broke a second later as the sniper-fire started again. This time, it was directed at them. One of their number caught a sniper round in the torso – not dead, but injured enough to stay down. Another was clipped in the leg. The rabble began to back up.

There was a big observation port in the side of the cloning vat. Armourglass plated, it was supposed to allow the techs to see the half-formed sims inside. It was an obvious weak point in the vat's construction. A round hit that window, and it shattered immediately. Glowing liquid poured across the factory floor. Sims in various states of growth sluiced out, directly onto the Spiral.

"What's that fluid composed of?" I asked Harris, watching the scene with a mixture of horror and amazement.

"Nothing good," said Harris. "But it is caustic when oxygenated."

The mob were covered in sticky blue gel. Bodies were already smoking, exposed skin on fire.

"Up!" came a shout. "Use ladder!"

Novak was there, braced on the catwalk. Stolen sniper rifle in both hands, aimed down at the Spiral agents. He'd given up shooting, now that the tangos had something else to think about.

There was a maintenance ladder beside one of the operational cloning vats. I realised that it would take us high enough that we could clamber onto the nearest gantry, get up to Novak's position. He waved a hand to us, pointing out the route we should take.

"Let's go," Harris said. "Those fumes are probably toxic."

The chemical stink had got a whole lot worse; enough that it made my eyes flood with tears. That and the smell of burning flesh from the injured Spiral made for a potent atmosphere.

One hand over the other, I clambered up the ladder. The Ikarus suit whined in objection – left leg refusing to straighten – but I made it up to the top of the vat. The structure was sealed with a metal lid, the sniper's prostrate body not far from the ladder, head shattered like a broken egg. Up close, I could see that the man's throat had been opened up, too. Whether it was that or the fall that had killed the asshole, didn't really matter.

"Up here," beckoned Novak.

Another ladder led to the network of gantries and catwalks from which technicians could oversee the factory floor, and Novak crouched there, waving us on.

"Where have you been?" I asked, accusatively, as I grappled my way up to him.

"Have been here." Novak looked me over, no doubt taking in the injury to my neck, the lacerations to my face caused by the fight in Storage. "Something happened, yes?"

"Something happened is right," I said. "Riggs is in Simulant Storage. He has sims, and he has weapons."

Novak's chest puffed out at that, his lip curling into a sneer. "Is bad."

Gunfire started again beneath us, yells from more tangos as they entered the chamber.

"Is Warlord here?" Novak said, wearing interest across his face. "On farm, yes?"

"I don't know," I said. "And right now, I don't really care."

"We need to get back to the *Paladin*," said Harris.

Novak gave a perfunctory nod, as though not quite committed to that idea, but said, "Through here. Service duct, yes?"

There was an open hatch at the end of the gantry; an unlit hole that led into the warren of tunnels and shafts in the deckhead. I glared at my wrist-comp – spattered with Spiral blood – and realised that none of this was on the schematics. That didn't seem to stop Novak. The big Russian tossed away the sniper rifle – useless in the narrow confines of the service ducts – and crawled in, hunching his shoulders to access the tunnel.

Harris and I followed.

The tunnel was tight, dark and even hotter than Simulant Processing; lit by pale emergency bulbs set into the ceilings, flashing intermittently and suggesting exit routes. We crouch-scrambled along on hands and knees in single-file, with Novak on point, then me, and Harris at the rear, covering the retreat with his PDW. For all the good that would do: the illuminated control panel showed LOW AMMO.

"Where were you, Novak?" I hissed in the dark, unable to let it go. "I ordered you to search Simulant Processing."

"So?" he answered.

Novak's sizeable bulk almost blocked the passage. He turned his head in my direction, eyes catching the emergency lights. I could see the cogs working in his head; considering whether he should lie to me, whether it would be better to just come clean.

I glared back at him. "That's not even an answer."

"I search Processing," he said. "But is no good." He shrugged, nodded down at the factory beneath us. "There is nothing here but robots. Is no use."

"An order is an order," I rebuked.

"But I do find something in crew quarters," he said. He paused, dangling a small metallic item between his finger and thumb. It was, I realised, a crudely fashioned Black Spiral pendant, hanging from a metal chain.

"I find this," he said. "In the girl who fight's locker."

Mori: the girl from the Command Suite. That made sense. She'd called in back-up, not from Alliance forces, but from the Black Spiral. The Spiral had either been nearby through coincidence, or their ship had already been en route to Darkwater. Neither was particularly encouraging.

"Figures," Harris said, grunting as he crawled. "I suppose she was a convert."

"Jesus Christo," I said. "Is there anywhere they haven't infiltrated? This place is supposed to be secure."

Novak shrugged again, sliding the pendant back into his suit and moving off. "Times change, yes?"

"They'll know that you're back, Harris," I said. "Riggs will have extracted, shared that intel. It'll make you a target all over again."

"I'll worry about that later," Harris said.

"Did you find any weapons, Novak?" I asked.

"Just a couple," he said. "But no guns."

I noted that Novak's armour was taped with new holsters and sheaths, each holding a bladed implement of some sort. He had maybe a dozen knives secreted across his body.

"Is okay here," Novak chattered away as he crawled. "That planet might've looked like home," he said, sucking in a mouthful of the noxious atmosphere, "but this place smells like it."

Although the light was low, and I couldn't see much further than the hand in front of my eyes, I could taste the smoke in the air. A headache like nothing I'd ever experienced had started to build in my temples, making me nauseous. I wished that I hadn't lost my helmet back in Simulant Storage.

"Just keep moving," I replied. "Which way to the Docks? The fastest route."

Novak halted at an intersection, considering. "This way," he finally answered.

"Are you sure about that? Riggs is probably right behind. He'll have a bio-scanner, and he'll know where to find us . . ."

"Am sure," Novak said.

I tried to activate my own bio-scanner, but the device flashed with Korean text, and showed an error that I couldn't interpret. Must've been damaged during the firefight in Processing.

"You better be right about this."

"We go through here," Novak said. "Through black place."

"The dark module?" I queried.

"Yes, that is right."

"Have you been in there?"

"You tell me not to," Novak said.

"That's not what I asked."

Novak shook his head. "Not yet. Access tunnel leads to module. We go through, then out into mess hall. Leads right to Dock."

I stared at the big Russian.

"Probably," he added.

"Comms are still down," Harris said, tapping his wrist-comp. It also showed an error message. "The Spiral must be using some sort of jamming tech."

"Whatever the Spiral have got, it must be pretty advanced."

"I just hope that the *Paladin* is still in one piece," Harris muttered.

I repressed the fear that we'd dragged our sorry asses across Darkwater only to find that the *Paladin* had been lost to the Spiral. Lopez and Feng hadn't been far from the docking bay. Once they had realised something was happening to the station, they should've fallen back to the *Paladin*.

Surely. Hopefully.

"Keep trying to make connection with the *Paladin*," I suggested. My own communicator had been lost in Storage.

In the relative quiet of the shaft, I heard Harris' heavy, pained breathing. He grunted with irritation as we crawled onwards.

"Are you okay back there?" I asked.

"Other than getting a prime view of your ass, I'm doing fine," he said. "Don't worry about me."

But I did. Harris had seen better days, and I knew that he would be struggling to keep up.

"Slow down, Novak."

"I said that I'm doing fine," Harris said. "It comes to it, you leave me. Right?"

"It won't come to that," I said. "You're the one with the Watch connections. If anyone can unite what's left of the Alliance in the face of this exodus . . ." I sighed. "Then it's you."

"Elena has instructions," he continued, "to get you and your squad off this station."

"That's crazy talk," I said, looking back at Harris now. "We're all leaving. No one gets left behind, and that's—"

I swallowed. The sight was actually almost impossible to behold. Harris didn't say anything at first, just grasped his stomach, frozen still.

"Take the gun," he eventually muttered. "We can't sit here all day."

"You—" I started. I felt weak with a sense of unreality, because – for the second time that day – I couldn't accept that this was actually *happening*. I tried again: "You've been hit."

"It's a fucking flesh wound, Jenkins. Stop making a big deal of it."

Harris clutched his stomach with one hand. The light was too low to properly evaluate his condition, but something had gone all the way through his Ikarus suit. Struck the armoured plates at his stomach and made a ragged hole there. The flexible element of the armour was wet with blood, liquid seeping between Harris' gloved fingers.

He looked more angry than scared, although I could tell that the wound was painful. Hell, I'd taken a round to the stomach before, and still had the scar to prove it. I knew that he'd be in some serious hurt.

"Christo damn it, Harris!" I said, more loudly than I'd intended. "You should've said something!" To Novak, I shouted, "We need to get out of this shaft and get a medi-kit, now."

Novak looked on. "Maybe the dark module has one."

"The lifer is right," Harris said. "And like I keep saying, I'm fine. I can move."

The tactical situation had changed. Although they'd almost killed me, my injuries suddenly seemed to pale in comparison. Harris was the one in immediate danger. In all the time we'd served together, I couldn't remember a time when I'd actually thought that the old man – Lazarus himself – might actually die. And yet here we were, crawling through a smoke-choked air shaft in a space station that was rammed with Black Spiral terrorists, and Harris had been hit.

"You're not dying in here," I promised. "We're not giving the Spiral that victory."

Harris' forehead was beaded with sweat, and not just as a result of the rising heat around us. "That might not be your choice, Jenkins."

Novak braced at the end of the shaft, waiting patiently and ready to open the hatch in the roof. He grinned at me. The aching in my head had grown so that it almost blotted out everything around me, and I tried to shake it away. *Maybe this is something worse*, I thought. *Maybe being strangled and beaten and almost killed just isn't enough shit on one woman's doorstep . . .*

"Ready?" Novak asked.

"On my mark," I said. "Three, two . . ."

". . . one!"

Novak popped the hatch; swinging it upwards on a hinge. Even in power-assisted armour, the cover was big and heavy. In Novak's hands, though, the metal plate opened with ease. He scrambled up and out, immediately searching for cover. I went next.

We were in a corridor. I squinted into the dark, reading words printed on the bulkhead. The dark module suddenly had a name.

"Specimen Containment," I said. "Restricted access."

"We do not count," Novak decided, scouting the next junction.

Harris staggered out of the tunnel, waving off my assistance, one hand still to his stomach.

"Looks deserted," Novak decided.

"There wasn't anyone in here when we boarded the station," Harris said. "But Nadi said that she couldn't breach the security protocols to access this sector's AI."

I remembered that Feng and Lopez had run a scanner-sweep of the whole station. There had been no one hiding in here, and none of the techs had raised an alarm about the module. Still, that the module had its own AI was concerning enough.

"Well," I decided, "at least the Spiral haven't breached these chambers yet. We can take a breather here, and regroup."

"Don't bother on my account," said Harris.

I knew from the base schematics that the dark module was located broadly in the middle of Darkwater, where the station's arms met. We were still a distance from the docks.

"This way," Novak said.

A long corridor stretched out ahead of us, in the same red light. The walls on either side were glass, segmented into cells. Dozens of little prisons; currently in darkness, but capable of being observed in relative safety from the main corridor. Beside each cell window, though, was a shotgun in a glass cabinet marked with BREAK IN CASE OF EMERGENCY. A bad feeling welled up within me.

"What is this place?" I asked Harris. My skin had started to creep, to crawl. "If you know, now's the time to tell me." I turned to him. "No secrets, Harris."

He gave me a hard stare. "I . . . I don't know. The Watch had heard rumours, but . . ." he swallowed. "Nothing more than that. Other than it's obviously a Science Division facility, I honestly have nothing else to tell you."

I cautiously took a step towards the nearest cell, my gun up and aimed inside.

"Holy Christo . . ."

Pure dark launched at me.

Despite his condition, Harris dragged me back from the observation window, and lowered my weapon.

"Shooting that thing is *not* a good idea, Jenkins," he said firmly.

What I saw inside the cell was difficult to properly describe. Not because I couldn't see it – I could barely take my eyes off the thing – but because words fail to convey the horror of it. A spiky black mass, sharp and fluid and moving: that's about the best that I can do. Phantom-like, it seemed to warp in and out of reality, its outline defined one moment, then transparent and ghostly the next. It hovered, then became indistinct and fluid. As I watched, the thing inside the cell lashed against the reinforced window. Again and again, in a concerted effort to escape. It threw a dozen spear-like tendrils at the glass, then withdrew, and started once more.

I got instant recall of the surveillance feed that Elena and Harris had showed me on the *Paladin*, of the Harbinger-infected Krell. That was what this thing's attempts to escape reminded me of.

Novak stopped. "What the hell *are* these things?"

A dozen or so lifeforms were trapped in individual cells, all acting in exactly the same way. We were in some serious shit.

"Reapers," I said. "These are Shard Reapers."

I'd seen a lot of bad things in my Army career. When you sign up for Simulant Operations, you're pretty much agreeing to seeing, shooting and hopefully killing the worst the galaxy has to offer. And the thing inside that cell: it was that. Not the actual construct, although that was dangerous enough, but what it represented.

It was a small part of the machine-mind. The Reapers were Shard weapons, and there was no plausible reason why Science Division should have them in containment on Darkwater.

See, everyone likes to think that the Shard are gone, and that their technology is dead, inert. That suits the likes of Senator Lopez, Alliance Congress, General Draven and all the other pen-pushers who direct military affairs. But the truth is a lot more complex. The Shard were a race of intelligent machines. They were capable of incredible feats of engineering, on a cosmic scale. The Shard Gates are just one example, offering instantaneous travel between the stars. But not all Shard tech is so helpful.

The Shard Reapers more than demonstrated that point. They were xenotech machines designed with one purpose in mind: to kill. Sci-Div had concluded that the liquid-metal composition was in fact a poly-alloy, an advanced nano-technology. Each Reaper was actually a supramolecular entity, its unique construction making it impervious to most forms of weaponry, extremely adaptable, and almost impossible to destroy.

Novak had drawn a knife from his sheath, but as he watched the Reaper shifting in the cell, he lowered it with a defeated look on his face.

"Why are the Shard here, now?" I asked. "Promise that you've told me everything, Harris."

"I really don't know," he answered. "I'll need to report this back to the Watch. Maybe someone there has answers. We'd – we'd heard that the Spiral were tracking certain black ops science projects."

"Is this why the Spiral are here?" I asked. Then, before I could get an answer: "What would the Spiral want with Shard Reapers?"

Harris just grimaced at me. "I think you can figure that out for yourself."

"They can't be controlled," I said, shaking my head. "Surely they know that!"

Novak had lost interest in the murder-machines, and was already retreating back up the corridor. The Russian knew when he was out of his depth.

"We try different route," he said. "Is too dangerous—"

The deck listed sideways, and the hatch at the other end of the corridor was suddenly breached.

CHAPTER EIGHTEEN

REVEALED

The corridor was immediately flooded with a cloud of smoke and debris. Another layer of sirens – somehow more insistent, more threatening – filled the air, managing to cut through the gunfire and the shouting.

"Harris!" I yelled, falling back the way that we had come. "Get down!"

The closest cell window fractured. I guessed that the thing inside – the Shard – had been kept under pressure. Maybe that was how they liked it, or perhaps that was some added layer of security. Whatever. It wasn't working.

The blackness inside the cell coalesced and became solid. A tendril lashed against the window. The glass exploded outwards with the roar of escaping atmosphere.

"I've got this," Harris shouted back at me.

Harris had pulled a shotgun from one of the emergency boxes, and he fired the weapon. It was a semi-auto security model, nothing fancy, but loaded with something I hadn't seen before. He pummelled the shadow-thing that erupted from the cell with shot, and where the blasts impacted blue sparkles of electricity appeared.

"EMP rounds," Harris said, already backing up.

EMP: electromagnetic pulse. The Alliance Army made a flavour of grenade that did the same thing – disrupted electronic equipment, scrambled advanced tech – but I'd never seen EMP shotgun shells. When Harris hit the Reaper, it froze, lost consistency for just a split second. Given that the Reapers were basically very sophisticated bodies of nanites, it was the ideal weapon to use against such an enemy.

"We go now!" Novak said, grabbing my arm. I hadn't really seen Novak frightened, and this was all new to me. I didn't much like it.

At the other end of the corridor, I could see a half-dozen Spiral tangos advancing through a wall of smoke. One paused in front of a containment cell window, then raised her weapon—

The window shattered. The Shard construct inside pierced the tango's body with one of its many tendrils. The black spear lifted her off the ground, went right through her—

And punched through the opposite cell window.

Darkwater's AI woke up.

"Alpha alert. There is a containment breach. Alpha alert. There is a containment breach. All hands, abandon this facility . . ."

Except, of course, that wouldn't be possible. We'd fired every evac-pod the farm carried, and now the only way off this bucket was the *Paladin. Or the* Firebird, I thought.

Rather than retreat, the remaining Spiral whooped in approval. The Reaper inside the cell launched itself free, slashing and tearing at another convert. Some of the tangos were overcome by a religious euphoria. They were actually fucking smiling. Smiling, as their bodies were torn apart by spears of black light. Smiling, as their corpses were thrown against the walls.

The next window ruptured too, and the corridor was suddenly a matrix of shadows, a nightmarish spider's web. In an instant, every cell was open. Terror rose within me and crashed around inside my head.

"We must go!" Novak shouted again.

He had my shoulder, was shaking me hard. That was enough to bring me back to reality. A Shard tentacle rippled past me, another Spiral body slamming into the ceiling overhead. Harris fired again and again with his shotgun, his face contorted in pain as he took the recoil of the stock against his hip.

"Hatch at other end of corridor is open," Novak said.

I dared a look back as we went, and wished that I hadn't. It was almost impossible to say how many Shard constructs there were, because they moved together, intertwined at times. Shifted between ephemeral and solid.

My God, are those . . .?

They were absorbing bodies. Breaking them down. Arms and legs and heads extruded from the black mass as it invaded the corridor.

And something else.

Warlord stood at the end of the passage. Brazen, arrogant even; wearing the same exo-suit as when I had last seen him, back on the Krell ark-ship when he had followed us into the Gyre. I was vaguely aware that both Harris and Novak were yelling at me to get out of there, but I paused. Watched as Warlord – Clade Cooper – advanced towards us through the fog of war.

"Lieutenant Jenkins," he said. "Stand down."

He extended an arm in my direction, but there was no

weapon in his hand. Instead, his fingers were splayed, index finger and thumb twisted. Warlord flexed his wrist: as though his fingers were working some invisible mechanism.

"Never going to happen."

I answered him with a hail of fire from my PDW.

Okay, I never expected a burst from the PDW to actually kill Cooper. He seemed star-touched, capable of surviving the worst. Like Kwan, I guess. It was a special ability shared by complete bastards. But I never expected this.

My gunfire didn't even reach him. Instead, the bullets sort of suspended. A whirlwind of debris formed around Cooper; like he was the eye of a storm. For a second, I was disarmed. This made no sense. We'd fought before, on North Star Station, then again on the ark-ship. Warlord had proved to be a very capable opponent on both occasions – he'd survived going toe to toe with a simulant in a full HURT suit – but this was new. This was frightening.

But . . . There most certainly had been something wrong about the way that Cooper fought when I'd first met him. His speed seemed almost supernatural, almost unworldly.

Like Novak, I was out of my depth. And I knew it.

The corridor walls rippled with activity. The Shard Reapers weren't attacking Warlord. Instead, they hovered around him.

"My reality is no longer yours," Cooper growled.

He almost looked surprised. As though he couldn't believe this was happening.

You and me both, bud.

He was pushing his abilities, or whatever they were, to the limits. Like Pariah, he was changing. But what Cooper was becoming? I wasn't quite sure.

"What the hell are you doing, Cooper?"

"Making things right," he answered. "*Correcting* the galaxy."

"We changed it already. You're bringing a war down on our heads that none of us want! We won the war with the fishes!"

"You call this victory? A galaxy ruled by bureaucrats and administrators?"

Harris stirred at my shoulder. "We have peace, Warlord. We have—"

If Warlord was in the slightest bit surprised by Harris' appearance, he didn't show it.

"I have nothing!" he screamed back. "The fishes took everything from me, and there's no space for veterans like us in the new world order. You should know that more than anyone, Lazarus!"

"You're wrong," said Harris. His strength was already draining, his face turned ashen. "We *can* change things."

"We're the same, you and I. Leftovers. Forgotten." Warlord shook his head. "This isn't peace. This isn't resolution. This is *surviving*, and that's not enough. So I'm going to tear it all down." His eyes became steel, full of determination. "And I'm going to tear apart anyone who stands in my way."

Warlord kept his hand outstretched, and twisted his fingers again. The corridor warped around me. The deck rippled: caught in the aftershock of an earthquake. I stumbled. The Ikarus suit's sensor systems fluctuated, error messages appearing over the wrist-mounted controls.

"Clade Cooper!" Harris yelled. "I'm bringing you in—"

Warlord's brow knitted in consternation. He twisted his hand again.

The walls buckled, the structure of the station groaning. I slammed my mag-locks to the deck: only remained upright because of them. The Reapers were shifting, shifting.

They were under his control.

Harris broke the spell, Gaia be thanked.

He fired off a single round from his shotgun. EMP again; enough to interrupt whatever power Warlord was using. Making the most of the distraction, Harris grabbed for the grenade at my chest, and tossed it into the fray.

"Fire in the hole!" he yelled, turning away from the blast.

The corridor washed with bright light.

Using the carnage caused by the frag grenade as cover, we retreated back through the corridor network and away from Warlord. The hatches to Specimen Containment had all been blown.

"You've got to tell Elena," he started, the shotgun held in hands that were quickly losing strength. He staggered. "The Shard – the exodus . . ."

"We'll both tell her. It's not far."

Any suggestion of medical assistance was long gone. Survival was key.

"Mess hall," Novak said. "This way! It will be empty!"

"How do you know that?" I yelled back at him.

I took a second to get my bearings. We were at one end of a chamber that was filled with tables, chairs. Flashing STATION BREACH warnings set into the walls, indicators glowing to demonstrate the direction of vital locations . . .

Novak had been wrong. The Spiral were here too.

Novak launched himself at the closest tango and unleashed. A knife filled each hand: sweeping in long wet arcs across the man's throat, where the survival suit's collar-ring connected with the torso. The tango let out a scream, grappling with the gush of blood caused by the fatal injury. Novak slammed a foot into the body, and it toppled backwards. Crashed into a table, rifle clattering to the floor.

"Come on," I ordered Harris. I propped him up as we advanced into the mess hall. "Novak, we need some cover!"

Novak turned to me, eyes wide and frenzied, and for a moment I wondered whether he had actually lost it: whether he was consumed by the red mist. Blood streaked his face like war paint.

But a heartbeat later, the Russian did as ordered. He upturned the nearest table, making a temporary barricade.

Gunfire erupted from the far end of the mess hall. I ducked back, behind the metal table. Pulled Harris with me, and noticed how his reactions had slowed. Novak roared in defiance as rounds spanked against the tabletop, punched through the thin metal surface.

"Tables as cover only works in the movies," I said to Novak, above the din.

"Cover is for assholes," Novak replied.

"Assholes that want to stay alive," I answered.

The Spiral yelled orders in a language I didn't understand. My heart sank with each fresh pair of boots that entered the room. We had Riggs at our back, Warlord somewhere on the station, and now Shard Reapers roaming free . . .

I popped up, over the lip of the table. Used it to steady the gun. Fired once, twice. Both rounds hit tangos, sent bodies sprawling backwards.

But there were more. Agents armed with pistols and melee weapons advanced on us. Some screamed battle-cries, others chanted. One sprang across the room, brandishing a shock-baton. The figure looked different from the others; with a tattoo-filled face. My finger fixed on the firing stud as the figure bolted across tables, that heavy baton ready to smash my head in—

"No!" Novak yelled.

He pushed me aside, and grabbed the man's body as he

reached us. The Russian punched the tango in the face – hard, *very* fucking hard – and the figure crumpled into his arms. Novak proceeded to drag him behind the table-barricade, effortlessly wielding the heavy baton.

"What was that for?" I asked, competing with the gunfire.

"Is intelligence, yes?" Novak answered. "Is for prisoner."

"Since when did you care about intelligence, Novak?"

"First time for everything," he replied. The tango was unconscious, and Novak had him by the collar: holding his prize firmly. I didn't have the strength to argue with him.

"He's your responsibility," I said, by way of concession.

"Of course," Novak replied. "Here, take this."

He pulled a grenade from the tango's armour, and palmed it to me. It was another frag grenade.

"We're going to make a run for that door," I said, formulating some kind of plan. DOCKS glowed at me from above the hatch at the end of the chamber. "I'll throw the grenade, and Novak will take the baton."

"No," said Harris. "I'll take the grenade."

"No fucking way. I'm not leaving you."

I pulled Harris upright. A bullet punctured the metal skin of the tabletop, very close to his head. Sweat drenched his hair, dripped from the end of his nose.

"With me, Novak," I said.

Novak tossed away one of his knives – the blade broken by the savagery of the attack – and racked the shock-baton.

"Am ready when you are, ma'am."

"Grenade out!" I lobbed the grenade overarm, in the direction we intended to run. "Go, go!"

I was up first. Novak was at my side, dragging the prisoner with him. Quite why he was so sure that we needed a prisoner, all of a sudden, was beyond me. But if it kept the big guy in check, and it didn't end up killing us, I was willing to go along with it.

—*reach out, keep reaching, searching*—

I stumbled as the pain in my head almost felled me. I just about managed to stay upright, and kept going.

DOCK.

I fixed on that word.

Then we were out of the mess hall. Through the smoke, into another darkened corridor—

"Whoa, whoa!" came a deep voice.

Riggs blocked our path. Skinned and armoured, a plasma rifle across his chest. He grinned from behind the face-plate of his combat-suit.

"Come on," he said. "It's over, guys. We've got you."

"Back up!" I shouted at Novak, who was still dragging the prisoner along with him.

Tangos had sealed off our exit route. Fuck. Fuck.

Riggs nodded. "No one touches them. Not without my authority."

The Spiral agents didn't seem particularly agreeable to that. Like hungry dogs, they circled us. We'd killed enough Spiral that I knew they'd want payback. Warlord, and the mess we'd left of Specimen Containment, couldn't be far behind.

"You're an asshole," Harris growled, standing on his own. "We'll never surrender to you."

Riggs slammed a fist into Harris' stomach, with such speed and ferocity that I barely even saw it. Harris hit the wall, crumpling with another groan. I went towards him, aware that there was nothing much I could do—

The pain enveloped me again, and this time I doubled over. At first, I thought I'd been shot, or that Riggs or the Spiral had used some weapon on me. But this was in my head; an intense jolt. *A connection.*

"Stay there!" Riggs ordered, as though shocked by my presentation.

We are here, came the words in my mind.

Harris slid to the floor, gritting his teeth against the pain.

"We're going to be okay," I whispered to him.

"No, you aren't," Riggs said. "This is Warlord's station. This is Spiral territory!"

"Then show yourself," I muttered.

Riggs looked down at me. Some of his crew had similarly started to back up, the tables turning again.

"Who are you talking to, Jenk?" he asked.

"I've got company," I said.

Pariah appeared behind the traitorous bastard; a nightmare of shadow and bladed limbs and animosity.

"We are here," it said. "And Riggs-other should be prepared to suffer."

Riggs' mouth opened, simulated lips parting to say something. Maybe it was an order. Maybe a prayer. Whatever it was, he never got the chance.

Pariah was a thing to behold. It batted aside Riggs' plasma rifle. The weapon's casing smashed against the bulkhead. Then the xeno launched forward, delivering the momentum of its full weight into Riggs. One clawed appendage pierced Riggs' collar-bone, went right through the combat-suit's armour plating as though it were wet paper.

Riggs roared in pain, twisting his body. His hand went for the plasma pistol holstered on his thigh.

Another claw tore through Riggs' right shoulder. P pinned the asshole to the wall.

"Your species is over, fish," Riggs said, sudden and real venom in his words. His lips were wet with blood, and his body convulsed. Going into shock, despite the best efforts of the suit's automated medi-suite. "Your time is finished."

P cocked its head. "We are just beginning."

Riggs gagged on blood. Struggled to speak, but managed, "The Harbinger virus will finish everything. It'll bring this galaxy to its knees."

"Goodbye, Riggs-other," P said, as it tore the traitor in two.

P stomped clawed feet – every aspect of the alien seeming to scream armour, spikes, death and strength – and swatted aside another Spiral tango. The woman screamed. Crumpled against the wall.

"We go now," P said. "Jackal-others are this way, aboard craft that sails stars. Navigator-other is with them."

I took it that P meant Lestrade, but didn't have time to confirm. "Lazarus is hurt!" I shouted back. "He needs medical aid!"

"Leave me!" Harris countered.

"Carry him, P."

P gave a disdainful look at Harris, folded on the floor, his guts leaking from the hole in his stomach.

"Saved by a fish head," Harris said, swallowing. "Something else that I'll never live down, huh?"

"Other may not get to," P said. Another flick of its claw, another dead tango. "We are not saved yet—"

The entire corridor shifted on its axis.

"They're blowing the tethers," I said, words spilling out of me now. How did I even know this? "Warlord is scuttling the whole farm."

I grabbed for something, anything, for some purchase. Novak sailed past me, snagging a piece of exposed pipework in the bulkhead. The station almost capsized. The air suddenly tasted cold and pure: a far cry from the tainted atmo I'd been sucking down for the last few minutes—

Shit!

I reached for Harris.

Maybe it was the injury. Maybe it was age. Harris had got slow, real slow. His hand grazed mine, fingers slid through my palm.

"Harris!" I yelled. "*Harris!*"

The station rumbled again, and gravity fluctuated. Harris tumbled back towards the mess hall. When I lost sight of him, he looked barely conscious.

"He's gone." Novak hauled his prisoner by the neck. "And we should be too. Docks are through there."

"I'm not leaving him!" I screamed.

"There is no choice," P said.

Rounds impacted the alien's body armour, taking chunks out of the organic plate. P grappled with me, pulled me along. The volume of gunfire coming from the mess hall was too intense, too heavy.

"We can't leave him! We can't leave him!"

But that was exactly what we were doing. The dock loomed ahead.

"Onto ship," Novak commanded.

Except, I realised, this wasn't our ship.

We were in Beta Dock. The ship in the cradle, attached by an umbilical to the station proper, wasn't *our fucking ship*! Instead, the *Firebird* sat in the docking claw.

"This isn't the right ship!" I railed. "We have to go back, for the *Paladin*!"

P kept moving, absorbing weapons fire, covering me, but talking as it went. "The Jackal-others fell back here. The simulants have been loaded onto this craft. There is no other choice."

"But Elena, Nadi!" I started.

"They are on own now," Novak said, brusquely.

No matter how much I disliked it – there was no choice here. Going back was suicide. It was this ship, or none at all.

We closed on the open cargo ramp. Feng and Lopez were at the lock, waving me on. I couldn't hear them over the roar of weapons discharge, but I could see the determination on their faces. They had plasma rifles, probably plundered from the station's armoury.

Then I was aboard the *Firebird*, collapsed on the deck.

"Where's Colonel Harris?" Lopez asked me.

"He – we lost him!" I shouted. "We can't leave without him!"

The cargo bay was now stacked with dozens of copies of the Jackals: staring back at me with impassive, hooded eyes.

"It's done," Feng said, shouting to compensate for the noise, into a communicator at his neck: a direct line to Captain Lestrade. "We're all on the ship!"

"Hold on to something back there," came Lestrade's voice over the ship's PA. "I'm opening the docking claw in three!"

I looked back the way we'd come, at the skewed corridor, through the mass of moving bodies. Desperate for some indication that Harris had made it out. Through the haze of fire, the dense smoke that claimed the atmosphere, I saw a shape emerging.

"Wait!" I ordered. "Tell Captain Lestrade to hold position! I see Harris!"

But, of course, life isn't that fair.

It was Riggs, now in a shiny new combat-suit, plasma rifle drawn. A mindless swarm of Spiral cultists followed. *They're just like the Krell*, I thought, as I scrambled away from this man I had once called a lover. *We're becoming just like them.* Meanwhile, Shard Reapers, dark and malignant, swirled behind him. The impossible shadows reflected what I saw in Riggs' eyes, what I had seen in Warlord.

The station's docking bay suddenly and definitively decompressed. The *Firebird* was still open to the elements, and a hurricane of debris escaped the open bay. I grabbed for some cargo webbing, watched as the world outside was pulled into space. Crates, weapons, bodies: a swirl of detritus followed as we lifted off.

Riggs stood among the carnage, his face-plate now transparent, and watched as the *Firebird* launched.

He waved – fucking *waved* – as the ship left.

CHAPTER NINETEEN

AT WHAT COST?

Lopez, Feng, Pariah and I ran for the bridge. Novak had secured the prisoner, for what good that would do us, and Zero met us en route, laying to rest any fear that she had been left on the *Paladin*. Her face, though, was abject horror.

"Where's . . .?" she started, before stumbling over the words and trying again: "Where's Colonel Harris?"

"He's still on the farm," I said.

"Is he . . .?"

"I don't know. We lost him, but the Spiral are blowing the tethers. We couldn't go back."

Was he dead? I didn't know right now. The thought chilled me, was almost paralysing. It felt like the universe needed Lazarus more than ever. It felt like *I* needed him more than ever. I couldn't do this alone.

"Was that Riggs?" Lopez asked me, as we ran. "Back in the docking bay?"

"Long story," I said. "But it was him. What's the sitrep?"

"Zero told us about an incoming signal," Feng explained,

"and we fell back to the *Firebird*. Nadi redirected the simulants here as well."

"Smart move," I said. "Anyone injured?"

Lopez shook her head. "We did better than you, ma'am. None of the Jackals are hurt."

We burst onto the *Firebird*'s bridge. The module was compact, and packed with cutting-edge military tech. Lestrade had plugged himself into the captain's console.

"All hands, buckle up!" he barked.

The ship's thrusters roared, and she banked hard as she swept out of the docking clamp. Her inertial dampener field kicked in, but struggled to compensate for the extreme manoeuvre.

"Can you pilot this ship on your own, Captain?" Zero asked, fumbling with her seat straps.

"It's an Intruder-class," Lestrade said, as he manipulated the pilot controls. "Not a dreadnought. She's made to fly with minimal crew, but I won't argue if someone wants to help with the gunnery stations . . ."

The Intruder was smaller than most line vessels, designed with manoeuvrability and speed in mind. Captain Lestrade made the most of those characteristics as he evaded the storm of debris that surrounded the station.

"You heard the captain," I said. "Lopez, Feng. Take the posts."

We all slid into gunnery pods. Screens lit in front of us.

"Tracking hostile weapon signatures," Lopez said, already punching in weapons clearance. "I'm activating the flak cannons."

"Just do whatever you can to keep us alive," said Lestrade.

The communications console crackled to life with an incoming transmission. I understood enough of the console's read-out to see that it was the *Paladin*.

"Do you read, *Firebird*?" came Elena's static-riddled voice.

"We copy," I replied.

"You made it out. Very good."

"I'm turning on the farm's defensive systems," Nadi declared. "Brace yourselves."

The farm's weapon array came online, and began shooting asteroids out of the sky.

"You have to listen," I said. "Something happened on the farm—"

Elena spoke over me. "I'm broadcasting a data-packet to your ship," she said, her voice remarkably calm and composed. "Encrypted channel." My console showed incoming data, and I accepted the packet. No time to consider it now, but the *Firebird* would keep it on the data-stacks for later retrieval. "In case we don't make it out, this is the mission. Understand?"

"Solid copy." But of more pressing concern: "Did Harris make it off the station? Tell me that he's on the *Paladin*!"

"Say again?" Elena said, over the comm. Her voice was becoming harder to make out. "Do not copy."

I watched as the *Paladin Rouge* cleared Alpha Dock, at the far end of the station. Her thrusters glowed blue, trailing plasma. I rubbed my temples. I was so tired that I could barely think straight.

"Boost the transmission!" I ordered.

"This will have to wait," Lestrade yelled across the bridge. "We can't stay here."

Darkwater Farm was a complete mess. Several modules were open to the void – streaming debris into Thane's upper atmosphere – while intense fires were visible behind some view-ports.

"Lazarus might still be on board," Zero said.

"Or he could be on the *Paladin*," Feng offered.

Thane's angry surface spun beneath us, the yellow cloud cover spiralling in sickening patterns . . .

There was a bloom of light from the station.

"The station's remaining bolts are blowing," Lopez said. "The farm's going down."

One bolt, then another. Then a third. The enormous tethers holding the base in position whipped around in zero-G. The reaction was immediate. Detonations rippled along the underside of the asteroid, through the upper levels of the station. The base tipped, lopsided, then began to career off-course. The entire facility impacted with the asteroid field, tumbling now. Its null-shield intermittently reacted, throwing surrounding debris into complete disarray. There were so many targets on my display that I could barely decide which to shoot first.

"We can't stay here," Lestrade repeated. "If the station's energy core cooks off, and we're still in the blast radius . . ."

Yeah, he really didn't need to finish that sentence. Anyone with even a passing knowledge of power tech knew that being within range of a failed quantum-energy containment core was a *very bad idea.*

"Get us the hell out of Dodge," I decided.

Then Darkwater hit Thane's upper atmosphere, and immediately began to burn up. It was pulled down into the gravity well, glowing hotter and hotter, caressed by the poisonous atmosphere . . .

"Energy core cooking off," Zero declared.

There was a sudden and brilliant flash of light. So intense that the *Firebird*'s view-screens polarised to protect our eyes. The hard radiation sensor chirped a warning, despite our distance from the detonation.

The *Firebird* made hard burn out of the band of rocks. Thane glared back at me. An electrical storm was developing on the surface – chain lightning coursing through the upper atmo, perhaps a reaction to the station's demise. Visibility was very quickly deteriorating, the *Firebird*'s electronic eyes becoming less reliable.

"I got another signal incoming!" Lopez yelled. "Moving up fast on our six!"

"The Spiral aren't done yet," Captain Lestrade said, still hunched over his console. "They're giving chase."

"I've got an ID," Zero said. "The *Iron Knight*. She's unregistered, but her profile is marked as shoot on sight for Alliance forces."

We hadn't known her name then, but we had seen the *Iron Knight* before. Both at Daktar Outpost, when the Jackals had first crossed swords with Warlord, and then in the Gyre, when Warlord had attacked the Silver Talon ark-ship. She was a blunt, ugly vessel; in appearance resembling an older-pattern freighter. But I saw now, reading the data-stream from the *Firebird*'s advanced sensor-suite, that she was much more than that. Her chassis housed dozens of active weapons systems, and she was equipped with a fusion and Q-drive. Her null-shield ignited, repelling debris and asteroids, and she powered on through the mess that polluted Thane's upper atmosphere.

At least I had no doubt that Warlord and Riggs had made it off Darkwater. They were unquestionably on that ship.

"She's not alone," Zero said. "I'm reading more hostiles incoming."

Five hot targets appeared on our tail, keeping pace.

Missiles flickered across the tactical display. Something hit our null-shield, and the resultant storm of debris sent a shudder through the *Firebird*'s belly. A dozen warning alarms filled my console, and a siren sounded across the bridge.

"I can't get a lock!" Lopez said.

"Me neither," added Feng.

"They're closing," I yelled.

I locked a targeting solution into my console, and fired off another railgun round. One of the ships suddenly banked, but the pilot obviously wasn't as good as she thought she was. The small vessel slammed into an asteroid, exploded.

The other four ships kept coming. A wave of kinetics hit our null-shield, the *Firebird*'s AI broadcasting protests direct to my console.

Lestrade banked starboard. He was flying the ship like we were in an atmosphere, dipping and weaving between asteroids. The hull began to creak, and outside I saw that we were actually clipping atmo, the pure black of space giving way to a foul yellow . . .

"Got one!" Lopez hooted.

Another Spiral ship went down, became an incandescent ball. Still, that left the *Iron Knight* and three others, and they were tight on our ass.

". . . drawing off fire, *Firebird*," Gustav's voice came, fluctuating between clarity and indistinct static. ". . . luck . . . Good sailing."

The *Paladin* appeared on the tac-display. She nosed through the moving terrain, seeking a safe path. Took out another fighter with a missile, leaving only two. Dipped low, hull positively glowing white as it clung to the upper atmo.

"You know what you have to do, Captain Lestrade," Elena said, her voice trembling with what I took to be G-force. "Execute your orders."

"Understood," Lestrade said.

The *Firebird* turned hard, trailing gunfire from the flak cannons. The Spiral ships peeled off, swooping, dodging, weaving. *Paladin* disappeared back into the asteroid field, chased by a swarm of smart missiles.

"*Paladin!*" I roared. "Come in, *Paladin!*"

There was no reply. Lopez scattered the Spiral fighters with the *Firebird*'s flak cannons, and Feng launched another volley of missiles.

"They're attracting the Spiral's fire," Lestrade said. "This is our chance."

There was obvious reluctance in the captain's voice, and although I didn't know him well, I knew that he wouldn't leave the *Paladin* behind without reason. But we were damaged, and the Spiral fleet was still a force to be reckoned with.

"Hard burn, all hands," Captain Lestrade said, with resignation.

"*Iron Knight* is pulling back," Lopez said. "She's focusing fire on the *Paladin*."

"Maybe . . ." Zero said, "maybe they think Lazarus is onboard."

I didn't know whether I wanted that to be true or not.

At what cost do you measure victory?

My current state of existence seemed to be running from one catastrophe to the next, but some catastrophes were worse than others. We'd scored a victory – obtaining the simulants – but they had come at a terrible cost.

I sat on the bridge for a long time. Listening to the gentle chime of the radar, the ping of the lidar. Other, more exotic sensors probed the dark, searching for any hint of a comms transmission, an energy signature, a distress beacon. Watching the tactical display and the view-ports, I almost wished that something would come after us. At least that would break the quiet, and give us a definitive answer.

But there was nothing. No sign at all of the farm, of the Spiral, of the *Paladin*.

Of Lazarus.

Pariah perched in one corner of the bridge, legs tucked

beneath itself, still dripping ichor from the multiple injuries it had suffered back on the farm. The xeno's bio-plating was ruptured in many places, although the flow of stinking black fluid that the creature called blood had been staunched by Zero's handiwork with a medi-pack.

"Can you sense anything?" I asked.

The alien regarded me coolly. "Nothing. The same as the last time Jenkins-other posed the question."

I sighed, turned back to my console. I was Army, not Navy, and I barely knew how to use this tech. But most of it was automated, thankfully, and Captain Lestrade had set the sensor-suite's search parameters.

"I'm only asking," I said.

"We understand," said Pariah. "We merely observe. We will inform Jenkins-other if the situation changes."

"You do that," I said. "Captain; send another transmission. All frequencies."

Captain Lestrade nodded. He hadn't moved from his post in the two hours since we'd left Thane.

"*Paladin Rouge*," Lestrade said, "this is UAS *Firebird*. Requesting response."

The gentle pop and crackle of background radiation sounded across the communicator.

"Again," I said.

Captain Lestrade repeated the broadcast another half-dozen times, but we both knew that there would be no result. He'd been sending the same transmission every few minutes since our retreat.

"They can't be gone . . ." Zero whispered. "They made it out. Surely."

"I wish I could believe that," Lestrade muttered. He didn't seem to want to make eye contact with anyone. "But there's no reply to the hail."

"Perhaps their communicator module is damaged," Zero said, ever the optimist.

"Then why aren't we seeing any evidence of their drive-trail?" Lopez asked.

"Their engine could be damaged," Zero suggested, searching my face and then Lestrade's, looking for some support for her theory. "Maybe they're still in orbit around Thane. We could go back, search for survivors."

This time Captain Lestrade shot her down. "The Spiral could still be out there, for all we know. We're one ship, and a damaged one at that."

Zero's face danced with emotion. "We can't let this happen."

Feng and Lopez were quiet. There was little that they could say, but Feng put an arm round Zero in a decidedly non-military way.

"Doesn't the Watch have resources?" Zero pushed. She wasn't going to let Harris go, no matter what the objection. "Can't you call in back-up, Captain? There must be someone you can trust."

Lestrade shook his head. "Sergeant, there is no one. This ship has a limited FTL transmitter, and the nearest Watch outpost is light-years away—"

"Bullshit!" Zero implored. "When I was a kid, Harris came back for me." She turned to me, desperation plastered across her features. "You found me, Jenk. You saved me on Mau Tanis."

"This isn't the time for your war story, Zero," I said.

"I'm not telling the story," Zero said, firmly. "I'm telling the truth. You, Harris, the Lazarus Legion: you saved a lost kid on a world destroyed by the Krell. And I joined up with Sim Ops because I wanted to give something back. Because I wanted to do something *good* with my life." Her words were impassioned, and she'd become animated. "How many people has he saved? How many worlds, ships, stations? Now we have a chance to do something for him."

"Enough," Captain Lestrade said. "There's no response from Thane. We have to assume that the *Paladin* is gone." He looked at me. "We all left someone behind out there, but you have a mission to execute." He tapped the console with one of his long fingers. "Dr Marceau gave me an order before we left Thane."

Zero made a distressed noise at the back of her throat. "We can't let this happen. We can't let it be."

Novak turned to Zero and said, "Am sorry about what happened to your Lazarus. Man is not to me what he is to you, but he saved us from Jiog. He is okay by me." Novak's eyes were hooded with what could've been sadness. "He did not deserve to get ghosted."

Lopez sighed. "The Spiral are going to pay. We have to make them."

Zero said nothing to that, only pursed her lips. In the space of a few days, she'd been hit by the double-revelation that her idol – the legend Lazarus – was alive, and also that he was probably dead. The kid deserved better. My Jackals hadn't known Harris, hadn't really fought with him, but they knew how important he was. Lopez, Feng, even Novak dropped their heads in respect. That Riggs had a hand in his condition made it that much worse.

"What's the *Firebird*'s situation?" I asked of Lestrade.

"We're moving out-system," he said. "The coolant system is fried, and we've got possible hull damage on E-deck." He flipped through some data on his terminal screen. "The flak cannon array needs some maintenance as well. But most importantly, the quantum-drive is still operational. From the look of things, the *Firebird* has a very fast drive."

"That was some good flying back there," I said, with a weary sigh.

"I did ten years as a combat pilot," he muttered. "They might change the systems, make things easier for the pilot, but the controls more or less work the same."

"If things had been different, none of us would've made it out," I said. I took one final glance at the scanner-suite. Nothing had changed. "Take us to the system's edge," I ordered Lestrade.

"Aye, ma'am."

"What did the Spiral want out here, anyway?" Feng asked. "Why were they on Thane in the first place?"

I told the Jackals what we had found on Darkwater. Of the Shard Reapers, in the dark module. Novak had been the only one with me when we'd entered the module. I described as best I could Warlord's behaviour, his inexplicable abilities. But even as I did so, they began to sound unreal – as though whatever I had seen him do hadn't actually happened. Of course, none of the Jackals had faced the Shard. They'd heard the rumours, seen the after-action reports – such that Alliance Command had declassified – but never witnessed the horror. I hoped that they never would.

"Christo . . ." Lopez said. "But what did the Spiral want with the Shard?"

Novak sneered and sucked his teeth noisily. "Is easy. We can just ask them."

The bridge went quiet at that. I'd almost forgotten about Novak's prisoner – the man he had insisted on dragging aboard the ship. So much had happened in the last few hours that it was unsurprising, I suppose.

"Is in cell," Novak said. "Brig is word, yes? We have prisoner. He is Russian, like me."

"We have prisoner," I repeated, thinking on this.

"He's a potential mine of intel," Feng commented.

No one wanted to hear it, to move on to the next stage of our mission, but the reality was that we had no choice. Whether Lazarus lived or died, the Spiral were still out there.

"I will do three degree," Novak said.

"Three degree?" Lopez asked. "What's that?"

"Asking of the questions," Novak explained. "Is the three degree, yes?"

"Third degree," I said. "You mean give the prisoner the third degree."

Despite the situation, Lopez and Feng laughed. Novak didn't see the funny side of it; just shrugged his enormous shoulders.

"I speak Russian," he added. "You do not. I ask the questions."

"All right," I said, seeing a possible lead here.

"Good, good," Novak muttered. There was an eagerness in his tone that I wasn't quite comfortable with; his bruised and battered face suddenly brightened, as though the promise of violence was bringing him alive.

"Let's take a look at our friend and see what he can tell us."

CHAPTER TWENTY

THIS IS THE ENEMY

The *Firebird*'s brig was basically an open cell with an observation field covering one wall. That was currently tuned so that we could see in, but the prisoner couldn't see out: a one-way mirror. The cell's lights were extinguished, save for a single glow-globe that had been turned up to maximum brightness, shining down on the prisoner like a spotlight.

The Jackals were gathered on the other side of the obs field, evaluating the prisoner and considering what he meant. Only Pariah was absent, because I didn't think the fish would help in this situation. Whatever the Spiral really was, it was clear that the organisation hated the fishes.

"You think that the Spiral will come looking for their guy?" Lopez asked.

"I doubt it," I said.

"They couldn't track him, even if they wanted to," Zero added. She clutched a data-slate to her chest, monitoring the conditions in the room. "He's been scanned for covert tech, and he's not carrying anything."

"We'll keep an eye on the situation," I decided. "Not all concealed tech is easy to detect."

The metal in Feng's head being a prime example. I still wasn't quite sure why I hadn't told the others about that yet.

"So this is the enemy, huh?" Lopez said.

"He doesn't look like much," Feng muttered.

The prisoner was underwhelming, to say the least. A man of maybe thirty years standard, with a bald scalp stitched with tattoos and nerve-plugs. A hard, pale face; a nose that had been broken so many times that it had lost all shape. A scattering of whiskers over a pointed chin. None of it spoke of a good or decent life.

The tango had been strapped to a chair, lashed at the ankles and wrists with steel cable. He wore a survival suit, stained with blood and soot. That, like the asshole's face and head, was literally covered in iconography. Black Spiral symbols, kill-slogans, clan markings. A language that I couldn't read.

"He's a member of the Cult of the Singularity," Zero said. She had called up a series of images on her slate, and was cross-referencing some of the tattoos with those on the *Firebird*'s mainframe. "The Cult is a known affiliate organisation of the Spiral."

Everyone had heard of the Cult of the Singularity. It had been around for a while, causing trouble on and off since the discovery of the Shard. They were a prohibited organisation; one of several that worked with, or sometimes for, the Black Spiral. A proto-religious movement, the Cult had actually appeared before the emergence of the Spiral. They worshipped the Singularity, sought to bring about convergence of organic and machine. Exactly how they were going to do this, or why it was necessary, wasn't clear to many believers. But what better example of such a convergence, so the Cult preachers insisted, than the Shard: a species that represented the superiority of the machine. The Cult had been responsible for several terrorist atrocities in the Outer Colonies, all said to be in the name of the Machine.

Zero continued reading. "Many Cultists have been inducted into the Spiral. The primary Singularity Cult texts are said to have been endorsed by Warlord. That's what this intelligence bulletin says."

"We had a problem with the Cult on Proxima Colony,' Lopez said. They're almost as bad as the Spiral."

Zero swallowed, looking peakier that usual. "Do you think that the Cult and the Spiral were on Darkwater looking for the Shard? It seems more than a coincidence."

"How did they know the Shard were there?" Lopez questioned. "Wasn't it a black op? Nadi couldn't even break the security protocol."

"And if she couldn't do it," Feng said, with a shake of his head and a laugh, "then I doubt anyone could."

There were Shard Reapers in the dark module. They had attacked the Spiral, but not Warlord. He seemed to have some control over them; something that I had never heard of or seen before. How did he do that? There was only one way to find out. I opened the comms channel into the containment cell.

"You can proceed, Novak," I said.

The Russian was already inside the cell. He turned to look at the obs field, and gave a slow nod. I could sense the rest of my squad tensing up around me, Lopez already looking to the floor. This was about to get nasty.

"Speak Standard," I ordered. "I want to hear what this bastard has to say."

Novak grunted, and directed his attention to the prisoner. The Russian's footfalls were heavy and slow, sending vibrations through the deck as he circled the captive.

"This can be easy, yes?" Novak said to him. "What is name? Tell me now."

"I am nobody," the captive answered. His accent was sharp, Slavic.

Who were you? I wondered. A nobody with an axe to grind and a galaxy that had forgotten all about him. That was what the Black Spiral offered: a chance of transcendence, for the nothing to become something. It was a powerful incentive, and not one to be underestimated. Unsurprising, really, that people like this would unite under the Spiral's banner . . .

Novak rumbled a laugh. The sound was malicious, and sent a shiver up my spine. "That's how you started," he said. "But now you are somebody."

"It doesn't matter," the man repeated. He had bruises and lacerations all over his chest; souvenirs from Darkwater. "I am Spiral. I have no other name."

Novak rounded the tango slowly. A predator on the prowl, the Russian appeared to be savouring every moment of this confrontation. He wore a deep grin on his face; a smile that exposed his darkened teeth.

"I think I call you Martin. Is nice name. Is American name. We both know you not American though." Novak paused. "I am Russian. You are too, yes?"

The figure looked up, and there was some silent understanding between Novak and the tango. Another prickle broke on my skin.

"We are understanding each other?" Novak said. He was stripped to the waist, his muscled body also wet with sweat, his prison tattoos more extensive than those of the smaller prisoner. "I think you are from mother country too. Am I right?"

"It doesn't matter," the prisoner spat back.

"I am Alliance," Novak continued. "I am here for answers, yes?"

The prisoner scowled. "Fuck you. Is coming. Is happening, whether you like it or not."

"You think I care about that?"

"Warlord cares about all of us," the prisoner said.

Novak's reaction was instant. He pounded a fist into the left side of the tango's face. Martin's head cracked backwards. Bright blood and spittle sprayed from his mouth. Zero gasped, sympathetically.

Novak got right into the man's face. "Your ship is gone. We destroyed it. My officer, she kill it in poison atmosphere."

Martin snarled. The noise was wet and painful to listen to.

"You know this man Riggs, yes?" Novak said. "He was once like me." He thumped a fist against his chest. "He was Jackal."

Martin said something in a language that was probably Russian. Novak rewarded him with another roundhouse to the chest. Ribs snapped. I started to feel a bit sick.

"Now you tell me what I want to know," Novak said. "Why were you on Darkwater?"

Martin's head swung back and forth, strands of saliva and blood dripping from his ruined mouth.

"Supplies," he managed. "We needed supplies."

"Why Darkwater? Is special. Is farm."

"Warlord; he need special supplies."

"Like what?"

"You see them." Martin looked at Novak, though his eyebrows. "How you say? 'Reapers', yes?"

"Why does Warlord need Reapers? Does not make sense."

312

"If you cannot understand, then is your problem. No more talk."

Novak dealt with that with another blow to the tango's face.

Lopez moved back from the obs field now. "I can't watch this," she said.

"Feng, take Lopez out of here," I ordered.

"On it," said Feng.

He ushered Lopez out of the room, leaving Zero and I watching.

"All right!" Martin said. "I talk!"

"Why Darkwater?" Novak roared.

"Because we need sims, for Riggs."

"For the traitor?"

"Yes," Martin agreed. "For traitor."

"What was Warlord doing there?"

"He need medication," Martin said. "He cannot live without."

"What medication?"

Martin rolled his head. "No more questions."

"I say when to stop," Novak said.

"We will stop all of this. We will destroy Aeon, and we will bring Dominion to your world."

Novak cracked his knuckles. Stood behind the prisoner and produced something that reflected the low light of the glow-globe. It was one his precious knives. He ran the blade down his forearm, testing its sharpness. Martin seemed to tense up a little at that – who wouldn't? – but his lips were still sealed.

I hit the two-way comms switch set into the wall.

"Leave it there, Novak," I said. "He's told us enough."

Novak looked up at the screen. His face was remarkably open, and incredibly calm: like this was just another day at work for him.

"Make window dark," he said. "You do not want to be seeing this."

"I said, *leave it*!"

But Novak wasn't listening. He began to speak rapidly, in Russian, despite my order. Martin, grinning through a mouth of broken teeth and blood, answered in the same language.

Zero looked to me for approval. I nodded, and she very eagerly deactivated the window, turning the mirrored field opaque. Martin's defiance was short-lived and pitiful. Soon his pained screams, his pleading in Russian, filled the brig. Novak was making the most of this.

"You can go too, Zero, if you'd prefer," I said.

Zero shook her head. She frowned at me, unsure of whether she should talk.

"Go on. Spit it out."

She held out a data-slate. "This is linked to the *Firebird*'s AI programme," she said. "It speaks Russian."

I took the slate and looked down at the words forming there.

"It's a real-time translation of the interrogation," Zero explained. "He keeps saying the word 'Aeon', but the rest . . . Well, see for yourself . . ."

"Shit."

Novak wasn't asking about the Spiral. Not after his first few questions, anyway. The rest – shot through with untranslatable screams and wet gurgling noises – wasn't about the Spiral at all.

"Get out of here, Zero. I have a slight matter of discipline to deal with, and it isn't going to be pretty."

Zero got the message this time, and scurried out of the brig.

*

The interrogation didn't last much longer. Barely a few minutes after Novak's gig had been rumbled, the tango was dead. Leaving what was left of the body – which, admittedly, wasn't very much – Novak came into the brig.

"Does not know anything else," he said.

"Well he doesn't now, Novak. He's dead."

Novak shrugged. "They kill Lazarus, yes? I kill them. Is no loss."

"Except that you weren't asking about Lazarus, or Darkwater, or anything else to do with this mission," I said. "Just what exactly is your malfunction, trooper?"

Ichor and bloody fluid was liberally sprayed across Novak's chest and face. He wiped at it with a rag; a mechanic cleaning himself up after a particularly messy repair, rather than an executioner who had just killed a man.

Novak glanced up innocently. "Is done," he said. "Spiral were here for sims. They have no more operators, only Riggs."

"And you know this how?"

"Because I ask question," Novak said. "In Russian, yes? Maybe you not understand."

"Oh, I understand perfectly. I told you to speak Standard."

"My mistake."

I thrust the data-pad in front of Novak, and his gaze settled on it. There was a perceptible drop to his shoulders, a tell that I'd started to recognise.

"I know what you were asking him," I said. "Zero set up the ship's AI to translate your questions, and his answers."

"Zero make the error in words—"

"So you're saying that Zero made an error in every question you fucking asked?"

"Ah, yes," Novak said, slowly.

"Who are you, Novak?"

315

"I am Jackal," he answered. "I am soldier." He went quiet, and added: "I am Son of Balash."

"Tell me everything. No more secrets."

"I already tell you. Back on ark-ship, in Maelstrom."

"That wasn't everything," I said. I pointed to a line of text on the data-slate. "'Tell me where Major Mish Vasnev is?' you asked. 'On pain of honour as Son of Balash.' Who the fuck is Mish Vasnev?"

Novak sighed, rolled his head on his shoulders as though he were considering how best to answer that question, or whether he should answer it at all.

"Vasnev was member of gang," he finally said. "Back on Old Earth. In Norilsk."

That was where Novak had grown up, according to his service files. During our last mission into the Maelstrom, Novak had revealed to me that he had tried to leave the *bratva* – the gang that I now knew as the Sons of Balash – and how his wife and daughter had been killed as retribution. Novak was arrested for the murders, then tried and sentenced to life imprisonment in a Siberian *gulag*.

"More," I said. "I want *everything*, Novak."

"Vasnev was boss, yes?" he said, seeking some understanding in my eyes. "Was godmother. I was enforcer. Bonded, for life." He tapped a tattoo on his chest, something that looked like a feathered serpent, coiled with Cyrillic script. "That asshole – the Martin – was *bratva* too," Novak explained.

"That doesn't make sense," I said. "I saw how you treated Alexei, when we escaped Jiog. He was a Son of Balash."

Novak waved a hand dismissively. "That was different. He was like me." He pointed to another tattoo; markings around his left eye socket: a crude semi-circle that was almost certainly a prison tattoo. "He was exile. We are both Sons in exile, yes?"

I still wasn't getting this. "So you were exiled from the Balash gang, or whatever it's called?"

Novak looked at me plaintively. "This is not like life in California, in the San Angeles, ma'am. This is bad life. This is short life."

Life in the San Ang ain't exactly a dream, I thought to myself, but let it go. It was beyond argument that life in northern Russia was a good deal worse. The Russian Federation had taken a direct shelling during the Directorate–Alliance war. That had been generations ago, but the land still hadn't recovered. Some doubted that it ever would.

"I am exiled, yes," Novak continued. "I am exiled by Major Mish Vasnev."

"And you want to know where she is, why, exactly?"

Now Novak's presentation became stony cold, ice cold. "Because I want to kill Mish Vasnev. She . . . she give order."

Novak pointed out another tattoo. In the mess of iconography and picts that spread across his skin, I'd missed so many clues to his background. But now that I looked, they were all there. His history was spelled out on a flesh-canvas.

"Vali," I said, breathlessly.

The name that he had used on the train, back on Jiog. He had spoken it accidentally, or so I'd thought, when talking about Zero. In the heat of the moment, I'd dismissed that as a slip of the tongue, nothing more. Now, it took on a new significance.

"Who was she?"

"My daughter," Novak said. "My little girl. She was six years old, and very small. To have daughter in Norilsk is bad. Son is better, so elders say. But when I look in Vali's eyes, I know this is wrong."

I swallowed back regret. "She was killed, wasn't she? By this Mish Vasnev?"

Novak nodded. "Vasnev gave this order."

"And now Vasnev is working with the Black Spiral?"

Another nod. "And now I get chance to kill Vasnev. To avenge, you understand? To make right."

"You can't do this," I insisted. "Not now."

"Not you," Novak said. "But me, I can. I do this, yes?"

"You're a damned Jackal! You're an indentured soldier of the Alliance Army, Novak!"

"I do not give fuck about rest of galaxy," Novak said. "Mine is already gone."

I met Novak's gaze. It was calm, but also resolute. Was he so different to Warlord? Clade Cooper had lost everything once, too, and that had turned him into a monster. I realised then that I really didn't know Novak at all.

"I'm sorry about what happened to your daughter, Novak," I said. "And your wife, too. But while you're a Jackal, you obey orders. *Capische*?"

Novak didn't answer, but there was a slight upturn to the corners of his mouth. Smiling. He was smiling at me. I didn't like that reaction one bit.

"Something funny, Private?" I asked.

"Nothing funny," said Novak.

The words might be right, but the reaction and attitude weren't. I sincerely doubted that this talk was getting through to Novak, despite everything that had happened. It struck me, in that instant, that maybe Novak had something in common with Riggs as well. I didn't know either of them, not properly.

"It comes to it, I give the orders," I said. "I know that you've got your own agenda, but like I said: you're a Jackal."

"Vali, she was toughest cookie," Novak replied. "She would not quit. She would not stop, and I know this. So I will be Vali. I will not quit. Her favourite animal is dog,

318

yes? We even had one. Was mutt." He laughed, hoarsely. "Did bite. Did have the fleas. But was Vali's favourite. She love him." The rage had returned to his posture, to his expression. "I would do anything for one more minute with her. Just one minute. You understand this?"

"I get it," I said.

"I will be Vali's dog. I will be Jackal."

"You left your post aboard the farm," I said, all of Novak's various insubordinations now making a lot more sense, "and you lied to me about that prisoner. We have a chain of command for a reason. I need to know that I can trust every one of my Jackals. I need to know that you're with this."

"I am," said Novak. "But I will not let this be gone. Chance comes . . ." He shrugged. "I take shot."

"And if my order conflicts with your agenda?"

Novak's eyes narrowed. He was rubbing the knuckles of his right hand with his left. The action was far from calming or reassuring. "Then things get interesting," he said. "Very interesting."

"Not good enough. I need to know that the Jackals come first."

Novak gave a slow, and rather unconvincing, nod. "Of course."

I shook my head and sighed at him. But I realised that this was the best response I was going to get.

"Dismissed," I said. "Make sure that bastard's body is spaced."

"Yes, ma'am."

CHAPTER TWENTY-ONE

SOMETIMES THEY COME BACK

We were sixteen hours out of Thane.

The *Firebird*'s coolant leak had been stemmed. Captain Lestrade had initiated the ship's automated repair systems, and was satisfied that we weren't going to fall out of the sky anytime soon. The damage to E-deck wasn't as bad as the captain had first thought; Lopez and Feng had sealed the hull breach with emergency supplies. Other maintenance tasks would take time, but they could be done on the fly.

We made the jump to Q-space as soon as we could. Although that wouldn't make us impossible to track, it would make it more difficult for the Black Spiral to give chase. That was the objective: to outrun the terrorist fleet, and lick our wounds. It gave us some breathing space, at the very least.

I held a debrief, of sorts. Lopez and Feng had missed most of the action, and Zero had fallen back from the main station to the *Firebird*. Captain Lestrade had been posted there right up to the point of the station takeover. None of them had seen much. Zero went over our intelligence about the Shard once again, and started to make some enquiries of the

Firebird's mainframe, but I knew that she would find nothing. Whatever Warlord had become, he was as *sub rosa* as they came.

"I've never heard of anything like it," Zero said.

"Neither have I," I replied.

"I'll do some digging, but I don't hold out much hope. Maybe he was the product of a black op, something covert?"

"It . . . it was like he was manipulating time-space," I said. Then shook my head. "That sounded a lot less stupid in my head."

Zero smiled. "I get it. I'll look into it."

"You do that."

I needed rest, and desperately. My neck throbbed, the bruises already turning a deep purple. Fresh damage to my ribs. My entire body felt as though I'd been pummelled by gunfire, which was more or less accurate. But the mission was more important, and sleep could wait. Half a packet of uppers – military-grade amphetamines – saw off any prospect of shut-eye.

Elena's data-packet was the logical next step in the oper- ation. She'd sent that to the *Firebird*, in the closing seconds of the engagement around Thane. Whatever Harris and the Watch had planned, it would be in there. I hoped that it had some answers.

So I commandeered the *Firebird*'s briefing room, and settled in for the night. Of course, it wasn't really night. But like most military starships, the *Firebird* operated a day–night cycle, even during deep-space flight. The human body's got to have its rhythm.

"Here we go . . ." I muttered to myself. "Computer, open data-packet."

"Affirmative."

The smart-desk lit with tri-D graphics, with information

streams, with the badges and seals of several military agencies. The Watch's reach was far, it seemed, but Elena had trusted me, and everything in the data-packet had been decrypted ready for review. I found a carefully organised briefing, complete with telemetry, jump-data, collected evidence on the Harbinger virus. Intelligence on the subject of the mission, Dr Olivia Locke, the former chief xeno-archaeologist of Tysis World. Harris had endorsed her file with annotations, with possible references to other leads.

I felt a real sadness as I read those notes. I lost focus, and it all came crashing down on my shoulders.

"Jesus Christo," I said. Rubbed a hand across my temples. "What the fuck am I going to do, Harris?"

I didn't expect an answer, but the darkness replied anyway.

"You got anything to drink?"

Harris stood behind me. He was still wearing the battered Directorate Ikarus suit, still clutching his stomach. Looking as though he had just stepped off Darkwater Farm.

"How – what?" I started. Much like when I'd seen Riggs in Simulant Storage, I was struggling to process this.

"Don't get up on my account," he said. Collapsed into a chair, with a tired groan.

"What are you doing here?" I managed. "Did you get off Darkwater?"

Harris gave a toothy grin. "Yeah, sure, kid. I got off Darkwater."

"But how?"

"Ah, we could go through the specifics, if you like. Maybe I could explain how I managed to fight off the Spiral, made a desperate run for the *Paladin*. Elena waiting for me, arms outstretched. That'd be a good story, right? Or maybe I found an evacuation-pod, one that the Jackals missed, and jumped into that. A passing Watch patrol picked me up."

"Is that how it happened?"

Harris' smile became fixed, eyes glassy. His stomach was weeping blood now. "We both know that's not how it worked though. We both know that I didn't make it off that station. And we both know that I'm only in your head."

"So ghosts like to drink now?"

"Everyone's got to have a vice," Harris said. "Even ghosts."

"I'm so sorry, Harris. I let you down."

Harris shook his head. "No, you didn't. I came back for you, on Jiog, because I wanted your help."

"I should've stopped the Spiral on Darkwater."

"You did what you could, kid. *I* don't matter. Not any more. But you and the Jackals: you can make a difference. The *Firebird* is your ship now."

"It looks that way."

"Hey, she's a decent ship. You could do a lot worse."

"I'd gladly hand her over to you," I said. "I'm not sure that I can take the responsibility. I've fucked things up so many times that I've lost count."

"We all make mistakes. Learning from them is what matters."

"Being dead seems to have filled you with moralising bullshit."

"Maybe," Harris said. He sat up in the chair. I could almost hear his bones creaking. "But I'm out of the game. Over to you, Keira."

"Any last words of advice, then?"

"This is your war now," Harris said. "Be careful how you fight it."

"Is that all I get from my old commanding officer?"

Harris sighed, looked at me some more. "Maybe listen to your squad. That's what I used to do. Sometimes, just sometimes, they might be the ones with the answers."

"*Novak* has answers?"

Harris shrugged. "I'm not saying him, necessarily. But the lifer has his uses, I'm sure. Watch yourself out there."

"Is that supposed to be a joke?"

"What?"

"'Watch' yourself?"

He shook his head. "I don't get it. You're weird sometimes, Jenkins."

I woke up with a start.

In a heartbeat, I took in the chamber. I was still sitting in the briefing room. Elena's data-packet was open on the smart-desk in front of me, but nothing else had changed. Harris, of course, wasn't there. The chair in which he'd been sitting was empty. Everything else just as it had been, except Zero was also present.

"You were sleeping," she said.

"Right, sure," I said. "Fine."

"You okay? Your neck looks . . ." She let that trail off, but the look on her face was enough. I sure as shit wasn't going to win any beauty pageants until I got my injuries seen to.

But I just nodded. "It's not as bad as it looks," I muttered. "I was reading the data-packet. I must've fallen asleep."

Zero gave me a knowing smile. "That's nothing to be ashamed of. It's been a long day."

"It has."

"I brought coffee," Zero said, sliding a plastic cup across the desk in front of me.

"Thanks. This is exactly what I need."

"You were talking in your sleep."

"I . . . I do that sometimes," I said. "That, and snore."

"Your secret's safe with me, ma'am."

"Still no sign of the *Paladin*?" I asked, hopefully.

Zero pursed her thin lips and shook her head. "Nothing, Jenk." She nodded at the smart-desk, at the open data. "Looks like Colonel Harris was well prepared for the next stage of the operation."

"He was," I said. *He is*, I wanted to say. "But there's nothing in here about the Shard, or about what we found at Darkwater."

"I've run a search," Zero said, "and I can't find anything, either."

"That's hardly surprising, but thanks for trying."

A quiet stretched between Zero and me, and she stared down at her coffee cup. There was something that she wanted to talk to me about, I realised.

"Go on," I said, sipping the coffee. "Talk."

"Is it that obvious?"

"We know each other too well, Zero. Something's been bugging you for a while. Since Jiog."

She bit at her lower lip. "Yeah, it has. I tried to tell you before . . . before the farm. But the moment didn't, well, seem right."

"Well now's the time," I said. "Go on."

Zero tried to keep smiling, but the expression dropped. She looked away from me: to the view-port that showed space outside.

"When we were on Jiog . . ." she started, faltering, "Kwan – Commander Kwan – he was, well, talking about the Aeon . . ."

The Aeon: a name or word that seemed to be following us around. Kwan had seemed to think that it was linked to our mission to find the *Hannover*. He'd called it a weapon; had been determined to find it as a result. At the time, it hadn't meant anything to me. I'd figured that Kwan had gone

325

insane. But the prisoner had referred to it as well. That was beyond coincidence; the Aeon must have some significance.

I wasn't tired any more. It was as though I was using a simulant, and my senses had become hyper-focused. Zero's uneasiness only heightened my concern. Something snapped inside me. *Riggs had the* Hannover's *data-core; the ship's black box . . .*

"Tell me that you didn't . . ." I said.

The pieces all fell together. Suddenly, everything made sense.

Zero shivered. "Don't be angry with me, Jenk. Please don't be angry."

"Tell me what happened," I said, as firmly but compassionately as I could.

"When we were aboard the *Santa Fe*, I opened the *Hannover*'s black box," Zero said. Speaking quickly now, as though that would make this all better, as though I wouldn't be able to follow what she was telling me: "When we escaped the Gyre, before we Q-jumped into Directorate space, I opened the *Hannover*'s black box. I read the files. I know what the Aeon is."

I called a briefing. The Jackals sat around the table, Pariah and Lestrade included.

"I—I tried to tell you before," Zero stammered.

"It's okay. Just calm down."

Zero kept talking, like she couldn't hear me, waving her arms around to demonstrate her point. "So much has happened. We escaped Jiog, found Lazarus. I kept trying to think of the best way to put it, the best time to tell you. We haven't stopped running since we left Directorate space, and then we had to plan the raid on the farm, and then Lazarus – well, you know about him, and I just—"

"Zero, please calm the fuck down."

Zero went quiet. Her mouth opened and closed a couple of times – looking a bit like a fish gasping for air, somewhat ironically – but she eventually stopped doing that as well. She was shaking. It'd taken some nerve for her to admit this; I had to give the girl credit for that.

"Tell me from the top," I said. "What did you do?"

"After we escaped the ark-ship, in the Gyre," she said, slowly, methodically, "and Riggs started the Q-jumps back to Alliance space, I opened the ECS *Hannover*'s black box. I cracked the encryption, and downloaded the contents to the *Santa Fe*'s mainframe"

"We talked about this," I said, remembering our conversation aboard the *Santa Fe*. "I told you—"

"That you didn't want it to be your problem," Zero completed. "But I thought that I was helping. It . . . it seemed like a good idea at the time. I was trying to take some of the pressure off you, ma'am. I figured that if I could, you know, take responsibility for it, then it would—"

"Did you tell Lazarus about this?" I asked.

Zero gave a small shake of her head. "No. You're the first person I've told."

"What is all fuss about?" Novak blustered. "Why are we bothered that Zero look in box? Is just data, yes, and Spiral have box anyway. Is no big secret."

But Feng had already figured it out. "Commander Kwan used the redactor on Zero," he said. "He looked in her head, Novak. Whatever Zero knows, the Directorate will too. Kwan has that information. They also have the *Santa Fe*, and whatever was downloaded to the data-stacks. The Directorate have an intelligence lead, and it's for that reason they won't give up."

Feng steepled his fingers in front of him, all formal

suddenly. He tended to get that way, I noticed, whenever we talked about the Directorate. His expression was fixed, maybe even a little broken. *Are you sure it's such a good idea*, a small voice taunted me, *to have the Directorate errand boy in the room while you discuss classified intelligence?*

Fuck you, I answered. *He's a Jackal.*

Support for Zero came from an unlikely ally. Lopez piped up, "How was Zero to know that we'd be captured by the Directorate? She didn't know that they would go poking around in her head when she opened the *Hannover*'s box."

"The black box was classified intelligence," I said. "What in the Maelstrom were you thinking, Zero? You more than anyone on this squad appreciate protocol."

"It was a bad call," she started. "It was just . . . well, we'd come so far. Our mission had cost so much. The crew of the *Santa Fe*, Major Sergkov . . . It didn't seem right that we would never get to know the *Hannover*'s mission. This sounds like I'm making excuses, but I'm really not. I know that it was wrong."

Feng's lips tightened into an approximation of a smile, although the expression was more disappointed than humorous. "I guess that people are paid to know these things, Zero. There's a reason why the grunts aren't told everything."

Novak crossed his enormous arms over his chest. "Still do not see big deal."

"So, Zero, what did you find?" I asked, leaning forward.

"This is going to make it worse yet. Commander Kwan and his surgeon used the redactor on me, and I . . . I can only remember parts of the download."

"Then tell us what can remember, yes?" Novak said.

"I'll try. The *Hannover* was sent into the Gyre to search for an asset." Zero looked down at the table now. Her voice took on an even tone, as though this was a mantra she had memorised. "Something capable of countering the Harbinger virus. Special asset X-93: also known as the Aeon."

"How did they know about the Aeon?" I questioned.

"I can't remember that part," Zero said. She was almost in discomfort, in pain, as she rubbed her head: rubbed the burns caused by the redactor's probes. "I don't know if I ever knew."

"What is the Aeon?"

"A weapon," Zero intoned. "It can scrub whole planets, or send stars supernova. We're talking interstellar-level devastation. I remember that part well enough."

"Holy Christo . . ." Feng said. "Can you imagine the Directorate with that sort of power?"

"Unfortunately I can," I said. *All too well . . .*

"The Aeon was a weapon used to oppose the Shard," Zero said, "during the Great Conflict between the Krell and Machines."

"The Shard?" I queried.

"Yes," said Zero, nodding. "There was something . . . something about a planet."

"Tysis World?" I led.

"That name sounds familiar," Zero answered. "But I can't remember why, or how it fits into this."

"Does the Aeon mean anything to you, P?" I asked Pariah. The xeno listened on silently, watching Zero. "It does not," it said.

The answer didn't strike me as very truthful, for some reason. But it was hard to evaluate the alien's responses – everything came out in that same flat voice. Something grazed the edge of my consciousness though.

"What sort of weapon is this Aeon?" Novak asked.

Zero shook with an imaginary chill. "I don't remember that. I've tried everything to bring the memory back, but the redactor: I think it permanently deleted some information from my head."

"At least Commander Kwan didn't get everything," Feng suggested. "We interrupted the download."

"Small blessing," I muttered. That had happened almost by chance; given another few minutes, the process would've been complete, and Zero would surely be dead . . . But whatever Zero had downloaded to the *Fe*'s data-stacks: Kwan had that.

Lopez looked to me. "Ma'am, what about a hypno-debrief? Would that help Zero remember, or at least let us get the information out of her head?"

Hypnotic debriefing was an intensive interrogation method that allowed Science Division to pull memories out of an operator's head. It was a much kinder process than redaction, and the Jackals had been subject to such a procedure once before, after the disaster at Daktar Outpost. Although it could be very painful, it tended to get results, and in most cases it was reasonably safe. There was just one problem.

"That's not going to work," I decided. "Zero can't use the simulators."

Zero was a negative. She didn't have data-ports, and as such couldn't use the tanks. That was a requirement for a hypno-debrief.

Lopez's shoulders sagged. "Good point."

"It's not the first time that my not being able to mount a tank has caused an issue," Zero said, "believe me."

But Lopez hadn't meant it that way. "Sorry, Zero. Didn't mean to piss on your show."

"It's okay," she said. "I'd love to get in a tank, do what you do. But you know how it is . . ."

Zero pulled back the sleeve of her suit, to expose her bare

forearms; the scar tissue vivid and angry, despite it being years since the data-ports had been removed.

"So," Novak summarised, "Aeon is weapon. We don't know what. Directorate know about Aeon because Zero look in box. And Spiral know about Aeon because they have same box."

"That's the size of it," Zero said. "Except that, maybe, the Directorate know more about this Aeon than I do, because I can't remember some of what I read . . ."

"Does it feel better to come clean about it?" Feng offered.

"I guess so," Zero agreed.

"Anyone else got any secrets that they want to tell?" I asked, looking around the table. Even P seemed to wither a little under my gaze. "Because now is the time to tell them."

No one reacted to that.

"Good."

It suddenly struck me that whether my squad had secrets or not wasn't the issue. I had been keeping secrets from them. Feng's implant, for a start. Did this new intelligence relate to that at all? Why was he still carrying the wetware around in his head?

"It's down to us now," I said. "The mission has to continue. We're going to finish Harris' work. We're going to stop this war before it starts."

I called up data on the main display, and colourful tri-D projections danced in front of me.

"This is our current location," I said, pointing out a system towards the Former Quarantine Zone. "And this is our objective." Another marker sprang to life. "Harris' original plan was to acquire material from Darkwater Farm, then jump to Mu-98."

I flagged quantum-jump points that took us to Mu-98, on the very edge of safe space. The *Firebird*'s mainframe had been updated with the latest intelligence, and Zero and Captain Lestrade had managed to access all of it. What they found was less than appealing. More Krell incursions into human space, and specifically within the vicinity of Mu-98, but that wasn't the worst of it.

"Does the Spiral have *every* Shard Gate now?" Lopez asked.

"Almost," I said. "The only Gates under Alliance control are here, here and here."

I pointed out the disparate locations. They were in the Mu-98, Beta Tanis and Tripolis Binary systems. Even the Gates that we had used to reach Darkwater were now listed as contested territory. None of the remaining Gate systems held much in the way of resources, but they were rapidly becoming major chokepoints for the war. Militarisation was inevitable, and I could well imagine how these systems would look. In combination with the Krell exodus, the Spiral's seizure of the Shard Gates would inevitably trigger a refugee crisis. Population centres would swell, life support would become stressed as it was required to sustain numbers it had never been designed to cater for. Food, water, air: the basics would become luxuries.

"Our objective is Kronstadt, in the Mu-98 star system," I said. "Specifically, the capital city Svoboda."

Novak grew misty-eyed. "Kronstadt?"

"That's right," I said. "It's Russian-held territory. Federal space."

"This system is in great danger," Pariah suddenly interjected.

The xeno stirred from behind me. The alien had been completely still, almost silent, throughout the briefing. Now its back-antennae were writhing, agitated. All eyes turned to the alien as it stood at the table.

"Something to add, P?"

"Yes," it said. "We do."

"Then be my guest."

"There are Kindred beyond that Gate," P said, indicating the Shard Gate in the Mu-98 system. "They mass in great numbers."

"Good fishes, or bad fishes?" Novak asked.

"*Bad* Kindred," P said. "Infected Kindred. We feel them."

Lopez swallowed, uncomfortable. "You *feel* them across this distance? We're still light-years away."

P made a clicking noise at the back of its throat. "Irrelevant. The Deep is disturbed, and the infected bide their time. It will not be long before this world is taken by the Harbinger."

"I guess that means we're on the clock," I said. "The Watch has a contact operating in this sector."

An image appeared in tri-D; a woman with a bob of blonde hair. Pretty, but features a little too cultured – too symmetrical – to be fully natural, I decided. Like Lopez, this woman had been under the surgeon's laser. As such, her age was difficult to guess, but she was probably approaching middle age by the standards of the Core Systems. Other than her rank and former position, Harris had compiled limited information on the woman. Like Lopez again, she'd come from a privileged family; had in fact studied at Proxima Colony's oldest university. But she wasn't Proximan. I'd wager that she was from the Faeran colonies; the draw of her chin, and her body shape, spoke of someone who had grown up in low-standard gravity. She had a slightly unreal look about her; unnaturally lithe, skin almost porcelain. She wore a civilian smart suit, a respirator hanging around her neck, and the image was posed; her smile feigned, face turned so that the photographer caught her from the best angle. Jaunty: that was the word.

"The picture is from a dig on Tysis World," I said, turning to look at Zero. It was surely no coincidence that Zero was able to recall that planet, and here was a woman with another link to the same location. "According to Harris' files, she turned rogue and left Science Division shortly after this picture was taken."

"So she's not military then?" Feng enquired.

"That's right," I said. "Her name is Olivia Locke. She is – or at least was – a xeno-archaeologist."

"A xeno what?" Lopez asked.

"She studies dead things and what they leave behind," I explained. "Dead alien things."

"What do we want from her?" Feng asked. "Why would Lazarus, or the Watch, need an archaeologist?"

"She was Chief Science Officer on Tysis World," I said, reading from the files as I spoke. "A planet which boasts the very first evidence of Shard life. The dig there uncovered numerous relics, and led to the discovery of the Shard Artefacts themselves."

"This is some pretty deep intel," Zero said. "That material is supposed to be classified. So what happened to this Locke woman?"

"According to her service record, she just upped and left a few years ago. Abandoned the project. She was bound by the Officials Secret Act, but simply disappeared. Went into hiding."

"Like Lazarus," Zero offered.

I hadn't realised the analogy until Zero mentioned it, but she had a point. "Yeah, like Lazarus."

"I wonder what she had to hide," said Lopez.

"That's what we're going to find out. Since her 'disappearance', Dr Locke has been in sporadic contact with the Watch. She claimed that she had vital intel on the Harbinger virus that she would only disclose to Conrad Harris. She made contact with the Watch some months ago, real-time, and requested exfiltration from Kronstadt. This was before things got really bad down there."

"But if she'll only release the intel to Lazarus, how are we going to persuade her to give it to us?" Zero queried.

"I don't know, put bluntly," I said. "But we'll cross that bridge when we come to it."

"Can we trust this woman?" Feng asked. "Could be a trap, for all we know."

I could understand Feng's scepticism. We knew next to nothing about Dr Locke, or her supposed intel, and the Jackals were currently AWOL. We also had both the Directorate and the Spiral on our tail. But my instinct told me that we had to go with this; that whatever Locke offered was worth the risk.

"It was obviously credible enough that Harris wanted to investigate it." I paused, watching the holo in front of me. "And dangerous enough that he thought we'd need sims."

"So what is plan?" Novak asked.

I hadn't actually got that far, and it rather depended on what resources we had available to us. "Lopez, Feng: what's the status on our equipment?"

Lopez smacked her lips. "We got a proper haul off Darkwater, ma'am. Ten bodies each, all on ice, ready for transition."

"That, and the *Firebird* was already equipped for a recon and assault operation," Feng added. "The armoury has M115 plasma battle-rifles, Widowmaker sidearms, personal plasma pistols, frag and incendiary grenades . . ." He shrugged. "More than enough firepower, I'd say."

"You can *never* have enough firepower," I answered back.

"We don't have a dropship or a shuttle aboard," Feng

said, excitedly, "but that's not going to be a problem. We have something better. It's a combat-suit, but not as we know it."

He opened a data-slate, slid it across the desk in my direction. It showed a schematic of a particularly well-armoured suit, made bulky by an oversized thruster EVAMP – "extra-vehicular mobility pack" – on the back, and a triple-reinforced main body. It resembled a flying casket, with a small face-plate, a squat profile and chunky limbs.

"A Type V Pathfinder drop-suit . . ." I muttered. "Nice."

The Pathfinder was the Alliance's equivalent of the Ikarus suit; a mixture of one-man space craft and personal combat-armour. The principle was simple enough. The drop-suit was launched from a ship in low orbit, and deployed directly into the theatre of conflict from space. There was nothing subtle about the Pathfinder, and nothing particularly sophisticated either. The drop-trooper doctrine wasn't a new idea – hell, it had been in service since Harris was a kid, serving with the Alliance Army in his own skin – but the Pathfinder armour was an update on the idea.

"They even have a drone intelligence package, hard-linked to each suit," Feng said. "I think that we're going to like the Pathfinder."

The schematic showed the Pathfinder armour with a clutch of hand-sized spy-drones, which could be controlled directly via the armour's neural-link. I'd used them before, and knew how useful they could be in the hands of a trained operator. But that was the catch: the Jackals had never used this type of armour, and there wouldn't be time to train them.

"You're supposed to be qualified to use a Pathfinder suit," I said. "To the best of my knowledge, I'm the only one with a Pathfinder badge."

"We used the Ikarus suits on Jiog," Lopez said, defiantly,

"and that was in our own skins. I'm sure that a Pathfinder suit can't be that different, right?"

"Wrong," I said. "The Pathfinder armour has a direct neural-link with the simulant user. It's a difficult mistress."

The Jackals' faces all turned glum at that. They were still a green outfit, and we hadn't yet moved on to the big toys used by many Sim Ops squads. It didn't surprise me that Phoenix Squad had been assigned this sort of advanced equipment; they were a veteran unit. Deploying a green team like the Jackals with Pathfinder armour might well be throwing away bodies.

"How many suits do we have?"

"Twenty units," Feng said. "All fully charged."

"What a waste . . ." Lopez said.

"Whining isn't going to make me change my mind," I said. "Not only that, Lopez, but if we're expecting to get Dr Locke off Kronstadt, we'll need transport. The Pathfinder armour will get us down to the surface, but it won't get us back."

"There's no way this ship can take atmospheric flight," Captain Lestrade chipped in, putting to rest any idea that the *Firebird* could make a drop-off or pick-up. "She's not designed for atmo, for a start, but even if we could risk a drop, that repair job on E-deck isn't going to survive re-entry and exit."

"So how are we going to get onto Kronstadt, and back out?" Lopez asked.

"I'll think about it," I said. "There's still time before we reach Mu-98."

"The ship already has a Simulant Operations Centre," Zero completed. "One of the benefits of hijacking an Army Intruder, I guess. I'll get that arranged how I like it."

I winced at Zero's use of the word "hijack", but did my best to hide it. "Fine. Briefing's over, people."

The briefing broke up, but I still had work to do. Novak wasn't the only Jackal keeping secrets.

I needed to speak with Pariah.

We might've changed ships, but Pariah had simply transplanted its lair from one location to another, and the *Firebird*'s engineering room now stank to the Core and back; walls covered in fish guts. I shut the door behind me, and the overhead glow-globes flickered on.

Pariah was waiting for me. It blinked away the light.

"You weren't being honest back in the briefing room, P. I'd appreciate it if you told me the truth."

"Clarify," the alien said, tilting its head.

"I had a dog, when I was a kid," I said, pacing the chamber. "You know, it did that same thing."

"Did what?"

"Cock its head at me. I used to think that meant it was listening to me. Then, one day, someone told me that it meant it was trying to *look* like it was listening."

P tilted its head again. "We are not canine. We are Kindred."

"But which is it, P? Are you listening to me – understanding me – or just *pretending* to understand?"

Pariah paused. "We understand you without words, if that is what Jenkins-other means."

I rubbed my head. Sometimes, being close to the xeno gave me a deep headache. I used to put that down to the alien's scent, but wasn't so sure any more. Just as P was changing, maybe I was too.

"We've shared a connection," I said. "Aboard Darkwater, I felt you in my head. But I was in your head, too."

"Such is to be part of the Collective," P said. "To be immersed in the Deep."

"Exactly. When Zero told us about the Aeon, I felt something from you."

It hadn't been much more than a ghost of a feeling; tantalisingly close, then gone. Sometimes, I got the sense that Pariah was chasing these phantoms around its own head, searching for answers, trying to unlock forbidden knowledge. The Krell psyche was vast, unknowable. If I focused too hard, the Collective – the Deep – would drag me in . . .

"What is the Aeon, P?"

"We do not know," Pariah said. "Not yet. Not fully."

"Then tell me what you do know."

"It is something that the Collective has known of for a long, long time. Since the awakening, things have become clearer for us, but our knowledge is not always reliable."

"Back on Darkwater, when you assaulted the Simulant Operations Centre, you felt something. You knew that there were Shard specimens on the farm, didn't you?"

"We felt their presence," P said. "It was a wrongness. An absence. That is what the Machines represent to us: an absence of life."

"Are the Aeon and the Shard connected?"

"The Collective knows, but we do not."

"I need to know if that changes. I've fought the Shard before. I know what the Machines are capable of."

"As do we," P said. "Knowledge of the Great Conflict, of the time before the Alliance-others were even known to the Kindred, is deep knowing."

"Do you know why the Shard were on Darkwater?"

"We do not. We wish that we did."

"When we reach Kronstadt, you're not going to be able to come with us," I explained. "This is a populated Alliance world, not some backwater colony. You're out of this one, P."

I felt a nagging emotion ebbing from the xeno: like psychic bleed. P wasn't happy with my decision. It felt hungry.

"Understood," Pariah intoned, nonetheless. "We will await direction."

"Play nice with Zero. I want you to be shipboard security, our early-warning system. First sign you get that the Harbinger-infected Krell might break through the Shard Gate, I need to know. You get any weird premonitions or bad feelings; tell Zero."

P cocked its head again. "Affirmative."

I turned to leave, but Pariah called after me.

"What happened to Jenkins' canine-other?" it asked.

"The dog got rabies. We had to put it down."

CHAPTER TWENTY-TWO

WAR THINGS

My military career had taken me the length and breadth of the galaxy, but I'd never been to Kronstadt before. So I did my prep, because too often the devil of a military op is in the detail. I buckled down and accessed the *Firebird*'s planetary database, pulling up everything I could find on the planet and its star system. Zero would've been proud; and in fact, I found her digital bookmarks across the files, suggesting that she had already been here.

Although I'd never visited, I'd already heard of Kronstadt. The planet had a pretty unique reputation. It was a Type III stellar body, in orbit around a star with the rather catchy designation Mu-98. Kronstadt had an atmosphere, and during the Second Space Age it had been flagged by the Alliance as a location capable of supporting human life, without the need for extensive terraforming: throw up a couple of atmosphere grids, and call it a day. The Russian Federation had been the first nation out there, and had staked their claim on Kronstadt. But the Russian settlers had found Kronstadt to be nowhere near as hospitable as Science

Division had expected. The system's sun put out an unhealthy amount of radiation, and did something strange to the weather patterns. The star, the debris in the atmosphere, and a dozen other local variables meant that acid rain wasn't just an inconvenience on Kronstadt: it was a killer.

So why did the Russian Federation settle good ol' Kronstadt? During the Krell War – back when we'd been engaged in conflict with the fishes – the system had attracted the attention of both species due to the reliability of quantum-streams in this sector. Putting it simply, you could jump ships from the Core Systems, and then send them onwards to the Quarantine Zone where the real action was taking place. That made Mu-98 an important strategic location, and something worth holding on to.

We watched the *Firebird*'s long-distance scopes as the ship approached the edge of the Mu-98 system. The Jackals poised at tactical stations, Pariah crouched at the main display.

"Cutting thrust," Captain Lestrade declared. "We're in Mu-98's outer orbit."

We drifted, scopes and scanners probing the surrounding space.

"Are we still running dark?" I asked.

"Yes, ma'am," Lestrade said. "Our military transponder is inactive. We can watch, but we aren't being watched."

"Keep us so until I say otherwise."

"You can thank Zero for that," Lestrade said.

Zero gave a self-conscious smile. "I try."

"Train our long-distance scopes on Kronstadt," I ordered. "I want as much information on that planet as we can get at this range."

Soon Kronstadt appeared in all its glory, filling the tactical display. The planet was mainly grey and barren, slashed with bands of dirty cloud cover. A ripple of green around the equator – which I took to be indigenous flora, forced into retreat over the decades – was losing the struggle against relentless and planet-wide industrialisation, the result of human occupation. There were dozens of cities and major population centres; some domed, others open to the harsh environment, but all sprawling, out of control. Atmosphere grids that looked like huge skeletal umbrellas covered most of the southern hemisphere, restraining the weather system, providing breathable air. Used correctly, the atmosphere grid could be a remarkable terraforming tool. But the grids here weren't anything like those on Alpha Centauri, or the more affluent Alliance colonies. Badly maintained, collapsed in places so that the cities beneath could be seen from space, this technology had crippled the world's ecosystem. Just looking at Kronstadt, I could almost feel the chill of the wind against my skin, the choking fumes caused by rampant industry . . .

"You must be real proud," Feng said.

The comment had been directed at Novak, and the implication was obvious: *who would be proud of a world like this?* Novak, however, didn't take it that way at all. He sucked his teeth and nodded.

"Of course," he said. "This is mighty Kronstadt. Is shining jewel of Russian Federation's space programme, yes?"

"It's also the *only* jewel in the Federation's programme," Zero said. "The Fed doesn't have any other extra-solar colonies." Yeah, she had definitely been in the mainframe. She went on: "The planet itself has a rather chequered history."

Feng grinned, looked to Novak. "Russian, huh? So everyone sits around drinking vodka and smoking cigars?"

I shook my head. "No, but everyone does run around killing the shit out of each other. Criminal gangs are in control of most of the northern arcologies, and the south isn't much better. The Russians aren't picky about who governs this place. The Black Spiral, and many of the criminal organisations they count as allies, have support here."

Zero nodded, knowingly. "It's pretty lawless."

"Is just rough round edges," Novak suggested.

"That's a very generous assessment of Kronstadt's status," I said.

Lopez looked less than impressed as the tactical display built up a picture of Kronstadt. "It looks awful dirty," she muttered. "And why are there so many ships out here?"

"Is natural, for such busy port. Kronstadt is special."

"Real special," Lopez echoed. "Are you crying, Novak?"

Novak looked away. "No. Of course not."

"You are most definitely crying," Lopez said.

"Leave it. I am just . . . emotional, is all."

Lopez frowned dramatically. "The Big Man is emotional? Now I've heard it all."

Zero went on with her potted history of the planet. "Kronstadt was settled during the Second Space Age. It's been occupied for almost a hundred years, and there were once plans to expand out here. But times change, and priorities shift. The Russian Federation were struggling to cope with the Directorate, back on Old Earth, and they gave up on the extra-solar colonisation programme. This place is a relic of an earlier age."

"And what a relic," Novak said, wistfully, sounding as though Zero had just paid him the biggest compliment ever. "Was discovered by greatest Russian space explorer of all time, Rejeik Nikolai. Now, there was a real man."

"By the sound of things," Feng suggested, "being a 'Russian space explorer' puts this guy in a pretty small group . . ."

344

"What would you know, Chino?" Novak countered. "You will find not so much likings for you down there. Russians and Directorate normally do not mix."

Feng let the slight roll off. "So I guess you and me getting along is just a fluke?"

Novak didn't reply to that.

"The Russian connection is not the only reason Kronstadt is so special," Zero said. "It's also the most isolated remaining Shard Gate in the network."

She trained the *Firebird*'s scope array on the stellar anomaly towards the heart of the system. Pale blue energy spilled from within the rent in time-space. The colours projected from the open Shard Gate were so intense – despite being only computer reproductions of the real image – that I even shielded my eyes. I'd seen many Shard Gates before, but this one looked weirder than usual.

"Little bit of warning next time," I suggested.

"Sorry about that," Zero muttered. "This is the Kronstadt Gate."

"That's nice, real nice," Lopez said.

"It was discovered before the Alliance figured out how the Gates actually work, and what they are," Zero went on. "The original expeditionary force thought that it was a quantum rift. Of course, it doesn't demonstrate the same non-baryonic spectral output as a Q-rift, so I really don't know what they were thinking . . ." She shook her head, laughing to herself. "They must've been crazy. Of course, now we know otherwise. The Gate has been fully mapped: it leads directly into the Maelstrom."

Novak gave another sigh, pride leaking out of every pore. "Is best Shard Gate in whole Alliance."

"Soon, it might be the only Shard Gate in the Alliance," I added.

345

"It looks . . ." Lopez started, struggling to find the right word, then settling on: "*disturbed.*"

"It is," Captain Lestrade said. "This system is drenched with ship-to-ship communications, much of it unencrypted. Lots of sailors are talking about the Gate's emissions. It appears that they're at an all-time peak; as though the Gate is open, permanently."

Pariah became animated at that, lurching to the tactical display to absorb the data there. I could feel the wave of emotion coming off the xeno as it panned its head back and forth.

"The infected Kindred mass on the other side of the Gate," P explained. "But they are not the first to come here."

Dozens of bio-ships – or rather their remains – floated in the vicinity. Several blackened hulks sat in orbit around Kronstadt, absent of any detectable life signs. Readings suggested that just as many had been vaporised or reduced to nothing more than space debris. With a stab of sympathy, I realised that at least one ark-ship had been destroyed out here. The husk of that vessel had been drawn into Mu-98's orbit like another planet.

"The last war-fleet to come through was Red Fin," Zero explained. "They tried to make contact with the local Navy assets." She swallowed, nervously. "But it appears that the Alliance fleet has been issued 'shoot first' orders."

"So they weren't even infected?" Lopez sighed. "This is some bad shit."

"There have been several incursions," Zero continued. "Six recorded in the last month, in fact. The Alliance Navy are holding the line, but who knows when the next wave will come."

P looked up, a deathly serious expression on its face. "Soon," it said. "We feel them."

"They'll have some resistance when they get here," Captain Lestrade said. "The fleet is waiting for them. The Alliance Navy has a cordon around the inner planets."

There was a long moment of silence as the Jackals took in the mustered fleet; the final and only line of defence between the Krell and us. In other circumstances, I'd have found the Navy's battlegroup impressive. Three dreadnoughts were moored at high reach. Portable fortresses, the dreadnoughts were the flagships for the rest of the Alliance fleet. Then there were the battlecruisers, corvettes, gunships – and everything in between.

One of the Alliance dreadnoughts – a bulldog of a warship, with a battle-scarred hull and the name *Io's Last* stencilled on her hide – was tasked with overseeing the Gate. Even at this distance, we were registering a dozen active weapons signatures, trained on the Gate and surrounding space. A swarm of fighters, gunships and shuttles flitted about the enormous ship, creating a safe zone that covered Kronstadt's six moons, and space lanes between the *Last* and some of the other warships.

"Which brings us to our next problem," Captain Lestrade said. "The Navy has complete control of the Mu-98 system. Nothing is getting in or out, not without their knowledge."

The *Firebird* was still dark, but it was obvious that the Navy battlegroup were monitoring space traffic in the area. If we revealed ourselves to the Alliance fleet, there was a damned good chance that we'd be facing a court martial. We'd endangered Alliance personnel, stolen equipment, hijacked a ship. And for what reason? We were chasing unverified intelligence on the say-so of a dead man . . .

"So how are we going to do this?" Feng asked.

"Getting down there isn't going to be a problem," I said. "But we can't use the Pathfinder suits to evacuate Dr Locke.

347

The armour is a one-way ticket. Without a shuttle, we won't be able to get Locke off-world."

"Surely we aren't going down there in our real skins?" Lopez ventured.

I shook my head. My neck, ribs and everything else still hurt, and that wasn't an option. "Not even I am that crazy," I said. "We're going to treat this like an infiltration operation."

"Sounds risky," Lopez objected. "Too risky."

"Not if we use simulants."

"But how we do that?" Novak asked. "You say yourself; we have no shuttle."

I focused the tactical display on the nearest fleet of starships. It was made up of a dozen or so haulers and freighters, loosely grouped together for security. Not all of the traffic in the area was military.

"We're going to board a refugee ship and take a ride down to Kronstadt. Once we're on the surface, we'll find and secure the asset. Then we'll take another transport back into orbit, rendezvous with the *Bird*, and jump system."

Zero twisted her lip, thinking on that. "The *Firebird*'s neural-link array has a decent range. We would need to shadow you from a safe distance, to maintain connection with your simulants, but it's possible."

Captain Lestrade approved. "This could work," he said. "If we can get parked in a low orbit, we may even be able to watch you with the *Bird*'s scopes. That could provide some orbital intelligence."

"But the sims are assault-types," Lopez complained. "What about weapons and armour? There's no way a refugee ship is going to let us aboard in combat-suits."

"Girl wants her big guns, yes?" Novak laughed. "You want to try out this Pathfinder armour!"

"Of course I do," Lopez admitted, "but it isn't that. The sims are bigger, meaner, better than humans. We join up with a refugee fleet and bodies like that . . . Well, I can't see it working."

"We won't be in uniform," I argued. "We'll take some shipboard fatigues, maybe some sidearms from the ship's armoury. We can dirty the bodies up. The disguise won't be perfect, but if we encounter any trouble we can extract back to the *Firebird* and bail out."

Novak and Feng nodded in agreement – no doubt eager to make the next transition – but Lopez was still unsatisfied.

"How are we going to get aboard a civilian ship?" she queried.

"We will steal one," Novak suggested.

I shook my head. "No one's stealing anything. These are Alliance citizens, and those ships are all they have. We're not taking them by force."

I watched the dark outside, the ever-expanding morass of debris that circled the outer rim of Mu-98 system. Closer now, the *Firebird*'s AI had detected several emergency broadcasts. I selected one of those signals.

"We use an evacuation-pod. That's how we get aboard a ship."

Zero grinned. "This sounds like it might actually work."

Even Captain Lestrade looked a little bit impressed with my ingenuity. "The *Firebird* has four pods. We could modify one, remove the identifier. It wouldn't stand up to scrutiny – not for long – but it'd pass a cursory inspection."

"Then that's the plan, Jackals," I said.

Lopez crossed her arms over her chest. "Can I at least load up the Pathfinder suits, and fresh skins, just in case?"

It would be a wasted effort, but if it made Lopez feel better, what the hell?

"You do that, Lopez, although I hope we won't need them. Sixty minutes to transition, people."

Sixty minutes later, the Jackals were strapped into the emergency crash couches inside one of the *Firebird*'s evac-pods. I sat up front with Feng, watching space through the shielded view-port, with Novak and Lopez in the rear.

"Get settled in," Captain Lestrade suggested. "Running final checks."

"I take it this is going to be bumpy," Lopez griped.

"That's about right," I answered. "Try holding on to something."

"Real cosy . . ." Lopez muttered.

"Cosy" was an understatement: the evac-pod was made to contain six crewmen in real skins, not four simulants. Lopez fidgeted noisily behind me, unable to get comfortable in the safety webbing.

"At least now we know how Ving felt," Feng added.

"Great," sighed Lopez. "That's exactly what I needed."

"You're clear for launch," said Lestrade.

"Copy that. Good to go."

Zero remotely keyed the ignition sequence. "Launching."

There was a stomach-churning lurch as the pod fired from the *Firebird*'s belly. Without a gravity-drive, everything not strapped down was in freefall. Space slid by outside.

"That's a safe launch," Captain Lestrade said. "*Firebird* adopting retreat pattern."

The pod's console showed Lestrade's progress, as he took the *Firebird* into the cover of a nearby moon. The captain had a difficult line to walk, or fly as the case may be. He needed to be close enough to maintain the neural-link between the sims and our real bodies, but not so close that questions would be asked by any potential saviour.

We didn't want this to look like a scam or ambush, after all.

The pod slowed. My stomach settled.

I flexed an arm, felt the simulant muscles respond. Usually, when I made transition, the war-hunger filled me. This was different: there was no thrumming in my blood, and the body felt without purpose. I was made for war, not infiltration. No combat-suit, no null-shield: this was not the Sim Ops that I knew. We didn't even have proper weapons. Each of us carried a single Widowmaker pistol; a basic semi-automatic kinetic. I was the only one with a comms capability, via the wrist-comp strapped to my arm. Using that, I opened a channel back to Zero, in the *Firebird*'s Simulant Operations Centre.

"Comms check. Do you copy, Zero?'

"That's an affirmative. *Firebird* copies."

"We'll keep comms to a minimum," I decided. "Don't want any potential rescue ships becoming suspicious."

"Copy that," Zero agreed.

"I'll send a sitrep once we reach Kronstadt. But until then, comms-quiet."

"Understood."

I removed my ear-piece, folded away the device's stalk. The small communicator was usually my lifeline to the SOC, from which Zero could provide operational intel. That sort of data could make or break a mission. But fugees didn't carry military-spec comms tech, and so I had to let it go. If we really needed her, Zero could home in on the comm signal, send assistance via the *Firebird*. I hoped it wouldn't come to that.

"This is never going to work," Lopez argued. "We look like freaking giants."

"Lots of colonies have oversized gene-types," I said.

"Humanity comes in many shapes and forms, Lopez. Not everywhere is as boring as Proxima Colony. Boreham's World, for instance."

"Never even heard of it," Lopez answered. "Sounds made up."

"And you've heard of every occupied planet in the Alliance, huh?" Feng countered.

"Exactly," I said. "And as it happens, it is made up. But we're dealing with civilians, and no one is going to have the facilities to check our identities. All we need to do is get onto a ship."

Each of us was over six and a half foot tall; and Novak in particular was especially big. But beyond height and build, there was nothing to identify us as Army. We all wore ship-board smart-suits plundered from the *Firebird*'s lockers with the crew badges and insignia removed; of a type that were found on a million civvie starships.

"Are you worried people will recognise you?" Novak asked Lopez. "It happened on farm, yes?"

"This is different," Feng said. "Lopez got recognised because she was in her real skin." He turned to look at her now. "I don't think the Senator himself would recognise Lopez without all her bodywork . . ."

"Fuck you, Feng."

It was true that there was little risk of anyone recognising Lopez as she was now. Her simulant body was almost twice her real skin's mass, the features of her face a better copy of Lopez before she'd gone under the knife.

"Maybe the new haircut is making her cranky," Novak suggested.

"I think it suits you, Lopez," I said.

As a final precaution, I'd insisted on Lopez's hair being cut short. It didn't exactly reflect fashion on the Core

Systems, unless having a craggy bob – fringe quite obviously hacked with a pair of shipboard safety scissors – had suddenly come in style. The Core had some crazy fashions, but I doubted this was one of them.

"We're going to be on Russian soil," Lopez said. "You're the one who should be worried about being recognised, Novak. Probably all kinds of gangers down there. Maybe we'll meet some of those Sons of Balash assholes."

Novak narrowed his eyes and grinned. "Can only hope."

In his real skin, Novak was a walking skin-canvas. But his sim was completely tattoo-free, and it was almost disconcerting to look at the pale flesh of his face and head. His hair was shaven, showing the contours of his head.

"Coming up on the main refugee fleet," Feng said, as the evac-pod's thrusters cut.

"Activate our emergency beacon."

"Affirmative."

The fleet consisted of a dozen civilian ships. We sailed alongside them, unobtrusively.

"Requesting immediate assistance," I said, over the general channel. "Please respond. We are the survivors of an attack by a Krell bio-ship. Please respond. We have limited oxygen. We are able to offer this pod as salvage."

We waited.

A half-hour passed, and several ships went with it. They were ramshackle things, patched and re-patched, barely capable of flight. No one answered our distress call.

"What did I say?" Lopez said, confidently. "This isn't going to work. We should get recalled and use those Pathfinder suits—"

The console chimed with an incoming transmission.

"What do we have here?" I asked.

A small hauler crawled into visual range.

"Her name's the *Varyag*," Feng explained, as the ship's registration and identification data appeared on the evac-pod's flight console. The ship's flanks were battered and bruised, suggesting a lifetime among Mu-98's asteroid fields. "She's a prospector ship."

"This is *Varyag*," said a voice. The words were in Standard, but heavy with a Slavic accent. "We read you. The pod is available as salvage, you say?"

The fish has taken the bait.

"That's right."

"Do you have anything else to trade?"

I knew that this was coming, and we'd planned for it.

"We've got four power cells," I said. We had to play the part: the offer couldn't appear unrealistic or too valuable. Cells were pretty much universal currency among space travellers. "We're looking for safe passage to Kronstadt."

The voice sniggered. Someone else in the background laughed. "You and the rest of them, lady."

"Can you help us or not?"

"Four cells, you say? And we get to keep the pod?"

"You heard me. We need immediate pick-up. Can you help or not?"

There was a pause. "All right. You got yourself a deal."

"Turning our navigational control over to you, Captain."

I cut the comm, breathed a sigh of relief.

The *Varyag* was already manoeuvring on an intercept course. Soon our evac-pod was moving alongside the other ship: ready to be taken aboard.

"See, Lopez," I said. "All it takes is a little faith."

The *Varyag*'s captain – or the ship's operator, at least – met us in the vessel's dock. He was a little man with leathery skin and a thatch of wild, dark hair, wearing a spacesuit with no ship identifier, and carrying an ancient-looking pistol at his belt.

"Name's Bukov," he said, by way of introduction, as we left the pod. Despite his accent, he didn't look very Russian at all.

"I'm Keira Jenkins," I said. Knowing that these were civilian operators, I had no fear of using my real name. "We were running a mining operation out in the far-orbits. This is all that's left of my crew."

"They grow them big where you come from, then?"

"Something like that."

The man at Bukov's side – who I instantly tagged as Sidekick – sniggered noisily. A lanky shaven-head brute of a thing, with few remaining teeth, he made no disguise of the fact that he was the captain's bodyguard. Sidekick had poor-quality gang-tattoos liberally scattered over his face, and Novak eyed him warily. I could imagine him reading every marking on the ugly bastard's flesh as though it were a secret language that only they shared. Novak – in the sim – had no history to show the other man.

"We're from Boreham's World," I said. "Extreme height and build are genetic anomalies."

"Right, right. Sure."

"You want to make a thing of it?" Novak questioned. He glared at Sidekick, then at Bukov.

Sidekick snorted another laugh, but Bukov just shrugged. "Fine. What do I care?"

"What do we care?" repeated Sidekick, nodding.

"We were attacked by those infected Krell," I explained. "Our ship went down, and we had no choice but to evacuate. The rest of my crew were lost."

Bukov circled the pod, making it clear that this was what he was really interested in. It currently sat in a holding cradle, in the centre of a cargo bay, hull still creaking and groaning, taking the stress of adapting to atmosphere. The paper-thin explanation for our presence out here, and where we were from, were largely irrelevant to Bukov. I'd read this situation pretty much right.

"Profit is king," Bukov muttered, twitching his pug-nose at the pod. He barked commands in Russian to Sidekick. The bigger man began lashing the pod in place with some heavy chains. "Is good salvage."

Although Zero had done her best to scrub the pod's data-stacks, I knew that a proper examination would reveal its origin. I wasn't worried about that though: Bukov didn't look like the sort of guy to be troubled by such an enquiry.

"You have cells also?" he asked.

"As promised."

Novak hauled the energy cells from inside the pod, and dropped them at Bukov's feet with a loud thump. The captain inspected them cursorily and gave another shrug.

"Fine. We take you aboard." He turned his back, and started off into the ship. "Come, here is bridge."

The *Varyag*'s bridge was a tiny room at the nose of the ship, crewed by a handful of Russian sailors who didn't even bother to look up as we entered. The air was thick with cigarette smoke; Bukov sniffed the atmosphere as he entered, and yelled something in Russian at the pilot. She gave him the finger and carried on sucking on the stub of a cigarette.

"This is crew," Bukov said. "I run lean. Is less mouths to feed, better for profit." He shrugged again, which seemed to be something he did a lot. "Means we can carry more cargo. We do many runs. Good for business, yes?"

"Sure," Feng muttered.

"We have no trouble with the Chino," Bukov muttered. "Many on Kronstadt will do, you understand? You pay for ride, then no trouble for me. But I tell you of this just for warning."

"We know," Novak said. He fired something back at Bukov in his mother-tongue, and the other man answered, nodding slowly.

"Big one is Russian too, yes?"

"Am Russian," Novak said, with his trademark solemnity. "Am Norilsk. From Old Earth."

Bukov gave a noncommittal grimace, as if to say he didn't really care which part of Russia Novak came from.

The *Varyag*'s tactical display was an ancient two-D version, but showed just how desperate things in surrounding space had become. We circled through a cloud of ships, evacuation-pods and shuttles. Navy vessels flitted to and from Kronstadt, ignoring the pleas of other evacuation-pods that littered the sector.

"I . . . I've never seen anything like this," Lopez said.

"I have," I said. "Mau Tanis."

Zero's home colony. The ships in orbit. The death. The destruction. The complete loss of everything that tied a citizen to his or her world.

"We have to stop it," Lopez said quietly. "We have to do whatever we can to finish this war."

"Be quiet, Lopez," Feng said.

This was the sharp end of the exodus.

"What if people don't have pods to trade?" Lopez enquired.

Bukov looked at Lopez as though she were talking crazy. "Then they do not come aboard. Is not charity."

Novak grunted. "Some things never change."

"How far is Kronstadt?" I asked. "We've been in that pod

for three days, give or take. I'm not sure how far we drifted off-course."

"Is not far. Few hours, if cordon allows."

"We could do with some rest."

"Fine. Bed down wherever. Will let you know when we reach Kronstadt."

It went without saying that we weren't the only fugees on the ship. Captain Bukov was a capitalist, and in war he saw opportunity. He might run his crew lean, but the corridors and open cabins of the *Varyag* were crammed with civilians. A family from the Outer Rim. Another flight crew, out of a neighbouring system. A couple who proclaimed themselves Singularity Cultists, the last surviving members of a church from one of the local moons.

I watched two children – the offspring of the Outer Rim family – make their own entertainment with some metal chips that Bukov had given them. I've never been good with ages, and I couldn't tell whether these kids were five or ten. Of course, the fact that they were painfully emaciated and wearing oversized crew-suits didn't exactly help.

Lopez came to sit down next to me. She had hidden a ration pack in her suit when we'd left the evac-pod, and had distributed it to the children. They stopped their game, and enthusiastically shared Acturan insect-bites and Proximan cornbread.

"That was decent of you," I said, keeping my voice quiet, the conversation just between us.

Simulants could eat, *did* eat, but it wasn't necessary. The body would burn up fat, eventually turn against itself. That was kind of the purpose. We were disposable.

"I'm not always a heartless bitch," she said.

"I never said you were."

"The others do, though, right?"

I laughed. "I didn't think that you cared about what they thought."

"Maybe I don't," Lopez said. "They say that I'm a princess."

"Your callsign is Senator, last time I checked."

Lopez ricked her lip into a grimace. "You know what I mean."

"Look, your background is what it is. Don't let them get to you."

"I'm not, but that's my point: my background is important. Maybe . . ." she paused, shrugged, "maybe I can make a difference. Maybe I have a responsibility to change this, if I can."

"Perhaps. Do you think that your father would listen to you?"

"Probably not. But if I could try . . . then maybe I should?"

"Maybe."

The children were ravenously eating scraps of freeze-dried cornbread: devouring it as though it were a delicacy.

"They must be real hungry," I said. "I've eaten that cornbread. It tastes like shit."

I saw a little of Zero – of Zoe Campbell – in the eyes of the children on the ship. They, and their parents, were no longer people. They had become haunted, empty. This was the cycle repeating itself, as it would forever.

"This is what will happen," Lopez said, as she watched the children. "Unless we stop it, the war with the Krell will start all over again. It will be an eternity of war."

"It won't happen. We'll see to it."

CHAPTER TWENTY-THREE

SOMEONE'S DREAM

"We must land on planet," Bukov said. "My pilot; she is good. Ship can take atmosphere, no problem."

The pilot shouted a string of expletives in Russian, although Bukov ignored her.

"You stay, watch the show," Bukov insisted of us.

"To see the Motherland," Novak muttered, "it is truly something. Yes?"

He turned abruptly to Lopez and Feng, who gave autonomic nods.

"Sure thing," Lopez said, as though persuaded by the force of his conviction.

"Of course," Novak said, waving a hand at the display, "you are not seeing it in best light. War is not good for any planet."

If nothing else, Novak had that part right.

"Where will we be landing?" I asked Bukov. "We need to get to Svoboda."

"We use cosmodrome at Svoboda," he answered. "Is safest place for fugees. Biggest city on planet."

The *Varyag* fell in with other military and civilian traffic. The ship shuddered around us, as it grazed atmosphere, and the Jackals grappled with any surface they could to stay upright. Outside, space began to lose its vibrancy, the blackness of the void giving way to the thermosphere.

"Try not to hit anything," Lopez suggested.

"Yark is good pilot," Bukov said. "She never had crash yet!"

The entire bridge shook with renewed vigour, the *Varyag*'s space frame groaning. The sudden and violent motion had its effect on Novak, who turned a sickly green as the gravity well caught us. Other ships took the same descent pattern, their hulls glowing orange and white as they breached the planet's atmosphere.

Just then, the *Varyag*'s comms console began to blurt a warning.

"*This is a Type 12 Alliance outpost. Full identification will be required from all citizens before processing by traffic control. Transgressors will be detained and may be deported, or executed as appropriate.*"

The message repeated in Standard, then again in Russian. Meanwhile, a siren sounded across the bridge, screens flashing red with safety warnings.

"What's happening?" Lopez asked.

"Is fine!" Bukov insisted. "Is not problem!"

"We're being painted by targeting lasers," Feng said, peering at the nearest screen. "Pull us out!"

Bukov grappled with the console, pushing aside a scrawny young crewman. He jabbed buttons, yelled something into the machine.

"What's he saying?" I asked Novak.

Despite his obvious discomfort, Novak grinned. "He says that he has friend in Space Control. That he pay his tax, and wants to land."

The message loop abruptly ceased.

"Bukov, my friend!" answered the same voice. "You are back again so soon."

"Yes, yes. I come with gift, yes? Stop pointing lasers at us, or there will be nothing left to give you."

The other man laughed. "Of course. Safe journey, my friend."

The ship's descent pattern gradually evened out, although her hull kept screaming. We flew through a swirling mass of grey clouds, which eventually cleared to an even greyer sky.

"We are coming up on Svoboda," Bukov said, waving at the view-ports.

Although I had no headgear – no tactical helmet or scope array – at this range, with my improved simulant vision, I could make out more than enough detail to get a measure of the place. Nothing here was new, and nothing here was welcoming. The only flashes of colour amid the artificial landscape were from neon signs and noticeboards; some almost as tall as the crumbling starscrapers. The city was a collection of jagged towers, dilapidated habitation modules, crumbling factories.

The terraforming grid stretched over most of the settlement. What had probably started out as a miracle of civil engineering had seen better days, and parts of the grid had collapsed, fallen onto the city below. Closer still, the girders of the grid were spaced kilometres apart, easily wide enough to allow starships to pass through. Svoboda itself was visible beneath the grid.

There was a pained rhythm to the planet, and the city. Sure, the Krell were here, and the tension such a threat produced was so extreme that I could feel it through the *Varyag*'s tired hull: could sense the fear and anxiety from the population below. But the Krell presented just another way to die, on a planet where there were already millions of those. I was making a snap-judgement based on scant evidence, given that I'd never been here before, but the closer we got to the surface, the more my view solidified.

We flew low over a massed shanty town – an adjunct to the city, grown almost as large – and towards Svoboda's cosmodrome. That was on the perimeter of the city, beyond the atmosphere grid: an arrangement of landing pads and traffic observation towers, ringed by anti-air flak cannons that ponderously tracked incoming traffic. Even by the standards of an outlier colony, those were ancient, outdated pieces of hardware. *Someone forgot about Svoboda*, I thought. *And now it's too late to do anything about it.*

"We land," Bukov declared. "Svoboda beckons. Everybody out."

The *Varyag*'s cargo bay door gradually opened with a tortured groan, revealing the world beyond. The crew, and the ragged column of fugees, disembarked the old ship, and immediately entered the chaos that was Svoboda cosmodrome.

The place had been fully militarised, with a kilometre-long landing strip divided into a dozen pads. Most were occupied by shuttles and smaller freighters – capable of atmospheric flight – although many looked as though they had been parked for a long time, darkened hulls suggesting lengthy exposure to the elements.

Kronstadt was wetter and colder than it had appeared on the approach. A fine drizzle filled the air, and the light seemed all wrong. Not that natural light really seemed to matter; floodlamps were arranged around the perimeter of the airstrip, and the neon glow of the surrounding district was enough to support the muted light cast by Mu-98. Kronstadt enjoyed a twenty-six-hour day, and it was late afternoon, local time. Even so, the planet still felt dark, dismal. As a reminder that it was up there, and that it could make or break Kronstadt, the Shard Gate blazed through the cloud cover. It was brighter than the planet's star, and beneath the baleful alien glow Alliance Army troopers in exo-suits loaded starships, engineers in semi-powered rigs assisting with hull repairs. Everyone wore respirators, and my wrist-comp informed me that the atmosphere outside was loaded with trace toxins.

"About that air," Bukov said, rummaging in his pack. "You might want to use these."

He produced four very battered respirator-masks that covered the lower face. Nothing like proper military hardware.

"That pod will make decent money," he said. "So I give these for free, yes? Wear them outside."

"Thanks," Lopez said, eagerly strapping on her mask. We all took them and did the same.

A group of soldiers approached Bukov. Carbines at ease, they wore outdated Army BDUs – battledress uniform – but the urban camouflage package had failed, leaving the uniforms a faded and drab grey that nonetheless seemed to match Kronstadt pretty well. Their leader had a corporal's badge on one shoulder, a Russian Fed flag on the other, and the Alliance Army insignia all over his body armour. Everyone wore respirators and goggles.

"Corporal Vostok, my friend!" Bukov said.

The corporal kept his hands on his carbine. He looked us over, and the ragged mob of fugees behind Bukov, with obvious disdain.

"You have gift?" he asked.

"Of course, of course."

Bukov passed the man a universal credit chip, and he pocketed it. The soldier's mood seemed to brighten considerably.

"Only twenty this run, huh?" he asked.

"Only twenty," said Bukov. "My bones are run ragged, yes? I must pay tax to you, and then tax to port authority."

Vostok grunted. "Is not my problem, friend. What is with big ones?"

The Jackals fell in around me. They hulked over Vostok and his men.

"My name's Jenkins," I said. "We're the survivors of a mining operation. Our ship went down three days ago. Your friend here was good enough to rescue us."

"I will bet he was," said Vostok, his grin visible at the edges of the respirator mask. His accent was Russian, and his voice young, but of what I could see under his mask, his face was well lined and wrinkled. Maybe that was the effect of life on Kronstadt.

"Are you expecting reinforcements anytime soon?" I asked. That was probably too much for a civilian to ask, but I couldn't help myself.

"You are joking, yes?" Vostok said, garnering a smattering of tired laughs from his squad. "There's no one important down here. Not any more, anyway. Shit is bad, real bad. I'm not sure how much longer we're going to be able to hold the line."

We passed through a chainlink fence, towards a clutch of Army and Navy prefabs.

"The damned fishes just keep coming," Vostok said. "We're fighting them day and night. Have you seen what happens when one of their ships gets infected?"

"Can't say that I have."

"It's terrifying. They become – what is word?"

Another of Vostok's squad spoke up, "Colonised."

"Yes, that is it, *colonised* within hours of infection." The corporal's eyes loomed large behind his goggles. "Go all silvery, all crazy."

"So we've heard."

Lopez paused beside me, and I heard her say "Jesus Christo . . ."

In the scant little shelter between some of the port's structures, men and women were gathered. They were lined up in rows, all kneeling, hands on heads. Most were shivering. There must've been a couple of hundred of them.

"What are they doing?"

"Do not ask," Vostok said.

"Well, I *am* asking," Lopez countered. "What are those marks on their heads?"

Each quaking citizen had a luminous stripe painted down their skull. The civvies were wet through from the constant drizzle, but the paint must've been specialised, because it resisted the rain. They had been grouped together according to their stripe colour.

"Everyone wants a ticket out," Vostok eventually said. "Those that can afford it are red. Those that can't are blue."

"And the greens?" I asked.

Vostok's eyes smiled behind his mask. "They are the payment."

"You can't be serious," Lopez suggested.

Vostok just shrugged.

This was a world that Lopez hadn't seen before. She looked visibly shaken by the idea that people would pay everything they owned to get out of the system . . . But the truth was staring her in the face. Fear was in the air, thicker than even the pollutants that clogged Kronstadt's poisoned atmosphere.

"Why all the questions?" Bukov asked me. "I pick you up in pod. I bring you here. What do you really want?"

I thought about lying, about trying to keep up the pretence. But the Shard Gate, glittering down on us, bathing this planet in its exotic rays, reminded me that we were on a clock. The exodus was coming. This was an opportunity for intel which we couldn't afford to miss.

"We're looking for someone," I said. "A woman."

"I can get you plenty of women," Vostok said, interested suddenly. "But who, exactly?"

I opened my wrist-comp, and projected the tri-D image of Dr Olivia Locke into the air in front of me. Vostok examined it with a frown. One of the corporal's men made a guttural sound; the others laughed.

"Her name's Olivia Locke," I said. "She's a doctor. A xeno-archaeologist."

"Big word," Bukov muttered, rubbing his hands together to chase out the cold.

"Do you know her?"

"Hard to say," Vostok answered.

"Would another credit chip help?"

"It might."

I nodded at Lopez. Thankfully, we had money. Not much, but I hoped that we had enough to get by. Feng had searched Phoenix Squad's lockers aboard the *Firebird*, and discovered that Ving and his men had left funds on the ship. It looked as though they had been working out of the vessel, in fact, and we had made the most of that by plundering their possessions.

Lopez produced a chip from her pouch – probably a smaller denomination than that Bukov had already paid – and handed it to Vostok. The corporal didn't even bother hiding the bribe, but held it up, inspected it. Finally, he slid it into his BDU.

"I do not know her," Vostok said.

Lopez tutted in exasperation, but Vostok put up a hand to silence her protest.

"But I know someone who will," he offered.

"Go on," I said.

"His name is Antonis Vitali. He is ganger."

"And how will a ganger help us?"

"Nothing happens in Svoboda, on Kronstadt, without Vitali knowing about it."

Bukov, obviously annoyed that he had not been the one to make a quick buck out of this exchange, interjected. "Vitali is king of the Barrows, what locals call the *Kurgan*. Anyone want to know something, Vitali is man."

"And the Barrows is . . .?" Lopez muttered.

Vostok shrugged. "Where too many people end up," he said.

"And where a nice girl like you could make some money," Bukov added, with a lingering glance at Lopez.

She gave him a look that could kill, and I was suddenly glad that we were not in combat-armour. I suspected that she would've gone through with it had she been.

"How do we get to the Barrows?" I enquired.

"I give you directions," Vostok said. "No extra charge. Vitali has bar; place called Nikolai's Dream."

I pulled up a local map on my wrist-comp, and put it under Vostok's nose. He selected a site in the middle of the sprawling shanty district.

"Is maybe five kilometres," he said. "But be aware, the Barrows are gang territory."

"We can look after ourselves," Lopez muttered.

"I'm sure that you can," Bukov replied. "So, if you find your – ah, friend – will you need to leave planet too?"

"Maybe," I said, noncommittally.

"I can do run, back to space," Bukov said. He knew that we had money, and there was still some to be made from us. "Maybe find friend who can take to neighbouring system, if interested?"

"Would require exit papers, of course," said Vostok.

"Of course," I said. "We could pay the admin fee."

"Good, good," Vostok muttered.

"Then come back and see us when you are done," Captain Bukov concluded.

We trudged on through the rain, towards the cosmodrome's perimeter. A row of heavy armoured vehicles sat at the security gate. I made out the hulking outlines of battle tanks – the famous Turing MBT-900, with its multi-weapon turret, and heavy-bore main plasma cannon.

Feng whistled. "Are those automated tanks?" he asked.

Vostok nodded and sighed at the same time. "Sure. Most intelligent piece of military hardware ever made, or so they say. Full AI, requires minimal crew to operate." Vostok patted the hull of the enormous tank, producing a solid thump. "Equipped with the largest-calibre plasma weapon on any ground vehicle, dual gatling cannons in the turret, smart missile system, and a triple-strength null-shield." Vostok paused. "They are useless to us in this war."

"Why?"

"Their motherboards are fried, and I don't see us getting resupplied anytime soon. Maybe proper technician could get them up and running. But I don't see us getting one of those soon either."

Each of the tanks sat on its anti-grav sleds, hulls corroded, half-submerged in the wet mud.

"You seem to know lot about tanks for civilian, yes?" Bukov said.

"Yeah, well, everyone has a hobby," Feng replied.

"That they do," said Vostok. From what I could see of his face, he didn't really care who we were, or where we were going. He and Bukov were kindred spirits; that he had been paid was enough. "Good luck in your search," he said.

"Thanks."

"But here is tip for free: do not take too long." He nodded at the sky, where the Shard Gate was still shining. "The Gate will fall within days, of that we are sure. Soon, this will not be Alliance territory."

Through the labyrinthine streets and alleys we went, sticking to the shadows, avoiding the advertising drones and surveillance eyes. Although I doubted that anyone was looking for us that closely – not yet, at least – it never hurt to be careful.

The sun was setting in the distance, throwing a sickly pale light over the shanty town. The aura of oppression ramped up, and the rain intensified. It stung when it touched my skin, and I quickly learnt to avoid letting it get into my eyes, because that shit seriously hurt. It probably accounted for the high proliferation of bionic eye replacements in the passers-by; from crude mechanical jobs, to more advanced semi-organics.

Make no mistake: Kronstadt was a cruel, cruel world.

The streets were packed with citizens. They had a universal appearance, with long armoured trenchcoats, usually pulled up to the neck, bald heads polished to a gleam by the ever-present rain. No headgear seemed foolish, but it was also a show of strength. *I know this place, and I will not be cowed.* Near the cosmodrome, weapons tended to be concealed beneath outer clothing, identifiable by the incongruous bulge at the hip where a pistol could be holstered. But as we left the surrounding district, that quickly changed. Pistols, shotguns, machetes, whatever shit the folks used to kill each other down here: it was all worn quite openly.

Eager for some respite from the rain, we entered a covered market. The smell of human sweat and hot food cooking on open griddles mixed in the air, against a backdrop of white noise produced by a few hundred civvies packed into a tight space. Lopez approached the nearest stall.

"What is this place?" she asked.

"Weapons market," Novak said. "For gangs."

Sure enough, nearly every stall was devoted to weaponry. From rifles to pistols to grenades; new and used, foreign and domestic. The selection was quite bewildering. But it wasn't the items on sale that impressed me.

PRIVACY FIELD IN OPERATION, said a holo-sign over the market entrance. NO DRONES! NO CAMS! NO LAW ENFORCEMENT!

"We're cutting through here," I decided. "I'll use the privacy field to make contact with Zero."

"Just keep your hands off those knives, Novak," Feng suggested, as the big Russian eyed a stall dedicated to all manner of bladed implements.

"Will try," Novak said, very unconvincingly.

I used my wrist-comp to make uplink to Zero and the *Firebird*. Luckily, despite the privacy field, my military-grade transmitter operated just fine, and I cracked the protection in seconds.

"Do you copy, Zero?"

"I read," she said. "Signal is poor, but that's to be expected."

"I'll keep this brief. We're deployed on Kronstadt. We rode a civilian ship to Svoboda cosmodrome. We have a retreat route planned as well, using the same ship."

"Is it reliable?"

"Probably not, but we still have most of Phoenix Squad's credit chips."

"Copy that."

"What's your location?"

"We're in fixed orbit over the city," Zero explained. "It'll allow us to remain within neural-link range."

"Good work. How's P behaving? Any fresh intel?"

"Nothing. It's . . . it's been very quiet."

"Hopefully it'll stay that way," I said, as I jostled past a stall offering stun grenades and flechette blasters. I paused occasionally to take in some of the more esoteric tech. Mostly, it was low-grade and mass-manufactured: ideal for gang-on-gang warfare, but hardly sufficient to defend against a Krell invasion. "We found something that you might be interested in."

"That so?"

"Yeah. The cosmodrome has a troop of those old MBT-900s."

"Turing MBT-900s? The AI tanks?" she asked, enthused suddenly. "Those things are classics!"

"Knew you'd love it. But the garrison down here can't get them working. Some problem with the motherboards. Probably caused by all this damned rain."

Zero tutted over the comm-line. "I doubt the rain would cause that problem. Did they say whether the main antenna had been checked? If that's still operational, then the actual motherboard just needs a hard reboot. It's very resilient tech. Nadi had this technique, actually, where she—"

"Okay, okay," I said. "I get the picture. I just thought you'd be interested, is all."

"Oh, I am."

"You can tell me all about it when we make rendezvous. Until then, comms-quiet."

"Affirmative. Zero out."

"Jenkins out."

Feng was at my shoulder. "Is Zero okay?"

"She's fine," I answered. "All quiet up there."

Feng nodded, looking a little boyish. "That's good."

We cleared the weapons market, and emerged into the Barrows. Groups of young gangers in trench-coats, faces completely covered in ink, stood in the street outside. They watched us go, but did not follow.

"Hey, Novak, what's with all the tattoos?" Lopez asked. She had enough common sense to keep her voice low.

"Gang affiliation," Novak said. There was a certain wariness in Novak's eyes that I hadn't seen before.

"What sort of gang?"

"Many gangs. Sons of Balash, Kozha Brotherhood."

The zone around the cosmodrome had been populated by off-duty soldiers and sailors. Here, things were different. Not necessarily physically – although the buildings had gradually taken on a more dilapidated appearance, and we'd already passed several burnt-out shells. But the place's vibe was different. The aura was all wrong; from the way in which the auto-cabs never seemed to stop in the road, to the look that the last handful of gangers had given us.

But Kronstadt had worse to offer.

"You see that," Feng asked me, pointing as surreptitiously as he could at the fascia of a derelict building. "They're here, too."

"I see it," I said. "Stay sharp, people."

It only confirmed what we already knew, but that didn't make it any more palatable. A Black Spiral had been sprayed onto a shop front. The slogan PURGE THE FISHES was painted beneath, in sloppy Standard. Like I say, hardly surprising. This was fertile recruitment territory. The Black Spiral was just another gang to these people.

We passed by a street preacher, screaming a sermon in pigeon-Russian at the top of his lungs. He clutched a tattered holo-book in two metallic hands; bionics that reminded me of Harris' missing hand. The preacher looked like a semi-mechanical vagrant, and projected an aura of insanity.

"He is telling world that it will end soon," Novak muttered, almost under his breath. "That the Singularity Cult will come, and a machine tide will wash us all away."

"The Cult of the Singularity is a prohibited organisation," Lopez reeled off.

"I don't see anyone arresting this guy," Feng muttered. "He's attracting a big crowd."

"You want to arrest him," I said, "be my guest, Lopez. But I'd rather not get into a fight down here, if that's all the same."

The Barrows were tight, claustrophobic even. My combat senses were in overload; eyes darting over every rooftop. There were too many vantage points. This wasn't just paranoia. Shanties and abandoned buildings presented ideal ambush opportunities. Exfiltration in these circumstances would be far from ideal.

"I can't believe that people survive like this," Lopez said.

"Not everyone is a senator's daughter," Feng said.

"I'm lucky. I get that. You don't need to keep reminding me."

"Speaking of great men, we are in luck," Novak said. "We are about to see greatest cosmonaut ever: Rejeik Nikolai."

We passed into shadow. Craning my neck, I looked up at an enormous metal statue that stood astride the roadway: so big that it almost grazed the atmosphere grid overhead. At least a hundred metres tall. Dressed in an archaic spacesuit, Nikolai's upper body was barely visible; choked by the low-lying clouds of pollution. The figure was poised bravely, one hand on his hip, fish-bowl helmet under the other arm. The elements had corroded whatever compound the statue was made from, reducing the bronze-coloured metallics to a patina-blue.

"He founded the original colony," Novak said. "Was real genius."

"He founded this dump?" Lopez said. "That hardly makes him a saint."

I had the distinct feeling that nothing remotely saintly happened here.

We had reached Nikolai's Dream.

CHAPTER TWENTY-FOUR

APPLIANCE OF SCIENCE

The bar's name was printed in Standard, Russian, and even Chino: every language in a gaudy blue-and-red neon light. Augmented by a tri-D presentation of various glyph-like symbols that hovered over the heads of passers-by.

"What do the symbols say, Novak?" I asked.

"Are *fenya* symbols," Novak offered. "Is like gang-language. Means this place is safe house, for any *bratva*."

"All of the gangs?" Feng queried.

"They come to drink here, and can get information," Novak said. "Is not fighting place. Is good location."

"How very civilised," I muttered.

The building itself was dilapidated and run down; in not much better condition than the rest of the Barrows. Even so, a bubble of quiet, of relative calm, seemed to surround Nikolai's Dream. The effect was almost supernatural; as though the building were somehow capable of repelling the hustle and bustle of the Barrows. As we approached, I realised the reason why. The shimmer of a null-shield surrounded the bar front, projected in a field across the street. Although people came and went beneath the shield, the rain produced a rainbow-like effect as it made contact.

"Whoever this Vitali is," Feng concluded, "he has money. No one else here has that sort of technology."

"If he's so rich, why is he still living here?" Lopez asked.

"Power isn't like that," Novak muttered.

"It is where I come from."

"Russia, gangs: things are not same as Proxima," Novak said.

"Let's get this done," I decided.

Beyond the door – which, I noticed, was actually made from military-grade armourglass: another nod to the fact that Vitali wasn't your typical citizen – the bar was bigger than it looked from the outside. Separated into several booths and sub-chambers, almost randomly. Holographic images danced on the table surfaces, providing the only light inside the dingy cavern. A blue haze hung in the air, vibrating softly, with a life of its own. The stink of narco-sticks was strong, only made stronger by my improved simulant senses.

The place was busy, filled with off-duty gangers huddled over tables. Every weathered face in the joint sent a message: *you're not from here, and you're not welcome here*. There was only one way to deal with a situation like this, I figured. Brazen it out. I gave the closest clutch of gangers a disdainful look, and walked straight up to the bar. The Jackals followed me, Lopez and Feng keeping pace, Novak at his own speed, keen to take in his surroundings.

A tender – who was more machine than woman, with both arms replaced by the ugliest metal prosthetics I'd ever seen – zealously guarded a selection of spirits and drug-dispensers behind the bar. Her face was an immobile rictus of scar tissue, upper lip caught in a permanent scowl. She carried the tattoos of a Singularity Cultist alongside more obvious Russian stamps, and paid us no recognition as we approached.

But, unfortunately, others in the bar did.

"What you want?" came a voice from behind me. Splintered, heavily accented Standard. "Bar is closed."

I turned slowly to face a four-man team of gangers in full clan uniform. Identikit assholes in trenchcoats, eyes replaced with mirrored visors that reminded me a little of the eyes of Krell thralls. Each had a missing limb of one type or another. Hands went to weapons at their belts almost immediately.

"Really?" I asked. "It doesn't look closed to me."

"Private party," said another of the gangers. "You American, yes?"

"Alliance," I answered.

The third man sucked his teeth. "All Alliance here, although that hasn't helped us much."

That drew some sniggers across the bar, which had quietened a little: had now become focused on this confrontation.

Novak stepped forward. "We want to see Vitali."

"Vitali isn't here," said the first ganger.

There was probably a neat, clean way of doing this. A diplomatic method, which involved talking the fine young men down, and persuading them that – in the interests of protecting galactic peace – we really *did* need to see Antonis Vitali. But that would take time, and time was the one thing we didn't have. Sim or no sim, all of this subterfuge was beginning to give me a headache. It might be Harris' way, but it sure as damn wasn't mine.

"Novak," I muttered. "I'm going to need you to show them."

"Show what—" the first ganger started.

His words were cut off by the heel of Novak's palm being driven into his face.

The ganger yelped, mouth fountaining crimson. He slammed into the table behind him. Glasses, narco-pipes and credit chips scattered across the floor. Hand to mouth, the ganger was down and out.

The second blurted something in Russian, and produced his piece: a cheap-looking needle-pistol. Capable of firing small-calibre flechettes, the gun was almost silent – a popular choice among the criminal fraternity. Probably purchased from one of the street vendors.

Novak spat something back, the words tumbling from him as though they'd been stored somewhere deep for too long.

The ganger got the gun up, but that was where his act of protest ceased.

Novak put his left fist into the man's face. He'd shown restraint, as far as the first attacker was concerned. Now that weapons had been produced, a certain boundary had been crossed. Maybe it was part of Novak's criminal code – if such a thing could persist across the void between Old Earth's Norilsk and Kronstadt – but whatever it was, the big man wasn't taking any shit.

The ganger's face exploded in gore and teeth and spittle.

He managed to fire the needle-pistol. The weapon produced a sound like paper tearing, barely audible above the background music. It spat flechette-like projectiles into the table, into the space where Novak had just been standing.

Novak brought his fist down on the ganger's gun-arm. The pistol dropped to the floor.

The other two men were armed with similar pistols. They drew them faster than I would've expected, but not fast enough.

Even without combat-suits, our senses were sharper than those of any two-bit gang heavy. Feng and Lopez had their

Widowmaker pistols on the two survivors. The response was swift. Like a vid-feed on pause, the gangers froze.

But Novak was on a roll. He flicked open the catch of the sheath on his chest, and with a *swish* pulled a mono-knife. The blade hummed softly, emitting a pale blue light. He snarled, looming over the first ganger he'd taken down.

Before I could interject – because I sure as hell wasn't going to let Novak skin these sorry sons of bitches – a clap sounded from beside the bar.

"There is no need for violence," said a rasping voice. "This is not the place for it. This is a safe house."

The kid with the broken face crept away from Novak. He looked a lot younger with his teeth smashed in.

"Who the fuck are *you*?" Novak asked. He was amped, body tense.

"I am Antonis Vitali," he said. "And I believe that you wish to speak with me."

The barkeep – her face still caught in that scowl – hadn't moved the whole time we'd been fighting.

"Go through," she said.

Antonis Vitali was a small, wizened figure, made shorter by the hunch of his shoulders. He wore a black silk kimono, pulled tight at the waist by a cord, and pair of slippers. His features were taut, head smattered with fine grey hair, but skin surprisingly unblemished, eyes a deep green that matched the gems on the oversized rings that he wore on his fingers.

"There was no need for that," Vitali repeated.

"They start it," Novak muttered under his breath.

"They are young, eager," Vitali said. "They do not know what they are doing. Come."

We followed Vitali into a chamber at the rear of the bar.

The place wasn't exactly ostentatious, but it did speak of the same wealth as the rest of the establishment. A glass desk dominated the room, from which were projected various news-casts, Krell invasion predictions, even Navy and Army troop movements. The shelves around the chamber were stacked with an assorted collection of weaponry, of cryo-caskets containing Krell appendages. The stink of illicit narcotics was never stronger than here.

Where Vitali went, a bodyguard of two female gangers followed. These were mostly machines, and had dermal implants visible beneath every inch of exposed remaining skin. They watched us with the same silvered eyes as the gangers in the bar, but I got the distinct impression that these two – if it came to it – would be far more dangerous opponents. This was Vitali's inner sanctum and he would know how to protect it. The man himself might be old and weak, but he was a cat with claws.

"This is safe house, you understand?" Vitali waved his hands in the air, and the rings on his fingers reflected the low light. "Fighting should not occur here."

He slouched into a leather chair behind the desk. Peered at me through the glaze of a tri-D broadcast, narrowing his eyes in a way that reminded me of Novak.

"Now, who are you, and what do you want?" Vitali scowled. "I cannot help someone who I do not know."

"My name is Keira Jenkins," I said. Vitali might well sell us out to the authorities, if the price was right, but there was no time for a cover story any more. "And we're looking for someone."

Vitali's old face creased in an impression of a smile. "You are American; that much is obvious. What, I ask myself, would an American want with Antonis Vitali, on a world about to be invaded by the Krell?"

One of the tri-D feeds Vitali had been monitoring featured classified Naval intelligence; showed movement around the Gate. Whoever this guy really was, he had influence: this sort of material was not for public consumption. Vitali saw where I was looking, and his smile became more pronounced.

"You are military, Keira Jenkins?"

"Perhaps."

"I think so. You do not get to my position, as king of the *Kurgan*, without being able to read people. They say this is my skill." He tapped a finger to the side of his head. "That is what Antonis Vitali does best. He listens, he remembers, he reads people." He indicated an empty seat in front of his desk. "Please. Sit, Keira Jenkins."

I did as offered. Vitali nodded at one of his guards, who stiffly – woodenly – trotted to a drinks cabinet behind him. The woman poured two shots of clear liquid, and placed them carefully on the table.

"These women are my guardians," Vitali said. "They are automatons. Skin-apparitions."

"*Strzyga*," Novak suggested.

Vitali appeared amused by Novak's response. I noticed that the bodyguard's hair was plaited, sweeping over a muscled shoulder, but there was a luminous green stripe on her scalp. *Payment: bodies from the cosmodrome.* Lopez noticed it too, and I looked at her sharply, willing her not to react.

"That is an old word," Vitali said, "and I have not heard it in a very long time. Your man over there – the one with eager fists – he is Russian, yes? But he is not marked. Why is this?"

Novak grunted. "I am not who you think I am."

"Oh, I do not think you are anybody," Vitali muttered. "I think you are *no body*."

One of the feeds on the table began to dance with security footage of the cosmodrome. It showed the *Varyag* coming into port, and the Jackals, Vostok and Bukov walking through the compound. Feng hissed behind me.

"Not much happens in Svoboda without my knowing," Vitali said. "You are new arrivals to Kronstadt. I see before me a Russian ganger, without ink. A man of the Chino, accompanying an American." His gaze settled on Lopez. "And a girl who – despite her best efforts – looks too similar to Senator Lopez for it to be a coincidence."

"You've got this all wrong," I said. My hand was already on the butt of my pistol.

But Vitali gave an uncaring shrug of his shoulders. "Perhaps. Please, drink. You owe me that much. It is a long way to come if you really are nobodies."

I sank the drink in one go. It was vodka; very strong, nearly caustic-tasting. I wondered whether it was perhaps made from the same fluid as the acid rain that fell outside. I almost choked on the taste, and heard Novak chuckle. That the vodka had any effect at all on the sim was impressive.

Vitali drank too, then looked at me, evenly. "And that seals it," he said. "You are simulants."

Lopez tried to chortle a laugh in response to underline just how ridiculous the suggestion was, but the noise came out all anxious and nervous. I didn't even bother to react. I realised that we had been played.

"The drink was spiked, right?" I asked.

"Not at all, but while there are some capable of withstanding the effects of pure Kronstadt-brewed vodka, I do not think that you are one of them. Not in your real skin, anyway."

I wiped the back of my hand over my lips. "Then let's get to business. You know that we're here for a reason, and you know that we won't leave until our mission is executed."

Lopez wouldn't let it rest so easily, and pointed at Vitali. "You drank the vodka too, asshole."

Vitali smiled. "That is different. This is my world. We locals are used to it."

I slid the glass across the table. The guard refilled mine, and also Vitali's.

"We're looking for someone." I called up a picture on the wrist-comp. "An archaeologist. Her name is Dr Olivia Locke. She was working with Science Division, and her last known location was Kronstadt."

As I expected, Vitali's eyes gave nothing away. "People go missing on Kronstadt all the time, Keira Jenkins."

"Do you know this woman, or not?"

Vitali reached for a narco-stick – the tip already ignited, sending out a column of blue smoke. "Who is she to you? What is the price of this information, I wonder?"

Novak's hand smashed down on the table. The tri-D news-casts jittered with the force of the impact, and the desktop shattered. Vitali's brow creased in a frown of annoyance.

"Do you know where we can find this woman?" I asked again. "You might like to answer the question," I suggested, "before my friend here *really* loses his temper."

"Enough," said another voice.

A woman appeared at the back of the office. I couldn't tell whether she had been waiting there all along, or had just appeared. She had obviously heard enough of the exchange to make herself known.

"I am Dr Olivia Locke."

"Back, Olivia," Vitali said. "There is money to be made here. We can barter—"

"*Enough*," Dr Locke repeated, more firmly. "No more hiding."

She was tall, slender. Flanked by the two female body-guards, she was somewhere between a prisoner and a dignitary.

"You are not Lazarus," the woman said to me. "Where is he?"

"The situation's changed. I'm Lieutenant Jenkins. We're Alliance Army, Sim Ops. Lazarus sent us."

"That wasn't my question. Where is Lazarus?"

Dr Olivia Locke wasn't dressed like she had appeared in Harris' intel holo, and her appearance had changed. Her hair was shaven down one side, had now turned a dirty yellow. Her eyes were darker, too; pale white skin an agitated red. Kronstadt's atmosphere must've played hell with her complexion. But I recognised her well enough; her slender-boned appearance was pretty unique, striking enough that I was sure this was our woman.

"Nice set-up you've got here," I said, hand still on my pistol.

"There will be no need for violence. I am who I say I am."

"She is, she is," said Vitali. He looked despondent.

"You've done a lot to hide yourself," I said to Dr Locke.

"I paid Vitali well for the privilege."

"Of that we've no doubt," I replied. "But we'll stay armed. We've already been told once today that there's no need for violence, and that hasn't exactly worked out for us."

"Where is Lazarus?" Dr Locke repeated.

"Lazarus is gone," I said.

The words had an obvious impact on Locke. Her thin shoulders slumped. Jesus, this girl was tall. Easily seven foot, approaching the height of a sim in combat-armour. She was almost alien in her appearance.

"Dead?"

Forgive me, Zero. Saying it would make it real, but there was no point in denying the truth. I nodded. "Yes."

"Then things are worse than I thought."

Vitali arranged a private room, and activated another privacy field as a safety measure. It seemed that Svoboda had plenty of secrets, and privacy fields were not uncommon. The device carried a subsonic buzz in the air as we settled in plush leather seats around a black-glass table.

"Come," Vitali gestured. "You will be safe here."

I watched Dr Locke as she took a seat opposite me, and couldn't help but feel a little deflated. All roads had led to this meeting, but Locke herself didn't seem to amount to much. We'd come so far, lost so much, for a single science officer. I just hoped that she was worth it.

"I know of the Watch," Vitali insisted, fussing over another seat at the table. "You do not have to hide anything from me."

"If it's all the same to you," I said, uncomfortable with the Russian's presence, "we're on official military business . . ."

"Leave us, Antonis," Locke said. She was shaking. "Please."

Vitali groaned, and tossed his head, but didn't argue. He drifted past, together with his bodyguards, leaving the Jackals and Dr Locke in relative quiet.

"How did it happen?" Locke asked me, without preamble. Her voice had a strange sing-song accent to it, but was cracked with emotion.

"We raided a farm. Harris never made it out."

"And you saw him die? You actually saw Lazarus die?"

"As good as," I answered. "He's gone."

Dr Locke sighed. For someone who barely even knew Harris, she was taking this news very badly. There was proper distress in Locke's face, real despair in her reaction. I wondered what the limits of their relationship really were. That Locke even knew Harris was actually alive meant that she was privy to classified intelligence.

"There was no way that he made it off the farm," I added.

"We heard some chatter," Dr Locke said, staring at the glass now. "That a farm had been hit, but I didn't believe it."

"News like that tends to travel fast."

"Antonis has people everywhere," she said. "The Russians may not have many colonies out here, but their spy network is second to none. The *Kurgan* king has been known to exchange intelligence with the Navy and Military Intelligence if the price is right."

"And yet he didn't trade you in to either," I said. "Does he know who you really are?"

"Of course," Dr Locke said. "We . . . we have history together. A long time ago. Not all of Sci-Div's operations are official, and people like Antonis can sometimes come in handy."

"Is that why you came to Kronstadt?"

Dr Locke smiled coldly. "It is the perfect hiding place. If you have money, anything is possible."

"So we understand," I replied.

Locke looked up at me sharply. "Lazarus told me about you," she said. "That you were his second in command. That you were with him when he was Legion."

"I was. We served together for many years."

"Who did it? Who killed Lazarus?" Locke asked. "Was Warlord there?"

"You know about Warlord?"

"Everyone knows of Warlord, but I know more than most," Locke said, cryptically.

"I know who he was," I said. This was one of the joys

of being AWOL, I guess: I couldn't be shot for sharing classified intel. "Sergeant Clade Cooper. 1st Battalion, Alliance Army Ranger. His squad was called the Iron Knights, and they died on Barain-11. Cooper was the only survivor; captured by the Krell and immersed in the Deep. Family – wife and two children – killed while he was in captivity."

"He's a man of Command's making," Locke muttered. "They created him. After his capture on Barain, then his liberation by Alliance Special Forces, he became something else. Something . . ." She paused, sighed. "Something not quite human any longer. Warlord is one with the universe, in the worst possible way."

"What's that supposed to mean?"

"It means that he exists before, and after," Locke said. "He died on Barain-11, but Science Division brought him back, made him something new."

"How did they do that?" More importantly, "*Why* would they do that?"

"Because he was to be something else. They used experimental nano-technology to repair his physical wounds. That damage could be fixed. But the wounds in his head? Not so much. He is seeking to wake something up. Something that has slumbered for a very long time."

I shook my head. "He killed my friend. He's sentenced millions, billions, to death."

"He knows the Krell like no other human," Locke replied, as if that was any sort of an answer.

I too had seen the Deep. Just in fleeting, only for a second, but that was long enough. I remembered P's description – the ebb and flow of the Deep, the difference between being immersed in it, and becoming part of it. Somewhere in there, among the muddle of emotions and thoughts, was Clade

Cooper. He was *part* of the Deep. That made him a very dangerous enemy indeed.

"Lazarus told me that you had information," I said. "Intelligence important to the Watch. You wanted safe passage off Kronstadt in exchange."

That drew the doctor back to the now, seemed to refocus her thought-process. She looked over at my squad. That same evaluating gaze that I seemed to see a lot lately; weighing us up. The expression on Dr Locke's face suggested that – civilian or not – she knew who we really were.

"We're with the Simulant Operations Programme," I said. "We have a ship. We can arrange your exfiltration."

"Sim Ops," the doctor repeated. "That doesn't surprise me."

"We have a whole platoon in orbit," Lopez exaggerated.

Dr Locke saw right through that. "And yet you send only four green troopers in skins down to the surface?"

"Well, the lieutenant isn't green . . ." Feng said.

"Are you going to give us this intelligence or not?" I asked, angered by Locke's constant riddles. "In a matter of days, maybe less, Kronstadt is going to be reduced to slag by the Krell. The infected are massing on the other side of the Shard Gate. So you can help us, as Lazarus intended, or we can extract and leave you to it."

"How do I know that I can trust you?"

"I could ask you the same question. That information about the farm is restricted. We only knew about it because we were there. Isn't that proof enough?"

"My information," Dr Locke countered, somewhat self-importantly, "is crucial to the war effort. I can't just—"

"We're all that's left," I said. "And right now, we're your only hope."

Dr Locke looked as though she was still struggling to

come to terms with Lazarus' death, and whether she should share her intelligence or not. Finally, she made her decision.

"I know what is causing the Harbinger virus," she said, "and I know how to stop it. I only told the Watch that I wanted safe passage so that I could give the information to Lazarus. There is no cost, save the price that knowing this will put on your head. The Harbinger virus was someone's dream made nightmare, and the Aeon is someone's dream made real."

Aeon. That name again.

"We know all we need to know about the Aeon," I bluffed. "It's a weapon."

"You think you know about the Aeon, but if you're here – just the four of you – then clearly you do not." Locke smiled again. "The Aeon is much more than just a weapon. It is another intelligence. An *alien* intelligence. Military Intelligence has been tracking the Aeon for some time. They arrived towards the end of the Krell War; probably drawn to this sector by the activation of Shard technology."

The Hannover *was searching for another alien species*, I realised. *She was sent to investigate the Aeon . . .*

"And you know this how?"

My mind was buzzing, the neurons firing. Another alien species in the Maelstrom? The implications of that were staggering. Jesus, the Directorate had almost started a war with the Alliance as a result of Shard leftovers – had almost brought the whole universe crashing down on our heads by summoning the Shard back to the Milky Way, at the end of the last Krell War. What would they do with the discovery of another alien species?

"I was chief xeno-archaeologist of the Science Division expedition on Tysis World. We discovered a ruin there; a Shard facility. It proved to be the most intact example of

Shard technology ever discovered, and led to some impressive discoveries about the history of the Maelstrom. The machines' linguistics are really fascinating. They tell of many conflicts, but especially of a Great War between the organics and the mechanicals."

"The Shard and the Krell?" Feng asked.

That the Shard and the Krell had once been at war – that they had almost exterminated each other millennia before the Alliance and the Directorate had entered the galactic stage – was common knowledge.

"Oh, so much more than that," Dr Locke explained. As she began to talk about the findings, she became revitalised by her passion. "There were – or, perhaps are – dozens of other species in the Milky Way Galaxy. Glyphs on Tysis World describe the coming together of several of these races in a union, opposed by another conglomeration. Can you imagine it? A pantheon of organic species on one side – a great alliance, if you will – in opposition to a machine-pact.

"During the Great War, the organics and the machines fought over the Maelstrom. The machine forces were stretched too far apart. They eventually fell, but the organics were scattered, unable to rally. The organics scored a pyrrhic victory, for what is was worth. In the waning days of their existence in this sector, the Shard unleashed a weapon."

Dr Locke paused, looking over the faces of each of the Jackals in turn. We all understood what came next, but it was me who asked the question.

"The Shard created the Harbinger virus, didn't they?"

Locke gave a slow, mournful nod. "The Shard created a virus capable of not just crippling their enemy, but turning the Krell against each other. Collective warred on Collective. But the Krell had their own weapons."

"The Aeon . . ." I muttered.

Dr Locke nodded. "The Aeon were a great ally of the Krell; a species capable of killing planets, sending stars supernova."

And that was exactly what the Aeon had done, in the Gyre. That was why the *Hannover* was sent out there, into the dark: to find the third alien race. The parts were starting to slowly – but painfully and surely – fall into place. My head had started to ache again.

"The Shard called the Aeon the Great Destroyer," Dr Locke continued. "Command hoped that they were still present in the Gyre, that perhaps they were still active. The Aeon may prove to be the only counter to this virus."

Counter. That had been Harris' word, back in the war room. I wondered, again, how much he had really known . . .

"So this Aeon can kill worlds?" Novak grumbled. "I say let sleeping dogs lie."

"I think that they have already awoken," Locke said, "and I think that they are angry."

"Command already knows all of this," I said. The *Hannover* had been acting on Locke's information. "Why draw the Watch out here, all the way to Kronstadt?"

"Tysis World is gone. It was destroyed by the Black Spiral. The expedition's findings went with it, and I was the only survivor."

"Then what's your intelligence?"

Dr Locke pointed to tattoos on her shoulder. "*I* am the intelligence," she said.

And then I understood. The image on Locke's shoulder sprang to life, dancing both across – and under – her skin. A map: that was what this was. On the surface of her flesh, it looked like an electro-tattoo. But up close, I could see that it was far more complicated. A starmap, literally inked onto her flesh, stark against her white skin. It was incredibly detailed, and quite beautiful. Subdermal implants flickered beneath the skin, purpose unknown.

"I can lead you to the Aeon," she said. "*I* am the only surviving map. I can end this — "

Vitali appeared at the door, waving his hands furiously.

"Quiet!" he yelled. "Everyone, stay quiet!"

The privacy field continued to buzz in the background, but that obviously wasn't enough. Behind Vitali, the bar had fallen silent. He paused at the door to the chamber, and I saw into the main bar room. The lights had been dimmed, all patrons frozen in place.

"What's happening?" Lopez asked.

A stab of illumination – a spotlight – played across the street outside, visible through the Dream's glass windows. Bright white light spilled inside, throwing shadows across the bar.

"What have you done?" Vitali exclaimed. He jabbed a finger at me. "Who have you brought here?"

"No one! We weren't followed!"

Which, of course, I knew was too good to be true.

Outside, the light shifted abruptly, panning back and forth. It was being projected from something big and dark, hovering overhead.

"No way . . ." Lopez muttered.

The spotlight was mounted on a dropship.

The Directorate were on Kronstadt.

CHAPTER TWENTY-FIVE

SCIENCE OF VIOLENCE

The whole bar went quiet, even the music silenced. Everyone peered through the smoke-glass frontage, at the black shape dipping over Svoboda's ragged skyline.

"That's a Dragon-class," Feng muttered. The anger in his voice was real and hot. "There are four of them."

Because, after all, one is never enough.

"You're sure about that?" I asked.

"I'm sure," Feng said.

Dr Locke looked from me to Feng, then back again. "What's a Dragon-class?"

"It's a dropship," I answered, by rote. "Small, fast, well armed. Mainstay of the Directorate forces."

"That's a lot of Shadows," Feng said. "Each Dragon can carry a platoon."

"They must've come in on another transport," I said. "Which can only mean that the *Furious Retribution* is up there somewhere."

"You think that Zero has seen them?" Lopez asked.

"I doubt it. The *Retribution* will be running a full stealth package. Must've got through that Navy cordon. The Alliance fleet is looking for Krell ships, not Directorate."

"The furious what?" Dr Locke enquired.

"An old friend," said Feng. "Flagship of Commander Kwan, Bureau of Shadow Affairs. He's been looking for us."

Dr Locke's mouth dropped open in horror. "You've brought the Shadow Bureau to Kronstadt?"

"Not through choice," I said. "I can assure you of that."

Lopez sighed. "It's a long story."

"Too long for now," I decided. "Under the table. Keep back from the windows."

"No, no, no!" Vitali implored. "I've already said, this is a safe house. I cannot have exchange of fire in my premises."

"Well it's too late for that," I said. "The bar has a null-shield, right?"

"Yes."

"Then keep it at maximum amplification."

"The energy costs alone . . . !" Vitali complained.

I completed his sentence: "Will be significantly less than the cost of rebuilding this place after the Directorate are finished with it."

Vitali glared at me in a way that suggested he wasn't exactly in agreement with my assessment, but nodded at one of his bodyguards. She went towards the back office, yelling something in Russian.

"It's set," Vitali said.

The reprieve would be temporary, and I knew it. At maximum polarity, the null-shield would prevent a bombardment of the bar by energy or projectile weapons. But that was only the first problem. Kwan would send in Shadow commandos to sweep the city, street by street, and the null-shield wouldn't help with that.

There was a ripple of anxiety through the bar. The bravado

that the *bratva* had showed when we'd arrived had evaporated, to be replaced by obvious fear.

"And here come the ground pounders . . ." Feng said, his voice little more than a whisper.

The four dropships were poised overhead. Their armoured bellies opened, and they disgorged troops into the Barrows. Wearing Ikarus flight-suits, the Shadow commandos launched from the dropships in formation, thruster harnesses flaring bright blue against the darkening sky. The troops landed on rooftops, immediately deploying into the buildings below.

One dropship hovered so low that it almost seemed to be sniffing the Barrows. Its VTOL – vertical take-off and lift – engines were aligned so that the backdraught virtually flattened the surrounding structures. Locals had started to filter out onto the streets now, yelling and throwing make-shift missile weapons at the dropship. The flyer's searchlight panned the shanties, but otherwise took no notice. Broken bottles and bricks were of no concern.

"What's happening?" Dr Locke hissed. "What are they doing?"

"Quiet."

Then the Dragon spoke.

"We are looking for escaped prisoners," came a voice, carried by an amplification system in the dropship's nose. I immediately recognised Kwan; his voice unmistakable. "They are fugitives, and sworn enemies of the Greater Asiatic Directorate. You will produce them, or we will tear this world apart looking for them. This is the lead prisoner."

An enormous tri-D image of my face was projected from the dropship's belly, filling the sky above the Barrows. Looked like it had been taken during our incarceration on Jiog; painted in blue light, it flickered and hazed in the rain, but it was clear enough.

"You have a fan," Novak said.

"More like a stalker."

"This woman's name is Keira Jenkins," Kwan said. "We offer a reward to any who assist in her capture. But to any who stand in the way of the Greater Asiatic Directorate, know this: we will destroy you, and everything you stand for. That will be all."

The Barrows responded immediately. Small-arms fire impacted the dropship's belly, in response. A dozen minor engagements erupted from rooftops, from the streets, as gangers and Shadows clashed.

"Do you think that Kwan is actually down on Kronstadt?" Feng asked.

But I knew that Feng really wanted to know whether Tang – the Mother of Clones –was out there. She had been responsible for creating him and his kind, and had threatened Feng's new life. The hatred was writ large across his face. That aside, Feng being on the same planet as the Directorate presented its own problems: namely, the metal in his head.

Instead of voicing that concern, I just nodded, and said, "We can only hope."

"There's an army of them out there," Lopez complained. "We can't take them on. We don't even have any proper firepower!" She scowled. "We should've used the Pathfinder suits, just like I said."

Listen to your squad, Harris had told me. Maybe the old bastard had a point after all . . .

"You were right, Lopez."

My reaction caught Lopez by surprise. "Then what are we going to do about it?" she continued. "There are only four of us."

I searched the faces of the Jackals, and I liked what I saw. "We four need to become an army," I said.

"And how exactly are we going to do that?" Lopez asked.

"We're simulant operators. Let's make the most of it. Vitali, look after Dr Locke. Hold the fort until we get back."

I tuned the communicator on my wrist-comp. Opened a channel back to Zero.

"Zero, do you copy?"

"I copy. I'm receiving some worrying transmissions. What's happening down there?"

"Prepare to receive four to the SOC," I said. "And get a fix on this location."

My wrist-computer's transmitter lit. The device would act as a homing beacon. While it wasn't the strongest transmitter in the arsenal, and the beacon would quickly deplete the comp's power cell, it would do for these purposes.

"Solid copy," she answered. "I have your location."

"Tell Captain Lestrade to make burn for low orbit. Stay safe, but bring the *Bird* in as low as she can go. We're going to make descent using the Pathfinder suits."

Lopez's eyes lit with interest.

"Understood," Zero replied.

"We need to be in a position to deploy immediately. Extract us in five seconds."

"Copy that," Zero said. She started the countdown.

Vitali flapped his arms anxiously. "Where are you going? You can't leave us down here with the Directorate!"

"We'll be right back. Jackals, prepare for extraction."

The neural-link between me and my simulant was severed, and I extracted back to the *Firebird*.

I snapped my eyes open. The Jackals were all around me, each bobbing in their tanks, extraction data filling the overhead view-screen.

"Extraction confirmed," I said, for a record that no one would ever review.

Zero swivelled on her chair, turning to the squad.

"The fleet in orbit is chattering," Zero said. Her voice was projected into my ear by the communicator, frayed with tension. "Is our position compromised?"

"It's not us," I said. I ricked my neck, the respirator still clamped over my mouth. "The Directorate are down there. They have four Dragon-class dropships, and a boatload of Shadow commandos."

"Shit. Have you found Dr Locke?"

"Affirmative. She's holed up in a bar. We're going back down there."

Zero turned back to her console. "I've painted your last location via the wrist-comp, but how are you going to get the doctor off-world? We've already been through this; even if you use the Pathfinder suits, you don't have any way of getting back into orbit."

"The cosmodrome has transports," I said. "We met a contact. Like I told you, we have a possible retreat plan. It's the best we've got. For now, I want the *Firebird* to remain on-station." Over the general squad channel, I said, "Jackals, prepare for transition."

"Affirmative," the squad chorused.

"Send us back, Zero."

"Transition in three . . . two . . . one . . ."

Then I was in the dark. Sealed inside a drop-suit, ready for deployment. I made a mental note to thank Lopez for prepping the simulants. The only reason that we were immediately drop-capable was because of her insistence on readying the suits. She'd been keen to use the new armour, and had not only armoured the spare simulants, but also loaded them into the drop-bay. What had, only a short while ago, seemed like wasted effort, now appeared to be damned good planning.

"Transition confirmed."

The Pathfinder suit's internal diagnostics activated.

WELCOME, LIEUTENANT KEIRA JENKINS. DEPLOY SUIT?

"Hell yeah."

The Pathfinder was immobile, because the limbs had to be locked into position for what came next. I was unceremoniously shuttled into a firing tube, a lot like a missile in a launcher; exactly what I was about to become.

The Jackals reeled off confirmations, and Zero and Captain Lestrade were chattering in the background. No point in keeping comms silent now: we were running hot, and from here on in stealth was a distant memory.

There was a rumble around me, as the drop-suit slid into the launch tube. No time to worry. No time to think about the Jackals' lack of Pathfinder training. Maybe it was better this way; at least there was no expectation, no anxiety. I licked my lips. Just like Harris said – no time for regrets. Sometimes the best strategies were down to luck. I hoped this was one of those times.

"Green for launch," Zero declared.

Then, feet-first, I was fired out of the *Firebird*.

"*Wooohooo!*" Feng screamed, his voice warbling as his suit took the acceleration.

Lopez and Novak's bio-signs appeared on my HUD. They too had successfully launched.

Crisp, cold air filled my simulated lungs. More commands filtered across my HUD, confirmed that various systems were now online. The armour took care of everything. Automated thrust control initiated.

The Pathfinder's visor was polarised, made to shield the face from sight-threatening explosions and bursts of light, but I caught a glimpse of Kronstadt from space. What I saw wasn't pretty, not pretty at all. The Alliance fleet in high orbit was active. Missiles and lasers and railguns silently raked the void. It seemed a lot of activity for just one ship . . . But we weren't the Navy's focus. Who were they firing at?

"Fuck!" Lopez screamed, her drop-suit veering on my left flank.

Something exploded out there. Debris scattered across our flight path. The suits' navigational system responded, took us on a safer approach vector.

"You read me, Zero?" I asked, my own voice quivering as the suit threw me around. "Zero!"

"I copy," Zero finally answered, her voice warped with static. "There's a lot of interference in this sector. Be aware that—"

An Alliance warship exploded nearby. It was a long way off, but ships didn't just blow up. I could see very little at the speed I was travelling, but the suit was painting graphics across my HUD: uplinking to the wider intelligence grid. The armour didn't care whether we were AWOL or loyalist, and the fleet was literally bleeding data. Kronstadt was closer with every heartbeat, the atmosphere beckoning to us. I braced myself in readiness for the breach; just prayed that we could make it. Once we hit atmo, we would be safe from the war in space . . .

". . . you even listening to me?" Zero complained.

"I copy," I said, focusing again. It was easy to lose concentration during a planetary drop. "Say again?"

"The tactical situation has changed—" she started.

T MINUS TWENTY SECONDS UNTIL ATMOSPHERIC BREACH, my suit told me. ADMINISTERING COMBAT-DRUGS.

Something icy cold snaked into my bloodstream, and my

heart rate slowed just a little. The drop-shakes calmed for a moment. Another series of thrusters in the suit's enormous EVAMP fired.

I saw red-white comets in the periphery of my vision. Those were the Jackals, their clipped breathing barely audible over the comm.

"Say again, Zero?" I said. "Do not copy!"

There wasn't much between me and the void to begin with, but parts of the drop-suit were now beginning to shear off. To the uninitiated, that might be concerning, but it was all part of the technology. The outer armour acted as a disposable heat shield, and was shed as the suit made atmospheric entry.

". . . arriving . . .!" Zero said.

"Say again?"

I only got static. CONNECTION LOST, my suit informed me. PLEASE TRY AGAIN.

But something else brushed my mind.

Others come. They are here.

And then I saw exactly what had got Zero so damn freaked. It was, with the benefit of hindsight, pretty hard to miss . . .

The Shard Gate was split wide, spilling green light across near-space. Already, the outlines of Krell bio-ships and arks were visible, trailing organic material as they breached the barrier between time and space.

"Holy shit!" Feng exclaimed.

A barrage of unencrypted Navy chatter assaulted my ears:

"*Gate is open! Repeat Gate is open!*"

"*Class Six incursion inbound. All available vessels move to intercept—*"

". . . *assist! Require assist! There are too many of them! Falling back!*"

"Do not, repeat do not, fall back from that position. The cordon must be maintained—"

"This doesn't change anything!" I managed. "Our mission remains the same. We drop in, secure the asset, and pull out. Now, concentrate on getting down to the surface in one piece."

I came up to meet Kronstadt's atmosphere, and the shakes had me again. No amount of combat-drug could suppress the sensation in my gut, in my limbs, as I burst through the exosphere and plummeted down towards Svoboda: fixed on the beacon broadcast by my wrist-computer . . .

Through cloud cover.

Plummeting, plummeting, plummeting.

Like fallen angels. Angry fucking angels.

Thrusters fired again. More armour slewed off, smoking as it hit the atmosphere. Vertigo, and her close cousin nausea, almost made me black out. The Pathfinder dumped more drugs into my bloodstream, and I was grateful for every one of them.

I got a bird's-eye view of Svoboda. What we'd seen in orbit – the Shard Gate opening – had caused a sort of chain reaction on the ground. The cosmodrome was a mass of activity: shuttles and smaller craft already lifting off, mustering to support the fleet in orbit. Meanwhile, AA guns tracked all over the city's perimeter, spitting mass-reactive rounds at incoming targets.

"Danger close!" I roared. "Prep for evasive manoeuvre!"

My drop-suit jinked and rolled, banked and ducked. Tracer fire slid beneath me, and I ground my teeth with the G-force. The Jackals' suits did the same, barely escaping the friendly fire.

We closed on the Barrows. What with the lashing rain,

visibility was shot to shit, but my suit had multi-vision. I flagged the four Directorate Dragons. The Shadow commandos were identifiable by the flare of their jump packs, as they moved from rooftop to rooftop. They had deployed drones too, and swarms were flittering through the streets, building up an intelligence network. The Directorate had slid right past the Alliance fleet; an assassin's knife to the heart.

LANDING ZONE IDENTIFIED.

I picked out the statue of Nikolai, standing astride the ragged mess of warrens. There, very close by, was Nikolai's Dream, the barely visible blue dome of the null-shield still protecting the establishment. The suit selected a safe place to touch down, and I got ready to make planetfall.

"Sound off!"

There were a series of ragged responses.

"Give those dropships a wide berth," I ordered.

"I hear that," Feng said.

Then we were down. The remainder of the drop-suit's shielding fired, sending out a wave of deadly shrapnel. Debris pinged off surrounding structures.

I slammed both feet into the ground. The combined weight of me and my suit was a thing to be reckoned with, and the pavement cracked with the force of the impact. The Jackals landed in the same way, with a finesse that I hadn't expected of them.

"Null-shields up!"

The squad complied. Our shields ignited, overlapping, creating an impenetrable barrier.

"Who marked up the suits?" I asked. "Was that you, Lopez?"

Each of the combat-suits was stencilled with our call-signs, our rank identifiers and accolade badges. Although the suits often didn't come back with the simulants, it was a Sim Ops ritual, an old tradition. My heart swelled with pride to see my team badged up, proudly wearing the Jackals' colours. Sure, there was an argument that declaring who we were was no longer a good idea – especially since we were technically AWOL, and Kwan had put a bounty on my head – but whatever our status, we were still Jackals.

"We all did it," Lopez said. "Joint effort. Before we reached Kronstadt."

"We thought you'd like it," Feng replied.

"Good work," I said. "We ready for this, Jackals?"

"Affirmative," they answered.

"Deploy weapons."

I slid the M115 plasma rifle from its magnetic lock on my back. The weapon automatically slaved to my suit, targeting data filling my HUD. A steely calm spread through the squad.

"See," Lopez said, "that wasn't so bad, right? We all made it down in one piece; we can be trusted with the nice things every now and again, ma'am."

"We'll see about that."

The advanced targeting array activated, suggesting firing solutions and hostile movements beyond the limits of my senses. The suit carried lots of cutting-edge upgrades – each was equipped with its own flight of drones, for instance – but we weren't going to use those unless necessary. Sticking to the basics would probably be more than enough for the Jackals.

I plotted our next move through the Barrows. The suits carried sensor-fouling scrambler modules – designed to stop the user from being shot down during the descent – but our arrival hadn't been exactly *sub rosa*. Although we hadn't triggered any immediate reaction from the Directorate, it was only a matter of time before they responded.

"On me, into the bar."

CHAPTER TWENTY-SIX

AZIMUTH, FAITH, FIRE

Nikolai's Dream sat resolute amid the Barrows, but I could see a dozen or so frightened faces peering out at us as we approached. We double-timed it down the street, and then through the null-shield. Paused outside the door.

"Let us in, Vitali," I said.

The protective screen over the door slid back, and Vitali stood there. Although flanked by his two bodyguards, he was positively quaking.

The Jackals marched into the bar. Once again, every face in the place was turned in our direction, but this time for very different reasons. The armour still smoked from a combination of the drop, and the rain. We were monsters, so big that the bar could barely accommodate us.

"Sorry we made a mess of your bar," Feng said, without sounding sorry at all.

"It . . . it doesn't matter," Vitali stammered.

Our simulants lay in a pile on the floor, dead. The gangers had cleared a space around the skins, no one wanting to get too close. I reached down and deactivated my wrist-comp.

The locator beacon was now a liability. Both Krell and Directorate forces would be able to detect it.

Novak did his own recovery job. He unstrapped the varied blades from his corpse, and slid them into sheaths across the combat-suit. Lopez watched on, one eyebrow arched in disapproval.

"What?" Novak questioned. "Am recycling, yes?"

"Sure," Lopez said.

"Is just shame to lose perfectly good weapons," Novak insisted.

Dr Locke stirred from behind the main bar. She looked dishevelled, but in one piece.

"I've never seen a Simulant Operations team in action," she said. "It's quite something."

"You're about to see a lot more of us," I said. "We're going to exfiltrate you to the cosmodrome. We'll use the storm as cover, but you'll need to keep buttoned up while we're outside. It's raining hard out there."

"Understood," she said, grimly. At least she'd the foresight to get dressed in a survival suit, with a respirator and goggles strapped across her head.

"The Krell have breached the Shard Gate," I said. "We heard some Naval chatter on the way in. They're saying that it's a Class Six incursion."

"Class Six!" Vitali exclaimed, as though he actually knew what this meant.

"The fleet's moving to intercept," I said.

"They'll stop the Directorate too, right?" a ganger piped up. It was the guy whose nose Novak had broken.

"I doubt it," I said. "Their hands will be full with the Krell." I turned back to Dr Locke. "But it does mean that we can probably hitch a ride off-planet, if we make it to the cosmodrome."

Vitali paced the length of the bar, grumbling nervously, wringing his hands. In the midst of what was soon to become the hottest warzone in the galaxy, his silk kimono and slippers were ridiculously inappropriate. The look really didn't work for him.

I tried to open the comms channel to Zero, but it was still blocked. Quite what was causing that wasn't clear, and I didn't have time to find out right now. My inner ear vibrated with the thrum of an approaching VTOL engine: one of the Dragons, turning to investigate our arrival in the Barrows.

"You should go," Vitali suggested. He was doing his utmost not to make eye contact with me.

"I think that's a good idea."

"Here, through my office. There is an alley out the back."

We barrelled through the bar's back rooms with weapons ready, expecting to meet resistance at any moment. The corridors were too small for a properly armoured trooper, and I fought the urge to just smash my way through the walls. The pent-up energy in the Pathfinder's frame was hard to control.

"The cosmodrome is three klicks through hostile territory," I said, over the Jackals' comms channel. "Whatever happens, we're disposable. But Dr Locke gets out, right?"

"Affirmative," the Jackals responded.

"We need that map."

I popped a back-up communicator from a pouch on my belt. Sim Ops-class armour usually carried all sorts of useful shit, and the drop-suit was no exception – the user was often expected to survive solo in a warzone. I thought-commanded my armour to tune the comm to our general frequency, then passed it to Dr Locke.

"Take this," I said. "Keep it switched on at all times. It's going to get hot out there, and we'll need to stay in contact."

Dr Locke nodded, and slid the communicator into her ear with an ease that suggested this wasn't the first time she had used this sort of technology.

"Will do," she said. "Comms check?"

"We hear you," Feng answered.

Vitali led the way, his bodyguards still at his side.

"Where will you go?" Dr Locke asked him.

"Where is there to go?" he said. "I am the *Kurgan* king. This is my home."

"Thank you for everything you've done," Dr Locke said, and once again I found myself wondering about their relationship.

"It is nothing," he replied. "Through there. Go."

I patted him on the shoulder. "You're okay, Antonis."

"You can settle your bill when we meet again," he answered.

I smiled and nodded. "Will do."

But Novak: he paused there. Stood in front of Vitali.

"I am truthful to you, now," Novak said, drawing Vitali's attention. "When I say am no one, is not true. I am someone, and you will know who."

Vitali frowned, obviously torn between the need to preserve his immediate personal safety and the curiosity caused by Novak's sudden disclosure. Novak opened his helmet and stared down at Vitali.

"I am Son of Balash," he muttered.

Vitali smiled knowingly. "I suspected as much. You are of Kronstadt?"

"No. What I say of Norilsk; that is truth."

"Novak!" I yelled. "Button up – we're leaving!"

Novak ignored me. "I need information."

"Don't we all?" Vitali muttered.

"Come on, Novak!" Lopez yelled. "This isn't the time."

"Be quiet, girl!" Novak barked back at her. He turned to Vitali again. "Where is Major Mish Vasnev?"

Vitali's smile faltered a little. Suggesting that perhaps he was networked to his two automaton guards, the women at his sides dropped into combat stance: hands on knives at their belts. Vitali frowned.

"You do not want to know where Mish Vasnev is," he said.

"I do," Novak said. "And I will find her."

Shooting started behind us. I recognised the sound of a Directorate-issue assault rifle; the distinctive suppressed hiss. Shouts followed.

"No time, Novak!" I yelled. "We're leaving – *now*!"

"You really want to know?" Vitali said, almost hesitantly. Whoever Mish Vasnev was, the little man was obviously frightened of her.

"Tell me."

Then Vitali said something in Russian. Novak replied, in the same language. Nodded, satisfied. They spoke too quickly for my drop-suit to translate the words, except for the last few.

"Tell her that Leon Novak is looking for her."

Novak slid his helmet back into place. A flash of light spilled from inside the bar: an energy weapon discharging.

"Go," Vitali said. "We'll hold them back."

We emerged into a rain-drenched alleyway, and found that the storm had well and truly broken. Dr Locke pulled up her goggles, slid the respirator into place. Her survival suit covered almost all of her skin, but in this downpour I had no idea how long it would protect her.

I nodded towards the end of the alley. "Jackals, move out."

I thought-commanded my suit to plot the way to the cosmodrome, taking the fastest route through the Barrows. Battlefield intelligence was scant, and it wasn't going to be easy. A reminder of just how fluid the tactical situation had become slid overhead: a Krell bio-pod, on fire. It impacted somewhere in the city limits, making the ground quake.

"What the hell was that all about?" Lopez asked Novak.

"Not your business, Senator," he barked back. "Directorate are here. It is time for action, yes?"

Two Dragons had taken up position above Nikolai's Dream, and Kwan continued his address to the city, the promise of a reward looping over the streets, from the lead ship. We scouted the perimeter range of the ships' sensors, sticking to the tight streets so that it was more difficult to spot us from above.

Of course, that tactic didn't last long.

A Shadow suddenly materialised out of the darkness, right in front of me. At exactly the same time, my suit detected the figure's repressed bio-signs. The tech these bastards were packing was good; too damned good. But human nature is human nature, and the figure paused: perhaps surprised to see us wearing full drop-suits.

"Contact!"

The commando disintegrated in a hail of bright plasma. His assault rifle fired as he died, spitting a stream of rounds into the air. The Shadows used silenced carbines, but in the alleyway the noise was still alarmingly loud.

Two more troopers appeared at the end of the alley. My null-shield lit as I took hostile fire. Dr Locke took up a position behind my armoured bulk.

"Take the one on the left, Novak," I ordered.

Novak slid past, mono-blade to the Shadow's chest. He

planted the blade between the seams of two armour plates at the gut. The knife went in fast and silent. The Shadow flailed for a moment, then went down.

I grasped the commando on the right. Faster than fast, I had my own mono-knife up and slicing through reinforced polymer. The body sagged in my arms, and I slid it gently into the trash.

"What is word?" Novak queried. "'Handy', yes? You are handy with knife."

"Not too shabby yourself," I said, sheathing my blade. "Keep to the dark. Move."

The Shadows would be networked. They carried heartbeat sensors, probably had in-head communicators. They'd be homing in on our location, but right now, we had a head start.

To demonstrate the point, another Shadow touched down ahead of us, gracefully bouncing from the roof of an abandoned building. Had the commando seen us? I didn't think so.

I battle-signed the Jackals to hold, and the squad fell into a crouch. Dr Locke folded behind me, pulling the hood of her suit over her face.

"Drones," Lopez whispered.

"I see them."

This Directorate trooper was surrounded by a swarm of drones. Each individual unit was equipped with a camera, red-lit eye lenses visible in the rain. They were designed to provide networked intelligence, being directed by a human overseer. As we watched, the mechanical cloud split into two, hovering into the surrounding streets.

"He's going to look for his buddies," Feng said, his voice low.

"And he'll find them dead," Lopez replied.

More bio-signs were massing around us. The Directorate were closing in. We needed cover.

Across the road, the open fascia of a hotel gaped back. The building was bombed-out, and looked a lot like it might collapse at any moment: a printed fixture with the name HOTEL RESTOV had long since fallen into the roadway.

"We'll take a shortcut through that building," I said. "Move fast; on me."

As soon as the drones passed by, I darted into the hotel's open reception. Bricks and concrete crunched underfoot, but the noise was covered by the din of the pouring rain. Dr Locke next, then Novak, Lopez, Feng. Inside the reception, then behind some mildewed furniture. The once-gilded ceiling sagged in several spots, and more water poured in from holes in the plasteel structure. But it was dark inside, and out of the immediate sensor-range of the Directorate commando and the drone swarm.

"That was close," Lopez muttered.

"Can we rest for a moment," Dr Locke said, trying to catch her breath.

Whatever my opinion of her, she looked drenched and in pain. Where the rain had made contact with her face – the scant exposed flesh between goggles and mask – she had already developed uncomfortable burn marks.

"Only until that swarm passes by," I said.

Another explosion sounded. Felt like it had come from behind us.

"The Dream is over," Novak said.

I used the downtime to try to open a link to Zero. "Do you copy, Zero?"

The line hazed, popped, but SECURE COMMS appeared in the corner of my HUD. "*Firebird* reads. What's your status?"

"We're making progress, but it's slow. We have the asset. Any more activity in orbit?"

"The fleet is adopting a defensive line around Kronstadt. We've managed to get closer; Captain Lestrade says we're still dark."

"Stay hidden. Do not reveal your location under any circumstances."

"Affirmative."

"The Directorate are searching for us down here. There's an army of them."

"I'm detecting other ships jumping in-system as well," said Zero. "Captain Lestrade says that their Q-signature is not, repeat *not*, Directorate."

I frowned. "Well that's just great. Some good news would be appreciated, Zero."

"I'll do what I can from here." Was that excitement in Zero's voice?

"Unless you can get some guns on these bastards, I'm not sure you'll be much help, Zero," I said. "Jenkins out."

"Zero out."

Feng put a hand on my shoulder, interrupting the communication. "Ma'am," he said. "We've got trouble."

The Directorate Shadow prowled into the open reception area, and the drone swarm cautiously advanced around him. We were going to have to move, and soon. Novak, Feng and Lopez had also seen the approaching hostiles, and were prepared to bounce.

"Are you ready to move again?" I asked Dr Locke.

She nodded. "I think so."

I turned to the Jackals. Nodded at the decayed and half-collapsed staircase that had once dominated Hotel Restov's foyer.

"We're going to go up, through the hotel," I decided.

"We'll take those stairs. Use your EVAMPs. We reach the roof, then bounce to the next building. Got it?"

"And me?" Dr Locke asked.

"I'd suggest that you hold on tight."

Dr Locke grabbed my armour for dear life. "Fly friendly," she said.

"I'll try."

The Directorate advanced into the hotel. Six commandos now, all armed with heavy rifles. The drones started to separate, their electronic senses reaching out into the dark . . .

"Go, go!" I ordered.

I fired my EVAMP. The pack ignited, propelled me through the reception. I grappled with the bannister of the stairwell. Gunfire chased us, hard rounds pranging off the walls.

"Grenade!" Feng declared.

He tossed a frag behind us. The explosion sent a shockwave through the stairwell, but we all held on. Up another level. The rain was everywhere, clouding my vision. Lopez opened up with her plasma rifle. A hostile bio-sign on my HUD winked out of existence.

Drones flew by. Their red eyes tracked my movement, doubtless feeding their intelligence back to the commandos. One-handed, I fired my rifle. Plasma lit the corridor blue; dropped a wave of drones. I touched down, running now. Dodged a hole in the floor, through a curtain of rain water. Dr Locke screamed, her survival suit hissing as it made contact with the liquid.

"Feng, Lopez! Covering fire!"

The two fell back, in a combat-crouch, as the Shadows came up the stairs. They exchanged gunfire with plasma fire, the roar of weapons discharge filling the dead hotel.

I reached the next stairwell. My suit had started to map

the interior of the building, second-guessing possible routes to the roof. The corridors were wide, rotted carpet lining the floors. Doors on each side, a window at the end. That was floor to ceiling, and open to the elements, glass long since scavenged or removed—

Light stabbed at the window. The nose of a Dragon dropship was visible there, hovering low. Active VTOL engines threw out debris and rain water. Dr Locke put a hand to her face, the glare of the dropship's spotlight blinding without a proper tactical helmet.

"Desist," boomed Kwan's amplified voice. "We have the building covered."

A hatch in the Dragon's hull opened, beneath the cockpit, and a ramp lined up with the empty window. The platform extended. Only I was in a position to see what was happening, and the sight sent a spike of hatred through me.

Back on Jiog. The cold. The hunger. The torture . . .

My simulated skin crawled.

Commander Kwan, wearing his full exo-suit, strode down the ramp, the string of medals pinned to his armour jangling as he moved. The arrogant bastard wasn't wearing a helmet, despite the sulphurous rain, and his lip curled in disdain as he tasted the air. He was flanked by a squad of commandos, their rifles trained on me and Dr Locke.

"By the authority of the Greater Asiatic Directorate, and the Bureau of Shadow Affairs," Kwan declared, "I hereby authorise your detention."

"Who does she have with her?" asked another familiar voice.

Feng's mother.

Tang stood at his shoulder. She too was dressed in armour, but her suit had been modified with the addition of a dozen robotic appendages; some tipped with razor-saws to cut open armour, others with scalpels, more yet with sensory probes. Snake-like, the devices twitched and swayed, as though agitated. Tang still wore a mask over her lower face, her medical lenses flipped over her upper face: ready to commence torture at a moment's notice.

"We will see," Kwan said. His hand rested, threateningly, on his redactor: the interrogation instrument holstered like a pistol. "Shadows, secure the prisoners."

"You're not taking her," I said.

"The Aeon will finally be ours," Kwan said, balling an armoured hand into a fist. "This is a momentous occasion."

"You don't know what you're dealing with, Kwan!" I yelled back, trying to decide exactly how we were going to get out of this mess with Dr Locke intact.

"We know all that we need to," Tang said. She looked further down the corridor, to where Feng was braced. "Ah, my errant son. You are returned to us."

"He is a disappointment," Kwan said, "and will be the first to be executed."

Lopez and Feng were pinned down somewhere behind me, their combat-suits absorbing heavy weapons fire at an alarming rate. Novak was picking off targets opportunistically, but the Directorate were now flooding the hotel with personnel. Commandos appeared at every entrance and exit to the corridor, weapons locked on us.

"Desist," Kwan repeated. He drew the redactor now, and its many mind-probes quivered ominously. "We have risked so much to follow you here, into Alliance territory, but our prize cannot be denied."

"And this one," said Tang, her mechanical limbs shifting arrhythmically, "is of some importance to you?"

I looked at Dr Locke, and there was knowing in her eyes. "You can't let them get this map," she said, bluntly. "See to it."

"Surrender now," Kwan demanded.

I thumbed a grenade from my harness. One flick of the activator, and it'd be over. Back on the *Firebird*. But if we took that route out, Dr Locke wouldn't be coming with us. *Better that the Directorate don't take the prize*, I decided. Dr Locke would thank me for it in the long run. I retreated down the corridor, towards the other Jackals.

"You will do as ordered!" Kwan said, his eyes flaring with anger. "Weapons down, now!"

"I'm not going anywhere with you," I said. "These skins: they're disposable."

Kwan's face crumpled in annoyance. "You and your meat puppets."

Dr Locke drew up close to me. "But I'm not," she shouted. "And I'm the key to your Aeon."

"You are liars," Kwan said. "All liars!"

"Then you'll be fine with my activating this grenade," I said. I could see that information trickling into Tang's brain.

"We must have her," she said, robotic arms stirring. She looked like some sort of mechanical version of a Krell bio-form; multi-limbed and dangerous. "We must secure the Aeon! Shadows, detain the prisoners!"

But Commander Kwan was looking past me. Looking at Lopez and Feng, at the end of the corridor . . . Korean started to spill out of his mouth, spoken at such a rate that the words had to be machine-assisted. A translation appeared on my HUD: "*Azimuth, faith, fire. All-hallows eve, by the light of the cold—*"

Then, an enormous blast wave hit me, and the dropship hovering at the window disappeared in a ball of fire and heat.

CHAPTER TWENTY-SEVEN

COLD RETRIBUTION

"Do you read, ma'am?" Zero asked, her voice cheery-calm over the comm.

"I . . . I read."

I picked myself up off the floor, cancelled a dozen damage warnings on my HUD, and rolled to my feet. Miraculously, my armour was intact, and despite the intensity of the shockwave that had just hit me, so was my sim. My hand was still caught in a claw, armoured fingers curled around the grenade that I'd somehow managed to refrain from activating, even as the explosion had hit.

Dr Locke stirred beside me. She was the only member of the team without a bio-sensor, so I couldn't read her vitals, but she wasn't dead. In the circumstances, that was the best we could ask for. I'd protected her from the worse of the shockwave, using my armour as a shield.

"Dr Locke?" I asked. "You okay?"

"I'm . . . I'm all right," she said. Her face was striped with dust and debris, one goggle shattered. "But my arm hurts pretty bad."

She had been thrown into the wall by the explosion, and she rubbed her right arm at the elbow where it had made contact. I used my HUD as a rudimentary medical scanner, and saw that she had probably fractured the ulna.

"You'll live," I said. If it wasn't going to kill her in the next two minutes, then she was just going to have to deal with it. "It's not serious."

Dr Locke gasped at the pain, but nodded back at me. "If you say so."

"Jackals, sound off!" I called.

The Jackals rose from the wreckage. Our suits were networked, and I could read medical data on each of the team; I knew that they were shaken, but hadn't suffered any serious injuries.

"Present," Novak said, with a groan. He emerged from a pile of debris where the ceiling had fallen in. The Russian wiped dust from his suit's visor. "Just."

Lopez and Feng were further down the corridor, and in better shape. "Affirmative," both answered.

"Seal this down," I ordered. "Kill them all."

The Directorate had been thrown into disarray; black-armoured bodies cast about the floor with limbs in unusual angles. They might be elite Shadow agents, but the Directorate were no sims. A couple roused, trying to get up. Lopez and Novak saw to them, putting down any resistance with plasma rifle and knife. Novak recovered his rifle, checked it for damage.

"What . . . what just happened?" Lopez asked.

"I'm not sure," I answered.

"Don't worry," Zero said, over the comm. "It was only me."

"What'd you do, Zero?" Lopez said.

"Don't ever say that I'm no help on a mission," she replied. She sounded very pleased with herself.

A ragged hole had been blown in the side of the hotel, where the window had been. The whole structure listed dangerously, groaning with the enormity of the damage it had suffered. I was almost frightened to look outside, to see exactly what had happened, but curiosity got the better of me.

"Well, at least the dropship is downed . . ." Feng said.

The ship had crashed into the next building, its nose half-buried in the pavement. The fuselage was utterly shattered, the pilot and co-pilot's bodies sagging lifeless in the cockpit. Despite the rain, small fires had broken across the ship's ruined hull.

"Was that Kwan?" Novak asked me.

"It was," I said.

"He dead?"

"I hope so."

The wreckage contained several black-armoured bodies, but the heat from the burning ship, and the range to the targets, prevented me from make individual identification: Kwan and Tang might, or might not, be among the dead.

"That's going to be tough to walk away from," Lopez commented. She too was covered in dust, her armour dinked and dented in numerous places. Something else caught her attention. She pointed into the street. "What the hell is *that* doing down there?"

An MBT-900 tank was positioned at the end of the street. The tank was literally loaded with armaments; from the phallic plasma cannon mounted on its turret, to the smart missile launchers on its hull, and the bank of anti-personnel kinetics guns studding its flanks. The package was topped by a null-shield generator that encased the vehicle in a blue sphere.

"I have control of the motor pool," Zero said.

"We can see that," I answered.

"That . . . that is awesome," Feng muttered.

The tank had an anti-gravity drive, but something that big required a boatload of force to stay airborne. It hovered a foot or so off the ground, crushing stonework beneath its bulk as it pivoted on its axis to better track hostiles. The surrounding air rippled, the small bones of my ear vibrating in time with the thrum of its engine. We watched as the vehicle's weapon systems activated, firing missiles and plasma bolts into the surrounding streets.

"How the damn did you do that?" I asked.

"Easy. We're in orbit over the city. When you told me about them, I tried to initiate the remote link to Alliance ground vehicles."

I still couldn't actually believe that Zero had done it. "Nice work."

"I never doubted you, Zero," Feng said. "Now, could you send a shuttle our way?"

"I'm good," said Zero, "but I'm not that good." She gave a self-deprecating chuckle. "But if Captain Lestrade keeps the *Firebird* in this orbit, I can maintain control of all four tanks. I can clear a path to the spaceport."

"Fucking A, Zero. You're the girl."

"I try. It was actually easier than I thought it would be. Nadi taught me a work-around for some of the security protocols. It was as I thought: the motherboards weren't actually fried, you see. They just needed a reboot and soft upgrade, and, well—"

"Okay, okay. We get the message. Thanks for the save."

The Directorate were regrouping, and fast. Drawn by the explosion, a handful of Shadows stirred on the closest rooftop. They opened fire on the MBT with grenades, probably high-ex anti-tank munitions. The tank's null-shield rippled, repelling the impacts. It responded a second later, and a bolt of blue fire hit the building, which promptly toppled into the street.

"Get moving," Zero suggested. "There are three more dropships out there. Those tanks can take some serious damage, but they're still only ground vehicles."

It wasn't just the Directorate we had to be worried about. The outlines of bloated bio-ships wavered on the horizon, and the sky was filled with bio-pods. I could hear the shriek of infected Krell on the wind, above the churn and pop of the burning dropship and collapsing building. Kronstadt was dead. It was just a matter of whether we were going with it. Time was running out.

"Hold the nearest tank's position," I said. "We're hitching a ride."

Using our EVAMPs, we bounced into the street below. I popped another couple of Shadows with my plasma rifle, and Lopez laid down covering fire with a frag grenade. That kept heads down long enough for us to reach the tank. We dashed through the null-shield, and Zero opened an access hatch on the flank using the vehicle's remote control facility.

"Get in," I ordered Dr Locke.

She did as she was told, clambering inside. Given her height, that was no easy task. The MBT-900 plainly wasn't made to hold much in the way of a human crew. In theory it was fully automated, but because machines make mistakes just as easily as the rest of us, it had a back-up crew compartment.

"That's going to be cramped," Feng said, shaking his head.

The tank's interior was dark, lit only by the tri-D schematics that reeled off firing solutions and tracked enemy movements. I climbed in behind Locke, Feng following me, but there wasn't room for Lopez and Novak. The Pathfinder suits and Dr Locke's size made the small space even tighter.

"What're we supposed to do?" Lopez moaned.

"You're riding up top," I said. "It'll give you a chance to up your Directorate kill-count."

"Sounds like you're trying to sweeten the deal," Lopez griped, as she climbed into position on the hull.

Novak just grunted a laugh. "Up close and personal. Just how I like it."

"I'm transferring manual control to the tank," Zero said. "I've already plotted a course back to the cosmodrome, but if I lose connection, you'll have to take over."

"Fine. Feng, you're driving."

"Copy that," he answered. "Moving off."

The tank's enormous chassis was suspended on a dozen anti grav-plates, powered by an engine that was more than capable of taking the Jackals' additional weight. We shifted portside, tracking Directorate hostiles as they advanced on us through the Barrows.

NEW DEVICE ON BATTLEFIELD NETWORK, my suit said. COMMENCE SYNCH?

Do it, I thought-commanded.

Now, this was more like it. I could feel the tank around me, could sense movement through the walls of the shanties and ruined structures of the Barrows. And not just this tank; I sensed the other three that made up the troop, moving across the district as well, clearing a safe route to the cosmo-drome. All were engaging targets – both Directorate and Krell – and laying down a curtain of withering firepower.

Distance to the cosmodrome: two kilometres.

Just two klicks.

"Are we going to make this?" Dr Locke asked me.

"Sure we are," I said.

"Nothing can stand in our way," Lopez reassured her. Now that she and Novak were outside the vehicle, we were using suit-to-suit comms again. "We're Sim Ops."

"We're Jackals," Feng said. "And never forget it."

"Have you ever fired one of these things before?" Dr Locke persisted. "The tank, I mean."

"No," I answered. "I haven't. Have you?"

She shook her head, settled into the crew station beside me. "No."

"Then be quiet and sit still."

The smell of burning flesh from Dr Locke's exposure to the rain was almost overwhelming inside the cramped cabin.

"Hey," Lopez said, "back in the hotel, what exactly happened to you, Feng?"

"What do you mean?"

"Just before Kwan got wasted," she said. "He was spouting some garbage. Words that didn't make sense."

"Everything bastard says is rubbish," Novak said.

Feng focused on driving the tank, but he shook his head. "I . . . I don't know what you mean."

"Sure you do," said Lopez. "Kwan was talking about 'all-hallows eve', or something. What did he mean?"

"I didn't hear," Feng said.

It sounded a lot like Feng was trying to convince himself of that. His hands, even in his gloves, were shaking. Before I could ask any more questions, a dozen more hostiles appeared on the tank's scanner.

"We've got company!" Lopez declared. She had already started picking off targets with her plasma rifle.

"I see them."

Using the main gunnery console, I set most of the tank's weaponry to auto-fire – it was made to pilot itself, using an advanced AI module, after all – but took over manual operation of the plasma turret. I fired at a nearby shanty, and watched as a half-dozen Directorate bodies were backlit by blue fire.

We turned a corner, rolled over another building. The tank's frame shook, but held out. Plascrete toppled around us. The null-shield absorbed gunfire in the rear. I heard Novak howling, wolf-like, as the tank fired another volley of smart missiles. All around us, Directorate troops advanced, and were cut down.

"We've got two dropships overhead!" Lopez yelled.

"Where's the third?" I asked Zero.

"Already gone," Zero said. "The fishes took care of it."

"I'd say two dropships are enough of a problem though," Lopez added.

The MBT's sensors detected both surviving Dragons circling the building. They flew low, raking the structure with kinetics, pounding it with missiles. Although it felt like the whole damn thing was going to come down on top of us, the tank just rolled on and on, hull vibrating as it took impacts. Lopez and Novak both cursed.

"Hold on up there," I said. "Feng, keep us in cover, and drive through whatever you like to get us to the cosmodrome."

"Copy that," Feng said, doubled over the controls. Was he actually shaking, or was that just the movement of the tank? It was hard to tell.

TANK A-16 OFFLINE, my armour told me. Meanwhile, tank A-17 was taking heavy fire. Tank A-18 was almost at the cosmodrome now, and I saw that it was engaging Krell primary-forms, their infected outlines unmistakable. Primary, secondary and tertiary forms were flooding the city, pouring out of bio-pods.

We slammed through another wall. The tank barely lost pace, crushing debris beneath the heavy grav-plates. Novak and Lopez held on, cursing loudly.

"I meant what I said," Dr Locke muttered, over the *thump-thump* of frag missiles discharging. "Back in the hotel."

"Sure."

"I need you to promise." She tapped her shoulder, where the starmap was located. "It comes to it, you need to make sure that I don't end up in Directorate hands. I've seen what they are capable of."

"I'm kind of busy right now."

"I mean it!" she implored.

She'd pulled back her respirator and goggles, exposing her blistered skin. Her survival suit was torn in a dozen places, exposing her shoulder. The map glittered there, powered by her body's energy.

"This was meant for Lazarus," she said, "but I think that I can trust you."

The tank shuddered with an enormous explosion. A fire team in the rubble were equipped with a shoulder-mounted missile launcher – a TAC-76 support weapon. The tank fired a volley of self-guided flechettes in response, but it was too late. Fire rippled across the hull; sent us careening into another wall.

"Shit!" Lopez screamed.

"I have them," said Novak.

He leapt from the tank, and fired his plasma rifle on full-auto through the smoke and debris. Novak cut down the tac team, and the tank ploughed on through the Barrows, threatening to leave him behind.

"Novak, get back on the fucking tank!" I shouted. "Feng, keep us moving!"

WARNING! WARNING! SECURITY BREACH DETECTED, my suit told me. My HUD began to fill with error messages, broadcast directly from the tank. SYSTEM INCURSION.

And now, whether I wanted to admit it or not, it was undeniable that Feng was shaking. Something was very wrong with him.

"What are you doing, Feng?" I asked, grabbing his shoulder.

SYSTEM BREACH! INCOMING TRANSMISSION.

One of the Dragons, its hull smoking, chin-gun still spitting rounds, hovered a safe distance overhead. I saw it with the tank's eyes, watched as the holo-image of Tang's face appeared, projected above the Barrows. I took some small pleasure in the fact that she *had* been injured in the dropship crash, and by the way her face was messed up, pretty badly at that. She was bleeding from lacerations across the cheek, and most of what remained was burning from exposure to the rain. This transport had obviously recovered her, and no doubt Kwan, from the wreckage back at the hotel.

Tang's voice spilled out of the dropship, amplified so that it resonated across the Barrows. The tank's AI threw code across the main console, attempting to translate the transmission. Nonsensical sentences appeared on the viewer.

"Azimuth, faith, fire. All-hallows eve, by the light of the cold night. Dark is the sun's wet embrace. The science of violence calls to you." Then, in Standard: *"Come alive, my son."*

Everything around me seemed to stop.

The dropship gently quaked on its axis.

The metal in Feng's head.

Feng sat bolt upright. He jerked the control sticks of the MBT, and the tank careened starboard. We hit a pillar. The

429

hull roared, and truck-sized chunks of building came down on us. Lopez was still on the outside of the hull, and she shouted in protest. There was nothing I could do to help her. *Get clear!* I wanted to shout. But all I could focus on was Feng.

"What is he doing . . .?" Dr Locke started.

I didn't answer. My hand was already on my sidearm, the plasma pistol unlocked from the mag-strip on my thigh.

I was simulant fast, but so was Feng.

The tank's cabin was filled with noise: alarms whining, the engine squealing in protest, hull groaning with the force of the collision. Tri-D alerts were being projected from every console, plastered across the inside of my HUD.

But all of that was background, just static to distract me.

Feng was the main event.

Private Chu Feng – member of the Alliance Army Sim Ops Programme, Jackal, friend – was *activated*.

That was the purpose of the metal in Feng's head. A neural-plant, Maberry had called it. Physically, the device was in Feng's body aboard the *Firebird*. The activation code hit Feng's simulated ears, and the simulant down on Kronstadt relayed the string of words up the neural-link, to his real skin.

Feng's right arm twitched, as though he was no longer in control of it. Which, I guess, he wasn't. His head snapped in my direction.

I had my pistol up. I fired off a pulse, aiming for his shoulder.

In the closed space of the tank's cabin, it should've been impossible to miss. But Feng twisted sideways, and the plasma bolt hit the tank's drive console. The tank veered, crashed into a wall. Came to a stop.

"What's happening in there?" Lopez asked, over the comms.

Lopez had survived the crash. Novak had pulled back to the tank. The Jackals' bio-signs were stable: no serious injuries.

"Get in here!" I ordered.

Feng reached for his own pistol. The weapon unlocked with a loud *schnick*.

I slammed a fist into his arm. The armour plating on his wrist deformed, and he dropped the weapon.

"What are you doing, Feng? Stop this!"

Feng grabbed his mono-knife. The blade lit, bright. He swiped it, towards me; moving faster now.

I tried to dodge, but there was nowhere to move inside the tank, no way to avoid the blow. The blade sank into the chest-plate of my armour, the cutting edge piercing the medi-suite dispenser on my torso, working its way right through the Alliance badge on my breast.

"Stop!"

"You're hurting her!" Dr Locke yelled. "Why are you doing this?"

But Feng wasn't listening. He pinned me to a stanchion beside the crew hatch, both hands reaching for the hilt of the blade. It sank deeper into the armour plating, the powered edge sufficient to pierce my suit.

"Feng!"

Determination was blatant on his face. He ground his teeth, beads of sweat forming on his brow. His eyes – visible through the face-plate of his helmet – were black pools: pupils completely dilated.

"Fight it!" I screamed.

I forced one hand around the hilt of the knife, in an effort to stop him from ending me. Used the other to form a fist and slammed it against his helmet, so hard that the face-plate cracked. To my left, Dr Locke was crawling up the interior wall of the cabin, trying desperately to find some way out of the vehicle.

The crew hatch groaned open. Lopez and Novak peered inside.

Feng didn't even respond. The knife moved a millimetre further, and I could feel the heat of the thing against my undersuit.

"Get him off me!"

Novak ducked low, grabbed for Feng's shoulder. There was such little room to move that he had limited leverage, but he managed to grasp Feng and slam him against the damaged console.

I breathed a sigh of relief – yanked the smoking knife free of my chest. Lopez's mouth was still an "O" of surprise, unable to comprehend what she was seeing.

"He just went crazy," Dr Locke said. "He lost it!"

"He's been activated," I said. My medi-suite was busted, fluid weeping from the torso plate like blood from a wound. The only explanation I could muster was, "Feng has metal in his head."

Novak and Feng were going toe to toe. The Russian planted a fist into Feng's face, smashing the remainder of his visor. Back against the cabin wall. Novak went to punch him again, almost filling the tight space, but this time Feng rolled out from under him. He swept a foot at Novak's knee.

Novak yowled and staggered backwards, his left leg twisting in a way that would probably be debilitating if he weren't in a sim. Feng followed up with his left elbow, the limb turned into a weapon by his armour.

But Novak wasn't stupid. He followed the momentum of the kick to his leg, and ducked beneath Feng's elbow. Then he pulled up his right arm: a mono-blade in his hand. The knife glowed as it ignited. Novak brought it up, towards Feng's ribcage—

I stepped in. Grabbed Novak's knife arm.

"*No!* We can't kill him!"

Novak fought me. "He is *Directorate!*"

Lopez threw off her indecision, and shot Feng in the right leg. Without so much as a sound, he collapsed backwards over another crew station. His armour was shattered, bright red blood pouring from the injury.

"If you kill him," Lopez said, "he'll extract."

"So?" Novak said. He was still amped with battle-fury, just looking for something – *anything* – to kill.

"Zero's up there on the *Firebird*," I said. "And so are we."

"Ah, shit," Novak said, finally understanding.

Feng was sprawled across the console. He didn't look so much defeated as just readying himself for the next round. Even as we watched him, he went to stand up on his damaged leg. His bio-signs were spiking, alerts crawling all over my HUD.

"Then how do I stop him?" Novak said, as though this was suddenly all his problem. "Bad words?"

I looked down at the fluid leaking from my medi-suite. It gave me an idea.

Like most Sim Ops combat-suits, the Pathfinder armour was equipped with a neural-link. As squad commander, I could remotely access the medi-suite on every team-member's suit. *Dispense sedative*, I ordered, as the Feng-puppet barrelled towards Novak. *Give him everything you've got.*

WARNING! BEYOND SAFE OPERATIONAL LIMITS! COMBAT CAPACITY WILL BE IMPAIRED—

Do it.

The drugs hit Feng's bloodstream immediately. He shuddered. His eyes rolled back in his head.

Lopez caught him as he fell.

"Good night, Feng," she said.

"He cannot be allowed to extract," I said. "Not until we all do." I opened a comms channel to Zero. "*Firebird*, do you copy?"

"We copy," said Zero. "I see that the MBTs are all gone."

"That's an affirmative. Listen, we don't have much time. Feng has been compromised."

"Say again?" Zero replied.

"He's been activated by the Directorate. I can explain later. Right now, I need you to keep him sealed in his simulator-tank. Use a sedative at your end, if you have to."

The downers in Feng's blood would only sedate his simulant. He'd need an extra dose to his real skin once we broke the neural-link.

"Is he okay?" Zero asked.

"I don't know," I said. "Keep his neural-link open. If he extracts, do *not* make contact with him."

"Solid copy," Zero said, although I could tell that she wanted to know more.

"We're proceeding with mission plan. Jenkins out."

"Zero out."

"What do we do?" Lopez queried.

"It's not over until we're dead," I said. "We go on. We'll proceed on foot; it's not far to the cosmodrome."

Lopez didn't dissent, but stated the facts: "We're still a klick out. Even if we get there, are we sure we'll be able to take a transport?"

"We have to try."

I plodded out of the MBT's open hatch. The Directorate advanced through the ruins of the building, the Dragons' searchlights probing its remains. I fired off a volley of plasma, caught one of the Shadows, but another two appeared, forcing me back into the cover of the tank. Krell skulked at the edge of my vision, my suit identifying primary-forms – reduced to thralls by the infection – through the dense smoke.

"It's too hot out there," Lopez said. "We have to pull out."

Dr Locke met my eyes. "I understand," she said.

"We'll keep going—"

"No, you won't. Lazarus wouldn't have it any other way. He wouldn't want the Directorate to take my intelligence."

"You barely even knew the man—" I started.

"But I knew his legend."

I sighed. The shriek of advancing Krell was audible on the air, and another bio-pod screamed by above. I cast an eye over the tactical scanner. Both remaining dropships continued to circle overhead.

"We're finished," Dr Locke decided. "We have to face it."

"I'll make that call," I said. "If we don't get you off-world, Locke, this is all for nothing. The galaxy will burn. Warlord will win."

And Riggs too. It's him that you really want to see dead.

"It doesn't have to be like that," Dr Locke said, with an air of resignation to her voice. She ripped back the entire arm of her suit, fully exposing the starmap. "Look at me. Please."

Then I realised exactly what she was doing. My HUD read the data embedded in her skin, in her flesh. The map was much more than a tattoo. The visor of my helmet was almost overloaded with information as it read the subdermal data.

"Capture the image," she said. "Use your helmet."

The mission wasn't over. Not yet, not while we could still get this information off Kronstadt. I scanned the whole map. The amount of data contained in the graphic was incredible. The whole operation took a few seconds – during which the Directorate began to renew their attack, and my bio-scanner continued to fill with hostiles. Once it was done, I activated my suit's transmitter: sent the package to the *Firebird*.

"I wish there was something I could say," I told Dr Locke.

"Seek the Aeon," Locke told me. "That'll be enough. Do you still have that grenade?"

"Of course."

All around us, the Krell and Directorate clashed. The ground rumbled with incoming projectiles, the Dragon dropships gunning down bio-forms as they converged on our location.

"You want to do the honours?" I asked, as I produced the frag grenade. At this proximity, the blast would catch us all. The Jackals would extract, and Locke would be killed.

"You take care of it." Dr Locke smiled. "Make your own legend, Lieutenant Jenkins."

The world turned white.

CHAPTER TWENTY-EIGHT

SLEEPER: ACTIVATED

And then I was back in the simulator-tank.

"Secure Feng!" I ordered.

Some impressive lacerations pocked my chest, stomach, limbs, face – pretty much everywhere – but while the agony of being killed by a grenade was enough to slow me down, it wasn't enough to take me out. Obviously, none of the injuries were real: they were just ghostly stigmata, reminders of the real thing. I dragged my sorry ass out of the simulator.

Novak and Lopez were clambering out of their own tanks, with the same urgency. Zero had summoned Pariah, the alien looming over my tank.

"Help me out of here, P," I said. "We've got a situation."

Feng stirred more slowly, his eyes searching the insides of the simulator as though this were the first time that he had seen it.

"Keep him in that tank," I ordered.

"I'm on it," Zero said, her voice hoarse with emotion. "Don't give in to it, Chu!"

Any hope that the transition had somehow cancelled the Directorate override – or whatever it was that had seized Feng – was dashed as his eyes focused on Zero.

"*Please!*" Zero shouted.

Feng's hands formed into fists, and he began to pound the inside of the tank's canopy. The whole simulator shook.

"I told you to sedate him!" I said. I was trying to shake off the extraction; trying to think of something – anything – we could do to solve this.

"I've already done that!" Zero said. "I gave him a double dose!"

"Stand back," Novak roared. He was out of his tank, dripping wet with conducting fluid, cracking his knuckles. "I take care of him."

"Feng-other has become a liability," said P. "We will assist."

"Exactly," Novak agreed. "Fish pops canopy, I take out Feng—"

"No!" Zero said, blocking Novak's path. "You can't do this!"

"He's turned," said Lopez. She was armed, a Widowmaker pistol aimed at Feng's tank.

"He doesn't know what he's doing!" Zero implored.

Feng had found a sort of rhythm now. His biceps contorted, and a terrible new well of strength opened up inside him. He rained hammer-blows on the canopy. Although it might be capable of taking an AP round, it wasn't going to take much more of Feng.

"What's the alternative, Zero?" Lopez said. "We can't let him loose on the ship."

"There has to be some other way!"

Zero's console displayed the data-packet in all its glory. Complete astrogation data, a starmap to a destination inside the Maelstrom. Even as we watched, the *Firebird*'s AI verified the Q-jumps. It plotted a route through the Drift, past previously occupied Krell worlds, into Harbinger-ravaged sectors . . .

"Dr Locke was the real deal," I said. "This intel looks like it means something."

"Jenkins-other is correct," P deduced. "Directorate cannot be allowed to obtain the map. Feng-other must be terminated."

P cocked its head at Feng, and the pounding seemed to grow in intensity: as though Pariah were somehow anathema to Feng.

"Feng is sleeper agent," Novak said, bluntly. "Maybe working for Directorate all along, yes?"

Zero shook her head, in denial. "No way. Not Chu. He's different." She looked to me, her tired eyes beseeching. "We can help him, right?"

"I don't know," I said. "He . . . he has something in his head."

"How do you know that?" Lopez asked.

"Maberry told me. She found something on the medical scans, after Jiog. She thought that it was some sort of neural-implant."

"Then . . . then we can destroy the control!" Zero urged.

Her console lit with an incoming communication, from the bridge.

"What's happening down there?" asked Captain Lestrade. "This area is hot, and getting hotter."

The shudder of the ship's gravity envelope told me that he was performing a manoeuvre under thrust. The inertial dampener field worked to counteract the effects.

"We read you, Captain," I said. "The Jackals have extracted."

"Then you have whatever the damn you needed from that planet?"

"Zero is going to upload some astrogation data to the mainframe," I said. "I want you to lock it down. Maximum encryption."

"Understood," he answered. "The Directorate have left the surface. I'm tracking two dropships en route from Svoboda."

My skin prickled, and my ports ached. Something like a plan was starting to come together in my head.

"Keep the scopes trained on those ships," I said. "Can you track where they're headed?"

Zero's face illuminated with hope. Meanwhile, Feng continued his assault on the canopy. He'd already broken the skin of his knuckles, sending spirals of crimson into the blue amniotic inside the tank.

Captain Lestrade paused. When he spoke, he sounded almost reluctant to give me the answer, as though he knew where I was going with this.

"I can," he said.

"Then take us as close as you can to their destination."

"What the hell are we doing?" Lopez exclaimed. "This system is falling apart! If the Krell don't get us, then the Directorate will!"

"I'm looking after my squad," I answered. "Watch Feng."

"Where are you going?" Lopez questioned again.

"I'm going after the *Furious Retribution*," I said. "Prepare for transition. Send me back, Zero."

New body. New armour.

I made transition, and Zero fired me from the *Firebird*'s drop-bay just like before.

"Launch successful," I said, through gritted teeth.

"Phase one thruster igniting," Zero said. "We have you on the scanner."

"Keep eyes on me throughout."

But within seconds, the *Firebird* was a pinprick of light, lost among the sea of other vessels that populated the Mu-98 star system.

The suit's systems booted up. What I couldn't see with my eyes, I could sense with the scanner-suite. I drank in the intelligence.

Space was awash with transmissions, with a thousand individual conflicts. The Harbinger-infected xeno fleet was hundreds strong, pouring through the Shard Gate.

Ark-ships dominated the orbital lanes. Huge, bloated things, the arks were mobile colonies, capable of carrying thousands of Krell warriors, an innumerable variety of bio-forms. All infected, all rotten. The very arks themselves were polluted by the Harbinger virus.

Bio-ships of many types followed behind the arks. They drifted in-system, firing their living plasma engines, spreading destruction wherever they went. The ships launched clusters of bio-warheads, Seeker missiles that took on a life of their own, and sought out targets of opportunity whenever they arose. Each of those warships was lethally dangerous in its own right; in a shoal of this size, the fleet was unstoppable.

Meanwhile, more specialised Krell starships trailed in the main fleet's wake. Some were twisted, urchin-like things; advancing ponderously, dropping living minefields as they went. Other, smaller vessels clustered together; Needler fighters forming flight wings that took on their Alliance counterparts. A tide of smaller living ships infested the asteroid and debris fields, creating entrenched Krell positions.

The Harbinger fleet took damage, sure, but it just kept coming. Every few seconds, another ship blinked into existence. The Shard Gate swarmed with xeno activity. The infected Krell were mindless, rampaging through Alliance battle lines.

The Navy's response was uncoordinated, insufficient, never going to be enough. I'd seen some bad shit in my time, but in all my years of Army service, I'd never seen anything so catastrophic as this. The first, second, third lines of defence had all fallen. Thousands of Alliance troopers and sailors had probably already been lost. New stars formed all around me as starship energy cores cooked off, as plasma and laser and railgun fired into the void. Surely nothing could live through this? It was a massacre, pure and simple.

As I watched, as the Pathfinder suit continued to make burn across space, I realised the Harbinger fleet's target.

"The xenos seem to be focusing on Kronstadt," I said.

Even from space, I could see explosions rippling across Kronstadt's surface. The Krell were invading, landing en masse, without care as to their losses. What did the fishes want with the planet, I wondered? Was there something – or perhaps *someone* – directing their movements?

"Phase two thrust initiating," Zero declared.

My suit accelerated. It felt like I couldn't go much faster; as though the body would simply disintegrate with the force, the pressure, if I tried.

"How's Feng?" I asked, just to stop myself from screaming with the pain in every joint, in my ribcage.

"He's alive," Zero said.

If I was going to save him, I had to act fast.

The Pathfinder suit jinked through a debris field. I was coming up on one of Kronstadt's moons; small and grey, surface pocked by the artefacts of human industry. Data on my destination filled my HUD.

"The dropships were headed for the dark side of that moon," Captain Lestrade explained.

"I'm coming up on the objective. I . . . I think I see it."

There it was. The black mass of the *Furious Retribution*. Hiding something that big was no easy job, but Commander Kwan had made the most of the confusion, of the fog of war. The vessel's battle-worn hull was almost invisible against the dark of space, only the glint of red running lights, and of open flight-bays, suggesting that she was even operational.

"Initiating phase three thrusters," Zero said.

"Thanks for the heads up. Firing countermeasures."

The drop-suit's outer plating peeled off. I trailed debris, fake radio emissions, and sensor-fouling signals in an effort to baffle the *Retribution*'s defensive weapons package . . .

It was crunch time. Do or die.

You get wasted out here, you won't even feel it. Probably.

And then I was through the *Retribution*'s null-shield, and heading directly for her hull. The suit weaved, banked, yawed. The cold caress of combat-drugs flooded my system. I punched through the *Retribution*'s defence perimeter. My suit's retro-thrusters fired.

"I'm down," I said, breathlessly.

I stood on the outer hull of the warship, and marvelled that I was still in one piece. It sounded like there was clapping, cheering, over the comm channel to the *Firebird*.

I unhooked a demo-charge from my backpack, and smiled to myself.

I'm coming for you, Kwan.

An effective starship breach usually demands planning and careful execution, relying on strategy, timing and intelligence.

I didn't care about any of those things. Not today, not while Feng still wailed and thrashed in his tank. I wanted my trooper back, and nothing was going to stand in my way. I moved on instinct alone; let my emotions rule my actions. The Pathfinder suit's multi-vision selected a possible weak spot in the *Retribution*'s hull – where two armoured plates had been bolted together – and I got to work.

"Deploying charge," I said.

"Move to safe distance," Zero suggested.

"On it." I bounced down the black plain of the hull, using my mag-locks to stay attached to the ship. "Clear."

The charge detonated, and the hull exploded outwards, creating a rip in the ship's armour.

A crewman, wearing Directorate colours, spiralled past me, sucked out into space. Another hung on to the lip of the entry point, fingers clawing at the twisted metal, already freezing from exposure to vacuum. Atmo and miscellaneous crap escaped in a miniature hurricane.

I moved fast. Tore the crewman away from the opening, and threw him out. The body cartwheeled into the void.

"Sorry, asshole. You made your choice."

The hull breach led into a corridor, wide enough to accommodate my armoured bulk. Security lamps in the deckhead flashed red, indicating a high alert, but exposed to vacuum the place was eerily silent.

"I'm in," I said. "Heading for the flight-decks."

The dropships had just docked, so that was where Kwan would be.

"We're watching the vid-feed from your suit," Zero said. "Anything we can do to help, let me know."

"Solid copy. Deploying drones."

My drone swarm launched, a dozen hand-sized discs hovering off in every direction. They'd map the ship, direct me to the locations that mattered: through airshafts, service tunnels, into locations that I couldn't reach.

See what you can see, I ordered.

AFFIRMATIVE, the swarm responded.

I approached the next blast door. That was sealed shut, but it had a reinforced window set into the door. Through that I could see a half-dozen figures in hard-suits: Shadow commandos. I read their bio-signs on my scanner, but I didn't need that to smell their fear. Even in vac, they reeked of it. Of course, I'd lost the element of surprise, but that didn't matter any more.

I slammed my foot against the door with as much force as I could muster. The hatch gave way with a single blow, the next corridor decompressing just like the first. These guys stood firm, mag-locked to the deck, and opened fire on me.

I cleared the remains of the hatch, and waded in.

The firefight was brief and lethal. Not so much for me – I survived it with barely a scratch on my suit – but for the Directorate commandos. I took out two full squads of Shadows, maybe twenty troopers in all. But that was just an estimate, because it was difficult to tell exactly how many I'd killed from what was left of them.

"I've reached the next junction," I said to Zero.

"The first flight-bay isn't far from your location," Zero said, her excitement obvious. "Keep going."

"I always do."

Adrenaline and fury drove me on, but a security hatch barred access to the next corridor. Most of the ship would be in lock-down now; standard starship protocol in the event of a boarding action. That was exactly what had happened aboard the *Santa Fe* when the Directorate had invaded. Kwan was going to know how that felt . . .

"More bio-signs moving on your position," Zero said, reading my feed.

Nothing was going to stop me from reaching Kwan and Tang. I punched the hatch. The Pathfinder's servos whined, more than a little pissed with my lack of finesse, but the powered armour went right through the metalwork.

"Grenade out."

I tossed a frag through the hole in the hatch. It exploded a second later, clearing my path. Without pause, I ripped apart the door panels and made a gap wide enough to pull myself through. While it didn't do any favours to the Pathfinder's paint job, I didn't care: I knew that neither I nor my equipment was coming back from this.

"More incoming!" said Zero.

"I see them, I see them."

Yet more Directorate advanced behind me, trying to catch me in a pincer movement. Gunfire erupted, rounds spranging off the damaged hatch.

I thought fast. The suit still carried three demolition charges. Inside the *Retribution*, I knew that a single charge would be capable of causing significant damage. That would do, I decided.

I unpacked a demo-charge. Magged it to the wall, just as the first Shadow cleared the ruined hatch. He paused for a fraction of a second, glancing at me, the demo-charge, then back at me. His red-eyed goggles radiated confusion.

The charge indicator flashed amber.

The Directorate trooper pulled back, battle-signing to his comrades.

I turned and fired my EVAMP. Bounced down the corridor, the Pathfinder's bulk grazing the deckhead as I went.

The demo-charge activated, and the corridor explosively

decompressed. Bodies and equipment whirled around me – the response team in complete disarray. I braced against the wall, locking myself to the deck again, as the entire ship seemed to shake with the after-effects of the unexpected depressurisation.

"Holy Gaia . . ." Zero muttered.

I talked as I moved, plodding down the corridor. "You saw that, huh?"

"Of course we saw it."

I did a quick equipment check. I had a decent complement of grenades, as well as power cells for my rifle.

"I've got two charges left," I said. "I'm going to make them count."

"Good idea," said Zero. "It . . . it looks like you've hit some of the ship's internal components."

"I hope so."

"Life support is going down. The drones report shifts in oxygen levels across the *Retribution*."

I called up the drone intel network, and graphics on my HUD showed their progress. They had managed to map most of the ship now; from the bridge, at the *Retribution*'s nose, through to the flight-decks at her aft.

"I have a fix on Kwan and Tang," Zero said. "They're together. I'm flagging their location."

"You do that."

I rounded a corner, and met with hot rain from another security team. I tore a grenade from my combat webbing. Activated it, and tossed it at the defenders.

"Feng's in a bad way," Zero said. "His heart rate is off the scale."

"Tell him to hang in there."

The commandos kept firing, even as I killed them. One was torn apart by the explosion of the grenade. Another went down with a plasma pulse to the chest. There were probably more, but I didn't even register them.

"Corridor clear," I said. "Moving on."

I found myself in a pressurised area of the ship. Maybe a door somewhere had sealed this section, in an effort to preserve atmo, or maybe the Directorate were conducting emergency repairs to stop me from hulling the place. It didn't much matter: I had my objective. Characters glowed on the walls; directions to various locations around the ship.

FLIGHT-BAY ONE, my suit translated.

That was confirmed by the drones, now coordinating their surveillance efforts on the bay ahead. As well as being capable of vid-surveillance, the drones were equipped with audio receptors. I had to calm myself, to slow my pace, as I caught snippets of conversation. All in Korean, but my suit translated the words.

Kwan's voice: "*The agent is activated. We must move quickly to the next stage . . .*"

Then Tang's reply: "*I need assistance, and now!*"

She sounded in pain; a wet, lisping edge to her vocals. Her demand obviously wasn't being made of Kwan.

Then, from somewhere on the bridge, an urgent communication for Commander Kwan's attention: "*. . . presence of a massed xeno fleet. We cannot safely continue at this location. Advise immediate retreat.*"

Another speaker: "*Honoured Leader, we must move. Our ship has been breached . . .*"

The blast door to Flight-bay One stood in front of me.

"*Then scramble a response—*"

"*They have already reached the flight-deck—*"

I laughed at that. *There's only one of me*, I thought.

Then Tang again: "*Someone help me!*"

I slipped my last two demo-charges from my pack. Then

thought-commanded the activation sequences, and magged one into place on the doors.

"What's the other charge for?" Zero asked.

"You'll see. I'm going in."

CHAPTER TWENTY-NINE

WARGAMES

Flight-bay One's hatch blew in.

I stormed onto the deck. Two dropships were nestled in the docking clamps, their noses pointing to the sealed bay doors. Both ships had rear ramps open, and looked as though they had been in the process of unloading their cargo. A dozen or so Directorate Shadows in Ikarus suits, carrying heavy rifles like those they had used on Kronstadt, were deploying from the dropships.

Commander Kwan stood at the foot of the ramp. An aide at one elbow, and a commando at the other. They seemed to be hustling him; aware of an urgency that he obviously could not sense. I was pleased to see that he hadn't walked away from Kronstadt unscathed. On the contrary, one side of his exo-suit was damaged, the leg trailing behind him awkwardly.

Kwan wasn't the only one to have been scarred by Kronstadt. Tang stumbled out of the same dropship, clutching at the remains of her armour. Her surgical mask hung at her neck, and the skin of her exposed face smoked from exposure to the planet's rain. The many-armed surgical harness swayed around her.

The Directorate Shadows opened fire on me as I rolled into the bay. There was much yelling and confusion, which was fine by me. I scattered several Shadows with another frag grenade from my rifle.

"Desist!" Kwan yelled, firing his ceremonial pistol. Rounds sliced the air. "I command that you surrender yourself—"

"Shut up, Kwan. This is getting old. I'm giving the orders now."

The Directorate fell back into the open bays of their dropships. Kwan and Tang into one; most of the Shadows into another. My null-shield flaring bright, and taking more fire than I really should've been, I tossed an incendiary grenade into the cabin of the second ship. The resulting explosion was contained but lethal, shredding the armoured bodies with simple efficiency.

"Stop her!" screamed Tang, banshee-like. She and Kwan were at the mouth of the other dropship.

ARMOUR BREACH, my suit said.

Shit. An AP round had penetrated the armour at my thigh. I stumbled; took a volley from a fire team positioned behind some cargo crates at the edge of the chamber. More Shadows were breaching the bay now. Medical warnings danced across my HUD. I also saw another alert there: CONNECTION LOST. I'd lost my link back to the *Firebird*; perhaps as a result of damage to my armour, or some disturbance in surrounding space.

The world narrowed to a single point. To that chamber, to the hostiles that surrounded me. And to Kwan, cowering in the back of the dropship . . .

I focused on him. "I go, I'm taking you all out with me."

Kwan paused, stopped firing his pistol. His eyes widened with a mixture of anger and fear. He held up a hand, and the remaining Shadows ceased fire too.

I'd fixed the remaining demo-charge to the chest-plate of my armour, and now I tapped it. The display flashed to indicate that it was armed.

"Don't you people learn anything? I'm disposable. Whatever happens, I'm not coming back from this."

Something rumbled in the deck, and despite the Directorate troopers' discipline, several faltered.

"If I die, this charge goes off," I continued. "It's keyed to my vital signs."

The response was not what I expected.

"We're not your enemy," Tang said. She wrung her hands, her ruined face contorted in pain.

I laughed. "You sure look like it. You killed Captain Carmine."

"That was a necessity," said Kwan. His gun-arm was lowered, but he wasn't relaxed. If his fear was alcoholic, I could've got drunk on the terror that dwelt in his dark beady eyes.

"And so you come here for vengeance?" Tang asked, the accusation plain in her voice. "The Krell are everywhere! What does the loss of one captain matter to this war?"

"We demand access to the Aeon!" Kwan yelled.

"You don't even know what the Aeon is," I said. "And, now, you never will."

I took a step forward. I was barely five paces from Kwan, and my bones ached to reach over and tear him apart. Rifles clattered around me, brought to bear again. Tang shirked back into the dropship, almost falling over herself in an effort to get away from me.

"Deactivate my trooper," I ordered. "He's one of mine, not yours."

"The clone is an asset of the Shadow Bureau," Kwan said, self-assuredly. "He is property of the Asiatic Directorate, and nothing—"

"He has a name," I said. "*Feng*. I want him back. Deactivate him, or I blow a hole in this ship, and you all die."

Kwan shook his head. "Never. The Directorate does not barter with hostile agencies!"

"This isn't bartering. I'm making a demand. Deactivate him."

The deck quaked again. No telling exactly why that was. Maybe the ship was moving off, trying to make safe distance from Kronstadt. But the reaction of those around me – no doubt equipped with in-head comms systems, which would allow them to make direct contact with the *Retribution*'s bridge – told a very different story. The Directorate were spooked.

They come.

Pariah forced its way into my head, whether I wanted it there or not. The communication was loaded with urgency and menace.

"Deactivate Feng," I said. "I'm not going to ask again."

Tang broke first. She held out a conciliatory hand, the fingertips of her glove burnt, exposing charred flesh beneath.

"Assure our safety," she said, "and we can discuss the process."

That obviously struck Kwan as a surprise. He glared sidelong at Tang.

"Stand down, Surgeon-Major! These people cannot be reasoned with!" he implored. "They are animals!"

"The agent can be deactivated by a microburst transmission," Tang said, swallowing away her pride. "I can provide the access code, if you can assure our safe retreat from the Mu-98 system—"

Kwan's pistol was against the side of Tang's head faster than I registered.

"There will be no retreat," he shouted, spittle flying from his lips, "and there will be no surrender!"

He fired.

Tang's head exploded. The insides of her skull plastered the deck, and her surgical harness immediately lost rigidity. Her body slumped sideways.

Kwan snapped his pistol round. Aimed at me.

The hangar shuddered, and something inside the *Retribution* detonated. Had my rampage triggered a chain reaction? Maybe, but this felt more urgent, more dangerous. The *Retribution* had been hit by something, and she was going down. Troopers began to retreat around me, boots pounding as the Shadows' morale broke.

"Where are you going?" Kwan screamed at his men. "Any soldier leaving this ship will face the full penalty for desertion!"

Kwan fired at the closest Shadow, felling him with a shot in the back. Another scrambled past the corpse.

I knocked Kwan's pistol aside with the back of my armoured hand. Grabbed the torso plate of his armour and lifted him off his feet.

"Deactivate Feng! *Now!*"

"They will consume us all," Kwan raved. "Your Alliance does not have the strength to stand against them. Only the Greater Asiatic Directorate, united behind me – Supreme Leader Kwan – is capable of weathering this storm!"

Pariah was trying to make contact with me again. I could feel the alien's mind probing mine, transmitting a fresh wave of emotion. This was my only method of contact with the *Firebird*, but it was frustratingly imprecise. All I knew was that P was trying to tell me something.

"The agent is mine!" Kwan yelled. "The Aeon is mine!"

The deck listed. The dropship behind Kwan broke free of its docking clamp, the squeal of metal on metal filling the air as it slid sideways.

The rage spilled out of me, and I shook Kwan's body with bone-breaking force. He barely seemed to feel the assault. His face had taken on a manic expression, as though he knew this was over, and rather than escape it, he had chosen to embrace it.

"There's nothing that you can do to save—" Kwan started.

But before he could finish the sentence, the *Retribution* exploded. Deep within the hull, her energy core destabilised, and the entire warship came apart.

Kwan, Tang, and the remainder of the Directorate task force were gone.

And me?

I made extraction.

The simulation collapsed. My comfortable, warm simulator-tank waited for me back on the *Firebird*. I snapped open my eyes.

"Extraction confirmed," Zero said. "Neural-link severed."

But whatever had just happened to the *Furious Retribution* was also threatening the *Firebird*. This was a hot extraction. The simulator had already started to drain, with the purge command initiated. I sagged in the cradle of cables, and quickly unplugged myself. The *Firebird*'s gravity envelope shifted, suggesting that we were moving under thrust.

"Jenkins-other must get out of the tank," Pariah insisted. "There is no time."

"What the fuck just happened?" I asked. "Who wasted the *Furious Retribution*?" Then, as my eyes focused, and I re-adjusted to my own skin, "What's Feng's status?"

I got my answer from the adjoining infirmary.

"Settle down, Feng!" Lopez screamed. "I'm trying to help you!"

He was braced on a medical cot, strapped at the waist, and he thrashed his arms and legs around, smashing everything within reach. That included Lopez. I caught a glimpse of his face, of the pained expression in his eyes. He was fighting it, trying to break the neural-implant's control.

"For fuck's sake!" Lopez shouted again, dodging a flailing arm. "A little help here, people!"

"His pulse rate is dangerously elevated," Zero said. "I . . . I can't do anything else to stop it!"

"Then I'll have to do it myself."

Lopez punched Feng. Just one blow, but hard, to the face. He immediately went rigid, still, on the bed.

"What did you just do?" Zero called.

"I saved his life," Lopez said. She rubbed her hand, groaning to herself. "Feng can thank me later."

P stooped in front of my simulator, passing me a pair of fatigues, handling them between pinched claws like it didn't really know what the garments were for.

"They come," it repeated.

The ship's PA system chimed. A siren blared across the deck.

"Bridge; now!" Novak said, over the comm.

"What happened to the *Retribution*?" I asked again.

P looked at me, its alien features twitching, and the mental connection I'd experienced aboard the Directorate ship became crystal clear.

"Oh, shit," I whispered.

The wreckage of the *Furious Retribution* hung in space like a cloud, the trajectory of every last piece of her shattered hull plotted by the *Firebird*'s AI. Many of the evacuation-pods had been launched, and were either making progress towards Kronstadt's moons, or seeking refuge among the sparse asteroid belt. Very few of them were going to make it to safety.

"Well, that's the Directorate out of the game, at least," Zero managed. Despite her words, Zero didn't sound in the slightest bit pleased with that outcome. She looked shell-shocked; as though she couldn't process what was happening.

The Mu-98 system had changed beyond comprehension. The Krell – or, more specifically, those fishes infected with the Harbinger virus – had taken it as their own. Their vast fleet polluted the sector, already staking claim to the moons and the asteroid fields. It even looked as though they were building things in the more distant recesses of the system. Dark structures of unknown design were springing up on the *Firebird*'s tactical scanner.

"How . . ." I started, my voice catching in my throat, "how has this happened so fast?"

P cocked its head at me. "There is no answer for that," the alien replied.

Kronstadt faced the worst of it. The planet's orbital space was thick with the invading war-fleet, the objective of a dozen ark-ships.

"The Alliance fleet is finished," Lestrade said, from his post at the captain's console. "There's nothing that we can do to help."

"It's Jiog, all over again . . ." I whispered.

Most of the Naval fleet was gone, and the broken hulls of dreadnoughts and heavy cruisers lingered on the scanner. Emergency broadcasts and mayday transmissions bubbled from the communications console, but the cries for help were going unanswered. Those Alliance vessels that had survived the initial attack were in retreat.

Novak was dumbstruck. He watched on in silence, both hands clutched at the armrests of his chair. To add insult to injury, the Harbinger-infected Krell seemed to be focusing their efforts on the population centres on Kronstadt's surface. At this distance, titanic warships were rendered like flies on the *Firebird*'s scanner, but they were massing around Svoboda, and the other major ports and cities of Kronstadt. Already, the planet's surface was blackened, almost withered. Whatever ecosystem remained on Kronstadt was collapsing, soured by the influx of Krell.

"Feng's out," Zero said, reading the latest results from medical via a console on the bridge. "Looks like he's dropped into some sort of deep coma. Maybe it's as a result of the activation." She shrugged, all out of ideas. "It's above my head, Jenk."

Lopez trailed behind, still rubbing her hand from punching Feng. Almost a full house now, to witness the death of a planet.

"What are they even doing down there?" Lopez asked. "What do the Krell want with Kronstadt?"

"They are killing it," Novak eventually said. "They are killing the planet."

"That is correct," P said. "The atmosphere is being contaminated. The world is becoming uninhabitable, for both species."

"That's not the worst of it," Captain Lestrade said.

"Can it get worse any worse?" Lopez asked.

"It already has," P answered.

The *Iron Knight*. Warlord's ship was right there, on the scanner; moving under hard thrust.

"It was the *Knight* that took out the *Retribution*," Zero explained. "We tracked her arrival through the Shard Gate. She came in with the Krell."

"The *Knight* is a damned cargo ship," I said. "How did she take out the *Retribution*?"

"She's not alone," Captain Lestrade answered.

Individually, the starships weren't much – more transport ships, a couple of light cruisers, some older-pattern military vessels – but combined, it was a different story. Strength in numbers made the insurgent convoy a significant threat. This was what the Spiral had been massing since the start of their activities: a fleet. Manned by fanatics, equipped with the spoils of their campaign. That included advanced military tech – weapons that they had put to good use in their surprise attack on the *Furious Retribution* – and I knew that we could not underestimate the Spiral any longer. They'd hit the *Retribution* hard, with munitions that could breach her shielding.

"Pull us out," I said, definitively. "Maximum thrust."

"We're already moving out-system," said Captain Lestrade. "But there are bogies everywhere."

It was testament to the captain's piloting abilities that we hadn't already been hit. The ragged column of infected Krell invaders had virtually no logic to their deployment, making their flight path difficult to predict and out-manoeuvre.

"Retain stealth," I added.

"Aye, ma'am."

"Can we make for Q-space?" Lopez asked.

"That's the plan," Lestrade explained. "We'll reach the nearest quantum-jump point in T minus two minutes . . ."

There was no point in suggesting that we try to get more out of the engines, because I knew that Captain Lestrade would be doing all he could to get us out of this mess as quickly as possible.

"What's our destination?" Zero asked. "We should know where we're heading."

"Anywhere but here will do me right now," Lopez said.

"We'll jump to Indra-16," Lestrade said. "We can regroup from there, and—"

A chime sounded across the bridge.

"We're being hailed," Captain Lestrade said. He looked up, exhaustion showing on his features. "The *Iron Knight* has found us." He looked at me with grim realisation. "What are your orders?"

Running stealth meant nothing to the Black Spiral. It was pointless to question how they had found us. Getting out of this situation alive: that was what mattered now.

"Open a channel," I said. "Let me speak with them, but keep us moving. I want safe clearance for Q-jump as soon as we can."

Warlord's face filled the tactical display. He wore his exo-suit, a respirator at his mouth, a hood pulled up over his head, making his features difficult to see.

"This is the UAS *Firebird*," I said, as bravely as I could. "We're retreating from this system—"

"Lieutenant Jenkins," Warlord said. Voice a wet rasp; scything through me. The sound had a similar effect on the Jackals. Even P bristled, grew tense in expectation of violence. "You made it out of Thane system, then?"

No thanks to Riggs, I wanted to say. Instead, I replied: "I can promise you that we will respond in kind to any act of aggression." I was painfully aware of just how hollow a threat that really was.

Warlord knew it too. "That's an Intruder-class starship. Long-range recon and deep-drop. It has a limited offensive weapons package. It won't be enough."

"Just let us go, Cooper."

That needled him, just a little. "I am no longer Clade Cooper. I left that name behind me when I shed my humanity."

"Sure. You're not human any more: you're less than that."

"I'm much more," he muttered.

Without warning, Warlord pulled back his hood. Revealed a face that was crippled by scarring, a mask of keloid tissue and hypertrophic damage. The injuries were almost ritualistic in their precision. As though his face had literally been taken apart, and stitched back together. Just as Dr Locke had described: a man rebuilt, with Sci-Div treating his flesh like building blocks. Only his eyes were original. They blazed with the intensity of dying suns, fighting against inevitable entropy.

I'd seen part of that face before, on Daktar. It seemed almost deliberate that his upper features could pass as normal; that only when he chose to reveal it would the horror become visible.

"What happened to you, Cooper?" I found myself asking. I couldn't stop the words from tumbling out.

"I've tasted the Deep, Jenkins," Warlord said. "I was part of their damned Collective. That came with a cost: it destroyed my body. What the Alliance found on Barain-11? It was a husk, nothing more. I was *gone*. And for the longest time, after the Army recovered me, I wished that I was dead. But your Science Division, with their thirst for knowledge, rebuilt me. They made me what I am. They created something *better*."

"You . . . you're a monster."

Warlord smiled. The scars around his mouth almost resembled lips, but not quite. "And *you* are nothing. Your squad is nothing. How easy it was to turn one of your number; to use him against you. Disciple Riggs still lives."

The mention of Riggs' name hardened my resolve. I regained some of my composure.

"Send him a message from me," I said. "Tell him that next time I see him, I'm going to kill him."

"Like we killed Lazarus?"

"You can't kill what can't die," I said, resolutely. Zero looked at me approvingly.

"We destroyed Darkwater," Warlord continued. "And we dashed his ship to Thane. He, and the Watch, are nothing. Dominion comes."

Unless we can stop it, I thought. We had the star-data to find the Aeon. Warlord didn't know that; not yet.

Captain Lestrade's bald head was dotted with perspiration. Throughout the conversation, we had continued at maximum velocity. The *Firebird* was arcing cross-system, heading towards the invisible Q-jump point, while the *Iron Knight* and her fleet were heading in-system towards Kronstadt. Our trajectories would pass, but fleetingly . . .

"This system, and these stars, belong to us," Warlord said. "This is Black Spiral territory. We bring the Krell here, to show you their true face."

"I think we get the message."

I looked over at Zero now. She had settled into the navigation console, and was counting down the distance to the jump point. We were almost there . . .

"I'm sure that you do," said Warlord. "But just in case, this should make my point."

And then it appeared. A single bogey on the *Firebird*'s scanner, moving fast. Almost on us.

"Stealth missile inbound," Zero said.

Warlord, and the Black Spiral, had been stealing equipment from research stations. I remembered now that Harris had told me as much, during our meeting aboard the *Paladin Rouge*.

"Shields," I ordered. "Now!"

The missile appeared on the tactical display; so close that it was detectable no matter what stealth package it ran. This

462

had been how the Spiral had taken down the *Retribution*, with experimental military-grade tech.

Warlord smiled again. "Goodbye, Lieutenant."

"Closing on jump point!" Captain Lestrade hollered.

"Fuck you, Warlord," Novak said, slamming a fist into the console in front of him. "I do not die like this. I do not die without knowing face of woman who kill my family!"

There was no answer from Warlord. The connection terminated in a flurry of static and feedback; ionic interference caused by the incoming warhead.

"Jump now!" I ordered. "Do it!"

"In three . . . two . . ."

"Go! Go!"

CHAPTER THIRTY

HAVE FAITH

"Does that hurt?"

"Of course it hurts. Everything hurts."

I sat up, and got an instant head rush. Had to pause for a moment to recover my senses. Nice long breaths, in and out. In and out. Calm. Thunder still rolled around my head; either the after-effects of medication, or I was shaking off a helluva hangover.

I was in a cot, with clean white sheets. In a room with white walls. Yeah, there was a lot of white in here. Everything was new, shiny. Clinically clean. I didn't recognise the location, but instinctively knew that I wasn't aboard the *Firebird*. A monitor and scanning apparatus sat beside me, chiming softly, graphics showing my bio-rhythms.

I pulled back the bedsheets, did a bodycheck. Both arms, both legs; all my own. Other than the usual collection of bruises, scrapes and healed bullet-holes, there was nothing new. I probed my injured ribs, and found that they felt a little better. That was good; it made breathing more comfortable. I wore Army-regulation underwear, freshly laundered.

Memory came back to me in waves. This was not what I'd been wearing when we'd jumped – or not? – from the Mu-98 system. What had happened to the *Firebird*?

More importantly, what had happened to the Jackals?

"Hello?" I called.

There was no immediate answer. I unplugged the various cables attaching me to medical monitors, both intravenous feeds and data-cables to my ports. There were little stabs of pain as I removed each. The air was cold against my skin. Colder still was the deck beneath my feet, as I got out of the cot. Gravity felt just slightly off, a tell-tale that I was in an artificial-G envelope. That sold it for me: I guessed that I was on some sort of starship. A hospital ship, or a vessel with a big medical wing, would make sense. But *whose* ship? That was the real question.

The chamber's hatch chimed, and I froze expectantly, aware of how vulnerable I was. If we had been captured by hostiles, I had no weapon, no cover.

There was a military officer at the door. He paused at the room's threshold, as though he didn't want to enter without an invite.

"You're awake then? That's good. You've been out for a while."

I made a quick assessment of the officer: American accent, Core Worlder. Wearing khaki uniform, an Alliance insignia on his chest. A halo of grey hair around an otherwise bald head, and a stern face. Older than me by a couple of decades, he had the badge of a full bird colonel on his shoulder.

"You're Military Intelligence," I suggested. "Right?"

He smiled. "I don't think that matters right now."

"Where am I?"

"You're aboard the UAS *Saratoga*."

"Where's my squad? Did they make it?"

The guy pulled a tight grin. "You want answers. I understand that."

"Damn straight I want answers."

"Help her, Captain," the officer said.

Another figure lurked at the hatch now, behind the anonymous Mili-Intel man. It was a simulant, in full combat-armour, towering over both of us. My heart plummeted as I saw who it was.

"Yes, sir," said Captain Ving, with all the vitriol of an angry teenager. He thrust a folded pair of shipboard Army fatigues in my direction, held the uniform in armoured hands.

"They've got you running laundry duty now, Ving?" I said. I couldn't help myself. "Glad to see that you made it out of Thane."

"Wish I could say the same about you," Ving muttered. Then, to the officer: "I told you she would be trouble. We should've left her where we found her, sir."

"Quiet, Captain Ving," said the officer. "She's going to be essential to the war effort. Please, Lieutenant, get dressed. The others are waiting for you."

"You mean the Jackals?"

The officer looked vaguely amused. "Get dressed."

I did as ordered, and realised how weird it felt putting on the Alliance Army uniform. Captain Ving and the Mili-Intel officer escorted me across the *Saratoga*.

They took up posts at the back of the chamber: out of view, making it clear that they would play no part in what was to follow. I got the feeling that Ving was here as security, to make sure I wasn't going to do anything stupid. Well, they didn't need to worry about that, but I could understand the reasons. They weren't the only security in here, either. A man and a woman in dark suits joined us. Their broad

466

sim-like physiques and dark glasses undeniably screamed Special Security Service. They watched me carefully, but offered no introduction.

I found myself in a long, rectangular conference room, with a smart-table that stretched the whole length. A viewport open to space filled one wall, and a familiar figure stood there, watching the stars drift by.

General Enrique Draven. Head of the military effort in the Former Quarantine Zone. My commanding officer.

The general wore full uniform, even a service cap, with his greying hair escaping from beneath. The old man's shoulders rose and fell as he took long breaths, but he otherwise stood still, his back to me.

I had an overwhelming sense of *déjà vu*. This situation was painfully similar to the dressing down I'd received from General Draven, following the debacle at Daktar Outpost. That briefing session had resulted in our mission into the Gyre, and had started this whole chain of events. Now, as I stood here, things had come full circle. I was back before General Draven and about to face the consequences of my actions . . .

But things had changed. I found a new strength. No regrets, no remorse. I'd done what needed to be done, whether Command agreed with me or not.

So, I stepped up to the desk, and snapped a salute.

"Lieutenant Keira Jenkins, reporting, sir," I said.

General Draven paused for just a second, then turned to me. His heavy grey moustache twitched, and his jaw danced, but his eyes were more sad than angry. It wasn't an expression I'd expected, and it instantly disarmed me.

"At ease, trooper," he replied. "Sit, if you will."

"I'll stand, if it's all the same."

"Of course." Draven kept his hands locked behind his

back, chest puffed up. Much like Kwan, Draven had a respectable ribbon of medals and accolades on his chest. You don't get to be head of Sim Ops without picking up a few shinies along the way . . .

"May I ask the status of my squad, sir?" I asked. If I was going to be strung up by Draven, I at least wanted to know what had happened to my team.

"We'll get there, Lieutenant. We should talk before we discuss Jenkins' Jackals."

I stood straight. "Yes, sir."

"We're still working on the intelligence download from your ports," General Draven said. He looked at me through his bushy eyebrows. "That will take some time, but preliminary analysis suggests that you've had quite the adventure."

"That . . . that's a diplomatic way of putting it, sir," I said. This wasn't the response I was expecting; not at all. "We . . . we didn't report in."

Draven nodded. "That was a major breach of protocol, but understandable, in the circumstances. I note that you claim to have met Lazarus."

"That's right, sir. He was working with an agency called the Watch."

Was that a smile on Draven's lips? "Interesting."

I swallowed. "You know about the farm, about Darkwater?"

"We know about the farm. We know that the facility was compromised by at least one Black Spiral agent. For your information, she was the only casualty. The rest of the station's staff was recovered by a Navy patrol."

"That's good," I said. I genuinely meant it: we hadn't intended to kill or hurt anyone. Not permanently, anyway.

Ving grunted behind me. He'd been wronged, and whatever Command's position on our actions, I knew that he wouldn't let it go.

"Everything you know," Draven said, "we know."

"So I've been hypno-debriefed?" I asked. I reached for the data-port at the nape of my neck. That would explain the headache.

"Of course. You've proven to be a highly valuable source of intelligence. You – and your squad – were primary observers to what happened at Kronstadt."

Tri-D projections appeared on the surface of the smart-desk; holos of the Mu-98 star system, of Kronstadt and her moons. All gone now; stripped bare by the Krell. Spiralling black constructions – shapes that reminded me of the Shard Reapers on Darkwater – seemed to pollute space. As though the Krell was replicating the Harbinger virus, on some massive, galactic scale.

General Draven saw where I was looking. "To date, we haven't been able to identify what those things are, but it appears that the infected Krell are *building* something. Science Division tells me that it's composed of organic, and inorganic, materials. The same pattern has been observed in all Harbinger-infected star systems. Those images are being recorded by remote probe, the very last Alliance assets in the Mu-98 system."

"What happened to the *Firebird*, sir?"

"We recovered your ship from Indra. It appears that you jumped Mu-98 just as the system went down." Draven paused, thought on that for a half-second. "It's amazing, really. The damage your ship suffered was . . . well, it should've sent the energy core critical."

"How did you find us?"

"I ordered a relief force," General Draven said. "But by the time reinforcements arrived, there was nothing to relieve. The task force dropped back to Indra, and picked up your transponder. Personally, I'm surprised that you even made Q-space in what was left of that ship. The Mu-98 system is

469

gone." He sighed, disappointed. "It was the last operational Shard Gate. Thankfully, your ship's mainframe survived. We've been able to recover the data-core."

So they knew everything. What with a hypno-debrief, and the *Firebird*'s data-core, there was nothing left to hide. I decided to front up to this.

"I want you to know, sir," I said, "that whatever the Jackals have done, has been on my orders."

Once again, Draven's reaction was disarming. His expression was amused rather than hostile.

"You've done something that no one else could, Lieutenant."

"So . . . so I'm not in any trouble?"

"No, Lieutenant Jenkins. You're not."

"Why?"

"You have some friends in very high places. Or, at least, your squad does."

General Draven's eyes shifted to the other end of the room. A figure emerged from the corner of the conference room, and came to stand beside me. The smell of strong, expensive cologne wafted up my nose; a pheromonal scent that spoke of wealth and power and everything in between.

Senator Lopez, Secretary of Defence for the whole damned Alliance, stood just a few feet from me. He was tall, slender. Sharply handsome, with a chiselled chin, perfect cheekbones, and bright, almost exhilarating eyes. He wore a dark business suit complete with a Proximan spider-silk tie, and polished Italian-leather shoes; an ensemble that probably cost as much as the ship in which we were travelling. Well, I guess that explained the Security Service agents. They were Senator Lopez's bodyguards.

"I'd like to thank you, personally," he said, "for bringing my daughter back to me." He held a hand in my direction.

I shook his hand, which I know wasn't appropriate, but I couldn't think of anything else to do. The whole meeting had taken on an air of unreality.

"Welcome back into the fold, Lieutenant Keira Jenkins," he said, in his broad, warm voice: a voice that had reassured billions that *everything's going to be just fine*. "It's a pleasure to finally meet you."

"And . . . and you, sir," I said. Here was the man who had wanted to shut down Sim Ops, was going to be responsible for navigating the coming war, and was Gabriella Lopez's father . . . There was much I wanted to say to him, but right there, right then, I simply couldn't find the words.

Senator Lopez had no such compunction. He strode around the smart-desk, a hand shifting over its surface to call up new data. The security agents tracked his movements like automated guns.

"Thanks to you, and your squad," he said, "we have everything we need to fight this war."

Images of other star systems, all polluted by the same black, twisting constructions, sprang from the table. Shambling war-fleets composed of bio-ships and arks, but also other, more familiar shapes. Human vessels – more angular, instantly distinct from the contoured outlines of the Krell vessels – sailed with the infected.

I drew my own conclusion. "Warlord is leading the Harbinger fleets."

Senator Lopez nodded. "That's right."

"This has been his plan from the start," General Draven added. "To infect the fleets, and turn the Krell on themselves. All out of some misguided sense of revenge."

"On a grand scale indeed," the Senator said, his eyes reflecting the light cast by the holo. "The Maelstrom will burn."

"But those constructions," I said, focusing now on the spiralling masses that developed in the infected systems, "they don't look Krell. They . . . they look like . . ." I didn't want to complete the sentence, but I couldn't stop myself. "They look like Shard technology."

The Senator turned to Draven and gave a smile. "You told me that she was good, General, but not this good." Now back to me: "You've only witnessed the Shard a few times, as I understand it?"

I nodded. "That's correct, sir."

"Science Division believes that these constructions are a by-product of the Harbinger virus," Senator Lopez explained. As Secretary of Defence, the constraints of military intelligence classification obviously weren't for him. I expected the Mili-Intel officer to step in at any moment and silence the conversation, but that didn't happen. Instead, Senator Lopez continued: "The Harbinger virus is a Shard construct."

I realised something. Back on Darkwater, I'd suspected it. Elena's summary of the virus, of what it was capable of, and how it infected – usurped – the Krell's sentience . . . It made a terrible kind of sense. Dr Locke's intelligence had merely confirmed it for me.

"Dr Locke was privy to some of that," Senator Lopez said, continuing to circle the table, "and she was probably the pre-eminent expert on the Shard. She knew more about them than anyone I'd care to name."

"She's gone," I said.

Senator Lopez looked up. "Oh, we know that sure enough." He tapped the side of his head. "Your hypno-debrief was very useful in that respect. As General Draven says, coupled with the *Firebird*'s AI, we know what you know."

Another image appeared on the smart-desk. It almost filled the room, and I struggled to repress my reaction.

An alien ship.

But not Krell, and not Shard. Something else.

"The Aeon," I whispered.

Senator Lopez gave another impressed nod of his head. "Right again. You're on a roll, Lieutenant. The ECS *Hannover* was tasked with searching for traces of this alien species. Command thought that they'd found something in the Gyre. Turns out that it wasn't the Aeon after all, and we lost the *Hannover* as a result. Dr Locke had already left Science Division by then – already taken her work underground. And so we were chasing our tails, following up any possible lead."

"Why do you need the Aeon, sir?"

The Senator stared at me for a long moment. It was that same evaluating look – weighing me up, testing my worth – that I'd experienced many times since Draven had first sent us into the Gyre.

"We're mounting a resistance, Lieutenant, and the Aeon are the key to finishing this war once and for all."

It wasn't until several hours later that I finally got to see the Jackals. I visited them on the *Saratoga*'s medical deck.

They sat together in one of the patient lounges: unguarded, except for a single Military Police officer on the hatch. I guess, after what we'd just been through, that was the least we could expect.

And there they were. The full team: Zero, Novak, Lopez, Feng. Even Pariah, coiled in one corner of the room. The xeno's presence alone probably justified the guard on the door.

Novak stood first, and hesitantly plucked at his uniform. "Do I need to change for prison overall?"

I swallowed and shook my head. "No, Novak. You don't. None of you do. We're . . . we're going to be okay."

"Really?" Novak asked, as though he couldn't accept that.

"We have a supporter."

"My father is onboard," Lopez said. Her hair was freshly washed, and she looked a little more like the old Lopez: an air of nobility had returned to her features. "I tried to tell them we'd be all right, ma'am."

"We had to hear it from you," Zero said. "What are they going to do with us?"

"It seems that we're being . . . well, I guess the word is reactivated."

Feng sat in the corner of the lounge, looking the palest and most withdrawn of the group. He still had a medical monitor on his arm, and wore a hospital gown rather than fatigues. As I looked at him, I realised what a poor choice of word that had been. According to General Draven and Senator Lopez, Feng's return to the Alliance was because of his deactivation as a sleeper agent.

"Even me?" Feng asked. Hopefully.

"Even you," I said. "Senator Lopez says that they've managed to remove the neural-implant." I produced a small metal vial that the Senator had given me, and tossed it to Feng. He reached out and caught it: held it up to his face. There was a bright sliver of metal inside. "The *Saratoga*'s medical staff are the best around, apparently. You can keep that as a souvenir."

Feng grimaced. "I'm sorry, ma'am. I . . . I didn't know." He struggled to find the words, the guilt painted across his young features. "I could've ruined everything."

"But you didn't," I said. "And it's my fault, not yours. Maberry found out about the metal in your head when we were on the *Paladin*. I didn't tell you because there wasn't anything we could do at the time. I'd hoped that it would come to nothing."

"Guess you were wrong about that," Lopez muttered.

"He's back now," Zero said. "That's what counts."

Feng looked away. "It was Surgeon-Major Tang, wasn't it? She put that in my head as a failsafe."

"I think so," I said, based on what Senator Lopez had told me. "But now it's gone. You're cleared for duty. Science Division says you're in the green."

Novak laughed. "That is what they say before, yes?"

"I think they mean it this time."

"So I'm not a danger any more?"

"Not to us," I muttered.

"Have the Directorate issued a response, after what happened at Kronstadt?" Zero asked.

I shook my head. "The remaining Executive has denied any knowledge, and hardly any news got out of Mu-98 before the system went down. For all intents and purposes, the Directorate . . ." I shrugged. "Well, they're out of the game."

Again, we should've felt some relief at that. Should've felt some pride, for what it was worth. But it was hard to feel much, after what we had been through. I was overwhelmingly numb, and I could sense that the Jackals felt exactly the same.

"How did we get out of Mu-98, ma'am?" Lopez asked. "We've talked about it, and none of us remember. My father refused to discuss it."

"From what I can piece together," I answered, "the *Firebird* jumped out-system. We used the Q-point to take us to Indra. The relief force found us by pure chance."

"Christo, that is lucky," Zero said. "I mean, Indra isn't a busy system."

"Our transponder was active." I waved a hand in the air, indicating the ship around us. "The *Saratoga* happened to be in the area, and picked us up. Captain Lestrade must've activated it, just as we jumped."

Zero nodded. She didn't seem very pleased with that explanation, but didn't question me further.

"Senator Lopez says that we're heading to Sanctuary Station."

"What's happening there?" Lopez asked. She was rubbing her arms, where her data-ports were located.

"The Alliance is mounting a resistance. And, if we want, we're going to be part of it."

Lopez looked around the room, at the rest of the squad.

"I think we'd like that," she said.

Pariah loomed over the squad, fluidly uncoiling itself from the corner of the room. Its pungent odour hung in the air, but it was strangely reassuring. None of the Jackals seemed to even notice it.

P stared at me. "We think that we would like that a lot."

My squad talked late into the *Saratoga*'s night cycle, until eventually the medtechs insisted that Feng get some rest. The squad retired to their bunks, leaving Zero and me drinking bad coffee, watching space through the lounge's open view-port.

"Something's bothering me," Zero said, being more direct than usual.

"If it's just one thing, then in the circumstances I think you're doing okay . . ."

Zero shook her head. "I get you. But this is serious."

"Go on."

She sighed. "You said that the *Firebird* was recovered in Indra-16, right?"

"That's right."

"And they found us because our transponder was switched on?"

That had been what General Draven and Senator Lopez had told me. "Correct."

"Well, I was on the bridge just before we jumped. We all were, but I was on the navigation console."

"And?"

"The *Firebird*'s transponder: it wasn't activated. We were running dark in the Mu-98 system, remember?"

I'd ordered Captain Lestrade to deactivate the *Firebird*'s transponder. We had been trying to avoid Alliance forces . . .

"Maybe the captain turned it back on," I suggested.

Zero didn't look convinced. "When we first got aboard the *Saratoga*, Captain Lestrade had his own cabin. They sent him back to the Core."

"So? He wasn't military. I guess he'll get his own debrief."

"I spoke with him, before he left." Zero's expression hardened. "He never mentioned turning on the transponder, or activating the mayday call, Jenk."

"So what are you suggesting?"

"Someone, or something, *did*," Zero said. "Maybe, maybe . . . we had some help out there."

I gave a tired laugh. I could tell where this was heading. "You just won't let this go, will you?"

"I think that someone was looking out for us."

"And you think it's him, right?"

She nodded. "I think it's him."

"Well, if that's what you want to believe, then who am I to stop you?"

Zero sat back in her chair. She looked almost contented, having got that off her chest. "If it was him, I guess he's gone back underground."

"I guess so," I said.

There was a cough behind me. The anonymous Military Intelligence officer, accompanied by Captain Ving, stood at the hatch.

"There will be time for discussion later," he said, his tone patronising: that of a concerned uncle. "You should all rest now. There's a lot to be done."

EPILOGUE

A single armoured figure.

The background was indistinct: perhaps a starship, or maybe a space station. Nothing that could reliably identify the location of the broadcast. No, the speaker was too good for that. He knew that countless intelligence analysts would be poring over this footage, examining it in every detail. Looking for some precious morsel that could be used to track down the man himself . . .

And there he sat.

Wearing his trademark exo-suit, the armour scuffed and worn. Every dink and scratch and scrape a reminder of the Black Spiral's war against the Alliance. Face encased within the skull-marked battle helmet, visor fully polarised so that no feature of the man inside could be seen.

"You know me," he started. "I am the Warlord of the Drift."

Voice wet, retchy. Damaged? He sounded sick.

"I am salvation. I am He Who Cares, and I urge you to take up arms. Your masters have traded your freedom for an alliance with the xenos. And where has that got them? Where has that got *you*?"

A dramatic pause.

"The border systems burn. Your so-called Quarantine Zone is in flames, and your defences are nothing to the alien fleets. There is no peace among these stars."

He sighed. It was a weary, care-laden sound; somehow not the expression of a terrorist warmonger. His words were in contrast to that impression.

"There can be no negotiation. The xeno fleets will not be stopped, and you are not bargaining chips in a petty political game. Now is your time. If you have been forgotten, if you have been downtrodden, then the Spiral welcomes you."

He extended a powered gauntlet towards the camera. Reaching out to anyone who was listening.

"Your war begins," he said.

The broadcast ended as abruptly as it had begun.

ACKNOWLEDGEMENTS

Writing is said to be a solitary experience, and it really can be, but I'm lucky to be surrounded by many supportive people. Friends and family are important when you need a break from the frontline; just as the frontline is important when you need a break from reality.

As ever, I'm grateful to my wife Louise for her invaluable feedback and acting as beta-reader for early versions of the story.

Equally, I'm thankful for the continued support and assistance provided by my agent, Robert Dinsdale. Robert's been with me from the start of my writing journey, and his advice and commentary on every book I've had published so far has been truly priceless.

The same goes for my terrific editor, Anna Jackson. She has been my editor throughout the Lazarus War and the Eternity War, and I'm appreciative as ever for her efforts. The same goes to all of the Orbit team.

Finally, and most importantly, I'd like to thank my readers. I really could not have done this without you; especially those readers who have stayed with me throughout my first trilogy and read into my second. I hope you'll stick with me into the next book, and onto wherever my writing takes me next.

Until next time: over and out . . .

Look out for

THE ETERNITY WAR: DOMINION

by

Jamie Sawyer

The Krell War has begun. The Black Spiral terrorist organisation, and their mysterious leader Warlord, have unleashed a deadly virus across the Maelstrom. There is nothing that can stop the alien fleets as they invade Alliance space . . .

Except for, maybe, Lieutenant Jenkins and her Jackals. The Jackals are now veterans of the Simulant Operations Programme – having operated simulant-bodies in some of the hottest warzones the galaxy has to offer – and back in Alliance territory, they have new weapons, new armour and new bodies. Jenkins' Jackals are given a secret assignment: to investigate the Aeon – a potential ally in the escalating conflict, and a force that might shift the gears of war in favour of the Alliance.

But there are many agencies interested in the Aeon, and too many sides in this war. Jenkins is going to have to trust her squad, the alien Pariah, and her instincts, as she makes the call that will make – or break – this war once and for all . . .

orbit

www.orbitbooks.net

extras

www.orbitbooks.net

about the author

Jamie Sawyer was born in 1979 in Newbury, Berkshire. He studied law at the University of East Anglia, Norwich, acquiring a master's degree in human rights and surveillance law. Jamie is a full-time barrister, practising in criminal law. When he isn't working in law or writing, Jamie enjoys spending time with his family in Essex. He is an enthusiastic reader of all types of SF, especially classic authors such as Heinlein and Haldeman.

For a glossary of military terms used in this book, visit www.jamiesawyer.com.

Find out more about Jamie Sawyer and other Orbit authors by registering for the free monthly newsletter at www.orbit-books.net.

if you enjoyed
THE ETERNITY WAR: EXODUS
look out for
FORSAKEN SKIES
Book One of the Silence
by
D. Nolan Clark

FEAR THE SILENCE

After centuries of devastating interplanetary civil war, mankind has found a time of relative peace.

That peace is shattered when an unknown armada emerges from the depths of space, targeting an isolated colony planet. As the colonists plead for help, the politicians and bureaucrats look away.

But battle-scarred Commander Aleister Lanoe will not abandon thousands of innocents to their fate.

CHAPTER ONE

Flying down a wormhole was like throwing yourself into the center of a tornado, one where if you brushed the walls you would be obliterated down to subatomic particles before you even knew it happened.

Racing through a wormhole at this speed was suicide. But the kid wouldn't slow down.

Lanoe thumbed a control pad and painted the yacht's backside with a communications laser. A green pearl appeared in the corner of his vision, with data on signal strength rolling across its surface. "Thom," he called. "Thom, you've got to stop this. I know you're scared, I know—"

"I killed him! I can't go back now!"

Lanoe muted the connection and focused for a second on not getting himself killed. The wormhole twisted and bent up ahead, warped where it passed under some massive gravity source, probably a star. Side passages opened in every direction, split by the curvature of spacetime. Lanoe had lost track of where, in real-space terms, they were—they'd started back at Xibalba but they could be a hundred light-years away by now. Wormspace didn't operate by Newtonian rules. They could be anywhere. They could theoretically be on the wrong end of the universe.

The yacht up ahead was still accelerating. It was a sleek spindle of darkness against the unreal light of the tunnel walls, all black carbon fiber broken only by a set of airfoils like flat wings spaced around its thruster. At his school Thom had a reputation as some kind of hotshot racer—he was slated to compete in next year's Earth Cup—and Lanoe had seen how good a pilot the kid was as he chased him down. He was still surprised when Thom twisted around on his axis of flight and kicked in his maneuvering jets, nearly reversing his course and sending the yacht careening down one of the side tunnels.

Maybe he'd thought he could escape that way.

For all the kid's talent, though, Lanoe was Navy trained. He knew a couple of tricks they never taught to civilians. He switched off the compensators that protected his engine and pulled a right-hand turn tighter than a poly's purse. He squeezed his eyes shut as his inertial sink shoved him hard back into his seat but when he looked again he was right back on the yacht's tail. He thumbed for the comms laser again and when the green pearl popped up he said, "Thom, you can't outfly me. We need to talk about this. Your dad is dead, yes. We need to think about what comes next. Maybe you could tell me why you did it—"

But the green pearl was gone. Thom had burned for another course change and surged ahead. He'd pulled out of the maze of wormspace and back into the real universe, up ahead at another dip in the spacetime curve.

Lanoe goosed his engine and followed. He burst out of the wormhole throat and into searing red light that burned his eyes.

Centrocor freight hauler 4519 approaching on vector 7, 4, −32.

Wilscon dismantler ship Angie B, you are deviating from course by .02. Advise.

Traffic control, this is Angie B, we copy. Burning to correct.

The whispering voices of the autonomic port monitors passed across Valk's consciousness without making much of an impression.

Orbital traffic control wasn't an exacting job. It didn't pay well, either. Valk didn't mind so much. There were fringe benefits. For one, he had a cramped little workstation all to himself. He valued his privacy. Moreover, at the vertex between two limbs of the Hexus there was no gravity. It helped with the pain, a little.

Valk had been in severe pain for the last seventeen years, ever since he'd suffered what he always called his "accident." Even though there'd been nothing accidental about it. He had suffered severe burns over his entire body and even now, so many years later, the slightest weight on his flesh was too much.

His arms floated before him, his fingers twitching at keyboards that weren't really there. Lasers tracked his fingertip movements and converted them to data. Screens all around him pushed information in through his eyes, endless columns of numbers and tiny graphical displays he could largely ignore.

The Hexus sat at the bottom of a deep gravity well, a

place where dozens of wormhole tunnels came together, connecting all twenty-three worlds of the local sector. A thousand vessels came through the Hexus every day, to offload cargo, to undertake repairs, just so the crews could stretch their legs for a minute on the way to their destinations. Keeping all those ships from colliding with each other, making sure they landed at the right docking berths, was the kind of job computers were built for, and the Hexus's autonomics were very, very good at it. Valk's job was to simply be there in case something happened that needed a human decision. If a freighter demanded priority mooring, for instance, because it was hauling hazardous cargo. Or if somebody important wanted the kid-glove treatment. It didn't happen all that often.

Traffic, this is Angie B. We're on our way to Jehannum. Thanks for your help.

Civilian drone entering protected space. Redirecting.

Centrocor freight hauler 4519 at two thousand km, approaching Vairside docks.

Vairside docks report full. Redirect incoming traffic until 18:22.

Baffin Island docks report can take six more. Accepting until 18:49.

Unidentified vehicle exiting wormhole throat. No response to ping.

Unidentified vehicle exiting wormhole throat. No response to ping.

Maybe it was the repetition that made Valk swivel around in his workspace. He called up a new display with imaging of the wormhole throat, thirty million kilometers away. The throat itself looked like a sphere of perfect glass, distorting the stars behind it. Monitoring buoys with banks of floodlights and sensors swarmed around it, keeping well clear of the opening to wormspace. The newcomers were so small it took a second for Valk to even see them.

But there—the one in front was a dark blip, barely visible except when it occluded a light. A civilian craft, built for speed by the look of it. Expensive as hell. And right behind it—there—

"Huh," Valk said, a little grunt of surprise. It was an FA.2 fighter, cataphract class. A cigar-shaped body, one end covered in segmented carbonglas viewports, the other housing a massive thruster. A double row of airfoils on its flanks.

Valk had been a fighter pilot himself, back before his accident. He knew the silhouette of every cataphract, carrier scout, and recon boat that had ever flown. There had been a time when you would have seen FA.2s everywhere, when they were the Navy's favorite theater fighter. But that had been more than a century ago. Who was flying such an antique?

Valk tapped for a closer view—and only then did he see the red lights flashing all over his primary display. The two newcomers were moving *fast*, a considerable chunk of the speed of light.

And they were headed straight toward the Hexus.

He called up a communications panel and started desperately pinging them.

Light and heat burst into Lanoe's cockpit. Sweat burst out all over his skin. His suit automatically wicked it away but it couldn't catch all the beads of sweat popping out on his forehead. He swiped a virtual panel near his elbow and his viewports polarized, switching down to near-opaque blackness. It still wasn't enough.

There was a very good reason you didn't shoot out of a

wormhole throat at this kind of speed. Wormhole throats tended to be very close to very big stars.

He could barely see—afterimages flickered in his vision, blocking out all the displays on his boards. He had a sense of a massive planet dead ahead but he couldn't make out any details. He tapped at display after display, trying to get some telemetry data, desperate for any information about where he was.

Then he saw the Hexus floating right in front of him. Fifty kilometres across, a vast hexagonal structure of concrete and foamsteel, like a colossal dirty benzene ring. Geryon, he thought. The Hexus orbited the planet Geryon, a bloated gas giant that circled a red giant star. That explained all the light and heat, at least.

He tried to raise Thom again with his comms laser but the green pearl wouldn't show up in his peripheral vision. Little flashes of green came from his other eye and he realized he was being pinged by the Hexus. He thumbed a panel to send them his identifying codes but didn't waste any time talking to them directly.

The Hexus was getting bigger, growing at an alarming rate. "Thom," he called, whether the kid could hear him or not, "you need to break off. You can't fly through that thing. Thom! Don't do it!"

His vision had cleared enough that he could just see the yacht, a dark spot visible against the brighter skin of the station. Thom was going to fly straight through the Hexus. At first glance it looked like there was plenty of room—the hexagon was wide open in its middle—but that space was full of freighters and liners and countless drones, a bewilderingly complex interchange of ships jockeying for position, heading to or away from docking facilities, ships being refueled by tenders, drones checking heat shields or scraping carbon out of thruster cones. If Thom went through there it would be like firing a pistol into a crowd.

Lanoe cursed under his breath and brought up his weapon controls.

Centrocor freight hauler 4519 requesting berth at Vairside docks.

Vairside docks report full. Redirect incoming traffic until 18:22.

Valk ignored the whispering voices. He had a much bigger problem.

In twenty-nine seconds the two unidentified craft were going to streak right through the center of the Hexus, moving fast enough to obliterate anything in their way. If there was a collision the resulting debris would have enough energy to tear the entire station apart. Hundreds of thousands of people would die.

Valk worked fast, moving from one virtual panel to the next, dismissing displays and opening new ones. His biggest display showed the trajectory of the two newcomers, super-imposed on a diagram of every moving thing inside the Hexus. Tags on each object showed relative velocities, mass and inertia quantities, collision probabilities.

Those last showed up in burning red. Valk had to find a way to get each of them to turn amber or green before the newcomers blazed right through the Hexus. That meant moving every ship, every tiny drone, one by one—computing a new flight path for each craft that wouldn't intersect with any of the others.

The autonomic systems just weren't smart enough to do it themselves. This was exactly why they still had a human being working Valk's job.

If he moved this liner here—redirected this drone swarm

to the far side of the Hexus—if he ordered this freighter to make a correction burn of fourteen milliseconds—if he swung this dismantler ship around on its long axis—

One of the newcomers finally responded to his identification requests, but he didn't have time to look. He swiped that display away even while he used his other hand to order a freighter to fire its positioning jets.

Civilian drone entering protected space. Redirecting.

Centrocor freight hauler 4519 requesting berth at Vairside docks.

The synthetic voices were like flies buzzing around inside Valk's skull. That freight hauler was a serious pain in the ass—it was by far the largest object still inside the ring of the Hexus, the craft most likely to get in the way of the incoming yacht.

Valk would gladly have sent the thing burning hard for a distant parking orbit. It was a purely autonomous vessel, without even a pilot onboard, basically a giant drone. Who cared if a little cargo didn't make it to its destination in time? But for some reason its onboard computers refused to obey his commands. It kept demanding to be routed to a set of docks that weren't even classified for freight craft.

He pulled open a new control pad and started sending override codes.

The freighter responded instantly.

Instructed course will result in distress to passengers. Advise?

Wait. Passengers?

Up ahead the traffic inside the ring of the Hexus scattered like pigeons from a cat, but still there were just too many ships and drones in there, too many chances for a collision. Thom hadn't deviated even a fraction of a degree from his course. In a second or two it would be too late for him to break off—at this speed he wouldn't be able to burn hard enough to get away.

On Lanoe's weapons screen a firing solution popped up. He could hit the yacht with a disruptor. One hit and the yacht would be reduced to tiny debris, too small to do much damage when it rained down on the Hexus. His thumb hovered over the firing key—but even as he steeled himself to do it, a second firing solution popped up.

A ponderous freighter hung there, right in the middle of the ring. Right in the middle of Thom's course.

It was an ugly ship, just a bunch of cargo containers clamped to a central boom like grapes on a vine. It had thruster packages on either end but nothing even resembling a crew capsule.

Lanoe had enough weaponry to take that thing to pieces.

He opened a new communications panel and pinged the Hexus. "Traffic control, you need to move that freighter right now."

The reply came back instantly. At least somebody was talking to him. "FA.2, this is Hexus Control. Can't be done. Are you in contact with the unidentified yacht? Tell that idiot to change his trajectory."

"He's not listening," Lanoe called back. Damn it. Thom was maybe five seconds from splattering himself all over that ugly ship. "Control, move that freighter—or I'll move it for you."

"Negative! Negative, FA.2—there are people on that thing!"

What? That made no sense. A freight hauler like that would be controlled purely by autonomics. It wasn't classified for human occupation—it wouldn't even have rudimentary life support onboard.

There couldn't possibly be people on that thing. Yet he had no reason to think that traffic control would lie about that. And then—

In Lanoe's head the moral calculus was already working itself out. People, control had said—meaning more than one person.

If he killed Thom, who he knew was a murderer, it would save multiple innocent lives.

He reached again for the firing key.

There had to be an answer. There had to be.

Instructed course would result in distress to passengers. Advise?

Valk could see six different ways to move the freighter. Every single one of them meant firing its main thrusters for a hard burn. Accelerating it at multiple g's. If he did that, anybody inside the freighter would be reduced to red jelly. Unlike passenger ships, the cargo ship didn't carry an inertial sink. The people in it would have no protection from the sudden acceleration.

Centrocor freight hauler 4519 requesting berth at Vairside docks.

The ship was too stupid to know it was about to be smashed to pieces. Not for the first time he wished he could switch off the synthetic voices that reeled off pointless information all around him. He opened a new screen and studied the freighter's schematics. There were maneuvering thrusters here, and positioning jets near the nose, but they wouldn't be able to move the ship fast enough, there were emergency retros in six different locations, and explosive bolts on the cargo containers—

Yes! He had it. "FA.2," he called, even as he opened a new control pad. "FA.2, do not fire!" He tapped away at the pad, his fingers aching as he moved them so quickly.

Instructed action may cause damage to Centrocor property. Advise?

"I advise you to shut up and do what I say," Valk told the freighter. That wasn't what it was looking for, though. He looked down, saw a green virtual key hovering in front of him, and stabbed at it. Out in the middle of the ring, the freight hauler triggered the explosive bolts on all of its port side cargo containers at once. The long boxes went tumbling away with aching slowness, blue and yellow and red oblongs dancing outward on their own trajectories. Some smashed into passing drones, creating whole new clouds of debris. Some bounced off the arms of the Hexus, obliterating against its concrete, the goods inside thrown free in multicolored sprays.

On Valk's screens a visual display popped up showing him the chaos. The yacht was a tiny dark needle lost in the welter of colourful boxes and smashed goods, moving so fast Valk could barely track it. But this was going to work, a gap was opening where the yacht could pass through safely, this was going to—

There was no sound but Valk could almost feel the crunch as one of the cargo containers just clipped one of the yacht's airfoils. The cargo container tore open, its steel skin splitting like it was a piece of overripe fruit. Barrels spilled out in a broad cloud of wild trajectories. The yacht was thrown into a violent spin as it shot through the Hexus and out the other side.

A split second later the FA.2 jinked around a flying barrel and burned hard to follow the yacht on its new course, straight down toward Geryon.

Enter the monthly
Orbit sweepstakes at

www.orbitloot.com

With a different prize every month,
from advance copies of books by
your favourite authors to exclusive
merchandise packs,
**we think you'll find something
you love.**